BONES OF THE LOST

KATHY REICHS

SCRIBNER

NEW YORK   LONDON   TORONTO   SYDNEY   NEW DELHI

SCRIBNER
A Division of Simon & Schuster, Inc.
1230 Avenue of the Americas
New York, NY 10020

First Scribner hardcover edition August 2013

SCRIBNER and design are registered trademarks of The Gale Group, Inc.,
used under license by Simon & Schuster, Inc., the publisher of this work.

For information about special discounts for bulk purchases,
please contact Simon & Schuster Special Sales at 1-866-506-1949
or business@simonandschuster.com.

The Simon & Schuster Speakers Bureau can bring authors to your live event.
For more information or to book an event, contact the Simon & Schuster Speakers Bureau
at 1-866-248-3049 or visit our website at www.simonspeakers.com.

DESIGNED BY ERICH HOBBING

Manufactured in the United States of America

1   3   5   7   9   10   8   6   4   2

Library of Congress Control Number: 2013020074

ISBN 978-1-4391-0245-9
ISBN 978-1-4391-1283-0 (ebook)

DEDICATED TO

Susan Moldow

Sage publisher, cat-lover,
and cherished friend

ACKNOWLEDGMENTS

First and foremost I offer profound thanks to every member of the United States military, past, present, and future. The steadfast dedication, courage, and strength of our troops inspired this book.

Heartfelt thanks to the USO (United Service Organizations) and the ITW (International Thriller Writers) for making possible my trip to Kyrgyzstan and Afghanistan. The camaraderie and patience of my fellow travelers—Sandra Brown, Mark Bowden, Clive Cussler, Andrew Peterson, Jeremy Wilcox, and Mike Theiler—made the long flights, early mornings, and late nights infinitely easier than they might otherwise have been. A special shout-out to Andrew Peterson and Andy Harp for answering dozens of follow-up questions.

Dr. William C. Rodriguez and Dr. Sue Black helped with details of forensic anthropology.

I appreciate the continued support of Chancellor Philip L. Dubois of the University of North Carolina–Charlotte.

Sincere thanks to my agent, Jennifer Rudolph-Walsh, and to my editors, Nan Graham and Susan Sandon. I am eternally indebted to Susan Moldow. I hope the dedication says it all.

I also want to acknowledge all those who work so very hard on my behalf, including: Paul Whitlatch, Roz Lippel, Lauren Lavelle, Daniel Burgess, Tal Goretzky, Kara Watson, Greg Mortimer, Mia Crowley-Hald, Erich Hobbing, Simon Littlewood, Glenn O'Neill, Caitlin Moore, Tim Vanderpump, Jen Doyle, Emma Finnigan, Maggie Shapiro, Tracy Fisher, Michelle Feehan, Cathryn Summerhayes, and Raffaella De Angelis, and the whole rambunctious Canadian crew.

I thank my family and friends for tolerating my moods and absences. Paul Reichs's comments on the Marine Corps, JAG, and the Article 32 process, and on the manuscript in general, were tremendously useful.

ACKNOWLEDGMENTS

As always, thanks and hugs to my readers. I love that you read about Tempe, attend my signings and appearances, visit my website (KathyReichs.com), like me on Facebook, and follow me on Twitter (@kathyreichs). You guys are awesome!

If I left anyone out, I apologize. If the book contains errors, they are my fault.

BONES OF
THE LOST

PROLOGUE

Heart pounding, I crawled toward the brick angling down to form the edge of the recess. Craned out.

More footfalls. Then heavy boots appeared at the top of the stairs, beside them a pair of small feet, one bare, the other in a platform pump.

The feet started to descend, the small ones wobbly, their owner somehow impaired. The lower legs angled oddly, suggesting the knees bore little weight.

Anger burned hot in my chest. The woman was drugged. The bastard was dragging her.

Four treads lower, the man and woman crossed an arrow of moonlight. Not a woman, a girl. Her hair was long, her arms and legs refugee thin. I could see a triangle of white tee below the man's chin. A pistol grip jutting from his waistband.

The pair again passed into darkness. Their tightly pressed bodies formed a two-headed black silhouette.

Stepping from the bottom tread, the man started muscling the girl toward the loading-dock door, pushing her, a hand clamping her neck. She stumbled. He yanked her up. Her head flopped like a Bobblehead doll's.

The girl took a few more staggering steps. Then her chin lifted and her body bucked. A cry broke the stillness, animal shrill.

The man's free arm shot out. The silhouette recongealed. I heard a scream of pain, then the girl pitched forward onto the concrete.

The man dropped to one knee. His elbow pumped as he pummeled the inert little body.

"Fight me, you little bitch?"

The man punched and punched until his breath grew ragged.

Rage flamed white-hot in my brain, overriding any instinct for personal safety.

I scuttled over and grabbed the Beretta. Checked the safety, thankful for the practice I'd put in at the range.

Satisfied with the gun, I reached for my phone. It wasn't with the flashlight.

I searched my other pocket. No phone.

Had I dropped it? In my frenzied dash, had I left it at home?

The panic was almost overwhelming. I was off the grid. What to do?

A tiny voice advised caution. Remain hidden. Wait. Slidell knows where you are.

"You are so dead." The voice boomed, cruel and malicious.

I whipped around.

The man was wrenching the girl up by her hair.

Holding the Beretta two-handed in front of me, I darted from the alcove. The man froze at the sound of movement. I stopped five yards from him. Using a pillar for cover, I spread my feet and leveled the barrel.

"Let her go." My shout reverberated off brick and concrete.

The man maintained his grasp on the girl's hair. His back was to me.

"Hands up."

He let go and straightened. His palms slowly rose to the level of his ears.

"Turn around."

As the man rotated, another fragment of light caught him. For a second I saw his face with total clarity.

On spotting his foe, the man's hands dipped slightly. Sensing he could see me better than I could see him, I squeezed further behind the pillar.

"The fucking slut lives."

You'll die, too, fucking slut.

"Takes balls to send threats by e-mail." My voice sounded much more confident than I felt. "To bully defenseless little girls."

"Debt to pay? You know the rules."

"Your debt-collecting days are over, you sick sonofabitch."

"Says who?"

"Says a dozen cops racing here now."

The man cupped an upraised hand to one ear. "I don't hear no sirens."

"Move away from the girl," I ordered.

He took a token step.

"Move," I snarled. The guy's fuck-you attitude was making me want to smash the Beretta across his skull.

"Or what? You're gonna shoot me?"

"Yeah." Cold steel. "I'm gonna shoot you."

Would I? I'd never fired at a human being.

Where the hell was Slidell? I knew my bluff was being sustained by coffee and adrenaline. Knew both would eventually wear off.

The girl groaned.

In that split second I lost the advantage that might have allowed him to live.

I looked down.

He lunged.

Fresh adrenaline blasted through me.

I raised the gun.

He closed in.

I sighted on the white triangle.

Fired.

The explosion echoed brutally loud. The concussion knocked my hands up, but I held position.

The man dropped.

In the murky gloom I saw the triangle go dark. Knew crimson was spreading across it. A perfect hit. The Triangle of Death.

Silence, but for my own rasping breath.

Then my higher centers caught up with my brain stem.

I'd killed a man.

My hands shook. Bile filled my throat.

I swallowed. Steadied the gun and stole forward.

The girl lay motionless. I crouched and placed trembling fingers on her throat. Felt a pulse, faint but steady.

I swiveled. Gazed at the man's mute, malevolent eyes.

Suddenly I was exhausted. Revolted by what I'd just done.

I wondered. In my state, could I make good decisions? Carry through? My phone was back at the house.

I wanted to sit, hold my head in my hands, and let the tears flow.

Instead I drew a few steadying breaths, rose, and crossed what seemed a thousand miles of darkness. Climbed the stairs on rubbery legs.

A single passage cut right at the top. I followed it to the only closed door.

Gun tight in one clammy hand, I reached out and turned the knob with the other.

The door swung in.

I stared into pure horror.

PART ONE

I'VE BEEN HELD PRISONER BEFORE. IN A BASEMENT, A MORGUE cooler, an underground crypt. It's always frightening and intense. But this captivity exceeded all others for pure physical pain.

The jurors' lounge in the Mecklenburg County Courthouse is as good as such facilities get—Wi-Fi, workstations, pool tables, movies, popcorn. I could have applied for a waiver. Didn't. The judicial system called, I came. Good citizen Brennan. Besides, given my line of work, I knew I'd be excused from actually serving. When I'd planned today's schedule I'd slotted sixty, ninety minutes max, cooling my heels.

Heels. Follow my leap here. In my business exciting footwear is Gore-Tex hikers that breathe, maybe wellies that don't land you on your ass. Buying, much less wearing, murderous high heels is about as likely for me as finding Giganotosaurus remains behind Bad Daddy's Burgers.

My sister Harry had talked me into the three-inch Christian Louboutin pumps. Harry, from Texas, land of big hair and mile-high stilettos. You'll look professional, she'd said. In charge. Plus they're marked down 60 percent.

I had to admit, the burnished leather and snazzy stitchwork did look great on my feet. Feel great? Not after three hours of waiting. When the bailiff finally called our group, I near-tottered into the courtroom, then into the jury box when my number was called.

"Please state your full name." Chelsea Jett, six minutes out of law school, four-hundred-dollar suit, pricey pearl choker, heels that left mine in the dust. A new prosecutor, Jett was cloaking a case of nerves with brusqueness.

"Temperance Daessee Brennan." Make it easy on both of us. Excuse me pronto.

"Please state your address."

I did. "That's at Sharon Hall," I added, just to be affable. Nineteenth-century manor, red brick, white pillars, magnolias. My unit is the annex to the carriage house. Can't get more Old South than that. I offered none of that.

"How long have you resided in Charlotte?"

"Since I was eight."

"Does anyone live at that address with you?"

"My adult daughter has at times, but not now." The bracelet Katy gave me hung loose on my wrist, a delicate silver band engraved MOM ROCKS.

"Your marital status?"

"Separated." Complicated. I definitely didn't add that.

"Are you employed?"

"Yes."

"Please state your employer."

"State of North Carolina." Keep it simple.

"Your occupation?"

"Forensic anthropologist."

"What is the educational requirement for that profession?" Stiff.

"I hold a PhD and am certified by the American Board of Forensic Anthropology."

"So you perform autopsies."

"You're thinking of a forensic pathologist. Common mistake."

Jett stiffened.

I offered a smile. The counselor didn't.

"Forensic anthropologists work with the dead for whom normal autopsies are impossible—the skeletal, mummified, decomposed, dismembered, burned, or mutilated. We're consulted on many issues, all of which are answered through analysis of the bones. For example, are the remains in question human or animal?"

"That requires an expert?" Restrained skepticism.

"Some human and animal bones are deceptively similar." I pictured the mummified sets awaiting me at the MCME. "Fragmentary remains can be especially difficult to assess. Are they from one individual, several, humans, animals, both?" The bundles I was not examining because I was sitting here, feet bloating like corpses in water.

Jett flicked a manicured hand, impatient for me to continue.

"If the remains are human, I look for indicators of age, sex, race, height, illness, deformity, or anomaly—anything that might be of use in establishing ID. I analyze trauma to determine manner of death. I estimate how long the victim has been dead. I consider postmortem body treatment."

Jett raised one questioning brow.

"Decapitation, dismemberment, burial, submersion—"

"I think that covers it."

Jett's gaze dropped to her scribbled questions. A long, long list.

My eyes found my watch, then wandered to the unfortunates still waiting to be grilled. I'd dressed to look respectful, to project the image expected of a representative of the Mecklenburg County Medical Examiner's Office. Tan linen pantsuit, silk turtleneck. Such was not the case for all my fellow captives. My personal favorite was the young woman in a tight sleeveless turtleneck, jeans, and sandals.

Not haute couture, but I suspected her feet felt better than mine. I tried to wiggle my toes inside the torturous pumps. Failed.

Ms. Jett took a deep breath. Where was she headed? I didn't wait to find out.

"As forensic anthropologist for the state, I'm under contract to both UNC Charlotte—I teach an upper-level seminar there—and to the Office of the Chief Medical Examiner in Chapel Hill and the Mecklenburg County Medical Examiner here in Charlotte. I also provide expertise to the Laboratoire de sciences judiciaires et de médecine légale in Montreal." Read: I am busy. I consult to police agencies, the FBI, the military, coroners, and medical examiners. You know the defense attorney will excuse me if you don't.

"Do I understand correctly? You work regularly in two countries?"

"It's not as odd as it sounds. In most jurisdictions, forensic anthropologists function as specialty consultants. As I've stated, my colleagues and I are only called in on cases where there's insufficient flesh for an autopsy, or the remains—"

"Right."

Jett finger-scanned the endless lineup on her yellow pad.

I stretched—*tried* to stretch—my unhappy phalanges.

"In the course of your work with the medical examiner's office, do you come into contact with police officers?"

Finally. Thank you.

"Yes. Often."

"Prosecuting or defense attorneys?"

"Both. And my ex-husband is a lawyer." Sort of ex.

"Do you personally know anyone involved in this litigation, the defendant, his family, the police investigators, the attorneys, the judge—"

"Yes."

And I was excused.

Ignoring my protesting pedal digits, I hobble-bolted from the courtroom, across the lobby, and out the double glass doors. My Mazda was at the farthest corner of the parking deck. Arriving ten minutes past the eight A.M. hour demanded on the summons, I'd grabbed the first space I could find, halfway to Kansas.

After a fast limp across a traffic lane, I rounded a row of vehicles and found my car closely flanked by a humongous SUV on the driver's side and even more closely wedged on the passenger side. Sweat glands pumping, I wriggled between the two sets of handles and rearview mirrors, butt and chest skimming the grimy doors and side panels squeezing my torso. My classy tan linen now looked like I'd taken a roll in a landfill.

As I wedged the door open and squeezed behind the wheel, something clinked at my feet. A sensible citizen—that is, a citizen in sensible footwear—would have stopped to identify whatever automotive adornment had been dislodged. I focused on my escape, fingers searching for keys in the zipper pouch of my purse.

Feet aflame, I jammed the keys into the ignition and bent sideways to tug at my right shoe. The thing gripped as though grafted onto my flesh.

I tugged harder.

My foot exploded from its casing. With much twisting and maneuvering, I repeated the process on the left.

Settling against the seatback, I eyeballed a pair of spectacular blisters. Then the hated Louboutins in my hand.

My hand.

My wrist.

My bare wrist!

Katy.

A familiar stab of fear pierced my chest.

I pushed it away.

Focus. The bracelet had been in place in the jury lounge, in the
jury box.

The clink. The little silver band must have caught on something
during my slither along the SUV.

Cursing, I squeezed back out and slammed the car door.

The human brain is a switching station that operates on two
levels. As a reflex order fired to my hand, a neural connection was
already taking place in my cerebellum. Before the door hit home, I
knew I was screwed. Pointlessly, I tried the handle, then checked the
position of all four lock buttons.

Cursing even more colorfully, I reached for my purse. Which was
lying on the passenger seat.

Shit.

And the keys? Dangling from the ignition.

I stood a moment, pant cuffs waterfalling over my bare feet, suit
streaked with dirt, underarms soggy with sweat. And wondered.

Could this day get any worse?

A muted voice floated from inside the car. Andy Grammer singing
"Keep Your Head Up," announcing an incoming call on my iPhone.
I almost laughed. Almost.

I'd told my boss, Tim Larabee, that I'd be at the lab before noon.
In the jury lounge, I'd phoned to update my ETA to 1:00 P.M. My
watch now said 2:00. Larabee would be wondering about the mummified remains awaiting my evaluation.

Maybe it wasn't Larabee.

Hell. So now what? There was no one I wanted to tell I was standing shoeless on a parking deck, locked out of my car.

But you gotta keep your head up . . .

Right.

I scanned the lot. Full of vehicles. Devoid of people.

Break the car window? With what? Frustrated, I glared at the glass. It countered with an image of an angry woman with really bad hair. Clever.

But it was. My eyes took in the glass that no longer snugged tight to the frame. A worn or missing tooth in the window regulator, Jimmy, my mechanic, had said. Dangerous. Enough gap for some kid to drop a wire and be halfway to Georgia before you realize your car's been boosted.

Seriously? I'd said. A ten-year-old Mazda?

Parts, he'd said solemnly.

Was a coat hanger too much to ask? I scanned the detritus collected where the deck's pavement met its back wall. Pebbles, cellophane wrappers, aluminum cans. Nothing likely to get me into the car.

I moved along the wall, gingerly positioning my feet. Though the blisters now looked like patches of ground beef, I soldiered on, cuffs dragging on the filthy concrete.

Mummified bones at the lab growing older by the minute.

Given all the delays, I'd be at the ME office until well into the evening. Then home to a cranky cat. Microwaving whatever was left in the freezer.

But you gotta keep your . . .

Can it.

Then I spotted a glint in the debris two yards ahead. Hopeful, I inched toward it.

My prize was a two-foot segment of wire, perhaps once part of a jerry-rigged arrangement such as the one I envisioned.

After a fast hobble back to the Mazda, I created a small loop at one end and fed the wire through Jimmy's gap.

Working two-handed, face flat to the window, I tried to drop the loop over the button. Each time the gizmo seemed well positioned, I pulled up sharply.

I was on my zillionth loop-and-yank when a voice boomed at my back.

"Step away from the vehicle."

Shit.

Clutching the wire firmly in one hand, I turned.

A uniformed parking attendant stood three yards from me, feet spread, palms up and pointed my way. His expression was one of nervous excitement.

I smiled what I hoped was a disarming smile. Or at least calming.

The attendant did not smile back.

"Step away from the vehicle." The guy's hair was blond, his face flushed a shade of red just a tick down from that of my blisters. I guessed his age at maybe eighteen.

I beamed a "silly me" charmer. "I've locked myself out of my car."

"I'll need to see ID and registration."

"My purse is inside. The keys are in the ignition."

"Step away from the vehicle."

"If I can manage to catch the lock I can show you—"

"Step away from the vehicle." Blondie had quite the repertoire.

I did as ordered, still holding on to the wire. Blondie gestured me further back.

Eyes rolling, I increased the distance. Let go. The wire slid inside onto the car seat.

Irritation overcame my resolve to be pleasant.

"Look, it's my car. I've just left jury duty. My registration and license are inside. I need to get to work. At the medical examiner's office."

If I hoped the last reference would do it, I was wrong. Blondie's expression said dirty barefoot woman with burglary tool. Dangerous?

"Call the ME office," I snapped.

A beat. Then, "Wait here."

Like I was a flight risk with no shoes and no wheels.

Blondie hurried off.

I leaned against the Mazda, fuming, shifting from damaged foot to damaged foot, alternating between checking my watch and scanning the pavement for my bracelet. I began to pace the parking lot. Finally I heard the sound of an engine.

Seconds later, a white Ford Taurus rolled up the ramp.

Could this day get any worse?

It just had.

2

PULLING CLOSE, ERSKINE "SKINNY" SLIDELL REMOVED HIS KNOCK-off Ray-Bans, lowered his window, and eyed my flopping pant legs, devastated feet, and disheveled hair. A smile lifted one corner of his mouth. Though the Charlotte-Mecklenburg PD Felony Investigative Bureau/Homicide Unit has more than two dozen detectives, somehow I always end up with Skinny. And the pairing is always a test of my fortitude.

It's not that Slidell's a bad investigator. Quite the opposite. But Skinny views himself as "old-school." In his mind that means Dirty Harry Callahan, Popeye Doyle, and Sergeant Friday. I've seen Slidell question witnesses. Always expect "just the facts, ma'am." But Skinny's not a "sir" and "ma'am" kind of guy.

Several years back, Slidell's partner, Eddie Rinaldi, was killed in a sidewalk shoot-out. No one blamed Slidell. Except Slidell. Thinking Skinny could use some diversity awareness, the department partnered him with a Latina lesbian named Theresa Madrid. To the surprise of all, the two got along.

Recently, Madrid and her partner had adopted a Korean infant, and Madrid had taken maternity leave. Slidell was temporarily working solo. Which he liked.

"Whoo-hee." The dolt actually said that.

"Detective—"

"You piss someone off?"

Later I might have chuckled about this episode. At that moment, I saw nothing but lousy choices. Argue with the parking twerp. Hike to a phone, then wait for AAA. Deal with Slidell.

"How did you know I was here?" Cool.

"I was with Doc Larabee when he got a call." Slidell leaned over and opened the passenger-side door. "Get in."

Drawing a lungful of fresh air, I slid into the seat.

"Lord in heaven, doc. Don't know I've seen anyone that ratty in years."

"You should get out more."

"What the hell were you—"

"Mud wrestling. Pull over there." I pointed to where my car was.

"Hate to see the other guy."

"I'll post a video on YouTube." I jabbed an impatient finger in the direction of the big SUV.

Slidell proceeded as directed.

"Stop!" My hand came up. "No, up behind that van."

"I know what happened. Some dude tuned you up for trying to boost his car."

"If I could boost a car, I wouldn't be here." I hopped out. The blisters looked like two red eyes staring up at my face.

If the bracelet hadn't been a gift from Katy, I'd have cut my losses and split. Someday I'd tell her about this. Then we'd laugh. Maybe.

I slid between my car and the blue mammoth, eyes on the pavement. Bingo. The bracelet lay beneath the two abutting mirrors, in the least accessible spot possible.

Sucking in my gut, I wedged between the door handles and down into a squat. Shoulders twisted sideways as far as they would, I reached out and snagged the bracelet. Then, careful not to set off alarms, I hauled myself up and made for the Taurus.

Slidell watched my performance without comment. Apparently I'd crossed the line from amusing to pitiable.

I got in and slammed the door.

"Where to?"

"The ME office." Snapping the bracelet onto my wrist.

"Happy to swing by your crib."

"My house key is in my purse. In my car."

"Shoe store?"

"No, thank you." Curt.

"No problemo. I'm headed back there anyway."

I could have asked why. Instead I sat facing the side window, attention focused on blocking the olfactory record of Slidell's passion for the deep-fried and overgreased. Of coffee supporting white colonies of mold. Of sweaty sneakers and oil-stained caps. Of stale smoke. Of Skinny himself.

But I wasn't exactly aromatic either.

Slidell exited the deck, kinked over to East Trade, and hung a left. Several minutes passed in silence. Then, "Who snuffed Fluffy, eh?"

I had no idea what that meant.

"Who popped the pooch?"

Great. Slidell knew about my mummy bundles. More grist for the comedy mill.

"Who capped the—"

"I've been asked to examine four sets of remains to verify that they are nonhuman. Should that be the case, archaeologists will date, authenticate, and send the materials on to . . . somewhere."

"Why's this litter of dead Chihuahuas—"

"The bundles are from Peru, not Mexico."

"Yeah, sure. So, how come these pooches get the ME treatment?"

"Customs officials snagged them at the airport. Some bonehead's been accused of smuggling them into the country. The illegal import of antiquities is a crime, you know."

"Ee-yuh." We rode a few more moments without talking. Then, "Ol' Dom Rockett got lassoed by the feds."

Though curious, I waited, knowing Slidell would expound.

"Dom Rockett, king of folksy shit from around the world."

"The whole world?" I couldn't help myself.

"South America, mostly. Our amigos down there got enough shit for the world."

Slidell is definitely fair-trade offensive.

"Junk bracelets, rings, crap to loop around your neck. Llama-mama shawls, wall hangings. Fleas from overseas."

"You're a poet, detective."

"Word is ICE thinks Rockett's expanding his horizons, maybe branching out to include real antiques." Slidell was referring to the

U.S. Department of Homeland Security's Immigration and Customs Enforcement. "Unreported ones."

I said nothing.

"Wouldn't surprise me. The guy's pond scum."

"You know him?"

"I know of him. Scum knows scum."

I didn't ask what that meant.

"Can you turn up the air?"

"Feet won't get cold?" Deadpan.

I shot Slidell a don't-go-there look. Which was pointless, since the Ray-Bans were fixed on the road.

Slidell reached out and flipped a button, then hammered the dash with the heel of one hand. A blue light flickered and tepid air oozed from the vents.

"If what you say is true, Rockett might have thought he could sell the mummy bundles to a museum," I said. "Maybe a private collector."

"I'm sure ICE will be querying his ambitions. Turd will roll on whoever he's dealing with."

Past I-77, West Trade swung west, then cut east again. Slidell took the curve fast, shooting paper bags and carry-out cartons across the floor in back. My mind threw up images of foodstuffs long gone. Fried chicken? Barbecue? Scavenged roadkill?

Finally, curiosity won out.

"What were you up to with Larabee?" I asked.

"Hit and run came in this morning. Female. No ID."

"Age?"

"Old enough."

"Meaning?" Sharper than I'd intended.

"Mid to late teens."

"Race?"

"Wetback. You can take that to the bank."

"No name, but magically you *know* the girl's Latina, and therefore undocumented?"

"She's moving with no ID and no keys."

Rather like I was, I thought, but didn't say it.

Seconds passed.

"Where was she found?" I asked.

"Intersection of Rountree and Old Pineville roads, just south of Woodlawn. Doc Larabee's putting time of death somewhere between midnight and dawn."

"What was she doing out there?" Mulling aloud.

"What d'you think?"

I was thinking Old Pineville was one deserted stretch in daytime, let alone in the middle of the night. There was a smattering of small businesses, but none that would attract a teenage girl.

"Any witnesses?"

Slidell shook his head. "I'll do some canvassing once I'm done with Doc Larabee. My guess, she was out working."

"Really."

Slidell shrugged one beefy shoulder.

"Unidentified teenage girl, that's what you know. But you've got her down as an illegal turning tricks. That speed detecting?"

He mumbled something.

I blocked him out. After years of practice, I've gotten better at it.

My gray cells offered a collage of images. A young girl alone in the dark on an empty two-lane. Headlights. The impact of a bumper.

"—Story?"

"What?"

"Do you remember John-Henry Story?"

The change of topic confused me. "The fire death last April?"

Six months back I'd examined fragmentary remains found in the aftermath of a flea market explosion and fire. I'd determined the victim was white, male, forty-five to sixty years of age. The bio profile fit John-Henry Story, the owner of the property. Story had told witnesses he was going to that location and had not been heard from thereafter. Personal items were found with the bones. A cell phone? Wallet? Watch? I couldn't remember details.

Though the ID was circumstantial, the ME had decided it was enough. Arson investigators had probed and tested, but the barn was so old, the destruction so total, an exact cause for the blaze was never determined.

Story's death had been big news. Prominent businessman burned to death in a building with inadequate alarm and sprinkler systems. The media had jumped on the issue of public safety at underregulated markets and gun shows. Eventually the press turned to something else, the furor fizzled, and Story's flea market reopened elsewhere.

"Ee-yuh." Skinny's favorite utterance. It drove me nuts.

For years the Mecklenburg County Medical Examiner was located at Tenth and College, in a redbrick box that was once a Sears Garden Center. For years the city fathers had talked of relocation. For years nothing had happened. Then, miraculously, the plan moved forward.

At a cost of eight million smackers, a replacement facility was built on government land in an industrial area northwest of uptown. Boasting seventeen thousand square feet, the new building is four times the size of the old. Epoxy floors, Corian walls, miles of stainless steel. Instead of only two, pathologists can now perform four simultaneous autopsies. The new setup includes a pair of rooms for analyses requiring special handling due to decomposition or potential contamination.

The stinkers. My kind of cases.

And the spanking-new building is conscientiously green. Sophisticated energy recovery systems. HVAC with air ducts up to forty inches wide. Though all the action takes place on the first floor, parts of the building had to be two stories to accommodate it all.

Yet the atmosphere is reasonably peaceful. The office and public areas are done in soft blues and earth tones. The windows are large and solar shades and light shelves maximize daylight intake and minimize glare.

In other words, our new digs are the bomb.

I waited as Slidell pulled through the black security fence, circled the flagpoles, and slipped into a parking spot. Killing the engine, he threw an arm over the seatback and a wave of odor my way. Then he shifted to face me.

"John-Henry Story had holdings all over Mecklenburg and Gaston counties. Story Motors. Story Storage—"

Store your stuff with Story. The slogan popped into my brain unbidden. It had been an annoying but effective ad campaign.

"—John-Henry's Tavern. The list is longer than my coon dog's tail."

"You have a dog?"

"You want to hear this?"

"Story's death was ruled accidental. Why are you bringing him up now?"

Slidell fixed me with a dramatic stare while reaching inside his jacket. Which was mustard and brown. With one deft move he pulled a Ziploc from the pocket of his shirt. Which was a shade of orange probably called melon.

Forcing my eyes not to roll, I leaned sideways to examine the contents of the baggie.

And felt my brows lift in surprise.

3

SUN GLINTED OFF THE PLASTIC DANGLING BETWEEN SLIDELL'S thumb and forefinger.

I waited for his explanation.

"Vic had a purse. Screeching pink, size of a burger, hooker strap."

"I carry a shoulder bag." Slidell's sarcasm was, as usual, turning me surly. As was his jump to the conclusion that the hit-and-run victim was a prostitute.

"Hot pink? Shaped like a freakin' cartoon cat?"

"You're sure it was hers?"

"Thing was lying in the weeds, three yards from the body. Hadn't been there long. We're checking for prints. But, yeah, I'm sure it's hers."

"This was in the purse?" I indicated the object enclosed in the Ziploc.

"Along with one tube of come-fuck-me red lipstick."

"Cash?"

"A ten and two ones. Forty-six cents. Loose. Like she just jammed it in."

"Anything else?"

"Nada . . . except—" He waggled the baggie. The Amazing Slidell, Magician of Mecklenburg.

I took the bag and studied the plastic rectangle inside, certain I'd misread the tiny black letters on its surface.

I hadn't.

"What the flip?"

"Thought it might interest you."

The yellow-and-brown US Airways club card had an expiration date of February of the upcoming year. The account was in the name of John-Henry Story.

"She had John-Henry Story's airline club pass?"

Slidell nodded.

"How?"

"Insightful question, doc. And here's another. Story crisped six months back. Where's his plastic been in the meantime?"

This wasn't making sense.

"What we got here is Story dies, but his card lives on. Or goes into suspended animation," Slidell said. "I checked. Last time he used the lounge was six weeks before the fire."

"Where was he going?"

"I'm working on that."

"Was anyone with him?"

"One guest."

"The girl?"

"They don't enter that information."

Slidell drew another Ziploc from his pocket. "And this was also in her purse."

I examined the slip of paper through the plastic. On it was scribbled: *Las clases de Inglés. Saint Vincent de Paul Catholic Church.*

I looked at Slidell. He looked at me and shrugged.

I moved to gather my belongings before exiting the Taurus, but, of course, I had no belongings. No shoes, no purse, no house or car keys, no phone, no cash, no cards.

Another time I could have called Katy for the spare key she keeps for my place.

Oh, God. Katy.

"Listen, thanks for swinging by for me. I—"

"—owe me one? Don't worry about it now."

Now? Great.

I hiked up my pants, eased from the Taurus, and hurried to the vestibule door. Stepping up onto the smooth concrete floor was as close to pleasure as I'd come all day. I paused a moment, taking relief from the cooling stone.

Waiting in my office were scrubs and sensible shoes. Soon I'd be reasonably presentable.

As with Slidell, my appearance wouldn't shock so much as amuse those inside. I'd arrived looking, and smelling, worse.

Except for Mrs. Flowers. She would signal disapproval by the briefest narrowing of the eyes, by a flurry of rearrangement of her already meticulously ordered desk.

I nodded at Mrs. Flowers through the reception window. After buzzing me in, she motioned me over with a finger waggle.

Though Mrs. Flowers has a first name—Eunice—to my knowledge she's never been addressed as anything other than Mrs. Flowers. The name so suits her I've wondered at times what she'd be called if she'd married a suitor named Smith or Gaspard. She is a peony of a woman, full-bodied, with pale pink skin that must have seen pampering since the stroller. The perfect complexion's one flaw? Mrs. Flowers colors in the presence of the opposite gender.

Blusher or not, Mrs. Flowers has the skill and motivation to keep every document filed and accessible, every report typed, proofed, and delivered promptly, all while answering the phone and triaging members of the public who show up at her window. Given a staff of three pathologists, numerous death investigators, the occasional specialty consultant, and myself, it's quite a feat.

"My word." Mrs. Flowers's upraised hand dropped to her yellow silk blouse.

"It's a long story," I said. Don't ask, I meant.

One carefully plucked brow arched slightly, but she let it go.

"Dr. Larabee wishes to see you." Southern as Tara. "He's in the main autopsy room."

"Thanks."

Two small hallways, called biovestibules by those who designed them, connect the administrative and public sectors of the building with the autopsy area. I passed through one, pausing briefly to check the erasable board.

Four new cases. A single-vehicle accident near Optimist Park on North Davidson, elderly male driver DOA at Carolinas Medical

Center. A sixteen-year-old female with a gunshot wound to the head, found beside a Dumpster on Shamrock Drive. The Peruvian mummified remains awaiting my assessment. And the teenage hit-and-run victim from Old Pineville Road.

Slidell's Jane Doe.

I beelined for the ladies' and did what I could with my hair and dirt-crusted face, then shifted to the locker room to change into scrubs. Last stop, my office for Band-Aids, antiseptic, and the spare Nikes I keep under the coat tree. Ten minutes after arriving, I was ready to roll.

When I pushed open the door of the large autopsy room, Tim Larabee was standing beside one of the two stainless steel tables. He wasn't cutting or weighing, not dictating, not even looking down at the remains.

Shielding her from me? From Slidell? From the many who would probe and photograph and analyze and dissect her?

Odd thought. But true. The cold process had begun. And I would take part.

X-rays glowed from light boxes mounted along one wall. Cranials. A full-body series.

A pair of boots sat on one counter. Tan vinyl, with high heels and red and blue flowers running up the sides. Soles caked with mud. Cheap.

And small. Maybe size five. Tiny feet striding in very big-girl boots.

Clothing hung from a drying rack. A red blouse. A denim miniskirt. A white cotton bra. White cotton panties with pale blue dots.

Slidell stood by the rack, feet spread, hands clasped and V-ing down over his genitals. He wasn't assessing the clothes or the body. He didn't acknowledge my entrance.

I felt a new wave of irritation, squelched it as I kicked into scientist mode. First rule: block mind-set. Don't suspect, don't fear, don't hope for any outcome. Observe, weigh, measure, and record.

Second rule: block emotion. Leave sorrow, pity, and outrage for later. Anger or grief can lead to error and misjudgment. Mistakes do your victim no good.

Nevertheless.

I looked at the bruised and distorted young face, and for a moment pictured the girl alive, slinging her pink kitty purse onto her shoulder. The strap slipping because the meager contents provided no ballast.

A dark stretch of road.

A hammering heart.

Headlights.

White cotton panties with pale blue dots. The kind Katy favored throughout middle school.

"Slidell give you a rundown?"

Larabee's question snapped me back.

"Hit and run. Not yet identified."

"Take a look." Larabee crossed to the X-rays. His face looked drawn and gaunt, even for him, an obsessive long-distance runner with no body fat and hollows in his cheeks the depth of ocean trenches.

I joined him. He slipped a ballpoint out of the breast pocket of his scrubs and pointed at a defect located approximately mid-shaft in the left clavicle.

At the third and fourth ribs inferior to it.

Stepping to the next film, he ran the pen down the arm, over the humerus, the radius, the ulna. The hand.

"Yes," I said to his unspoken question.

I followed as he moved on, to a posterior angle of the pelvis. He didn't have to point.

"Yes," I repeated.

To an anterior-posterior view of the skull. A lateral view.

A cold fist started closing on my gut.

Wordlessly, I returned to the body.

The girl lay on her back. Larabee hadn't yet made his Y-incision, and, except for the bruises, abrasions, and distortion due to fractures, she might have been sleeping. The hair haloing her head was long and blond, one clump held high with a plastic barrette shaped like a cat. Pink. The kind little girls love.

Focus.

I gloved and examined the ravaged flesh, ghostly pale and cold to the touch. I palpated the arm, the shoulder, the hand, the abdomen, felt the underlying damage evident on the X-rays in glowing black-and-white.

"Can we turn her over, please?" My voice broke the stillness.

Larabee stepped to my side. Together we tucked the slender arms tight to the body and rolled it by the shoulders and hips.

My eyes traveled the delicate spine and small buttocks. Took in the tread marks imprinted on the flesh of the painfully thin thighs.

The fist tightened.

"What's this?" I ran one finger over a discoloration on the girl's right shoulder. Maybe five inches long, the bruise appeared as a series of dashes.

"Hematoma," Larabee said.

"It's a patterned injury," I said. "Any idea what made it?"

Larabee shook his head.

I looked at Slidell. He looked back but said nothing.

"May I see the CSU photos?" Stripping off and tossing, not so gently, my latex gloves.

Larabee collected a stack of five-by-sevens from the counter and handed them to me. Frame by frame I viewed the desolate spot where the girl had lived her last moments.

The photos told the same story.

It was no accident.

The girl had been murdered.

4

"Murdered?" slidell's bark ricocheted off the stainless steel and glass surrounding us.

"Legally that would imply intent," Larabee said.

"Screw legal definitions." I jammed a finger at the devastated body. "Some bastard killed this kid."

"What the hell are you talking about?" Slidell was shifting surprised eyes between Larabee and me.

I gestured Slidell to the X-ray showing the left arm bones. Larabee joined us and offered his pen. I took it and pointed to the humeral shaft, four inches below the shoulder joint.

"See this dark line?"

"A broken arm don't mean the kid was capped." Slidell was peering at the gray-and-white image, doubt crimping his already dubious expression.

"No, detective. It doesn't." I shifted to indicate the hand. "Note the medial and distal phalanges."

"Don't go all jargony on me, doc."

"The finger bones."

Slidell leaned in and studied the illuminated fragments at the tip of my pen.

"The middle phalanges should look like small tubes, the distal ones like tiny arrowheads. They underlie the fingertips."

"Looks like wood shavings."

"The bones have been crushed."

Slidell made a noise in his throat I chose not to interpret.

I moved on to the cranial X-ray.

"There are no skull fractures. But note the mandible, especially the mental eminence." I would leave discussion of soft-tissue injuries to Larabee.

Slidell pooched air through his lips.

"The chin," I explained.

"How come it's called mental when the brain's up top?"

"Some people think with their mouths."

Larabee smiled. Almost. My sarcasm was lost on Skinny.

"Fine." Slidell's skepticism was turning his tone gruff. "Her chin's broken, her arm's broken, and her fingers are smashed. How's that add up to murder?"

"The tread marks on her thighs tell us this is a vehicular death. But it's no regular hit and run. The victim wasn't standing along the side of the road. Not hitchhiking. Not waiting on the shoulder for a ride from a friend. She was hit square in the back."

Larabee nodded in confirmation of the conclusion he too had reached but had yet to voice.

Slidell continued staring at the film.

"Picture this," I said. "She's walking, maybe running. A car comes at her from behind. Maybe she tries to escape. Maybe not. Either way, the car plows into the backs of her legs."

Slidell said nothing. Larabee kept nodding.

"She goes down hard, arms outstretched. Her chin impacts the pavement. She's forced beneath the chassis. The left tires roll over her left hand, crushing her fingers."

"You sure about this?"

I gestured an upturned palm at Larabee.

"Typically, a pedestrian hit by a vehicle is slammed onto the windshield or thrown sideways and outward, receiving injuries to the head, upper torso, or legs," he said. "This victim has no cranial or thoracic trauma consistent with a windshield impact or rapid deceleration angled to the left or right."

Slidell still looked unconvinced.

I snatched up the crime-scene photos, chose two, and handed them to him. He studied both, then slowly exhaled through his nose.

"No skid marks."

"Exactly. The driver never hit the brakes."

"Sonofabitch."

I turned to Larabee.

"You're putting PMI at seven to ten hours?" I was asking about postmortem interval.

"To be safe. The body arrived here shortly after nine this morning. Air temp last night dropped to forty-eight. I observed lividity, but still got blanching. Rigor—"

"Whoa, whoa. Back it up, doc." Slidell pulled a pen and small spiral from his pocket and began taking notes.

Larabee indicated the body. "Notice the purple mottling on her belly, the fronts of her thighs, the undersides of her arms, and the right half of her face?"

Slidell glanced up, resumed scribbling.

"That discoloration is called lividity. It's due to the settling of blood in the body's downside once the heart stops beating. When I pressed a thumb to her flesh, the vessels were pushed aside, leaving an area of pallor."

Slidell twisted his mouth to one side.

"A white mark," Larabee simplified. "After about ten hours the red blood cells and capillaries would have decomposed sufficiently so blanching wouldn't have occurred."

"And rigor's when the stiff gets stiff." Slidell pronounced it *rigger*.

Larabee nodded. "When the body arrived, rigor was complete in the small muscles, but not in the largest ones. Her jaws were locked, but I could still bend her knees and elbows."

"So she died more than seven hours before she got here, but less than ten." Slidell did the math in his head. It took a while. "Sometime between eleven and two."

"It's not a precise science," Larabee said.

"What about stomach contents? Once you get her open?"

"Ninety-eight percent of her last meal would have left her stomach within six to eight hours of ingestion. With luck I might find some fragments, corn, maybe tomato skin, in a rugal fold in the gastric mucosa. I'll let you know."

"What about vitreous?" I was asking about fluid drawn from the eye. "Can you test for potassium?"

"I took a sample, but it won't really narrow the range."

"How close was she to the light rail?" I asked Slidell.

"She was on the shoulder, on the side opposite the railway."

"How often do trains pass during those hours?"

"Last one runs by there just after one A.M. The next isn't until five A.M."

"What about metallic spray?" I asked Larabee. "Or oil. Did you find any deposits on her skin or hair? On the clothing?"

He shook his head. "Unlikely airborne residue would travel that far, but I'll double-check. What are you thinking?"

"The presence or absence of train residue might narrow the time frame."

Larabee spread two sinewy hands, palms up. "Worth a try."

I turned back to Slidell. "How was she found?"

"A call came in a little after seven A.M. Teacher on her way to work noticed what she thought was a mannequin, pulled over, thinking she could use a dummy for the school play. Tossed her cornflakes, then dialed 911."

I picked up the scene photos and worked through a progression of shots moving from far to near.

The first several showed a stretch of empty road not different from what I'd pictured in my mind. On the right, the raised light-rail tracks threw long, postdawn shadows over the embankment, the shoulder, and the pavement below.

On the left, maybe eighty yards distant from the yellow crime-scene tape triangling the body, stood a small stucco building fronted by a gravel lot.

"What's that?"

"A party supply store. Been empty for months."

"And that?" I pointed to a one-story, windowless structure.

"Some sort of self-storage outfit."

The next series zoomed in on the body and its immediate surroundings. Rountree Road coming in from the west. Old Pineville running north and south. On the latter lay one of the tan vinyl boots. My eyes traversed the pavement.

Paralleling the right shoulder was a swath of grass and foxtails that yielded to tangled underbrush as the ground sloped to a trench beside the supporting wall of the light-rail platform.

Back on the Rountree side, I noted an irregular smear of dirt and a spray of pebbles on the gravel shoulder, what looked to be a crumpled paper cup, and a beer can. Specks of white peeked from the tangled weeds. Litter?

"Think there could be anything useful there? Prints on the cup or can? Something in the trash?"

Slidell licked a thumb, flipped pages, and scribbled in his spiral.

In the next series, the girl was covered by a red wool blanket, a corner of her skirt and one leg visible along the left side. The limb twisted outward from the hip at an impossible angle. Beside it, not on the foot, was the other boot.

The mound below the blanket looked pitifully small. Tracing its contours I could see that the other leg lay straight, with the foot crooked unnaturally toward the head. One arm appeared to be outstretched. The position of the other was unclear.

Bands of anger and sadness squeezed my chest. I drew a deep breath.

"Who covered her?" I knew it hadn't been CSU. No way trained technicians would risk transferring fibers or disturbing trace evidence.

Slidell spit-thumbed pages in his notepad.

"Lydia Dreos."

"The teacher?"

"Yeah. I forgot that part. She had the blanket in her trunk."

In the next several photos the girl lay exposed, with the blanket folded inside a plastic evidence bag beside her. Her skin looked ghostly white against the backdrop of oil-darkened gravel, blacktop, and mottled vegetation.

A thought struck me.

"She had no jacket."

I sensed Slidell shake his head.

"It was forty-eight degrees last night." I added the obvious.

No one replied.

I moved on, through close-ups of the battered face, the crushed hands, the sad little boots.

"The height of the hamstring bruising will allow us to estimate front-bumper height. We should be able to narrow vehicle type from that," Larabee said.

"Find any paint on her?" I asked.

"None," Larabee said. "But there's a smear on the purse. Black. Could be from the vehicle. I'll send it off for analysis."

"Any scraping on her back from the undercarriage?"

"No."

"Do you have a maximum anterior-posterior body width? For vehicle clearance?"

"Pelvis nineteen point one centimeters. If she's lying flat on her belly."

"Injuries to the chin and fingers suggest that was the case," I said.

"What's that in inches?" Slidell asked.

"Seven and a half."

"Nothing on wheels rides lower," Slidell said. "'Cept maybe a skateboard."

"Anything noteworthy about the bruising across her thighs?" I asked.

"Two inches top to bottom," Larabee said. "No patterning."

"So no grill," Slidell said.

Good one, Skinny.

Slidell finished jotting. Punctuated his note with a tap of the pen. Then, "So lemme get this. The kid's running—"

"Or walking," Larabee cautioned.

"The bumper slams the back of her thighs. She goes down. Her chin smacks the pavement. Her arms fly out. The vehicle rolls over her, crushing her fingers."

I could see her in the darkness, a silhouette backlit by double beams fast closing in. Lungs burning. Heart hammering. Goose-bumped skin slick with sweat. High-heeled boots wobbly on her feet.

"So what killed her?"

"Though I see no fracture, the cranial X-rays suggest devastating trauma. When I open her skull I'm certain I'll find subdural, subgaleal, and intracerebral hematoma accompanied by massive edema in the parieto-occipital region."

Slidell just looked at him.

"A blow to the head caused bleeding into her brain."

Slidell thought about that. "The kid's hit from behind and goes belly down with her brain busted bad. How's she end up so far off the pavement?"

"Perhaps the force of the impact."

"Or?" Slidell picked up on something in Larabee's tone.

"Hematoma doesn't necessarily cause death right away."

"You suggesting she might have dragged herself some?"

Larabee nodded glumly.

"If the bastard had pulled over, the kid would have lived?"

"Medical intervention might have saved her life. Might have."

Intent or not, that's murder in my book. I didn't need to say it.

I see violent death on a regular basis. I know the cruelty and stupidity and insensitivity of which humans are capable. And yet, every time, the same question.

How?

How could someone run down a kid and leave her to die? Unless that was the plan.

The men watched me walk to the drying rack and pick up the skirt. The skirt that would have ended just above the impact site.

I turned to Slidell.

"Have this tested."

"For what?"

"Paint."

"What are the chances—"

"DNA, parsley, fucking life from Mars! Just have it tested!"

Many males are embarrassed in the presence of strong female emotion. Most have mastered the art of nonreaction. The averted eyes. The shifting feet. The unneeded cough.

Slidell went to his fallback, the pointless wristwatch check.

Larabee returned to the table and, unaided, repositioned the girl on her back.

"I'm sorry." I was. "That was uncalled for."

"I'm sure you noticed these." Larabee proceeded as though my outburst had never taken place.

I rehung the skirt and walked to his side. Slidell followed.

Larabee lifted and rotated one of the girl's arms.

Angry ridges snaked the flesh of her inner elbow.

"Well, that goes to motive." Slidell was so close I could smell his sweat and hair oil. "Kid probably crossed her pusher and the prick took her out."

"There's something else," Larabee said quietly.

5

"KILL THE LIGHTS, PLEASE."

Slidell clumped to the wall, back to the table.

Larabee clicked on a small UV light and directed it toward the girl's inner left thigh.

A scatter glowed blue-white on her skin.

Semen.

As Larabee slowly moved the beam, some stains fluoresced more intensely than others.

"Multiple donors?" I asked.

"We'll need DNA to confirm," Larabee said. "But that's my impression."

"We talking rape?" Slidell's mouth was right at my ear.

"I found no vaginal tearing or abrasions. No sign of anal entry."

"So we're back to my first guess." I heard Slidell straighten. "The kid was on the stroll."

I bit back a response.

Larabee thumbed off his flash. "Get the switch?"

Slidell did.

"Think you can narrow the age estimate?" Larabee spoke to me as the fluorescents buzzed to life.

"Has Joe taken dentals?" I was referring to Joe Hawkins, most senior of the lab's autopsy techs.

Larabee indicated a brown envelope lying on a countertop light box.

I crossed to it and poured the small black squares onto the box's viewing plate. After pushing the on button, I arranged the films anatomically and studied the illuminated dentition.

"All four second molars are in occlusion, with the roots fully formed down to the tips. That puts her, minimally, above twelve. The third molars are unerupted and show little root development. I'm not an odontologist, but, dentally, I'd say she's in the range of thirteen to seventeen."

The men waited as I continued to study the X-rays.

"Left first molar's got a mean abscess. Lots of caries, but not a single restoration."

"No evidence she ever saw a dentist." Larabee got my meaning.

"So I don't bust my ass chasing dental records." Slidell parked his hands on his hips. "An abscess. Wouldn't that hurt like a sonofabitch?"

"People have different thresholds for pain," Larabee said. "But yes, probably. What are you thinking?"

"Maybe she went to one of those free clinics. You know, looking for drugs or something."

"Good idea, detective."

Like a mail-order toy, the human skeleton comes with assembly required. Most bones are present at birth but lack the knobs, bumps, and borders that make them complete. Throughout infancy and adolescence, these fiddly bits, called epiphyses, appear and fuse to the shafts or main bony elements. The fusion takes place with age predictability.

I shifted my attention to the skeletal X-rays. More than a decade of working with me had made Joe Hawkins savvy to the exact views I needed. As usual, he'd nailed them.

I started with a plate showing the girl's hand and arm bones. Slidell's insistence she was a hooker had my nerves on edge. Knowing it would annoy him, I went all "jargony." Petty, but I did.

"The distal radial epiphysis is in the process of fusion, the distal ulnar epiphysis has recently fused. The rest of the hand bones are complete."

I moved to a film showing the shoulder and left arm.

"The acromial epiphyses are present on both scapulae, but remain unfused."

I pointed to the broken humerus.

"The medial epicondyle and the distal composite and proximal epiphyses are in the process of fusing."

On to the pelvis.

"The iliac crest is present but still separate." I was referring to a sliver of bone that would eventually form the superior border of the hip bone.

The upper leg.

"The femoral head and trochanter are fused. The distal epiphysis is in the process of fusing."

Lower leg.

"The proximal and distal epiphyses of the tibiae and fibulae are in the process of fusing."

The foot.

"The proximal phalanges—"

"So what's it all mean?" Slidell cut me off.

"She was fourteen to fifteen years old when she died."

Far too young to catch a hint of what life had to offer. Fifteen years. She should have had eighty.

Rotten teeth. Needle tracks. Semen stains. Fifteen crappy years.

For a full minute the only sounds in the room were the fluorescents overhead and the air whistling in and out of Slidell's nose.

"Might be I could work the clothing, track down where it was sold." Slidell shoved his notepad into his jacket. "Boots might be a goer."

My mind had moved from how to who. Who had left this kid facedown on the asphalt? A drunk too impaired to see her in the dark? Too callous to stop? Or a killer fully intending the result?

"Anything else?" Barely trusting my voice.

Larabee gave a tight shake of his head.

Nodding to Slidell, I returned to my office. Sat at my desk. Antsy. Uneasy.

Slidell was a good cop. But he had a habit of falling captive to defeatist mind-sets. Convinced the girl was undocumented, a prostitute, and a junkie, would he devote sufficient energy to finding her killer?

Yes, he would, I admitted to myself. Druggie hooker or not, the kid turned up dead on Skinny's patch, and he would look upon it as a personal challenge.

Then why so anxious?

Katy? My abandoned vehicle and purse? The goddamn blisters? Whatever.

I crossed to the bathroom and splashed cold water on my face. Took a look in the mirror. Assessed the face looking back.

Intense green eyes. Weary, but determined. A few starbust wrinkles at the corners, well earned. Chin and lids holding firm. Dark blond hair yanked into a pony, not having a good one.

"Right, then. Peruvian dogs."

The image in the glass mouthed the same words. Nodded the same nod.

I bunched and tossed my hand towel and headed out.

While the new MCME facility is immense, the same is not true of my office. Were a realtor to advertise it for rental, she'd use descriptors like "cozy" and "snug." My desk takes up most of the space. File cabinets, coat tree. If Larabee steps in, it's crowded. If the visitor is Slidell, forget about breathing.

I'm good with the square footage. It's mine. No one encroaches. Mostly I use it for writing reports or examining files. Like the one lying on my blotter.

I sat down and opened the cover. On top was a form requesting an anthropology consult. I skimmed the contents.

Case number. Morgue number. Police incident number. Investigating officer, agency. Larabee was the requesting pathologist.

I skipped to the Summary of Known Facts. The brief, handscrawled paragraph contained nothing I hadn't heard from Slidell. Suspicion of smuggled antiquities, objects confiscated at Charlotte-Douglas International Airport. Dominick Rockett.

I moved on to Description of Specimens. The items in question were identified as mummy bundles. Four in number. Peruvian in origin. Possibly Inca. Likely obtained from a cemetery.

My eyes dropped to the final section: Expertise Requested. The boxes beside "Exhumation," "Biological Profile," and "Trauma Analysis" had been left unchecked. Beside the category "Other" were six scribbled words: *Analysis and written report. Human remains?*

I set the form aside and thumbed through the stack of paper-clipped photos.

In the first three, the bundles lay side by side, wrappings intact.

Though desiccated and discolored with age, each seemed in pretty good shape. Fair enough. The Peruvian desert would have provided a reasonably dry environment, a burial context kind to preservation.

The next several photos showed one of the bundles partially unwrapped. I could see what appeared to be a shriveled dog's head, eyelids closed, fur still covering one flattened ear.

I dug back to my grad-school days, to a course on South American archaeology. And came up with little beyond the basics. Fifteenth century. The Andes Mountains. Machu Pichu. The Quechua language. Inti, the sun god.

I lined up the photos. Stared. A gaggle of brain cells coughed up an article I'd read maybe five years earlier. *National Geographic?* The Chiribaya, a pre-Inca population living in the Osmore River valley, some five hundred miles southeast of Lima. The Chiribaya had interred their dogs along with their dead.

I booted my laptop, opened Google, and entered a few key words. Peru. Canines. Mummies.

Yep. The Chiribaya buried their dogs between the graves of their dearly departed. Some with blankets and food for the long journey onward.

Now I understood my involvement in the case. I was to make sure there were no human bones caught up in those bundles.

According to the case board, the dogs were here. I could walk across the hall and unpack them.

I didn't.

My thoughts kept drifting back to the hit-and-run victim, now under Larabee's scalpel.

My gaze fell on the photo closest to me, on a slash of white visible below the rolled gum of the unwrapped dog. A tooth. Perfect after centuries.

Unlike the teeth of our young Jane Doe.

I reclipped the photos and closed the file.

Sat a moment.

Reopened the file.

Checked a name.

Picked up and dialed the phone.

6

"UNITED STATES IMMIGRATION AND CUSTOMS ENFORCEMENT. How may I direct your call?"

I asked for Luther Dew, the agent working the mummified-dog case.

ICE does not offer music to callers placed on hold. Bored and agitated, my mind started playing What Songs Would Suit? Ricky Nelson's "Travelin' Man"? Neil Diamond's "Coming to America"? Merle Haggard's "Movin' On"?

A recorded voice cut the game short.

"Special Agent Dew is not available to take your call. Please leave a message after the beep."

I left a message.

Glanced at my watch. The time was movin' on to 5:30 P.M. To be a travelin' woman I'd need my car.

I opened the file again and stared at the photo of the unwrapped dog. What were they called? Chiribayan shepherds? Looked like a snoozing spaniel to me.

My eyes shifted to the phone, willing it to ring.

It didn't. Of course.

My mind looped back to the Jane Doe who'd recently left Larabee's table.

Had I missed something?

Before I could consider the possibility, the landline shrilled its after-hours ring.

"Dr. Brennan?"

"Speaking."

"Due here."

Confused, I looked at my watch again. Had I forgotten an appointment?

"Luther Dew. Returning your call." The voice was high and somewhat effeminate. I pictured Truman Capote in bow tie and fedora.

"Thanks for calling back so quickly."

Noncommittal silence.

"I'm with the medical examiner's office."

"Yes. I just phoned you at this number."

"I'm working on the Peruvian mummy bundles."

"You're the anthropologist?"

"I am." Matching Dew's prim with prim. "I wondered if I might have some background on the case. On Dominick Rockett, the importer."

Dew gave an annoyed little click of his tongue.

"Sir?"

"Importers are legal and adhere to U.S. Customs regulations. They file proper paperwork. They bring in only what is allowed. None of that applies to Mr. Rockett in the matter of these artifacts."

Of *these* artifacts?

"Has your agency had other interactions with Rockett?"

"I am not at liberty to say."

Alrighty, then.

But I hadn't called Dew to talk about smuggling. His Peruvian dogs were simply my lead-in, a means to schmooze him for what I really wanted to know.

"Can you share anything on Rockett?"

"I cannot divulge the specifics of an open file."

And I don't give a rat's ass about Dominick Rockett.

"I understand, sir. But mummified dogs are unusual for this facility. I assume you got a peek at the one that was partially unwrapped?"

More noncommittal silence. But a hitch in Dew's breathing suggested he might be thawing.

"If that pooch opened its eyes and asked for Alpo, it wouldn't surprise me." I chuckled, congenial as hell. "He's that well preserved."

"Is he."

"These dogs were quite a score for your department."

"You wouldn't believe the items we confiscate." Did the prig actually sniff?

"I'm sure the array is impressive."

"Take rhinoceros horns. Traditionally, smugglers would grind them and hide the powder inside statues or other hollow objects. Now they're importing whole heads, declaring them as legal antiques. They sever the horns, replace them with synthetics, and think they're in business. How dumb do they think we are?"

"The Peruvian dogs came through Charlotte-Douglas, right?"

"Smuggling isn't limited to big cities. Contraband can arrive at any port of entry." Dew was opening up, though revealing only what was public knowledge. I knew the ploy. Had used it myself. "Did you read about the Tyrannosaurus bones seized up north?"

"Sir?"

"A semicomplete skeleton from the Gobi Desert. The imbeciles listed it on two different importation documents. As if we wouldn't check." Yep. Dew actually sniffed in disdain. "They declared reptile heads, broken fossil bones, and a couple of lizards."

"What was the tip-off?" I picked up and started flipping a pen on my blotter.

"The materials were wildly undervalued. But the flashing red was the information entered as country of origin."

"Which was?"

"England."

"Tyrannosaurus-on-Thames?"

"Yes. The Mongolians had a giggle over that." Delivered without a hint of a laugh.

"Good work."

"The American people don't fully appreciate what ICE does for international relations."

"I'm sure the Peruvian government is thrilled you recovered their artifacts."

"Which brings up a good point. Their head archaeologist is quite anxious to have the specimens returned promptly. And he very much hopes your examination can be as noninvasive as possible."

"Of course. I'm hoping I can see all that I need to with X-rays."

There was a long pause. Then, "I suppose I can share some facts, since you are involved in the case. The mummy bundles arrived as part of a shipment of pottery. Apparently Mr. Rockett thought we couldn't tell bones from ceramics."

"Seems pretty amateurish. Has Rockett been in the import business for long?"

"Since the early nineties."

"In all that time he's never been caught with illegal goods?"

"Mr. Rockett has either been straight, careful, or extraordinarily lucky. But the gentleman's luck ran out on this one. The bundles turned up in a random check."

"What's his explanation?"

"He says he bought them from a farmer who owns the land where his son dug them up."

"If he's a successful importer, why risk smuggling antiquities?"

"He claims he had no idea they were old."

Dew made one of those thinking-with-your-lips-or-teeth sounds. Deciding how much more to share?

"Are you familiar with Mr. Rockett's background?"

"Only that he collects and sells indigenous arts and crafts from South America."

"Have you met him, Dr. Brennan?"

"No."

"Seen him?"

"No." What the hell?

"Mr. Rockett is a veteran of Desert Storm. 1990."

"The first Gulf War."

"I'm not certain of the whole story. Perhaps a Scud missile, perhaps burning oil. Rockett suffered severe burns, leaving him badly scarred."

I said nothing.

"War is cruel, Dr. Brennan. Mr. Rockett returned to a country where no one would hire him because of his disfigurement. Or so he believes."

Still, I just listened.

"He couldn't find a job. He was frustrated. Then Mr. Rockett remembered the souks of the Middle East, the goods available for next to nothing. Jewelry. Clothing. Household items. He formulated a plan. Buy overseas, sell stateside at tenfold the purchase price. Trinkets for the undiscerning."

"Wouldn't Rockett have a military pension, and disability?"

"Of course. But his import business provides a nice subsidy."

"But the mummy bundles came from Peru."

"Some time back, Mr. Rockett shifted his focus to South America."

"Why?"

"Geographic proximity? Ease of operation? Personal safety?" I heard the swish of fabric, pictured impeccably clad shoulders rising in a shrug. "I really couldn't say."

"Americans aren't popular in the Middle East these days."

"Uprisings, revolutions, civil wars, kidnappings. Political instability negatively impacts any enterprise. Perhaps upheaval in the Middle East made South America more appealing."

"Let me ask you something." Casual, as though the thought had just entered my mind. "I've got a girl here, fourteen to fifteen years old, possibly Latina, possibly undocumented. She was killed in a hit and run near Old Pineville Road last night. We're having trouble getting an ID."

"Go on."

"She had a pink kitty purse and hair barrette, and was wearing a short denim skirt, red blouse, and embroidered boots."

"Sounds like any teenager. What makes you think she's illegal?"

"She had a note in her purse about English language classes at a local Catholic church. The note was written in Spanish, and the parish also holds Spanish language mass. That, plus the fact that she had no form of ID, no keys, makes the lead investigator suspect she's Latina."

"Sorry, but I do artifacts, not people. I specialize in the illicit importation and distribution of cultural property, and the illegal trafficking of artwork. Besides, if this girl has not been determined with reasonable certainty to be illegal, ICE would not be involved."

"Is there a colleague you could ask?"

"I'd help if I could. But unless you know your victim was undocumented . . . And even then . . ." Dew sounded distracted. "It's not as if we have a list of every person who enters the country illegally. It's quite the opposite. Sorry."

"Sure."

"When might you complete your examination of the mummy bundles?"

"Soon."

"Please keep me posted."

"Will do. And thanks for your time, Agent Dew."

My fingers lingered on the cradled receiver.

And my nerves buzzed with frustration.

Dew was a dead end.

Slidell had his mind glued to a theory.

Time to call it a day. A lousy one.

Again, the nagging thought. Had I missed something?

Without making a conscious decision, I got up and walked to the cooler, my rubber soles squeaking softly in the stillness. Cold air whooshed when I pulled open the heavy steel door, enveloping me in the smell of refrigerated flesh. I flipped on the light.

Six gurneys lined the walls, three holding occupied body bags. I checked tags until I found the one marked MCME 580-13. *Unknown*.

I was glad no next of kin ever saw this frigid crypt. No mother ever viewed her child stiff from the cold. No husband ever gazed on his wife labeled with digits and letters.

I swallowed. Partially unzipped MCME 580-13.

The girl's hair trailed like seaweed across her forehead, tangled and yellow.

Somehow wrong with her olive skin and dark lashes and brows. I looked closely at her roots. Noted a quarter inch of black at her scalp.

The girl's hair was bleached. Could Slidell be right?

On reflex, I brushed wayward strands from the girl's face. The pink barrette loosened and fell to the side of her head.

An image popped. Katy, blond curls in dual ponies, plastic barrettes holding unruly escapees.

I retrieved the girl's lone possession and clipped it firmly in place. My hand lingered as it had on the phone.

"You have my promise." My voice sounded brittle in the small icy space. "I *will* find your family. I *will* send you home."

Wanting to take a headshot, I reached for my iPhone.

Empty pocket.

My mobile was in my purse.

In my car.

In the courthouse parking lot.

The car I couldn't retrieve because I had no ride.

The car I couldn't drive because I had no key.

Cursing, I rousted up the Polaroid. After snapping the girl's picture, I spent one more silent moment studying her features, then rezipped the bag.

Back in my office, I scanned the photo and e-mailed it to myself. Then I gophered through my desk drawers, hoping for peanut butter crackers or a stale granola bar. Lunch at the courthouse had been a Snickers.

My food quest turned up zip.

Great. I'd return hungry and empty-handed to my town house. To a peeved cat. And an empty fridge.

I was Googling for locksmiths and taxi services when the phone rang again. The call changed my plans.

7

I DON'T NORMALLY TENSE AT THE SOUND OF PETE'S VOICE.

Janis "Pete" Petersons. My ex. Sort of. Long story.

I fell for Pete in college. He was wrapping up law school, a post-fratboy charmer. Good mind, good body, good prospects. Good talker.

Our marriage was dandy for almost twenty years. Might have lasted if Pete hadn't started sharing his charms with other women.

That aside—big aside, there—once we separated and time soothed the anger and hurt, I grew to like Pete's company again. In the parlor, not the bedroom. Though, truth be told, the old embers can still smolder now and again.

Like many former spouses, Pete and I remain permanently linked. There's our daughter, Katy, of course. And pets. When Pete travels, his dog, Boyd, is a guest at my town house. My cat, Birdie, bunks with Pete when I'm out of town. Sharing custody helps on both sides.

Over the years, Pete's ring tone has come to signal a discussion of Katy, or the exchange of details concerning animal transfer. Occasionally a request that our daughter wants filtered through her old man the softy.

Tonight was not the ordinary call.

Pete never dialed my office line.

Oh, God!

I saw the girl zipped in the bag across the hall. The girl who'd been left to die on the roadside.

I saw Katy.

"What is it? Has something happened?" Fingers death-gripping the receiver.

"Relax. Katy's fine. Where the hell have you been? I've been phoning you all afternoon."

"It's a long story. You're sure Katy's okay?"

"I Skyped with her this morning. Night there. Her unit was just back from a training exercise."

"How'd she look?"

"Wired. Tired. Bunch of GIs shouting nearby. How much can you tell?"

One year ago, Katy was a researcher at the public defender's office, bored, bitching, but safe in Charlotte, her single joy in life her boyfriend and absentee landlord, Aaron Cooperton. Out of college and completing a stint in the Peace Corps, Coop had joined the International Rescue Committee and volunteered for aid work in Afghanistan. He was on his way to Kabul to fly home to Katy when an IED blew up his convoy.

Katy was devastated by Coop's death. Unaware of her close connection to him, the Cooperton family had excluded her, even barred her from the private funeral they held in Charleston. Katy was left with no closure and no way to grieve.

I watched my daughter start her mornings red-eyed and ragged, drag through her days. I listened and did what I could to comfort. Took her with me on a working trip to Hawaii. Nothing helped. It gutted me to see her in such pain.

Maybe I should have guessed what was coming.

Suddenly Katy was sparkling again, enthused about life. The dark shadows under her eyes slowly faded. Her chin reclaimed its cocky tilt. When she visited, it was no longer for hours, but for minutes squeezed in between pressing commitments.

It was Pete who told me she'd enlisted. In a call like this. Katy had kept her plans secret until the papers were signed.

"Don't worry," she'd said when finally we'd talked. "I won't be in combat."

Right.

On May 14, 2012, the United States Army opened HIMARS, High Mobility Artillery Rocket System, and MLR, Multiple Launch

Rocket System, units to female soldiers for the first time. Early the next year, the military lifted its long-standing ban on women in combat.

Upon completion of her BCT, basic combat training, Katy requested MLR as her military occupational specialty, or MOS. Following AIT, advanced individual training, she was off to Afghanistan.

WTF?

I've consulted to JPAC, the military's central remains-identification lab in Hawaii. I can play the acronym game, too.

I brought my mind back to the current conversation. "But how did she seem?"

"Psyched. Talked about doing the same training as the men. Artillery. Cannon platoons—"

"Oh, God."

"She's a tough kid. She'll be okay."

"You're right. It's just—"

"I know, sugarbritches. You see violent death every day."

"Don't call me that."

"She'll probably end up a general."

"You think she'll make a career of the army?"

"That's not what I meant."

"Why do you suppose she chose not to enlist in an officer candidate program? She's a college graduate."

"I think it was the time commitment."

But Pete hadn't called about Katy. He'd have done that this morning after he talked to her. I waited for him to get to his point.

"So what's the long story?" he asked.

Really?

I summarized my adventures at the courthouse and was shifting to the hit-and-run case when Pete cut me off.

"Sounds like your day sucked. How about dinner?"

"What's the occasion?" Wary.

"Can't I ask a soon-to-be ex-wife to dinner?"

I had a hunch what he wanted. Wasn't about to get roped in.

"No way I'm playing marriage planner for Summer, so don't ask."

In midlife, most men lust after sports cars. Pete had set his sights on a trophy wife. Summer was my fiftysomething ex-husband's thirtysomething bimbo fiancée. Best in show for tits. DQ for lack of IQ.

"You know how she is," Pete said lamely.

I knew only too well. I'd agreed to mediate for Bridezilla once already. Ended up catching flak from both sides.

"She needs guidance."

She needs a muzzle and a tranquilizer dart. I didn't say that.

The wedding from hell, postponed twice, now loomed near. At least five million people had been invited. School friends, work friends, friends of friends. Facebook boasted fewer chums than Summer.

"The wedding's in less than two weeks."

"Wait a day. That will change."

"She's panicking."

"Give her a Valium."

"She likes you a lot."

"Look, Pete. Summer is your problem, not mine."

"I know, I know. It's just that I have depositions all week and a trial on the docket the instant we get back from Tahiti. I've been running around auditioning photographers, picking up thank-you cards, crap you wouldn't believe. Every day there's a new crisis."

Typical Pete. For two decades I'd shouldered most of the child-rearing responsibility because his professional calendar always came first. Car pools; dentist, doctor, and orthodontist appointments; gymnastics, ballet, and swim-team runs.

Maybe if you hadn't been so busy fussing over your baby bride's Barnum and Bailey three-ring you'd have noticed your daughter these past months, caught the signs she was about to make a dangerous decision.

I didn't say that, either. I waited, annoyed and anxious to hang up and phone for a taxi.

"Tempe. Are you listening to me? I need the papers."

The divorce agreement. I'd signed but not delivered it to Pete. Could have with little effort. So why the procrastination?

"Right. They're on my desk at home. I should have given them to you ages ago. Sorry. Of course, come and get them anytime. There's no need to take me to dinner."

"I want to take you to dinner."

I started to protest. Pete cut me off.

"I'll pick you up out front. And I promise. Not a word about the wedding."

"I don't think—"

"How was it you planned to get home?"

Side-out, Pete.

8

Fifteen minutes later, a shiny new BMW convertible swerved to the curb. Red with black leather interior.

Trophy wife. Trophy car. I fought an impulse to roll my eyes.

Less commendable was Pete's fashion sense. Sure, he could muster a suit and tie for court, but a golf shirt and khakis was his normal attire. My ex's guiding principle: comfy and cool.

As I dropped into the passenger seat, my brows rose at the sports jacket, blue shirt, and navy slacks.

"Don't we look snazzy." Excluding the sockless loafers.

"I'm having dinner with a lovely lady."

Orbital roll beyond my control.

"Nice wheels." Keeping it light.

"Got a good deal."

"Uh-huh."

"Took 'er up to Asheville over the weekend. Purred like a kitten. Summer squealed at every switchback. Almost squealed myself once or twice."

Squeals all around.

"Goes from zero to sixty in faster than you can say zero to sixty."

Pete understood I cared little about cars. I knew he was tiptoeing to avoid mention of the upcoming nuptials.

I grabbed the armrest as he gunned out of the lot, cut left, right, then left again.

"Zero to sixty," I said, smiling.

"Check out the sound system." Pete tapped something and Maroon 5's "Payphone" surrounded us in a moving cloud of noise that rendered further communication impossible.

Just past the Queens University campus, Pete winged onto the main drive at Sharon Hall, shot the tunnel of ancient magnolias past the white-columned manor house, and braked to a gravel-spitting stop in the parking area between the carriage house and its annex. Turning his head sideways, he gave me a two-brow waggle.

"Nice." I unbuckled my seat belt.

"I'll wait here."

"I've got to shower."

"No rush."

I held out a palm.

Pete pulled his keys from the ignition, removed one, and handed it to me.

"Thanks." I flipped the door handle.

"Tempe?"

"Yes?"

"Don't lock it in the house."

Pete's phone was out before I was.

The annex has a bedroom and bath upstairs, living and dining rooms, kitchen, a study/guest room, and bath down. Garden in back, grassy patch in front, patio to one side. Though cramped, the place suits me perfectly.

I let myself into the kitchen and flipped on the light.

"Bird?"

No cat.

"Here, boy."

Nothing but a soft ticking coming from the parlor.

I found Birdie under the sideboard holding Gran's clock. Though cats are said to lack facial musculature capable of expression, his message was clear.

"You mad?"

Pausing a moment for effect, Birdie rose, stretched, then padded toward me, cool but prepared to consider explanation. And dinner.

I bent and scratched one furry white ear.

"Sorry, champ. But tonight's menu is a bit subpar."

Returning to the kitchen, I plucked two eggs from the fridge, mixed in a tin of sardines, and heated the combo. When the mess congealed I scraped it into his bowl.

One thing about Bird, he does not hold grudges. All sins forgiven, the feline dived in.

Since I often spend my days with decomp and biohazard, I've mastered the art of the quick cleanup. And amassed a spa-worthy array of soaps, gels, and lotions. Tonight I grabbed the nearest. Out and dry in five minutes, smelling of grapefruit.

Birdie walked in as I was pondering acceptable couture for delivering divorce papers. My eyes met his.

"Screw it."

I grabbed jeans and a black tee, added pale green seashell earrings and a black cotton jacket.

"What do you think?"

Birdie cocked his head but rendered no opinion.

I hurried down to the study, cat at my heels. As I snatched up the documents, Birdie did a figure eight through my ankles.

I glanced at my watch. Pete had been waiting a full twenty minutes.

The cat arched his back and lifted his tail. I scratched his ears and added a series of down-the-back strokes.

When I popped the Beemer door, Pete was still on the phone.

"Don't inhale while you're spraying." Pause. "Okay. But really, I've got to go." Shorter pause. "Yes, I'll call when I'm on the way. I love you, too." Sotto voce.

"Sorry. Bird—"

"No problemo. Ale House good with you?"

"Sure." It wasn't. Big-screen TVs. Fans cheering, groaning, coaching. Noise level at eighty-five decibels. "Is Summer having bug issues?"

Pete looked at me blankly.

"She needs to fumigate?"

"Oh, no." He shook his head. "She's spray-painting antique bottles to use in the centerpieces. Or some damn thing. It's supposed to look artsy."

Wedding talk. Nope.

A short, thrumming blast of Bob Marley, and we were at the Carolina Ale House, a multiscreened extravaganza on the ground floor of a steel-and-glass tower in the heart of uptown. Pete managed to secure a table away from the bar. Not quiet, but out of the no-talk zone.

A waitress greeted Pete with more teeth than a radial saw and favored me with a millisecond of eye contact while mumbling that her name was April.

"Fat Tire ale?" April beamed another dental stunner at my ex.

"Good memory." Pete did the finger-pistol thing.

I asked for Perrier and lime.

Pete chose the baby back ribs. I went for flatiron steak.

Food and drinks ordered, I pulled the documents from my purse and laid them in front of Pete. He glanced at them but did not pick them up.

A void stretched across the table, a bubble of quiet amid the din around us. So little paper. So few words for a love that had produced hopes, dreams, and a beautiful daughter. A love destroyed by an act of betrayal.

There should have been some ceremony. An unwedding? A rite of dissolution? Something beyond a Settlement Agreement and Verification. At least a better font.

"Sorry it's taken so long." I broke the awkward silence. "No excuse. I should have—"

"It's not a problem, sugarbritches. I'll have these filed before noon."

"Don't call me that." Reflex.

"Okay." The old Pete smile. "Cupcake."

Pete slid the papers into the snazzy jacket pocket, then patted my hand.

The touch. His skin on mine. So familiar.

I groped for neutral conversational ground.

"Your wrongful-death case, barrister? How's it going?"

"I won't know until my doctor gets deposed in the morning."

I told him about the criminal misdemeanor trial from which I'd escaped. He told me about a tooth that was causing him grief.

Mercifully, April arrived with our drinks. Pete chugged. I sipped.

"And you?" After another awkward pause. "How're things with Monsieur Le Dick?"

Monsieur Le Dick, Pete's flip name for Andrew Ryan, Lieutenant-détective, Section des crimes contre la personne, Sûreté du Québec. My colleague when I consult to the Laboratoire de sciences judiciaires et de médecine légale in Montreal. My on-and-off lover. Off now. Off forever?

"He's good."

"*Bon*." Pronounced "bone."

"Never speak French, Pete."

And don't ask about Ryan. Don't force me to voice my anxiety over his recent coolness. His distance.

If Ryan and I truly were finished, the split wouldn't be as wretched as the one from Pete. There would be no bitterness, no angst. No stunned child to whom an explanation was due. No moving out. No division of property. No standing in line at the DMV to record change of address. With Ryan, there'd be nothing but a murky trench of sadness.

I couldn't bear to talk about it. To think about it.

"I'm swamped with work here," I said.

"Anything interesting?"

"Four mummified dogs from Peru."

Pete cocked a questioning brow.

I told him about the confiscation by ICE at the Charlotte airport.

Our plates arrived and, for a full minute, we focused on salt and pepper, steak sauce, butter, sour cream, and ketchup. April asked if I needed more ice.

Inexplicably, my thoughts went to the child in the cooler.

"We've also got a teenage girl," I said to Pete. "Run down last night near Old Pineville Road."

"The parents must be devastated."

"We don't know who she is."

"Jesus. Larabee's case?"

I nodded. "There are a couple of leads. If Slidell would get off his fat ass. In his mind—"

"Which is small."

I smiled. "In his small mind, she's an illegal turning tricks."

"Proof?"

"A pink purse, needle tracks, and bad teeth."

"That's it?"

"Bleached hair, a dark complexion, and a Spanish note in her purse."

"Skinny thinks she's from south of the border."

I nodded.

Pete chuckled and shook his head. He'd met Slidell, knew how pigheaded the man could be.

The clamor of voices hushed. Then a multi-throated groan filled the room. Some sporting event was not going well for the home team.

Pete's ribs were stripped and stacked when he laid down his utensils and wiped his mouth.

"Can I roll something by you?"

"Sure."

"I have a friend, Hunter Gross. I don't think you know him. His nephew, John, is a marine second lieutenant."

"Semper fi." I snapped a salute.

Pete had served in the Corps, still kept the Marine flag on a small stand in his office. Every November tenth, he celebrated its birthday with his old OCC buddies.

"Until a few months ago, John was serving as a platoon leader in Afghanistan. As I understand the story, he and his men were ordered to search a village." Pete stopped, an odd expression on his face. "I'm not sure of the details, but the kid's been accused of murdering unarmed civilians."

"Jesus."

"Hunter says no way he's guilty."

"Your friend. The uncle."

"Yes."

"What's your take?"

Pete shrugged. "I'm not sure what to think. Hunter says the kid's a good marine, had plans to make a career of it, but I don't know him."

"Where is he now?"

"Cooling his heels at Camp Lejeune pending completion of an inquiry."

"Relieved of duty?"

Pete nodded.

"Hard." For something to say.

"Yeah. Hell on the family."

Cold-blooded killer? Incompetent leader? Good soldier, bad decision in the heat of battle? Tough one.

In the same place Katy was posted.

Pete bunched and tossed his napkin. Looked at me. Read my mind.

"You're thinking of Katy, right?"

I didn't respond.

"Katy's a private. She won't be leading anyone anywhere."

"She's in artillery."

"Behind the lines."

"Launching rockets at people who hate us."

"Not everyone in Afghanistan hates Americans."

"I know. But life's so . . . unpredictable over there. She could be killed on her way to breakfast."

"So could I."

"You know what I mean."

"Katy is a survivor."

He said it with such confidence I could almost believe him. Still. The images. Katy lying by a burning Humvee on a bleak desert road. In a body bag.

Like the girl in the cooler.

The hit-and-run victim had a mother somewhere, wondering where she was. Why she wasn't calling. Was someone assuring her that her little girl was well?

I gulped the last of my Perrier, now mostly melted ice.

"My car—"

"Off we go!"

Pete pantomimed writing. April and her teeth reappeared with the check.

We did our usual lunge. Pete got there first, paid cash, including a tip that could have financed a presidential campaign.

Five minutes of Rihanna, and we were at the courthouse parking deck. I got out and circled to Pete's side of the car. He lowered his window.

"So. Tomorrow we're officially free." Christ. Did I really say that?

"Yeppers." Equally lame.

We shared a clumsy through-the-opening hug. Lasting a moment too long?

"All the best to you and Summer."

"Thanks. Keep in touch?"

"Of course."

"Do you want me to wait until you're wheels-up?"

"I'm a big girl."

"But lousy with keys."

I dug out and dangled the spares from my desk. Returned his loaner.

Then Pete was gone.

My purse was still in the Mazda. The hated shoes.

Below, passing vehicles made soft whooshing sounds on Fourth Street. In the distance a drunk warbled "Lucy in the Sky."

I dropped one set of keys into my purse and pulled out my phone. Slidell answered after two rings.

"Yo, doc." In the background I could hear the play-by-play of a baseball game.

"How're you coming on the hit-and-run vic?"

"Tomorrow—"

"Have you canvased the neighborhood? There are a few shops along Old Pineville Road."

"Like I said—"

"What about body shops?"

"I'm on it."

"Clothing and boot shops?"

"On it."

"Clinics?"

No response.

"Did you drop by St. Vincent de Paul?"

"On it."

"On it when?" Slidell's cavalier attitude was pissing me off.

"Look, we got nada. We're going to get nada. If she's illegal, no one's gonna come forward. If she's on the stroll, no one's gonna come forward."

Deep down I suspected Slidell was right. Still.

"How about running her picture in the paper?"

"Did you hear what I just said?"

"Can't hurt, right?"

"Neither can tossing goat turds into the sea." Deep sigh. "Look, I ain't blowing you off. A few hours ago I caught an MP with ties to the mayor. Single mother, two kids, steady job at the Rite Aid. Gone. Chief says I got no life till the lady is found."

The line went silent.

I sat, irritated but not totally discouraged. Though sometimes slow out of the gate, Slidell usually came through in the stretch. Unless preoccupied. Enter high-pressure missing-person case.

I pictured the girl with the pink barrette.

I pictured Katy the last time I'd seen her, at Fort Hood the day she graduated from basic combat training. Instead of barrettes she wore camouflage fatigues, boots, and a black beret. Her body was rock hard, her long blond hair tightly knotted at the nape of her neck.

Throughout that day, I'd fought back tears of pride. Tears of dread.

The same dread I felt sitting alone in that parking deck.

What if Katy disappeared and no one bothered to find her? To determine if she was dead or alive?

The human brain is a switching station that operates on two levels.

As my hand turned the key, my higher centers sent up images of a lonely stretch of two-lane.

Instead of going home toward Myers Park, I wound through uptown toward I-77.

Took the southbound ramp.

Headed toward Woodlawn.

9

THE STRETCH OF OLD PINEVILLE ROAD I WAS DRIVING HAD ONCE been the main route from Charlotte to Pineville. But the town and the road had both seen better days. And busier. South Boulevard, to the east, now had all the action, and few motorists made this strip their final destination.

I flicked on my turn signal and tapped the brakes. Double beams bore down on my trunk. A horn blared and a large mass swerved around me, taillights like glowing red eyes in the darkness.

After reversing direction, back toward uptown, I pulled to the shoulder and studied my surroundings. No sidewalks. No traffic signals. Deadly for pedestrians.

Off my passenger side ran a broad strip of weeds and scrub vegetation. Beyond that, the tracks of the Lynx Blue Line, the first and only spur on Charlotte's light-rail system.

Had the girl come here by train? To what station? Woodlawn? Scaleybark? If she'd descended from a Lynx platform, might someone have seen her?

Had she come by car? On foot? Was she alone? With a companion? A kindly stranger who'd offered a lift? A burger? A drink?

And, above all, why? Why was she here? Larabee was placing her time of death at somewhere between eleven and two. What had lured a teenage girl to this isolated spot in the middle of the night? With no jacket in the chilly weather.

I knew the CSU techs had photographed and bagged every scrap of evidence. So why was *I* here after my long, frustrating, blister-raising day?

To see for myself. To hear. To smell. To sense the place.

Keys firmly in my pocket, I popped the door. A gust of wind caught my hair and flipped the hem of my jacket. Though summer lingered by day, come sunset the air was already turning cool.

I zipped up to my chin.

I was more warmly dressed than my Jane Doe had been. Why? An adolescent fashion statement? A rushed departure? Anticipation of an evening indoors?

I pictured the high-heeled boots and denim skirt. Meaningless. Kids dressed like that to hang out at the mall, attend school, or party with friends.

A train whistled softly in the distance. Not the light rail. A freight line on parallel tracks. Norfolk Southern? CSX? Aberdeen and Carolina Western?

Had the girl hopped from a boxcar and walked to Old Pineville Road? A long shot, but possible.

If the girl had arrived by car, it was doubtful she asked to be dropped here. Did the driver force her to disembark? Why? An argument? The conclusion of a cash transaction?

I thought about the semen stains.

Was the sex consensual? Was it followed by a disagreement, her slamming from a vehicle in anger? Was she raped, then tossed aside like last week's trash?

Was Slidell right? Had the girl tried to turn a trick and been run over by a renegade john?

I scanned the far side of the road, saw the black silhouettes of commercial buildings. Pewter-gray space between.

I thought about the US Airways club card in the girl's purse. About John-Henry Story. Why was she carrying a dead man's plastic? Had she been traveling with him the last time he used it? Going where? Had he given the card to her? Had she stolen it from him? It was nothing she could have used without him present. Why had she kept it?

The girl's body was found near the intersection of Old Pineville and Rountree, a short distance in front of me. Was she running when hit? Standing still? Walking? How far had she crawled after being struck?

A truck rumbled by, arcing wide to avoid my Mazda.

Note to self: Have Slidell check with truckers frequenting this route. Appeal to motorists driving here late last night. But he would know to do those things.

Did the girl see the vehicle that killed her? Did she try to avoid it, or was she hit before sensing danger?

I stood a moment, shivering, listening. The silence was broken only by the *tic-tic* of a wind-tossed wrapper. A muted car horn.

My nose took in the scent of oily cement. Exhaust. Dry leaves, the way they smell only in autumn.

I scanned up and down the pavement. On the opposite side, maybe a quarter mile behind me, I detected a faint blue-and-red twinkle I hadn't noticed before. Sliding behind the wheel, I hung a U-ey and drove toward it.

The twinkle came from a white stucco cube that probably began life as a filling station. Christmas lights rimmed a front window in which faded announcements covered most of the glass. Red lettering on the front wall identified the establishment as the Yum-Tum Convenience Mart.

The only vehicles present in the Yum-Tum's lot were a rusty gray pickup and an ancient red Ford Escort. I parked beside the truck and got out.

Through the iron-barred glass door I could see a single clerk behind a chest-high counter. An alarm beeped when I entered.

I noted ceiling cameras, one facing the counter, another in a corner, pointed at the door. Both looked old. I guessed they were programmed to rerecord every twenty-four hours.

If they functioned at all.

Note to self. Ask Slidell about security tapes.

A man in Bermuda shorts, high-top sneakers, and a Panthers jersey was paying at the register. While waiting him out, I took in more detail.

Beer, soft drinks, and milk in the coolers. Racks of salted this and fried that, with warnings of health hazards printed on the bags. Donuts under warming lights, glistening like plastic. Hot dogs revolving on a greasy rotisserie. The place was an intestinal terrorist attack.

Wordlessly, the clerk handed Bermudas his change. She had platinum hair, milky skin, and dark goth eyes. The effect was both tough and innocent. Like a preteen Halloween mishap.

As Bermudas exited, I plucked a pack of mints and approached the counter.

"Busy shift?"

"That it?"

"It is." I held out a ten. "Were you working last night?"

"I work every weeknight."

"So you saw the accident?"

The Morticia eyes rose to mine. Narrowed. "Sort of."

"What'd you make of it?"

"Why are you asking?"

"I'm with the medical examiner's office. I examined the victim."

"Like, her body?"

No, genius. Her argyle socks. "Yes, her body."

"You're, like, the coroner?"

"I work for the medical examiner."

"Like, at a morgue?"

Remove the word *like* from her vocabulary and the kid would be tongue-tied.

"Yes."

"I guess that's cool." She slammed the register and handed me my change. "Did you have to go to school for, like, decades?"

"Yes. May I ask your name?"

"Shannon King."

"Are you a student, Shannon?" I gestured at an anthology of short stories lying on the counter.

"I'm taking some classes at CPCC."

"That's very enterprising."

"My English instructor makes us keep a blog. It's a bitch, because, you know, I'm here every night, some afternoons. How much can you say about Cheetos and Pepsi?"

"Must make you a good observer."

King eyed me, uncertain if I was mocking her. Then, "I guess."

"The accident, for example."

"I saw zip. Heard nothing until the sirens."

"Really?"

"Look, I thought what you're thinking. I said to myself, Shannie, you must've heard something. Tires. Wham-o. Something. I didn't."

"Until the sirens."

She drew a breath, then her upper teeth came down on her lower lip.

"Except?" I prompted.

"I don't want to sound stupid."

Too late.

"Of course you won't," I said.

"I'm not sure. I may be, like, backfilling."

"Any little thing could turn out to be important."

"Maybe someone screamed. But not nearby. And it was more like a yelp. But it could have been a passing driver changing radio stations. Or a cat."

"Or a scream."

"Yeah, a scream."

"You didn't go out to check?"

"Yeah, I did. The store was, like, totally empty. But there was nothing. Same as every night."

"Did you see any vehicles slowing or accelerating rapidly?"

"Nuh-uh."

"It was good that you looked."

"Listen, I'll try to comb my memory." She shrugged, embarrassed at what she viewed as unbridled enthusiasm. "Might help my blog. That's all."

"That would be good."

"Or I can ask customers. Be cool about it, you know. Like, 'Did you see that accident Monday night?' The way you did with me."

I passed her the Polaroid I'd taken in the morgue cooler. "Have you ever seen this girl?"

"Is that her?" Staring at the photo. "The girl that got killed?"

"Yes."

"Holy shit. She's young."

"Yes."

"What's her name?"

"We don't know. We're trying to find out."

"I wish I could help." She started to slide the photo toward me on the counter. Stopped. "I could keep it. Show it around. You want I should do that?"

I considered, decided against it. Not with her alone here at night. No way I wanted her alerting the wrong person.

"I'll talk to the investigator in charge about getting you a copy."

"What's his name?"

"Detective Slidell."

"He'll call me?"

"He'll do that."

I handed her my card. "Please phone if you think of anything. Anything at all."

My hand was on the door when her question stopped me.

"What was she doing out here so late?"

"I don't know, Shannon. But I will find out."

Thirty minutes later I was home in bed.

10

T HAT NIGHT MY DREAMS WERE RAGGED SNATCHES, ALL FORGOT-
ten upon waking. Save one.

Ryan was walking down a shadowy road overhung with dark,
intertwined branches. His back was to me.

I called to him, but he didn't stop. A car approached from beyond,
illuminating his long, lanky form in the brilliance of its headlights.

Ryan turned. Slowly, his features morphed into Pete's.

The Pete/Ryan figure came toward me, twirling a folded umbrella.
When close, he poked my side with the tip, again and again.

I opened my eyes. Felt pressure under my rib cage.

Reaching beneath me, I felt something hard on the mattress.
Retrieved it.

My Latvian amber ring had slipped from my finger. Or I'd worried it off in the night.

Either way, one thing was clear. I'd lost weight. Not long ago the
fit had been tight. Stress poundage?

I lay a while, replaying the dream in my head. What would ol'
Sigmund think?

I pondered the Peruvian dogs. Considered the best approach.

Then I remembered something far more important. Wednesday
morning. Katy and I were scheduled to Skype at oh-nine-hundred, as
she'd put it. East coast time.

My eyes shot to the clock. Seven fifty-five.

I quickly showered, shampooed, and dried my hair.

As I exited the bathroom, my iPhone was singing. I reached it too late.

The phone icon indicated two voice messages. A third landed as I stood with the device in my hand. Seriously? In twenty minutes?

I ran through the list.

The vet's office had called with a reminder about Birdie's annual checkup.

Pete. No message. With congratulations on a successful divorce?

Shannon King. It took a moment for the name to click. The clerk at the Yum-Tum. King left a number and asked that I call her.

Time check. 8:20 A.M.

I pulled on sweats, barefooted down to my office, and launched Skype on my Mac. Katy wasn't online. Made sense. I was forty minutes early. It was only 4:50 P.M. in Afghanistan.

Birdie jumped up and nudged my hand from the keyboard.

"Sorry, Bird. Breakfast it is."

The cat followed me into the kitchen and watched as I concocted another feline gastronomic delight. Tuna with instant oatmeal. I vowed to hit the PetSmart that day for a case of canned food and a huge bag of crunchers.

Cat fed, I spooned French roast into the basket, added water, and clicked on the coffeemaker.

While Mr. Krups did his thing, I phoned Shannon King. She answered, sounding distracted. Or sleepy.

"Listen. I'm, like, combing my mind. Like we said."

How long could that take?

"Good," I said.

"But I'm coming up empty. I promise, tonight I'll be all over this."

"That's great." I checked my watch.

"And I was thinking. Like, maybe I could come to the morgue."

The morgue.

"Thank you for offering, but nonprofessional visits aren't allowed. It's a question of security and bio-protocol. But please let me know if you remember anything."

Returning to the study, I checked Katy's online status with Skype. Nope.

Fair enough. 8:28 A.M. here. 4:58 P.M. there.

To kill time I did a quick scan of my e-mail.

Three donation requests.

An ad for a natural way to burn fat.

A picture of Harry with an Irish wolfhound and her current squeeze. One was named Bruce, the other Albert. I'd no idea who was who.

An Exercise After Forty newsletter.

Nothing from Katy. Good. No cancellation.

Unable to sit still, I raced up the stairs two at a time. Exercise after forty.

Returning to the bathroom mirror, I dabbed on mascara and blush.

As though Katy would notice.

More after-forty exercise down to the kitchen. A refill on coffee, then I rechecked Skype.

No change. 8:42 here. 5:12 there.

I rolled my chair sideways and plucked an issue of *JFS* from the shelf above the desk. Scanned the table of contents.

Crossover immunoelectrophoresis for discovery of blood proteins in soil. Confocal microscopy for examination of fired cartridges. STR melting curve analysis for genetic screening. Detection of meglumine and diatrizoate from bacillus spore samples.

Though scintillating topics, nothing held my attention.

Time check. Nine twenty. Still no Katy.

Easy, Brennan. Bagram Air Force Base is the safest location in Afghanistan.

So Katy had assured me. Ditto Pete.

I sipped my tepid coffee and stared at the unchanging screen. Willing my daughter to appear.

9:40.

10:05.

Stomach knotted, I thought about the Jane Doe in the MCME cooler.

Maybe the girl's mother was drinking coffee as I was, trusting that her daughter was somewhere safe.

Easy.

Back to the journal.

No go.

For the millionth time I wondered about Slidell. I knew he'd go all

Dirty Harry about a kid being killed on his patch. That he'd pursue every lead. But he had his priorities.

The disappearance of a hard-working single mother who was locally known forced the death of an unknown probable illegal and possible hooker onto the back burner.

On screen, the digits in the upper corner changed to 10:22.

She's calling from a USO center, I told myself. Dozens lined up for the Internet. Troops talking to their wives, their husbands, their kids, their mothers. Lingering over good-byes.

Keep busy. Do your job.

I reduced Skype to the dock and entered a series of keystrokes.

In 2005, recognizing a need to address the dual problems of missing persons and unidentified remains, the National Institute of Justice held a giant meeting in Philadelphia called the Identifying the Missing Summit. Later, a deputy attorney general created the National Missing Persons Task Force and charged the U.S. Department of Justice with identifying and developing tools to solve missing-person and unidentified-decedent cases. The task force recommended the creation of a centralized data bank.

The National Missing and Unidentified Persons System, NamUs, resulted from that recommendation. NamUs is free, online, and available to everyone.

The NamUs home page appeared on my screen, with links to three databases: Missing Persons, Unidentified Persons, Unclaimed Persons. Hoping someone had reported my Jane Doe missing, I chose the first.

Search parameters appeared. I entered sex as female, race as white, age as adolescent. Leaving the category "ethnicity" blank, I filled in Date Last Known Alive, Age Last Known Alive, and State Last Known Alive. Then I hit search.

And got zero matches.

I changed the age descriptor to late teen/young adult.

Still no matches.

I entered Hispanic/Latino for ethnicity.

Nada.

Changed the age descriptor back to adolescent.

Nothing.

Disappointed but not surprised, I did the only thing I could. Taking information from my copy of the girl's ME file, I entered her into the Unidentified Persons database. Physical, medical, and personal descriptors. Clothing. Accessories. A brief summary of the circumstances surrounding her discovery.

There was so little to enter. No scars. No tattoos or piercings. No dental work. No implants. No deformities.

Just a normal, healthy teenager. Dead.

10:40. Still no ring from Skype.

Head to the office and get on with the mummy bundles?

I decided to give Katy a few more minutes.

I logged in to the Doe Network, the International Center for Unidentified and Missing Persons.

Same result.

I was finishing up when my iPhone sounded.

"Yo. Doc." Slidell was chewing on something.

"Yes." Staring at a picture of Katy taken two summers back at the Outer Banks. Wind-tossed and caught by late-afternoon sun, her long blond hair shimmered like gold.

"Spent some time with the brain trust out on Old Pineville Road. These dipshits couldn't find their own assholes if—"

"Did you learn anything useful?"

"You kiddin' me? Checked out a party junk store, a U-store facility, a garden center looked like it specialized in mold, and a dozen other shitholes holding on by suction cups. Welding shop was my personal favorite. Chick at the desk must've spent a whole lotta time sucking fumes. Could've waltzed the corpse in with me and Dumbella wouldn't have taken notice."

"No one recognized the photo?" I'd sent Slidell a copy of my cooler Polaroid.

"No one knew shit."

"Did you visit a convenience store called the Yum-Tum?"

"Yeah. That was a treat."

"Did you ask about security tapes?"

"Camera's broke because the owner's broke. Fuckwit actually said that."

"Did any other businesses have CCTV or security cameras? Maybe one that might have caught the road, maybe even the accident?"

"Same story everywhere. The tapes are reused every twenty-four hours."

"What about the vehicle? Did you get a lab report back on the paint?"

"Oh, yeah. They put it right at the top of the priority list and sent the report over by limo."

"Did you try body shops? Ask if anyone brought in a car with damage consistent with a pedestrian hit?"

"You been drinking a lot of coffee this morning?"

Ignoring that, I told Slidell about my NamUs and Doe Network searches.

"No surprise there. Larabee sent her through every system on the planet. I checked MP cases. No one's reported a kid missing that fits her profile."

"How far back did you go?"

"Far enough. Clearly she ain't local."

"She could be a runaway."

For several beats no one said anything. I could hear muted traffic noises in the background. Slidell spoke first.

"The kid's moving under the radar. Carrying no papers. No keys. Nothing. The odds we hang a name on her ain't real good. What are ya gonna do?"

"We've still got to try."

"Chief's got my balls in a sling with this woman's gone missing."

"Double task, detective."

Slidell made a noise, then disconnected.

11:02. So much for Skype.

I typed an e-mail to Katy. *Sorry to miss you. Everything okay? Suggest another time. Love, Mom.*

On to the dogs.

But instead of heading upstairs to get dressed, I got more coffee and returned to my desk.

What are ya gonna do?

I dialed the SBI Crime Lab in Raleigh. Asked for Josie Cromwell in the Forensic Biology and DNA section. After a short delay she picked up.

"Ms. Cromwell."

"Hey, Josie. Tempe Brennan."

"How you doing, girl?"

"Good. And you?"

"Can't complain. Still know where all the bodies are buried?"

"A few. Are you busy up there?"

"Just sitting around, keeping my nails clean."

We both laughed. It was a quote from a man she'd recently beaten out for a project manager spot.

"How's it feel being boss?" I asked.

"Has its perks. So, what's happening? You coming up to Raleigh?"

"Sadly, no. I'm calling to ask a favor."

"Uh-oh."

"I've got a young girl, midteens, a hit-and-run victim. Struck from behind and left to die."

"Lord in heaven." I could see Josie shaking her head, short black dreads bobbing with the motion.

"I'm not sure how committed the lead detective is. He thinks she's illegal, probably in the life."

"Just another dead hooker."

"We've got prints, but the kid's not in any system. We can't find an MP with her profile. We swabbed for DNA, of course."

"Which is useless until you have a name so we know who to contact for comparison."

"Exactly. But the pathologist found semen. We're hoping that might lead somewhere."

"I hear you. But the backlog here is freaking out those higher up the pay scale."

"Any chance you can goose my girl up the queue?"

"I'll do what I can. Which is probably not much."

"Tim Larabee is submitting the samples." I gave her the pertinent case information. "I'm in your debt."

"You better believe it."

Still, I didn't log out to head to the lab.

I returned to my e-mail and opened the picture I'd scanned and sent to myself and Slidell the previous night. The girl lay in her body bag, pale and still.

I wondered how she'd looked in life, when her spirit still lived in her face, and her quirks and mannerisms made her unique. The squint of an eye, the tilt of a brow, the lopsided upturning of one lip.

I opened a file labeled MCME 580-13, and saved the image to it. Then I attached and e-mailed a copy to Allison Stallings, a crime reporter at the *Charlotte Observer*. A few years back, Stallings had followed a string of satanic killings I was working.

Actually, Stallings had stalked Slidell and me. But she'd reported the facts accurately and fairly. In the end, I'd liked her.

After waiting ten minutes, I dialed Stallings's number.

"Who is she?" she said by way of greeting.

I repeated what I'd told Josie Cromwell, adding a few more specifics about time of death and the body recovery site.

"What do you want?"

"Can you run the picture and a short article? Might scare up a witness, or someone who knows her."

"Hang on."

I did. Far down the line, indecipherable snippets sounded like chatter from another galaxy. Stallings was back in less than five minutes.

"Sorry. My editor says not yet. If your kid's still a Jane Doe a week from now, he'll reconsider. But nothing front page."

"Thanks. I appreciate it."

We traded good-byes and disconnected.

Okay. Dogs.

As I was pulling on jeans, a blouse, and ballet flats, my brain posted an image of Slidell talking disdainfully of wetbacks and hookers.

Was he right? Was she illegal?

What are ya gonna do?

Firing back downstairs, I e-mailed the girl's photo to Luther Dew at ICE. Another long shot, but it couldn't hurt.

I sat a moment, thinking. About Slidell and his missing single mom. About my phone conversation with Luther Dew.

And I realized the obvious.

For my Jane Doe to have a name, I'd have to take the initiative.

I added text to the girl's photo and sent my work to the printer.

Flyers in hand, I set out.

11

THE ONLY CAR IN THE YUM-TUM'S LOT WAS THE GRUNGY FORD Escort from the night before, probably Shannon King's.

Grabbing a handful of flyers from the passenger seat, I got out and walked toward the door. A car rattled by behind me. Gravel crunched underfoot.

In daylight I could identify some of the neighbors. A tool and die company, an outfit with its lawns full of cast concrete, a screen printer's shop, a crumbling sprawl that looked like an old Motel 6 converted to apartments.

No phone, no pool, no pets . . .

Thanks, Mr. Miller.

The Yum-Tum's front window was blanketed with notices, some fresh, most yellowed and curling at the corners. I stopped to read a few through the grimy glass.

Missing cats and dogs, one parakeet. Good luck with that. An ad for a wet T-shirt contest at some bar probably long since belly-up. An author hawking her self-published book, *Mind over Weight*. Seriously? At Fat Cells R Us?

King was behind the counter, thumbing through a copy of *OK!* magazine. The clotted lids lifted when I jingled through the door.

"Hi, Shannon."

"Hey." Noncommittal.

"Wondered if I might post some of these?" I handed her a flyer.

She eyed the picture, read the few details I'd included about the accident, the victim, my contact information at the ME office, Slidell's at the CMPD.

"Okay." She hooked a thumb in the direction of the Motel 6. "Creepoids from the apartments might have seen something."

She dug below the counter, produced a roll of tape with hairs curling from the sticky side.

"Put it in the window."

"May I also hang one on the door?"

The dark brows puckered.

"You have my card. If the manager objects, tell him to call me," I said.

"What the fuck. I'll tell him the coroner insisted." She placed the flyer to one side of the counter, facing out. "I'll keep one here, you know, watch how people react. If they look, like, guilty or something."

Great. I had a kid in a cooler and my daughter in a war zone. I didn't need a bimbo junior investigator.

"That's fine, Shannon. But just observe. Don't engage anyone in conversation."

"You think I'm a moron?"

"Of course not."

I felt goth eyes on my back as I posted the notices and left.

The day was warming, the cloud cover starting to fragment. The sun's brief appearances warmed my shoulders and hair.

After removing my jacket, I drove to the Motel 6.

The complex, called the Pines, consisted of a long, rectangular box that appeared to have little motivation to remain standing. Paint that had once covered the cinder-block walls now looked like irregular bloodred sores. Each of the ten units had a single curtained window and faded blue door.

Rooms to let fifty cents . . .

I guessed that tenants at the Pines were mostly short-term, either hoping to move up or dropping down hard.

A few battered cars waited on the strip of pavement fronting the rectangle, like swayback horses tied outside a saloon. I nosed mine into the herd and got out.

No one answered my knock at the first six units. I slipped flyers under the doors and moved on.

Numbers 7 and 8 were opened by dark-skinned women claiming *no comprendo*. Ditto when I posed my questions in Spanish. Eyes fearful, they took their flyers and quickly withdrew.

At unit 9, a bare-chested man cracked, then slammed the door before I could speak. At 10, a voice bellowed, "Get the fuck gone!"

I did.

Driving Old Pineville and the small network of arteries surrounding Rountree, I tacked the girl's picture to trees, fences, and utility poles, to a barrier leading into woods where the Rountree pavement ended. I left her image at every business Slidell had visited. Most accepted my handiwork with skepticism. A few asked questions. The majority did not.

Discouraged, I worked my way along South Boulevard, then hit the three light-rail platforms closest to the spot where the girl had died.

I was *wheep-wheep*ing my Mazda when my iPhone announced an incoming call.

"Temperance Brennan." Sliding behind the wheel and clicking the belt with my free hand.

"Luther Dew."

"How can I help you, Agent Dew?"

"I had hoped you would be in your office." Reproachful?

"I'm on my way now."

"I wonder if I might stop by, perhaps in half an hour?"

"I haven't completed my analysis of the mummy bundles."

As in, I haven't started.

"Have you done radiography?"

"Yes." I'd asked Joe Hawkins to X-ray the crap out of everything.

"I'm wondering if I might have the films to aid me in composing my report."

"You're welcome to take photographs, but our office must retain the originals."

"That will be sufficient."

"Do you know where the MCME facility is located?"

"Yes. Half an hour, then."

Dead air.

And you have a nice day, too, Agent Dew.

As my palm smacked the gearshift, a warning growl rose from my gut.

Quick time check. Almost two. I'd catch a bite when Dew left. Maybe hop out for a burger and fries.

Who was I kidding? The chance of lunch was less probable than that of finding Birdie in an apron cooking dinner tonight.

Grab something at the Yum-Tum? I wasn't that hungry. Never would be.

I popped in a Scott Joplin CD, cranked the volume, and tapped the wheel to the beat of the "Maple Leaf Rag."

Twenty minutes and a Circle K stop later, I swung into the MCME lot. Mrs. Flowers buzzed me through, smiling as always.

I waited for her usual decorous briefing.

"You have no new phone messages. Dr. Larabee is out. No one else has requested time with you." The "i" in *time* was three miles long.

"Thank you. Someone from Immigration and Customs Enforcement will be here shortly. Special Agent Luther Dew."

"The mummified dogs?" The penciled brows lifted a millimeter on the powdered forehead.

"Has Joe completed the X-rays?"

"He placed them in the small autopsy room."

"Thanks. Please give me a heads-up before sending Dew back."

"Of course."

En route to my office, I glanced at the case board. Nothing new for me.

I was checking my inbox when the phone rang.

Great.

"Your special agent is here." No tremble, no quivery breathing.

Point of information. Though as refined as any Daughter of Dixie, in the presence of the tall, dark, and handsome, Mrs. Flowers not only blushes, she goes all Marilyn breathless.

So. Dew wasn't much to look at.

"Can you hold him ten minutes before sending him back?"

"Certainly."

In the small autopsy room, each light box held a film, and large brown envelopes lay beside three of the four plastic tubs.

Shifting from box to box, I flicked switches and viewed X-rays of the contents of the first bundle.

Good.

Removing those images, I moved on through the other three series. I was peering at the last film when footsteps clicked down the corridor.

I turned.

A pink beluga filled the open doorway. No fedora, bow tie, or suspenders.

Dew wore a white shirt, blue tie, and pinstriped navy suit. A very large one. I put him at six two, minimally three hundred pounds.

I stepped forward and extended a hand. "Tempe Brennan."

"Luther Dew." Firm grip, but not a testosterone crusher.

Dew's eyes flicked past me, came back.

"Thank you for making time." The high voice sounded wrong emanating from the supersize body.

"Of course."

Again, Dew's gaze went to the X-rays. I noted that his eyes had oddly violet sclera.

"Please." I gestured him to the nearest light box. "Come closer."

Dew's fleshy neck stacked into layers as his head tilted left then right to make sense of the superimposed long bones, ribs, and other anatomical parts.

"It doesn't look human," he concluded.

"Canine all the way. Note the snout, the teeth, the tail vertebrae." I pointed to each.

"The others are similar?"

I nodded. "Though I've made only preliminary observations." Now there was an understatement. "One appears to be a puppy."

Dew spent a few more moments studying the compressed skeleton glowing white on the film.

"I appreciate your limiting your examination to noninvasive methods."

"Unless I spot something suspicious I shouldn't have to disturb the wrappings."

"The Peruvian archaeologists will appreciate that." Dew pulled out and waggled a small point-and-shoot Nikon. "May I?"

I switched X-rays until he'd photographed all four sets. Then he shot pics of the unopened bundles.

When he'd finished, we both stood a moment, regarding the dogs.

A thought struck me. What the hell?

"The hit-and-run victim we discussed remains unidentified."

Dew looked down at me blankly.

"The girl that Detective Slidell suspects is undocumented. Would you like to view the body?"

"I really don't see how that can be useful."

"We're here. She's here. What can it hurt?"

Before Dew could object I led him into the cooler, centered the proper gurney, and unzipped the bag.

To his credit, Dew didn't leave. Nor did he show any emotion.

A moment passed. Then, "This is very sad, but I really can't help. Is there somewhere we can talk?"

I rezipped the girl and we moved to my office. Dew filled a good hunk of it. I waited for him to divulge what was on his mind.

"As part of its investigation, ICE has begun examining Dominick Rockett's finances."

Dew took my lack of response as nonunderstanding.

"We are looking at Mr. Rockett's bank records, purchase histories, tax returns, for example. Among other things."

The guy talked like he was reading from a training manual.

"The gentleman has assets difficult to explain by the totality of his pension and disability income combined with the proceeds from his import business."

"Meaning?" I knew what it meant. But it seemed Dew needed feedback.

"Dominick Rockett may be a larger player than we suspected."

"You think he's a smuggler?"

Dew shifted a lot of poundage in a surprisingly elegant manner. "These dogs may be the tip of a very lucrative and disturbing iceberg."

My stomach chose that moment to voice another notice of need.

I reddened. Dew might have. I couldn't tell, his face was already so flushed.

"But I've engaged you too long." Dew rose.

"You'll keep me in the loop?" I asked.

"Certainly. You've been very cooperative."

Cooperative? What was I, a suspect?

"Thank you." I pulled a flyer from my purse. "Perhaps you'll float a few questions about my Jane Doe?"

Dew was studying the photo when the landline shrilled.

"I'm sorry to interrupt." Mrs. Flowers sounded tense. "But the caller is insistent. And sounds rather upset."

An image of Katy flashed in my mind.

"I'll take it." Mouth dry.

As I mimed "sorry" to Dew, the ambient sound on the line changed.

"—picture on the flyer?" The voice was low, the connection awful.

"Are you referring to the notice about the hit-and-run victim?" I asked, baffled.

"—girl dead?" The caller sounded female.

"Yes. She is dead."

"—hurt her—scared—"

"Scared of what?"

Garbled static.

"—all were—"

"Ma'am. Can you hang up and call me back?"

"—wrong—had to tell someone."

"Do you know who the girl is?"

Click.

Dial tone.

12

"IF YOU'D LIKE TO MAKE A CALL, PLEASE HANG UP AND—"

I depressed and released the button, then punched in Mrs. Flowers's extension.

Busy.

Again.

Still busy.

Come on. Come on.

The caller had sounded guarded. Did she break the connection? Did someone else?

"I'm sorry." To Dew. "That may have been a tip on my Jane Doe."

"I understand."

This time Mrs. Flowers answered.

"I apologize f—"

"The last caller. Do you have a number?"

A pause, then, "I do."

Dew watched as I jotted the digits. Then, "Again, thank you, Dr. Brennan."

"I'll let you know when you can collect the dogs."

Dew was barely through the door when I hit Slidell on speed dial.

"Yo." In the background, Waylon Jennings was advising a trip to Luckenbach, Texas.

"Can you trace a number?"

"Lemme guess. *Dancing with the Stars* finally rang and you lost 'em."

I told him about my flyers, then about the anonymous caller. Braced for a lecture. Which didn't come.

"Shoot."

I shot.

"Gimme five."

Three minutes later, Slidell was back. Sans Waylon.

"Pay phone. Who knew they still existed? Most of those booths are now pissing—"

"Where?"

"Seneca Square Shopping Center."

"South Boulevard, near Tyvola." My heart threw in a few extra beats. Seneca Square wasn't far from the site of the hit and run.

"Ee-yuh. I'll float a few questions. But unless your tipster dialed naked in a tiara, the chances of anyone noticing are probably zilch."

Slidell was right. Which irritated the hell out of me.

"Any news on the vehicle?"

"No."

"What about the smear on her purse?"

"The FBI's mostly a jokefest of Fuckaround Frankies. But their paint data's the shits."

Slidell really did have a way with words.

"Forty thousand freakin' samples, but ours didn't hook up."

"What we sent wasn't paint?"

"Yeah, it was paint. But not from a car."

"From what, then?"

"Fuck if I know."

"What did the report say?" Barely masking my annoyance.

"Bunch of crap about solvents, and binders, and pigments, and additives. Methyl this and hydrofluoro that. Why can't these fart-wads just speak English?"

"You'll have someone figure out what the stuff is?"

"Yeah, yeah."

"How long will it take?"

"As long as it takes."

When we'd disconnected, I closed my eyes and replayed the mysterious call in my head. Female, saying the hit-and-run vic was scared. Accent? The connection was too lousy to tell.

Did the woman know my Jane Doe? If so, why not give me her name?

Scared of what?

The caller sounded frightened herself.

Frightened of what?

Everyone has access to a mobile or landline these days. Why use a pay phone? To maintain anonymity? Erroneously thinking the call couldn't be traced?

Had the woman disconnected or had someone cut her off? Had she meant to say more?

At that moment my stomach definitely said more. Loudly.

I fired to the kitchen for a Diet Coke, returned, pulled the top item from the stack in my inbox, and read as I chewed the PowerBar I'd scored at the Circle K.

The form reported on human bones discovered on the shore of Mountain Island Lake. Amelogenin testing showed the remains were those of a male. Definitely not Edith Blankenship, a missing woman the cops thought they'd found. Terrific. So where was Edith? And who was the guy from the lake?

I wrote a brief report, attached the form, and placed both in a bright yellow folder in my outbox. No reason for the color, except that I liked it.

Next I responded to an invitation to the upcoming meeting of FASE, the Forensic Anthropology Society of Europe. Sounded great, but who had the time?

Enough paperwork.

Bunching my PowerBar wrapper, I shifted to the small autopsy room to undertake a more detailed examination of the mummy-bundle X-rays. I was on pooch three when the phone rang.

"Your special agent is back." Mrs. Flowers was speaking with lips close, hand cupping the receiver. "Shall I send him to you?"

What the hell? Dew had been gone little more than two hours.

"Yes, please."

Dew and I reached my office door at the same time. Again I noticed that, despite his size, the man's every move was executed with grace and efficiency.

I dropped behind my desk and gestured to the chair opposite. With Dew again in it, the thing looked as if it had been designed for toddlers.

"Long see, no time."

Dew either missed or chose not to acknowledge my joke.

"I have information that might be of interest to you."

"About my Jane Doe?"

"About Dominick Rockett."

"The somewhat less than legal importer."

Still not the slightest hint of a smile.

"Dr. Brennan, you are an accomplished professional. In our very brief encounters I have sensed that you care deeply about your work. More importantly, I believe you are a moral and honorable person. Opening the mummy bundles would have made your job infinitely simpler. Yet you chose not to. I respect you for that. And I trust you."

Straight Capote, effeminate and proper.

"I feel duty-bound to share certain knowledge that I withheld during our previous conversations."

Dew shifted as if to lean back. Changed his mind, accurately distrusting the carrying capacity of the chair.

"In the course of our investigation we have discovered that Mr. Rockett has holdings in a company called S&S Enterprises. Since S&S is a privately held entity, little information is publicly available about its structure, activities, or shareholders."

"What does S&S do?"

"The interesting thing is not what the company does. What has caught our attention is the size of Mr. Rockett's holdings. Based on what we've ascertained thus far, it seems his interest totals upwards of a hundred thousand dollars."

"Pretty big bucks."

"As we discussed earlier, Mr. Rockett's officially reported earnings are modest."

"Money from his military pension and his import business."

Dew nodded. "Thus, we must question the source of income allowing such a substantial position."

"ICE thinks the guy's dirty."

Dew continued as though I hadn't spoken.

"There is another fact my colleagues and I find intriguing. Another reason I feel I should take you more fully into our confidence."

Dew looked down at his hands, which lay motionless in his lap. Back up at me.

"Until recently, one of the owners of S&S Enterprises was a local entrepreneur named John-Henry Story. I believe this is a person with whom you are familiar?"

"The John-Henry Story who died in a fire last April?"

"I am told you identified Mr. Story's remains?"

I nodded, too shocked to answer.

Shocked but pleased. It was the link that could bring ICE on board.

"I also have something to share," I said. "You recall the girl you viewed in the cooler?"

Dew's oddly lavender eyes narrowed.

"The kid run down and left to die?"

Dew started to speak. I raised a silencing palm.

"When found, that kid had John-Henry Story's airline club card in her purse."

Dew straightened a cuff but said nothing.

"Are you hearing me, Agent Dew? Dominick Rockett, your suspected smuggler, was involved in S&S Enterprises. S&S Enterprises was owned, at least in part, by John-Henry Story. My Jane Doe was carrying Story's plastic when she died."

Dew's face remained unreadable.

"Surely it would be useful to your investigation to know who this girl is."

"Does your detective—" Dew rotated one enormous pink hand.

"Slidell."

"Is Detective Slidell not convinced this youngster was a prostitute?"

"I fail to see the relevance of that."

"There could be many explanations for this coincidence you describe, none having to do with Dominick Rockett."

"I don't believe in coincidence." Cool.

Dew waited a very long time before answering.

"As I've explained, my mandate is to investigate the illicit importation and distribution of cultural property." Ever so patient. "At present our focus is on Dominick Rockett's financial status as it relates to his potential culpability in such activities. Should it turn out that your victim was somehow connected, I will, of course, reconsider. But an airport lounge card in the purse of a suspected prostitute?"

Dew tipped his head and raised his brows. Seriously?

I fought the urge to kick his prissy but substantial derriere out of my office. Instead I smiled.

"Is there someone else who might—"

"At the moment we are woefully understaffed." Dew rose. "For now, regretfully, your girl's case must remain with local authorities."

My roommate was in the kitchen when I came through the door.

"Hey, Bird."

The cat sat, curled his tail around his legs, and regarded me with round yellow eyes.

I dropped my briefcase, squatted, and stroked his head.

He stood and arched his back. Looking hopeful? Expectant? Maybe just hungry.

More guilt. I'd yet to buy cat food.

Why hadn't I stopped at a supermarket? At least a convenience store?

Now I would pay the price for obsessing with work and ignoring household.

The cat, not so much.

Knowing the refrigerator was a dead zone, I went to the pantry. Birdie nosed through the crack as the door swung open. Placing his forepaws on the bottom shelf, he stretched to his full bipedal height and sniffed.

Right. Instant grits it is. With the remaining tuna.

Watching the cat devour his second supper of porridge *à la mer,* I had to smile. After two frustrating days, it was nice to please someone.

Quick check of my house phone. No messages.

Quick check of the produce bins. One three-pack of romaine lettuce going brown. Four shriveled carrots. A cucumber the consistency of Play-Doh.

The shelves held orange juice, Diet Cokes, plum preserves, olives, condiments, and a carton of milk ten days past its sell-by date.

The freezer offered one frost-covered burrito and a chicken potpie.

While the potpie heated, I logged in to Gmail.

Nothing from Katy.

Relax. She's fine. No news is good news.

Nothing from Ryan.

Why hadn't Katy contacted me? E-mail? Text? She knew I'd be crazy with worry. Daily communication wasn't possible, but she'd been so good. And she'd never failed to Skype at a prearranged time.

Gran's clock bonged eight. Though tired and anxious, I forced myself to stay busy.

The rest of the e-mails were either ads or matters of no urgency.

I ate the pie, which was heavy on legumes and light on poultry. Washed the cat dish. Paid a few bills. Watched an episode of *Boardwalk Empire* with Birdie purring in my lap.

Fought the urge to check Gmail every ten minutes.

At ten I showered and hit the sack.

Sleep? Who was I kidding?

No toe testing or tentative wading. My brain dove straight into a whirlpool of anxiety.

Who was the dead girl? Why was she out with no identification or keys in the middle of the night? Had someone removed the contents of her purse?

Why lift her ID but leave John-Henry Story's club card?

That one I could answer. The card was in the purse's lining. But why? Was the girl hiding it? Did someone take her ID but miss Story's card? Her killer?

What value could an airport lounge card have? It was not a credit card.

Story had been dead six months. Slidell said the card hadn't been used in that time. Couldn't be used without Story.

Another possibility broke through.

Could John-Henry Story still be alive? If so, had he faked his own death? To gain what?

And. More disturbing. If Story hadn't died in that warehouse, whose bones had I examined?

I turned on the light and checked my phone for an e-mail or text from Katy.

Shit.

Lights out.

Neurons in gear.

John-Henry Story was fifty-one when he died. My Jane Doe was maybe fifteen. Had Story asked the girl to travel with him? For him? Where? For what reason?

The gray cells offered no hypotheses.

Somehow Story's card went from his possession to the girl's purse.

The pink purse lying in the dirt by her body.

I pictured a deserted road, a sloping shoulder, headlights slashing the post-midnight darkness.

And had another thought.

Was John-Henry Story connected to the hit and run?

Had he been the driver?

Whoa. Now that was a stretch.

A stretch based on zilch. Pure dream sequence. Nothing scientific about it. Even if Story had staged his own death, the fire was in April, long before the girl's murder.

Giving up on sleep, I threw back the covers and descended to the kitchen. Birdie padded along, confused but willing.

I heated a cup of water, dipped a peppermint tea bag, then poured the last of the milk into a saucer. Birdie lapped, unconcerned that his snack was a bit past its prime.

As I sipped tea, my thoughts took another route.

Dominick Rockett, the former soldier with the mutilated face. The importer caught with illegal antiquities. The investor in a company owned by John-Henry Story.

Where did Rockett get the funds to buy in to S&S Enterprises? Why that company? When? Before Story's death? Supposed death? Was Story a factor in Rockett's decision to invest?

Another coincidence?

Right.

Did Dominick Rockett know John-Henry Story? Work for him? With him? Doing what?

Was Rockett involved in the hit-and-run killing?

Suddenly the room felt chilly.

October. Winter really was coming. Soon it would be time to turn on the heat.

Placing my mug in the sink, I returned to the bedroom, my feline companion right at my heels.

I tucked under the covers, killed the light, and closed my eyes. Tried to clear my thoughts.

No Dominick Rockett. No John-Henry Story. No Jane Doe.

My higher centers began another loop.

The afternoon's call.

Who was the woman on the phone?

Assuming the call was legit, what had frightened the dead girl?

Was the caller also afraid of this person?

Birdie leapt up, circled, and nestled into the crook of my knee. I ran my hand down his back, grateful for his unquestioning loyalty.

Flashbulb image. Charred fragments. So fragile I'd had to spray them with polyurethane before attempting to tease them from the ashy matrix in which they were embedded.

John-Henry Story?

If so, what was Story doing in that barn so late at night? Was he that hands-on involved in the business? Was he having financial difficulties? If so, might he have torched the place? Accelerants flame fast. Did he miscalculate and find himself trapped? But the arson investigators wouldn't have missed that. There would have been evidence of accelerants, containers.

I pictured a figure backlit by fire and smoke. Panicky movements. Flames catching his clothes, his hair, his skin.

If Story didn't die in that blaze, who did? A worker? A vagrant, asleep in the wrong place at the wrong time?

Round and round.

Questions leading to more questions.

No answers.

And where the hell was Katy!

13

I AWOKE TO RAIN BUCKETING DOWN OUTSIDE MY WINDOW. AND A feeling I'd slept too late.

Yep. My clock radio said 8:42.

Eyes half open, I snagged my iPhone and scanned overnight e-mails.

No update from Katy.

Quick calculation. Midafternoon in Bagram. She'd be busy.

Knowing I should wait, I sent a message.

"Please check in. Mom."

Nothing from Ryan.

My sister Harry had fired off a foursome, the first landing at 2:42 A.M. The others had followed at five-minute intervals.

I speed-read to get a sense of the new crisis.

For a chuckle, I sometimes visit the website First World Problems. The contents are Harry's life in microcosm. The Angsts of Harriet Brennan Howard Dawood Crone. Though I think she dropped Crone when she divorced husband number three. Or was he two?

New acquaintances are often shocked to learn that Harry and I are siblings. But despite our differences, which are epic, my sister and I share one fundamental trait. She is wired with the same bulldog drive that got me through college, grad school, and decades in a demanding and often heartrending profession.

What differs between us is the focus of our passion. For me it's the search for truth, recognition, and justice for the dead.

For Harry it's shopping. Shoes. Shades. Houses. Husbands. Deep down, I think the acquisition itself is irrelevant to my sister. What matters is the hunt.

Over the years I've pondered why Harry is the way she is. Why I'm the way I am. Clichéd as it seems, I've come to believe that our mother owns a big piece of the blame.

Looking back, I realize Mama swung on a pendulum beyond her control, one that moved her between wild elation and soul-bleeding depression. With each upswing, she'd take joy in wearing the latest fashion, knowing the right people, seeing and being seen at all the best parties, concerts, and restaurants. With the plunge would come tears, withdrawal, the closed bedroom door. Having achieved all she'd sought, Mama wouldn't give a damn.

My mother's moods bewildered me as a child. As an adult, I still don't fully understand.

And I worry there are hints of Mama's demons in my sister.

I've never discussed my personal issues with Harry. A battle with the bottle. A failed marriage. A daughter who'd volunteered for combat without asking my advice. A long-distance relationship with a man I couldn't get on the phone. Given my record, I was hardly in a position to counsel others.

I did listen, however. But this morning Harry would have to wait.

Wrong. The phone rang as I was heading for the back door.

"How're those styling stilettos we scored?"

"I wore them to court." Then threw them out.

"Bet you wowed the lovin' shorts off that jury."

"Mm. Listen, Harry. I've got to get to work—"

Undeterred, baby sister launched into a tale of woe involving a broken pool pump, algae, and back-ordered parts. Barely pausing to draw breath, she segued into a rant about a guy named Thorny.

"I thought you were dating an astronaut." Orange Curtain. First time I saw the name I assumed it was a typo. "Or a guy named Bruce."

"Orange had the brains of a budgie. Wait. That's being unfair to birds."

Shoulder-cradling the phone, I slipped outside and turned to lock the door. Bad move. The thing popped free and dropped to the stoop.

"—merchandise right there in my living room. What makes men so bloody proud of their genitals?"

"So Orange is out."

"Seven carats wouldn't get that bonehead back through my door."

"Have you made plans to visit Tory?"

Silence greeted my question.

The previous summer, Harry had learned that her son, Kit, had a now-teenage daughter, conceived when he was just sixteen. And I'd learned that I had a grandniece. Father and daughter now lived together in Charleston, South Carolina. Harry hadn't taken the news of grand-parenthood well.

"Harry?"

"Remember what an assclown Kit was in high school? How the hell's he going to parent a fourteen-year-old girl?"

"I'm sure he's matured. And Tory's a bright kid."

"You've said that."

"You're her grandmother."

"You've said that, too."

At the MCME, my phone was flashing like a strobe on speed.

I punched the code for my mailbox, thinking Slidell.

I got Capote.

Dr. Brennan. Could we please speak at your earliest convenience?

I'd felt upbeat following my conversation with Harry. Calm.

That tranquillity popped like a bubble in sunlight.

Why this negative reaction to Dew? Federal agents are renowned for their disdain of local law enforcement. But he'd exhibited no con-descension toward me.

Yes, Dew had withheld information. Yes, he'd refused to help with my Jane Doe. But I believed he truly felt he was doing his job.

So why did I distrust the guy?

Did I suspect he was playing me?

Because I'd tried to play him?

I dialed the ICE office, asked for Dew, was placed on hold by a weary-sounding receptionist.

A full minute later, Dew answered.

"I'm very sorry to keep you waiting, Doctor Brennan."

"No problem. What's up?"

"S&S Enterprises."

"The privately held company."

"I hate a closed door."

"Don't we all."

"This one wasn't locked as tightly as the partners might have wished."

I waited.

"The entity is a holding company for a number of properties and other holding companies. Fast-food restaurants. Convenience stores. A bar called John-Henry's Tavern."

I heard paper rustle, then Dew continued in his prissy, high voice.

"S&S is owned in large part by John-Henry Story and his younger brother, Archer Story. Lesser partners include Harold Millkin, Grover Pharr, and Dominick Rockett."

"So Rockett was one of a handful of players holding pretty big cards."

"Apparently. Whether he bought or earned his way into the partnership remains unclear. What is clear is that, at the time of his death, John-Henry Story was suffering some serious financial reversals."

Wasn't everyone these days? I thought. "Was S&S in trouble?" I asked.

"No. But Story wanted to infuse more capital for expansion, and he himself had no available cash. In addition to S&S, Story owned a pizza chain and four auto dealerships which were costing him a lot of money."

"In the Carolinas?"

"The pizza parlors are here. The dealerships were located in Texas and Arizona."

"Were?"

"Are you familiar with Saturn?"

"A different kind of car." I still remembered the early ads.

"Pontiac launched the brand in the mid-eighties in response to the success of Japanese imports in the U.S. At first, sales were good."

"As I understand it, Saturn never really kept up with R and D."

"So I've read. In any event, sales declined. In 2010, General Motors discontinued the brand. Many dealers suffered significant financial losses."

"John-Henry Story was one of them."

"Yes. And the pizza franchise is bleeding money."

I leaned back in my chair and considered Dew's update.

"Which way do you think it went? Story knew Rockett had money, so he brought him in to shore up the S&S capital reserves? Or Rockett got word S&S wanted cash and seized the opportunity to buy in cheap?"

"With either scenario, the question remains the source of Mr. Rockett's cash."

"Maybe Rockett worked for Story or for one of the other partners and was paid with a piece of the action."

"Maybe."

"Does Rockett admit to knowing Story?"

"I've yet to pursue that line of questioning." Starchy stiff.

"Have you asked him about his interest in S&S?"

"I wish to avoid goading Mr. Rockett into seeking legal counsel. At present he thinks his only issue will be a fine for failure to report proper value and provenience of an import entering the country."

"Smart. Don't hit him until you have all the facts."

I heard a hitch in Dew's breathing. "Here's an interesting fact. The further I delve into the Rockett investigation, the more your name comes up."

"My involvement with Rockett's mummified dogs, with John-Henry Story's remains, and with the hit-and-run vic who had Story's airline club card."

"Precisely."

"What do you make of that, Special Agent Dew?"

"I am hoping you will give that question some thought."

"Likewise."

"I look forward to your report on the Peruvian bundles."

"Topping my agenda."

After disconnecting, I phoned Slidell.

Voicemail.

Was the man avoiding me? Refusing to answer when my number came up on his screen?

Whatever.

I went to the stinky room and finished viewing the fourth set of mummy X-rays. All dog.

Relieved that my first impression had been correct, I returned to my desk.

No message light. No e-mail from Katy or Ryan.

While composing a report for Dew, my thoughts kept looping to Rockett and Story.

Had either man met my Jane Doe?

Frustrated, I saved and minimized the ICE report, logged on to Google, and called up images of John-Henry Story. I'd seen some pictures back when the fire took place, remembered only that the purported victim was unimpressively short.

Rodent was the first word to coalesce in my mind.

An *Observer* photo taken four months before Story's death showed a short, wiry guy with thinning hair, gaunt cheeks, and dark, beady eyes.

Rattus rattus.

Another shot caught Story at a Panthers game. In another he was outside a Consigliore's pizzeria, waving at the camera.

I contemplated doing a full search on Story, opted to complete my doggie report.

Slidell finally called at noon.

I briefed him on what I'd learned from Dew.

"Deep dish went deep shit."

I ignored that.

"The hit-and-run vic had Story's card in her purse. Rockett was a minor partner in Story's company, S&S."

"Where's a two-bit smuggler get cash for an investment like that?"

"Alleged smuggler. What I want to know is, what's the link between Story and Rockett? And does one or both of them connect to my Jane Doe?"

"Soon's I get this MP—"

"We need to check out John-Henry's Tavern, see if Rockett's been there with Story. Or if either was ever there with my Jane Doe."

"Why doesn't Dew haul Rockett in and sweat him?"

"Other than the mummy bundles, he's got dick at this point. Dew's convinced the dogs are just the tip of something big, and doesn't want to spook Rockett into lawyering up."

I heard a phone ring in the background. Voices. A deep sigh.

"I told you, doc. The chief's on my ass to find this—"

"You saying he doesn't care about the kid in my cooler?"

"I'm not saying that. Look, I been working the body shops. No one's seen a vehicle fits our bumper-height estimate with front-end damage."

"What about St. Vincent de Paul?"

"No one at the church ever heard of this kid."

"Clinics?"

"Ditto."

"Clothing? Boots?"

Silence hummed across the line.

"It's been two days, Slidell." He knew as well as I the importance of the first forty-eight.

"I'm not sure I see the upside of visiting this joint."

"At least we'll be doing something."

"Scratching my ass is doing something."

"Do you know John-Henry's Tavern?"

"Yeah. A real slice of heaven."

"We need to check it out."

"For what?"

"For whatever is there." Slidell's attitude was cracking my resolve to stay cordial.

"I'll hang up now unless you got something else to say."

"Never mind," I snapped. "I'll go myself."

"No you won't."

"Okay. I won't."

"Goddammit."

For a full ten seconds, I listened to air whistle in and out of Slidell's nose.

"Give me half an hour."

14

SOUTH END, JUST BELOW UPTOWN CHARLOTTE, IS A MIXED HUNK of turf with serious ambitions up the social ladder. And climbing fast.

The neighborhood dates to the 1850s when the construction of a railroad line connected the Queen City to Columbia and Charleston, South Carolina. Over the decades a manufacturing community sprang up along the tracks, fired largely by a booming textile industry.

Fast-forward to the waning years of the twentieth century. Largely ignored by a town viewing itself as the face of the New South, South End had little to offer beyond abandoned mills, warehouses, and a minor league baseball park. But come the nineties, cagey developers saw dollar signs.

Today, South End is a mélange of condos, lofts, and renovated industrial leftovers housing restaurants, shops, studios, and a broad spectrum of design-related industries. Want a plumbing fixture, fabric, or upscale lamp? South End is the answer to your needs.

But traces of the hood's past remain. The Design Center of the Carolinas, the headquarters for Concentric Marketing, and the Chalmers Memorial Associate Reformed Presbyterian Church breathe the same yuppie air as seedy garages, abandoned factories, weed-covered acreage, and a strip club.

John-Henry's Tavern was located not far from the intersection of Winifred and Bland. Flanking it on both sides were lots with entire eco zones thriving in the cracked concrete.

Opposite was a windowless bunker covered with graffiti and enclosed in chain-link fencing. A sign warned NO TRESPASSING. Nothing indicated the structure's name or explained the purpose of its existence. Junk covered a raised platform that might once have been a loading dock. Rusty beer kegs. A table made of slapped-together boards. An old piano with a black skull spray-painted on a silver moon on its upright portion.

Slidell swung a left into the tavern's small parking area, which may have been paved. Or not. A coating of dirt and gravel rendered the issue moot.

"This place saw a lot of action back in the sixties." Slidell shifted into park and cut the engine.

"I'd have guessed the twenties."

"Beach music, shagging, that kinda shit. For a while the owners brought in truckloads of sand, strung lights in the yard. Young assholes pretended they were at Myrtle Beach grooving to Maurice Williams." Pronounced *Moe-reese*.

"When was that?"

Slidell slid a toothpick from the right to the left corner of his mouth. "Late seventies."

A smile tugged at my lips. "You bust some moves here, detective?"

Slidell looked at me as though I'd told him the world was made of Gouda.

What was I thinking? Slidell's soul probably had liver spots by his sixteenth birthday.

"Who comes here now?" I asked.

"Older assholes."

"What's that?" I tipped my head toward the building across the street.

"Back in the day it was a mill of some kind. Been abandoned since the fifties. Rumor was the property was going condo. Project went south, I guess. Now the dump's mostly a pain in the ass 'cause of squatters."

For several moments we both evaluated our target.

Save for a Coors sign glowing in the rain-blurred front window, the small brick bungalow might have been a private home. Iron handrails bordered the two stairs leading up to the stoop. A chimney jutted from the far end, suggesting the presence of a fireplace inside.

The front door, once red, and the trim, once white, were faded and peeling. I'd been by this old building. When?

Before Katy had hired on with the Public Defender's Office she'd briefly tended bar at the Gin Mill, a trendy Irish pub a few blocks over on Tryon. Perhaps I'd taken a wrong turn after dropping her off.

Slidell's Taurus shared the parking area with a pickup and five cars whose odometers undoubtedly showed very high numbers.

I was about to comment when a man in sweats rounded the building and walked with questionable balance to a white Honda Civic. Slidell and I watched him climb in and drive off.

"Ready?" I asked.

Taking Slidell's grunt as affirmative, I stepped out into rain that had dwindled to a slow, steady drizzle. All around me were the sounds of dripping water.

After heaving himself free, Slidell hiked his pants, checked the back of his waistband, and rolled his shoulders. A glance left, then right, and he strode onto the stoop and through the door. I followed.

As expected, the tavern's management invested little in lighting. Or cleaning. The air smelled of stale beer, human sweat, grease, and smoke.

As my eyes adjusted to the dim, my mind logged details about my surroundings. From the tension in his back, I knew Slidell was also assessing.

Wooden tables with unmatched chairs filled the space where we stood. A jukebox rested against the wall to their right. A mirror in a heavy gilt frame hung above and beside it. Beyond them straight ahead a bar formed an L, its short side facing the tables.

I spotted a second entrance far back to the left, opposite the terminus of the L's long side. At the moment, that door was propped open with a dark shape that looked like a gargoyle or garden troll.

A series of bulletin boards ran along the wall from the rear entrance to the near end of the bar. Above them were painted the words STORY BOARD. On them were tacked at least a billion photos.

To our right, an archway gave onto a room holding roughly a dozen more tables, all empty. A narrow corridor led deeper into the house, presumably to toilets and the kitchen.

A trio in work clothes and steel-tipped boots occupied a four-top in the main seating area. Three hard hats lay at their feet. Three hamburger specials mounded their plates.

Two men and a woman sat at the bar, backs to the photo gallery, empty stools equidistant between them. The men wore hoodies, jeans, and running shoes. Both had logged enough miles to have shagged at the tavern in its Myrtle Beach days. Both were drinking beer.

The woman wore black stretch pants and a pink tee that warned, STOP LOOKING AT MY BOOBS. With her fried gray hair and sagging face she looked old enough to have mothered the men. Her glass held something the color of tea, probably bourbon.

Though the bartender matched Slidell in poundage, his weight was distributed along more orthodox lines. And much more compactly. Maybe five ten on tiptoes, he had rheumy blue eyes and a shaved skull. Tattooed on his forearm was some sort of bird.

Having memorized the layout, Slidell crossed to the bar.

"How's it going?"

Rheumy eyes continued drying his hands on a rag.

Slidell made a show of looking around. "I see business is booming."

"What'll you have?"

Slidell shifted his toothpick. "Little more hospitality?"

"You're a cop."

"You're a genius."

The three laborers went quiet. The beer drinkers shifted on their stools.

Boob woman eavesdropped unapologetically.

"License is in order." Rheumy eyes hooked a thumb at the wall behind him.

Slidell placed both palms on the bar, spread his feet, and loomed.

"How 'bout we start with a name?"

"How 'bout we start with some ID."

Slidell badged him.

Rheumy eyes slid a glance at the shield and looked up at Slidell.

"Name? Or am I starting out with questions too high up the grid?"

"Sam."

Slidell raised both brows in a go-on expression.

"Sam Poland."

"How long you been working here, Sam?"

"What's this about?"

"Whadja do, Sam? Jump some girl's bones?" Boob woman guffawed at her own wit, then knocked back a slug of her drink.

"Zip it, Linda." Poland gestured Slidell down the bar, closer to where I'd paused. "Who's the chick?" Nodding at me.

"Lady Gaga. We're getting an act together."

Poland's jaw muscles bulged, but he said nothing.

"So, Sam. How long you been working at the country club here?"

"Twelve years."

"Tell me about Dominick Rockett."

Poland studied the rag in his hands. Up close, I could see they were red and splotchy. I suspected eczema.

"I'm talking to you, dickwad."

"This is harassment."

"Rockett drink here?"

Poland shrugged.

"What's that supposed to mean?"

"A customer looks old enough, I don't ask for ID."

"Guy's face looks like he washed it with a blowtorch. That help?"

"I might've seen someone like that."

"Sitting with John-Henry Story?"

"Who?"

"You know, Sam. I'm starting to think you're trying to waste my time. People waste my time, they piss me off."

"Sorry I can't help."

"You saying you never heard of John-Henry Story?"

Poland shrugged again.

Moving with astonishing speed for a man of his bulk, Slidell reached out, finger-wrapped Poland's neck, and brought him forehead to forehead.

Around us the room went totally still.

"I find that odd, Sam. Being Story's the man used to cut your checks."

Poland struggled to free his head. Slidell held him like a vise.

"I can walk out to my car and run your name through every system in the city, the county, the state, and the universe. You got an outstanding warrant? Unpaid taxes? Late child-support payment? One single slip, your dick is mine."

Slidell's words sent droplets of saliva onto Poland's face. They glistened blue and green in neon oozing from signage behind the bar.

Even Linda had nothing to say.

Thinking Poland might speak more freely with me out of earshot, and wanting to avoid spittle, I moved toward the bulletin boards and feigned interest in the photos.

The collection looked as if it stretched back beyond the Nixon years. Some snapshots had old-fashioned scallopy edges. Some were standard drug-store-issue prints. Some were Polaroids not holding up well.

I fingered through the layers, digging out an image here and there.

A creased black-and-white showed an old Chevy coupe with whitewall tires, its fedoraed driver arm-draping the door. A color print featured a kid in a boater with an LBJ hatband. Another captured a Kodak moment inspired by four bare buttocks.

Dozens of pictures dated to the tavern's Myrtle Beach days. In shot after shot couples danced under looping strands of lights, gathered at tables, or mugged at the lens in shoulder-to-shoulder camaraderie.

There were shots of New Year's Eve celebrations, balloons festooning the fireplace, ceiling, and walls. Of diners in shorts and sundresses dappled by sunlight at patio tables. Of drunks in green hats, shamrocks, and beads.

Men in coveralls. Women in stilettos and spandex. Couples snugged together like spoons. Businessmen in suits. Twenty- and thirtysomethings in full-body Nike or Adidas. Athletic teams in uniform. Quartets and sextets of college students.

Over the years the fashions and hairstyles changed. Long bangs. Wild perms. Shaved heads. Pierced noses and lips. It was like sifting through layers at an archaeology dig.

Behind me, Slidell continued hammering at Poland. The beer drinkers and Linda remained silent. The workers had resumed conversing in low tones.

As I moved from board to board, I wondered how the collection had come to be.

Whatever its history, the allure had faded in recent years. Few images looked like products of the digital age.

I was at the end of the last board when I spotted Story. Or was it?

Moving discreetly, I pried the tack loose with a thumbnail and studied the photo.

Oh, yeah. *Rattus rattus.*

Story was beside a woman in a sparkly green halter creating va-va-voom cleavage. Both were raising champagne flutes. She was smiling. He was not.

A blond kid sat one barstool down from the woman, leaning at an angle that suggested at least twenty beers. The date embroidered on his varsity jacket was two years back.

Pumped, I burrowed through more stratigraphy.

Pay dirt.

I knew the terrible price of war. I'd seen images of veterans in full dress uniform, heads high, ravaged faces proud. Speaking at rallies. Arm in arm with their beautiful brides.

I'd been told Dominick Rockett's burns were severe. Still, I was unprepared.

On the left, Rockett's brows and lashes were gone, and his forehead hung bulbous over a lidless orbit. His lips were bloated and skewed, and his nostril melted into a cheek the consistency of congealed oatmeal.

On the right, save for hair loss and an unnatural smoothing of the skin, his face appeared normal. A knitted tuque was pulled low on his forehead.

I felt pity as I viewed the destruction. The image in the mirror every morning of Rockett's life. In his mind when a stranger looked away. When a child stared or screamed in fear.

Dear God. What a price.

My eyes moved from Rockett to the other man sharing his table. Wiry, with gaunt cheeks and small rodent eyes.

Casting a quick glance behind me, I thumbed the second snapshot from the board and slipped both into my purse. Then I crossed back to the bar.

Slidell had released Poland but was still grilling him. The beer drinkers and Boob woman remained focused on their beverages.

"—telling you, man, I don't know."

"You don't know much, do you, asshat."

After a round of my not so subtle throat-clearing, Slidell graced me with a glance. I tipped my head toward the door.

Slidell frowned, then hit Poland with two more questions. Got more nothing, but the point was made. Dirty Harry was in charge.

Slapping a card on the bar, Slidell gave the usual instruction about phoning. Then we left.

Back in the Taurus, I pulled out the purloined pictures and identified the players. Slidell studied the faces without comment. Which surprised me.

"So Story and Rockett are drinking buddies," he finally said.

"I don't know about that. But this proves they're acquainted."

"What say we poke at that?"

"Oh, yeah. But remember. Dew doesn't want Rockett spooked."

"Right."

We were rolling before my seat belt clicked home.

15

Rockett LIVED OFF HIGHWAY 51 IN ONE OF CHARLOTTE'S FAR southwestern tentacles. During the first half of the drive, Slidell briefed me on what he'd learned from Poland. Which was practically zip.

After some prodding, the bartender admitted he'd seen the tavern's owner a few times. Said Story hadn't been a drinker, hadn't been interested in getting to know his employees.

Poland had the impression Story usually came with men, and that the visits had been more business than pleasure. Wasn't sure, since Story hadn't been a smiley guy.

Poland hadn't a clue who'd started the photo gallery. Or maintained it. Said the collection traced to well before his tenure.

"Apparently Story and Rockett weren't all that concerned with discretion." Throughout the trip, I'd been wondering what that implied.

Slidell turned to me, a Chiclet halfway from his palm to his mouth. "Meaning?"

"Why allow their picture to be posted on that board?"

"Dumb shits probably didn't know."

Maybe.

Thirty minutes after leaving South End, Slidell hooked a left past a sign announcing LES FLEURS. Pretentious, I know. But Charlotteans like their neighborhoods christened.

Houses in Les Fleurs were mostly ranches and split-levels dating to the sixties and seventies. Most had meager square footage, detached garages, and some variation on the theme of pastel siding.

The streets were curving, tree-lined, and named after flowers. As Slidell wound from Marigold to Poppy to Rockett's address on Azalea Court, I noted that every backyard was fenced, every front lawn mowed and edged. Here and there a bike or scooter lay abandoned on a walkway or propped against a staircase, porch, or foundation.

It was a hood that made you think of kids, dogs, and retirees. What did Harry call houses like these? Starter-ender homes.

Slidell pulled to the curb in a cul-de-sac shaded by two magnolias and a towering pine. Behind each magnolia was a ranch, one salmon, one green. Below and behind the pine was a brown two-story that New Englanders would call a saltbox.

"Anything strike you weird about this place?" Slidell had looped the court to park facing out, and was scanning the street we'd just driven down. His jaw was working double time. The gum was making wet popping sounds.

I followed Slidell's sight line. Saw nothing but closed doors, blank windows, and a lot of azalea bushes, none in bloom.

"Looks pretty quiet."

"Damn quiet."

"We're on a cul-de-sac in the burbs on a rainy Thursday afternoon."

"La-dee-da. Cool-day-sac." Slidell freed his belt. "Guy lives on a freakin' dead end."

Flashbulb image. The face in my purse.

I felt a wave of pity, followed by unease. Would Rockett be as disfigured as the snapshot suggested? Was that why he lived on a "freakin' dead end"?

"Rockett's place isn't flashy."

"Squirrel's either a piss-poor smuggler or one cagey sonofabitch."

"Did you check how long he's lived here?"

"Deed's been registered in his name since 1991."

"So he bought the property shortly after his retirement from the military. Mortgage?"

"No."

"He could have saved up. Or inherited money."

Slidell worked a molar with a thumbnail, then resumed chewing. "Wonder what the neighbors think of his gardening skills."

He was right. Maybe it was the perpetual shadow cast by the pine. Maybe lack of interest. The emphatically green lawns to either side ended abruptly at the boundaries of Rockett's patchwork of dirt and grass.

"Let's roll."

"Remember," I warned. "Dew will be pissed if we goad Rockett into hiring an attorney."

"Ee-yuh."

I climbed from the Taurus and headed toward the house, raindrops gently cooling my face. I focused on the sensation to clear my head.

Of pity for Rockett.

Of thoughts of Katy and IEDs.

The door, painted brown to match the siding, had a black wrought-iron knocker in the shape of a cannon. Slidell banged it. Banged again.

In the distance, traffic hummed on Highway 51. No sound came from inside.

Slidell was about to whack away a third time when a lock rattled. His body tensed as the door swung in.

So did mine.

It had not been a trick of unkind light. And the scarred flesh had experienced no rebirth or restoration since the photo had been taken.

Though the day wasn't cold, Rockett wore a black knit hat pulled low to the level his brows should have been. The fingers wrapping the doorjamb were waxy and pale and had no nails. Above the hand, the edge of a tattoo winked from the cuff of his long-sleeved tee.

Rockett looked at Slidell, then at me, the left side of his face frozen, the right side crimped in a scowl.

I forced my expression neutral.

Slidell held up his badge. "Charlotte-Mecklenburg PD."

Rockett's good eye flicked to the shield, returned to us.

"What do you want?" Gravelly, but deep.

Slidell hit him with the old saw about asking a few questions.

"About what?"

"You want we should do this in front of the neighbors?"

"You see any neighbors?"

Slidell crossed his arms and spread his feet. "Or we could do it uptown."

"You got a warrant?"

"Should I have a warrant?"

"You tell me."

The two men locked eyeballs. Which were at about the same level. But Rockett's neck was thick, his body all muscle. The definition under his tee spoke of hours in a gym.

Mimicking his unwanted caller, Rockett crossed his arms and set his feet wide.

A flush darkened Slidell's face.

"This really won't take long." I smiled, trying to defuse the macho standoff.

"Who the hell are you?" Holding his gaze on Slidell.

"Dr. Temperance Brennan. I—"

"Lady works at the morgue."

Rockett's right cheek may have twitched slightly at Slidell's response. A beat. Then he inhaled through his good nostril, exhaled slowly. I thought he'd send us packing.

"Ten minutes." Rockett stepped back.

Slidell spit his gum into the grass and entered. I followed, into a windowless foyer with checkerboard flooring, folding doors on the left, wall pegs on the right. A knitted cap hung from one, a black windbreaker from another.

Rockett led us into a parlor with a picture window that was curtained against daylight. The room's only illumination came from a flat-screen TV the size of a billboard. Sports highlights played soundlessly, bathing the room in jumpy kaleidoscope patterns.

A brown leather couch sat opposite the television. Flanking it were distressed wood-and-iron tables, maybe Restoration Hardware. Angled beside it was an elephantine recliner. The TV remote lay abandoned on one arm.

The room's back wall held shelving half-filled with equipment relating to the audio-visual setup. A ship in a bottle. A combo thermometer-barometer device. Photos, mostly of men in uniform. A framed patch. I recognized the Marine Corps anchor and eagle embroidered on a red circle at center. The words DESERT STORM arced above, and TASK FORCE RIPPER arced below.

To either side of the shelving, lining the baseboard, were larger objects. A metal breastplate. A carved tusk. A painted ceramic vessel. A battle-ax. Each artifact looked seriously old.

I caught Slidell's eye. He nodded. He'd noticed, too.

Rockett gestured toward the sofa but remained standing. So did Slidell. So did I.

"Clock's running," Rockett said to Slidell.

"Save the attitude."

Rockett's spine, rigid as a mast, went even straighter.

"What'd you say your name was?"

"Slidell."

"Fire away, Slidell."

"How 'bout we talk stolen dogs."

Something flickered in Rockett's good eye. Surprise? Relief? He said nothing.

Slidell waited.

At length, Rockett snorted, a dry, wheezy sound like air through a filter.

"You been talking to that fruit fly Dew?"

Slidell neither confirmed nor denied.

"You want me to react?" Rockett asked.

"You want to react?"

"Will it get you and Sister Wide Eyes out of here sooner?"

"Might."

"*Stolen* is the wrong word," Rockett said.

"Enlighten me."

"I bought the dogs from a farmer. Guy was so eager to sell he nearly peed his gauchos."

"ICE don't look kindly on relic smuggling."

"I didn't know they were old."

"That your hobby? Buying up mummified pets?"

"Dew's got no case."

I knew Slidell was leading Rockett, getting him to believe we were there because of illegal antiquities. Target lulled into overconfidence, Slidell would pounce.

As the men spoke I glanced across a corridor into what the architect had probably intended to be the dining room. Instead of table, chairs, and buffet, the room held a bench press, weights, chin bar, punching bag, treadmill, and elliptical.

"ICE thinks you're dirty," Slidell said.

"They've got nothing."

"Yeah?" Slidell jabbed a thumb over his shoulder. "You get that shit at the Walmart?"

"Everything I own is legal and documented. Someone wants to sell, I buy. Someone wants to buy, I sell."

"Could be that's the case. But from now on, you hit a border, a latex glove goes right between your cheeks."

"I'll say I'm a virgin, ask for gentle."

"You think you're smarter than me?" Slidell's tone indicated tightly controlled anger.

"Donkey piss is smarter than you."

That's when Slidell crossed the line.

"You got all your tax ducks in a row, asshole? 'Cause Dew is fine-combing your 1040s, your bank accounts, your credit scores, every plumbing bill you ever paid."

Rockett simply glared. With a hair less confidence than before?

"Screw with the IRS, you're looking at hard time." Slidell's face was hard. "You know Dew's wife is Peruvian? For him this is personal. And he's got contacts down there. You skate this bust, and I ain't putting money on those odds, you may want to think about shifting your base of operations. Maybe to Mars."

I doubted the wife story. And was certain Dew would disapprove. But I didn't interrupt.

"Every penny you ever earned, every dime you ever spent, Dew's running his pencil down the columns. He's calling your buyers, your suppliers, subpoenaing their records. Think Farmer Gaucho and his amigos will go to the slammer for you? Only question is how fast can they *hablo* to save their own asses."

Silence followed Slidell's rant. Rockett finally broke it.

"Why's my customs beef a concern of the Charlotte PD?"

"My turf, my call."

Rockett glanced at his watch, back at Slidell. "That it?"

"No. That ain't it. Tell me about your buddy, John-Henry Story."

"Don't know him." Rockett's face remained carefully blank. But the fingers of his unscarred hand curled inward.

"Lying to a police investigator will bring you serious grief."

What the hell? Slidell had already inflamed the situation. I pulled out the bar photos. Rockett glanced at them briefly, but offered no explanation.

"Special Agent Dew is aware of your position in S&S Enterprises," I said. "Of your association with John-Henry Story."

"No comment." Through lips barely open.

"You got any comment on how Story managed to torch himself?"

Rockett offered no reply to Slidell's question.

"Here's what Dew keeps wondering." Rainbow fragments of light danced the contours of Slidell's face. "Where's a two-bit importer get the bucks to play with the big boys?"

Still nothing.

"Local businessman up in flames." Slidell raised and lowered his palms, as though comparing objects for weight. "Two-bit importer with a shitload of cash."

"You saying I had something to do with Story's death?" Behind Rockett, a referee raised his hands above his head. "Are you fucking crazy?"

Seeing a possible crack in the smug self-control, I arrowed straight to the real purpose of our visit.

"Two nights ago a young girl was killed in a hit and run near Old Pineville Road."

I pulled out one of my flyers. Rockett gave it another of his nano-second glances.

"The girl wasn't killed on impact. She managed to crawl to the shoulder, where she died in pain some time later. Alone. Terrified."

"You're telling me this because?" Rockett's undamaged eye bore into mine.

"The girl had something belonging to John-Henry Story in her purse."

"So?" Cold as ice.

"Did Detective Slidell mention that he works homicide?"

The distorted face changed in a way I couldn't interpret. I dangled the flyer square in front of it.

"You were acquainted with Story. This girl was acquainted with Story. Do you know who she is?"

"Mary Fucking Poppins."

Anger burned in my chest. War hero or not, Rockett was repulsive.

"One other thing. The ME found semen on the girl's body. The samples are being tested for DNA."

Rockett shrugged. "Test away."

"The kid's got Story's plastic. Story's your partner and drinking pal," Slidell said, clearly sharing my disgust. "You're connected, asshole. Who is she?"

"Get the fuck out of here."

Slidell didn't budge.

"Here's one more fact, Mr. Rockett." My tone was glacial. "Yesterday I received a tip. The caller claimed to know the hit-and-run victim. Said the girl was scared."

"So?"

"Something or someone frightened this child." I waggled the flyer inches from Rockett's nose. "I *will* find out what or who that was."

With an angry swipe, Rockett knocked the paper from my upraised hand. I retrieved it from the floor and placed it faceup on the table.

"I will not stop until this girl is identified. Detective Slidell will not stop until her killer is caught. You lied to us about knowing Story. You must have had a reason to do so, and that ties you in."

"And remember, asshole." Thrusting his face into Rockett's, Slidell hiked his brows up, then down. "I'm fucking crazy."

Without another word we walked out and drove away.

And that was it.

For the next ten days I would learn nothing about the girl with the pink purse and barrette lying in the morgue cooler.

PART TWO

16

Saturday I woke with bed linens wrapping me like a constrictor. If I'd been thrashing in my dreams, I remembered nothing.

Birdie was nowhere to be seen.

I pulled the clock into bleary view. 8:45.

When breakfast is late, my cat either chews my hair or rattles a silk plant I keep on the dresser. He's good. Either ploy annoys me enough to get up.

Weird that Bird hadn't tortured me into consciousness. Too heavy-handed with the oatmeal and eggs?

But I'd bought his favorite on my way home the previous night. Iams. He didn't know I fed him the weight-control formula.

I rose on one elbow and looked around.

No cat.

Then I smelled coffee.

And heard muted music. "Good Day Sunshine"?

Puzzled, I pulled on sweats and headed for the stairs.

A box of donuts sat on the dining room table. Napkins. Plates and utensils. Butter and jam.

In the study, the Beatles were singing about needing to laugh.

I pushed through the swinging door into the kitchen.

Pete was at the counter, pouring juice from a carton.

"Sugarbritches." Big Pete grin. "I didn't wake you, did I?"

Is there a nonsarcastic answer to that question? My brain conjured none.

"What are you doing here?"

Then, panic.

Which must have shown on my face.

"Don't worry." Pete raised a calming hand. "Katy's fine."

"You've talked to her?"

"She's fine."

"That's not an answer."

Pete stowed the carton in the fridge and turned back to me. A smile twitched his lips as he took in my attire and disheveled hair. Probably a bed crease denting one cheek.

"Don't start." I gave him my squinty-eye warning.

"What?" Boyish innocence.

"It's much too early for a fashion critique."

"You look terrific, sugarbritches."

"Don't call me that."

"Here." Pete thrust a glass toward me. "It's loaded with vitamins."

"You sound like Anita Bryant." Accepting the OJ.

"She was right." Pete took a sip. Clarified. "About oranges. Cheers."

Pete tapped his brim to mine. We both knocked back our juice.

"Where's Bird?" I set my glass in the sink.

"Sleeping off the pâté."

"You gave him pâté?"

"Relax. It was chicken liver, not goose."

"The vet has him on a diet."

"He didn't mention that."

My eyes were still rolling when the cat strolled in. Pete picked him up.

Birdie purred like a Ducati cruising at eighty. He likes my ex. Always has.

"Did you know you've been robbed?"

"What?" My eyes flew around the kitchen.

"Your refrigerator's been stripped."

"You're hilarious."

"Seriously. It's empty."

"I've had a busy couple of days."

"The hit and run?"

"Mm. That why you're here? To make sure I'm eating?"

"Madam." Sweeping an arm toward the door. "Shall we adjourn for coffee and tarts?"

"I will not get sucked into your wedding drama."

"That's not why I'm here."

We both filled mugs, added cream, then moved to the dining room. Pete took the chair opposite mine at the table.

"Butter and jam?" I cocked a questioning brow.

"You never know."

"Yes. With donuts, you do."

I helped myself to a chocolate glazed with sprinkles.

Pete took no pastry. Didn't touch his coffee.

"Snooze you lose," I said brightly. "Should have bought more chocolate."

"They're all for you."

"What, no flowers?"

It was an old joke between us. Pete didn't laugh.

Alrighty, then.

As I waited for my ex to get to the point, another possibility entered my mind.

"Is there a problem with the divorce? Did I do something wrong on one of the form—"

"Everything's in order."

"Have you filed—"

"I will."

"The wedding is still on track?"

Jesus, Brennan. Why bring it up?

"There are some glitches. Nothing Summer can't handle."

Summer can't handle stirring yogurt without instruction. I didn't say it.

Birdie jumped onto the chair beside Pete. He ran a hand down the cat's back. Stared at the motion, distracted. Avoiding?

My gut clenched.

"You're not lying to me, are you? This isn't about Katy, right?"

"Only peripherally."

Heat flamed my cheeks.

"You said—"

"She's fine."

"Have you heard from her today?"

"No."

"Then you have no idea how fine she is." Sharp.

Pete continued stroking the cat. Continued watching his hand do it.

"Sorry. I didn't mean to bite your head off," I said.

Pete leaned back. Changed his mind and leaned forward, elbows on the table.

"There's a way you can see Katy."

"We were supposed to Skype—"

"In person."

"What? She gets leave? Already?" My donut froze in midair. "Oh, God. Is she hurt?"

"No."

"Has she been hospitalized?"

"No. Christ. Stop overreacting."

"Tell me the truth."

"I have no reason to believe that our daughter is anything but healthy and happy." Überpatient.

I studied Pete's face. Saw no deception. But a boatload of doubt.

Janis Petersons? Man of glib tongue and cast-iron nerves?

"What's going on, Pete?"

He lifted his mug. Set it down without drinking.

"You can go to her."

"Go to her?" I'd missed a connection somewhere.

"To Bagram."

"Bagram. Afghanistan?"

"Right."

This was not making sense.

"I know you worry, sugarbritches. I worry, too. Especially when days pass without word. I can't let on, of course, being manly and all."

Another old joke unacknowledged by laughter.

Pete continued, his tone different now. Deadly serious.

"I don't want to manipulate you. But I do want to persuade you."

Persuasion. The lawyer's stock in trade.

"Persuade me." Again I parroted, totally confused.

Pete drew a deep breath. Let it out. Laced his fingers.

"Okay. You remember my friend, Hunter Gross?"

I shook my head.

"The one I mentioned at dinner on Wednesday?"

At the bar with its volume on blast. "He's a marine," I said. "His nephew's a marine."

"Yes. John Gross. I've known Hunter for years."

"From your days in the Corps." I could never keep Pete's old marine buddies straight.

Pete nodded. "Hunter called me again. He's truly concerned about his nephew."

"Go on."

"I think I told you John's at Camp Lejeune awaiting an Article 32 hearing."

An Article 32 is the military equivalent of a grand jury. The purpose is to determine if sufficient evidence exists to proceed to court-martial.

"John's been accused of killing Afghan civilians." The story was coming back to me. "Which he denies."

"A court-martial will ruin the kid's career. Though that's the least of his worries. If found guilty, he could serve life in a federal penitentiary. Or worse."

"What's he supposed to have done?"

"According to the charge sheet, he shot two unarmed villagers during the search of a compound."

"What's his version?"

"It was dusk. The scene was chaos. The men came at him screaming about 'Allah!' One made a move as though reaching for a firearm. He claims he shot in self-defense."

"Turned out the men had no weapons."

"You've got it."

I thought about that.

"Gross is holding, what, an M16? The victims are unarmed? Yet they rush him? It doesn't make sense."

"Heat of the moment? Personal jihad?" Pete shrugged. "Who knows?"

"There has to be more to the story."

"Here's what I know. As a lieutenant and platoon leader, John had to make a lot of difficult decisions. With serious consequences."

Pete paused, perhaps recalling his own difficult choices while in service.

"One such decision involved a corporal named Grant Eggers. After repeated corrective interviews, John was forced to remove Eggers from his position as fire team leader. Eggers was furious, apparently bad-mouthed John at every opportunity, but never confronted him."

"Let me guess. Eggers is the one making the accusation." I went for a powdered-sugar frosted.

"Yes. He says the men weren't running toward John, but away from him. He claims John shot them in the back."

"Jesus."

"Yeah. Crazy ten ways to Sunday. Hunter is convinced his nephew is being railroaded."

"Why?"

"Uncle Sam isn't exactly beloved over there. Two unarmed civilians dead. An American marine the shooter. The locals want blood."

"Politics."

Pete shrugged. Who knows?

"The solution couldn't be simpler."

Pete reached over and brushed a thumb across my upper lip. I batted his hand away.

"Sugar mustache," he said. "Go on."

"The medical examiner checks the bullet entry and exit points."

"That's been impossible."

"Why?"

"The men are buried in a Muslim cemetery. NCIS has repeatedly tried to get access, but the Afghan authorities have repeatedly refused to allow either an exhumation or an autopsy. After a lot of diplomatic maneuvering, they've now reversed their position."

I had a sudden suspicion where this was heading.

"They've agreed to an exhumation," I guessed.

"Yes. But there's no guarantee they won't change their minds again. So speed is of the essence. The Article 32 hearing has been recessed to allow time for the exhumation to take place."

"Uh-huh."

"How well preserved do you think the bodies will be?"

"What was done with them postmortem?"

"Hunter's intel says the men were bathed, shrouded, and buried. Just laid on their right sides, heads toward Mecca."

"A year in the ground. No caskets. I'd expect advanced decomp, if not full skeletonization."

"U.S. experts will only get one shot at these bodies. If base personnel aren't top-notch, John could be screwed."

"Determining bullet trajectory is not rocket science."

"You know that. Will they? According to Hunter, this is John's best hope to clear himself. The defense wants a say in who will exhume and examine, and the prosecution has told them to propose someone who might be mutually acceptable."

"You want me to go to Afghanistan." Said with the enthusiasm I reserve for boils and sties.

"Yes. Your prosecution background will satisfy the government and the defense will go along with Hunter's recommendation."

Pete leaned back, eyes intense on mine. He'd presented his case. Now he waited.

Deep breath.

"Don't get me wrong, Pete. I feel for John and his family. But military physicians have a lot of experience—too much—with traumatic injury. Any doctor in Afghanistan will have seen hundreds of gunshot wounds."

"In fresh tissue. You just said it. The only thing left will probably be bone. That's you. That's your thing. You're the best. Plus, the Article 32 hearing is in North Carolina."

"I have commitments. I can't just take off for the other side of the world."

"You do it all the time."

"No, I don't."

"JPAC?"

Pete was referring to my role as a civilian consultant to the Joint POW-MIA Accounting Command, the military's central identification laboratory in Honolulu.

"That's different. Those visits are scheduled."

"That's another reason it has to be you. You know how the military functions, and your JPAC connection is another big reason the government will agree to you as the forensic expert."

"Pete—"

He reached across and took both my hands in his.

"I'm asking this as a personal favor. Please. Oversee the exhumation. Do the analysis."

"This is ridiculous. The logistics would be a nightmare."

He smiled. "You've already been cleared."

"By whom?"

"The DOD, the Pentagon, the friggin' White House."

"Are you kidding me?"

Pete pantomimed crossing his heart. "Digging up corpses on foreign soil is serious business, especially when they're evidence in the investigation of an American soldier."

"No way." I pulled my hands free. "I've got a teenage Jane Doe in my cooler and no one gives a flip. If I don't press her case, who will?"

"How's that going?" Not full-out sarcastic, but close.

"It's going." Clipped. Why was I even discussing this?

"It's your choice, of course. Stay here and keep pressing. Go to Afghanistan and help an American who's maybe getting screwed. An American who risked his life serving his country."

Pete paused to allow the unspoken implication its full impact. Katy.

"You can do either, buttercup. But ask yourself. Will staying here really help your Jane Doe?"

Annoying as it was, Pete had a point. Slidell would keep chipping away at the hit and run. Not as fast without me nagging, but he'd do the work. Luther Dew? No nagging needed there. The DNA? I could fly around the world and still beat the results to my inbox.

"John Gross needs one person he can trust to be impartial and competent. He needs the best."

"What if I find that these men were shot in the back?"

"Then I will have fulfilled a commitment to a friend, and you will have found the truth, wherever it leads."

Then Pete the litigator brought his argument home.

"The incident took place at a village called Sheyn Bagh. You'll go there to oversee the exhumation. You'll do the analysis at Bagram."

Where Katy is stationed. Again, it didn't need saying.

"I'll think about it."

Dear God, was I really considering this?

Pete passed me the donuts. I shook my head. He placed one on his plate, collected both mugs, and disappeared into the kitchen.

On the sideboard, Gran's clock tapped out its quiet metronome. Curled on his chair, Birdie snored softly. Out the window, a mockingbird trilled a Saturday-morning air.

Pete returned and set coffee before me. Took his chair. Waited.

At length, he asked, "Finished thinking?"

"No." I was.

"You'll go, right?"

"When?"

He pulled an envelope from the back pocket of his jeans, removed two papers, and laid them on the table.

I glanced at each.

Invitational travel orders.

An e-ticket on Turkish Airlines. Charlotte-Douglas to Dulles International. Dulles to Istanbul.

Leaving the next day.

17

THE REST OF THAT DAY WAS A NIGHTMARE OF ERRANDS, PACKING, and last-minute arrangements. Ditto Sunday morning.

Larabee had to be notified. Slidell. Dew. LaManche in Montreal. Katy.

I tried Ryan, got voicemail. Big surprise there. Message: Gone to Afghanistan. Let him think about that.

Not wanting an inquisition, I sent Harry an e-mail. An extremely vague one.

I asked a neighbor to bring in the mail and papers. Dropped Birdie with Pete. Filled a prescription. Bought socks.

You get the picture.

Packing was a challenge. The Weather Channel said it might be hot, might be cold. Terrific. Figuring I could peel down, I erred in the direction of the latter.

In addition to jeans, tees, and sweaters, I tossed in my usual crime-scene duds: khaki BDUs, khaki cap, desert boots, gloves. Saucy. I figured my hosts could supply any specialty gear needed.

Sunday morning I also loaded files onto my MacBook Air. A template for an evidence transfer form. A template for a forensic anthropology case form. The latest version of Fordisc 3.0, a program for the metric analysis of unknown remains. A number of online osteology manuals. All probably unneeded, but I wanted to be fully armed.

Last, I copied an article I was preparing for the *Journal of Forensic Sciences*. Unlikely I'd do any writing on this trip, but what the hell.

The taxi rolled up at four. I was at Charlotte-Douglas in thirty minutes, through security in thirty more.

Aviation miracle, the flight was on time. Three hours after leaving the annex, I was walking up a Jetway at Dulles.

After locating the Turkish Airlines gate, I found the Virgin Atlantic lounge and burrowed in for my three-hour wait.

Again, the gods were smiling. At 10:20 a voice announced my flight was boarding for an on-time departure.

Thinking international travel wasn't so bad, I queued up with my fellow business-class passengers, found my seat, stowed my belongings, and buckled my belt.

I do not sleep well in flight.

For the next ten hours I read, ate a reasonably good meal, tried a movie or two. Donned earplugs and eyeshades, reclined my seat, and tucked under the blanket. Sought positions in which all of my limbs enjoyed blood flow. Reoriented again and again. Raised the seat and turned on the light to read. Lowered the seat. Dialed up white noise on my phone. Tried another movie.

Again and again I thought about Jane Doe. Assured myself I hadn't abandoned her.

Deplaning in Istanbul, I felt like I'd rowed the entire fifty-five hundred miles.

The Turkish Airlines lounge was all gold and white, with circular arches separating bars, seating clusters, and food stations. The chairs and sofas would have looked stylish in any posh L.A. hotel. Wi-Fi. A pianist. Even a masseur. I could've lived in the place.

I snagged a few hors d'oeuvres, then checked my e-mail.

Katy and Ryan remained incommunicado.

Not so Harry. Now panicked.

Twenty-four hours had passed since my departure from Charlotte, almost none of that time spent sleeping. No way I was up to dealing with baby sister. I sent a follow-up message as vague as my first. Traveling. Catch up soon.

My next flight was aboard a 737 whose interior had never experienced a facelift. I got the bulkhead row, which meant a wall in my face in exchange for an extra inch of legroom.

The ride was bumpy. The coffee was Turkish and tasted like tar.

Five hours after taking off, the pilot put down at Manas International Airport in Bishkek, Kyrgyzstan, the transit center for U.S. and coalition forces moving to and from Afghanistan.

As we taxied through blackness, I attempted some math. My watch said it was 9 P.M. EST. Monday. I estimated it was Tuesday morning in Kyrgyzstan. That's all the precision my sleep-deprived neurons could muster.

A master sergeant named Grace Mensforth met me at the terminal. Medium build, brown hair, unremarkable features. The type witnesses rarely remember.

Mensforth introduced herself as my Air Force liaison. At my blank look, she explained that, though Kyrgyzstan operates the airport, the USAF runs the Transit Center. Thus her presence.

"How was your flight?"

"Uneventful."

"Best we can hope for, eh?" She swept an arm left. "Baggage is this way."

Mensforth led me across a cement-floored terminal that looked like the basement of a Stalinist factory. Boy-men in nine-foot peaked caps and long wool coats stood with automatic weapons slung across their chests.

My duffel was on the floor, a spot of tan in a sea of multicolored leather and speckled camouflage. I waded in and hoisted it free.

"Give me your passport." Mensforth held out a hand. "I'll handle the visa."

"Thanks."

"The red tape is unreal."

Slowly, the baggage area emptied. I stood, cold seeping through my Nikes, jacket, and jeans, fatigue weighing on my body like a truckload of sludge.

Finally, Mensforth returned.

"This your first trip to the Islamic Republic of Afghanistan?" Handing back my passport.

"And Kyrgyzstan."

"The Kyrgyz Republic. On to customs."

Again Mensforth arm-motioned "this way." I wondered if she'd been a maître d' in another life.

Fortunately, the line was short. As we progressed, body length by body length, Mensforth took a stab at conversation.

"*Kyrgyz* comes from *forty*. Forty tribes."

"Really."

We lurched forward.

Mensforth interpreted my listless reply as either aloofness or lack of interest. From then on we waited in silence.

Fifteen minutes after queuing up, I was following my liaison across a pitch-black tarmac. The air was frosty, the wind damp and penetrating.

Head lowered, Mensforth angled to a white Air Force van and opened a side rear door. I climbed in. A kid in uniform loaded my bag, then slid behind the wheel.

As we drove, tiny lights shaped up in the distance. I spotted no other vehicles.

My head throbbed. My stomach churned. Sleep would definitely take precedence over food.

The trip to the air base was mercifully brief, maybe five minutes.

As the driver paused at a checkpoint to answer questions and present ID, including my passport and orders, I stared at the canvas-and-mesh-surfaced wall outside my window.

"That Hesco?" I was curious, despite my exhaustion.

"Yes, ma'am," Mensforth said.

I'd read about Hesco. Made of crate-size units filled with sand and rock, then stacked three-high hard against each other, such barriers are strong but pliant. When ready to move on, base workers just empty the bags.

No idea why my brain dredged that up.

Finally, docs inspected and stamped, we cleared the gate.

The van wound past prefab rectangular structures, enormous Quonsets, what might have been a small mosque, a long, low arrangement that looked like a bar. Eventually, we pulled to the curb by a windowless, two-story number measuring about a hundred feet long by thirty feet wide.

"Female barracks." Mensforth hopped out and cut toward a metal staircase on the building's near end.

I followed. The kid trailed with my duffel on one shoulder.

We clanged up the stairs to a metal door. Mensforth gave me a key.

"You're in 204. Take the empty rack."

The kid dumped my bag and scuttled back down.

"You may luck out and have the room to yourself." Mensforth spoke in hushed tones. "The head's down the hall. I'll collect you at oh-eight-hundred."

Though the sky was still dark, I doubted dawn was far off.

"What time is it now?" I asked.

"Oh-four-thirty."

Hallelujah.

The room, barely eight by ten, held two wardrobe units and two single beds. I lucked out. Both pillows were empty.

After opening my duffel, I fired to the head. Back in the room, I peeled off my clothes, pulled on a tee and clean panties, plugged in my iPhone, set the alarm, and collapsed.

Church bells bonged.

Startled, I opened my eyes.

My brain groped.

Manas.

I clawed the phone. Killed the bells. Checked the digits.

7:45.

Shivering, I yanked on BDUs and boots, grabbed my toiletry case, and trudged down the hall.

Quick swipe at the teeth and hair. Different brushes.

At 0800 I opened the outside door. The sun was a low white ball in an immaculate blue sky. Frost coated the grass like a dusting of sugar.

Mensforth stood at the base of the stairs, a puffy brown jacket draped over one arm.

"Good morning." Breath coned from her mouth.

"Good morning. Bring my gear?"

"Yes, ma'am."

I collected my duffel and backpack and clumped down the stairs.

"Take this." Mensforth offered the jacket.

"You think it'll be that cold?"

"Better to have and not need, than to need and not have."

"My mother used to say that."

"Mine too."

We both smiled. I put on the jacket.

"Thanks."

"Thank Uncle Sam. Hungry?"

"Oh, yeah."

"Let's hit a DFAC." Pronounced *dee-fack*.

A different kid in uniform now manned the wheel of the van. Scarecrow thin, with buzz-cut hair.

As we drove, Mensforth briefed me on my upcoming travel arrangements.

"Your flight downrange is at noon, which means lockdown by oh-nine-hundred. You'll be issued IBA at the airfield."

Individual body armor. I was looking forward to that.

The kid made a couple of turns, then braked by a structure that looked like an aircraft hangar.

Mensforth and I presented ID and were admitted to the dining facility. After washing our hands at one of a score of taps, we entered the main hall. The air was thick with the smell of warming food. Sausage. Canned corn. Tortillas. Bacon.

Troops in camouflage and workers in civvies filled trays at hot and cold stations, salad and sandwich bars, burger grills, and dairy cases. Men and women of all ranks ate at hundreds of tables set out in rows.

Mensforth gave some instruction, which I missed, then left me on my own. I headed to a banquette that seemed to be drawing a decent crowd.

My instincts were good. Large metal bins offered standard Midwestern fare: eggs, bacon, toast, hash browns. I heaped my plate, added juice and coffee, then found an empty place at a table by a soft drink cooler.

Further down, on the opposite side, was a man in a uniform I didn't recognize. French? Polish? Beside him sat a twentysomething carrying a weapon half her body weight.

Banging trays, clanging utensils, and humming conversation vied with football play-by-play coming from wall-mounted screens. Now and then staccato laughter broke through the din.

Mensforth found me, and we ate without talking. She'd gone for some sort of burrito with a cheeselike overlay. Breakfast finished, we bussed our trays and headed for the airfield.

Flight staging took place in another hangarlike affair with TVs airing yet more football.

Troops sat crammed onto benches, either on cell phones or other devices or with eyes closed or numbly resting on a game. Observing them, I wondered, Is sport the new opiate of the masses?

Others slumped on duffels or slept tucked to the walls. Male or female, all looked weary. And wary.

Mensforth led me to a side room in which shelving and bins overflowed with IBA.

Personal protective gear is designed to protect your person. Which does not mean it fits your person. Especially if your person is of the double-X gender.

Outer tactical vests come in four colors—woodland green camouflage, desert camouflage, universal camouflage, and coyote brown, the khaki of the Marine Corps. Mensforth handed me a universal, size small. I removed my outer jacket and slipped into the gray-green beauty. Not bad.

Then Mensforth added small-arms ballistic inserts to the front, back, and sides. And handed me a helmet. The combined weight came to somewhere north of forty pounds. I felt and looked like a Hesco unit with feet.

And then we waited.

I dozed on and off, mostly sat listlessly watching game after game.

Wisconsin lost by a field goal to Minnesota. Badgers and Gophers? Really?

Oklahoma hammered the TCU Horned Frogs.

Okay. Maybe small furry mammals didn't make such bad totems.

The room grew thick with the smell of sweat, mildew, and dusty canvas. With the scent of exhaustion and fear.

At one point those around me began gathering their gear. Mensforth reappeared and told me to stay put. It wasn't my flight. Mine was delayed.

Just past four, Mensforth finally led me onto a bus crammed with marines. Fifteen minutes later, we were standing on the tarmac outside a plane that looked as if it had been designed to transport shuttles for NASA.

"You're going to be impressed." The shriek of aircraft engines forced Mensforth to shout. "A C-130J can carry three vehicles, or close to a hundred troops."

I eyed the plane's interior, estimated the space was maybe forty by nine by ten.

Not exactly business class. I didn't say it.

As I waited with what seemed like a thousand marines, crew off-loaded cargo onto palletized rollers, then flipped down flooring.

"Word to the wise," Mensforth said. "The heads on these babies aren't designed for our team."

"What's the flight time to Bagram?"

"Two, maybe three hours."

"I'm good." I planned to sleep.

At a signal from a camouflage-clad kid with a rag around his head, Mensforth plucked me from the line and led me onto the plane. The marines watched in hostile, exhausted, or good-natured silence.

Seating was on long benches arranged in facing pairs. Back support came in the form of red nylon latticework strapping.

Parachutes and other gear hung from the fuselage walls. Pipes, tubing, cables, and countless things I didn't recognize snaked overhead.

"Ass to the wall, you freeze," Mensforth said. "Ass to the center, you go numb."

Numb sounded good.

"You can lose the body armor."

Grateful to offload the extra poundage, I removed the hated jacket. Mensforth tossed it to the floor at the end of the bench, then showed me how to stow my helmet at my feet and my pack in my lap.

"Use 'em." Offering a small packet containing two orange earplugs.

I nodded.

"You'll be met at Bagram by a Captain Welsted."

I thanked Mensforth, wondered briefly if she knew the purpose of my trip. Then she said an odd thing.

"Watch your back."

"Got my trusty IBA." Tapping my helmet.

"That'll handle the bullets." Glancing left then right, she leaned close. "Be careful."

Before I could ask her meaning she said, "Have a good one."

Then she was gone.

The plane filled fast. A marine the size of a linebacker took the "seat" to my left. A black kid with spectacularly white teeth dropped down on my right. Opposite, I drew a guy who had to be seven feet tall. My knees met his lower legs at about mid-tibia. Snugly.

After a final round of shouting, the crew shut the hatch. I glanced at my fellow passengers. Most were male and in their twenties.

I heard a lot of "fucking" this and "fucking" that. Bravado. We were going downrange. In Pete's day the phrase had been "in country." Same idea. Same apprehension. We were heading to war.

I noticed a man three over and opposite, watching me intently. Asian. Maybe eighteen.

I smiled. The man looked away.

The engines thundered to life. I inserted the earplugs.

The ungainly craft lumbered skyward. Finally leveled.

I lowered my lids. Tried to sleep.

We pitched and dipped, engines throbbing out a deafening roar. Icy air blew up my back. Though shoulder to shoulder, shin to shin with my seatmates, a penetrating cold invaded my bones. Before long I felt desperate to stretch, or at least reposition. Knew there wasn't a chance.

Time passed. My brain lingered on that border between waking and sleeping.

Suddenly my body lurched at an angle that had to be wrong. Beside me, the linebacker tensed.

Adrenaline shot through me.

My eyes flew open.

The plane was dark as a tomb.

And plunging toward earth.

18

ALL AROUND ME WAS BLACK.

My left side was smashed against the linebacker. The kid with the teeth was smashed against me. Knowing it was pointless to fight gravity, I made no attempt to right myself.

Then the whine of the engines dropped. Our three-person sandwich unzipped slightly.

The wheels hit hard. Hit again, with less force. Again.

My heartbeat settled. We were rolling on terra firma.

After a short taxi, the plane jerked to a stop. The lights came on, the hatch opened, and outside air filtered into the fuselage, bringing with it the smell of fuel and exhaust.

We waited as pallets of cargo were unloaded, and then, row by row, collected our gear, moved rearward, and hopped onto the tarmac. My eyes swept a three-sixty arc, anxious for a sense of the strange land I'd heard so much about.

Overhead, a universe of stars winked in a boundless black dome. On the ground, nothing but darkness.

We all waited for the luggage pallets to be opened. Collected our gear. Then, unsure what to do, I followed the marines toward a square black shape on the horizon.

As we drew close, the shape crystallized into a one-story building. Standing at its door were a man and a woman, the former in civvies, the latter in camouflage fatigues and eight-pointed utility cover.

The woman was about my age, tall and solid but attractive in a no-nonsense, no makeup way. Her dark hair was knotted at the back of her cap.

Like Katy's.

No way. Focus.

The woman took the lead. "Dr. Brennan?"

I nodded, thinking the question pointless. How many fortysomething civilian females arrived at Bagram by military transport?

When the woman extended a hand, double bars were momentarily illuminated on her fatigues.

"Maida Welsted, base ops."

"Captain."

We shook.

The man shifted his feet. Signaling impatience? Annoyance? Welsted ignored him.

"I'll be handling field ops for the exhumation in Sheyn Bagh. All mission assets—team, vehicles, armaments, air transport." Welsted's English was softly accented. British? Anglo-Indian? Spanish? "You need anything, you go through me."

"Dr. Brennan has had a long flight."

The man was tall, maybe midthirties. A blue athletic cap covered what I suspected was a hairline heading south.

Welsted looked at the man. In the dim light escaping the door, I couldn't read her expression. But the man seemed to stiffen.

"I'm just saying, we can do this in the morning. She's been on a plane for four hours. Probably wants dinner and rack time."

The man's hand shot my way. "Scott Blanton, Naval Criminal Investigative Service."

Blanton's grip was firm, but no match for Welsted's.

Without a word, Welsted turned and crossed to a pair of men standing outside the depot at our backs. The younger wore jeans and a windbreaker with a White Sox logo. The older was in baggy linen pants, knee-length shirt, and voluminous sweater. Both had beards and unkept hair.

"Captain Welsted can be a bit stiff." Blanton smiled, revealing one upper incisor overlapping the other. "Texan, you know."

Not sure how to respond, I said nothing.

Behind Blanton, the men listened to Welsted, both overnodding. In less than a minute, she rejoined us.

"Let's get you to your B-hut." Without waiting for a reply, Welsted strode off.

Blanton shrugged, and, despite my repeated protests, took my duffel.

We boarded a van whose driver was indistinguishable from the pair at Manas. A short ride and a long security check brought us onto a base that, in the dark, appeared similar to the one I'd just left in Kyrgyzstan.

With one big difference.

Here I would enjoy no dorm-room comfort. No *toilette* down the hall.

My quarters consisted of one half of a B-hut, a plywood box in a maze of identical boxes, all squatting in a field of kiwi-size gravel. The interior, maybe eight by ten, contained two bunks, two slapped-together nightstands, a wooden wardrobe filled with shrink-wrapped cases of bottled water, and a table heaped with dusty magazines and ancient copies of *Stars and Stripes*. And, miraculously, a PC terminal that looked twenty years old.

That was the good news. The bad news?

The bath facility was an ankle-twisting football field away.

After informing me that we'd have a briefing with the head of base ops at 0900, Welsted took her leave.

"You want to get some chow?" Blanton asked.

Though exhausted, I'd had nothing but granola bars and Diet Coke since breakfast.

"Sure."

I dumped my gear. As we walked, I told Blanton about Katy. He said he'd look into tracking her down.

A quick burger and chips and I was back at the B-hut.

"Breakfast at oh-eight-hundred?"

"I can find my way."

"Things look different in the light."

"Sure. I'd appreciate an escort." I did.

"Maybe I should have contact info in case there's a change of plans?"

Doubting they'd be functional, I gave him my mobile number and e-mail address.

After a touchdown run to the toilet, I set my alarm, positioned my flashlight on the nightstand, and collapsed into bed.

My last thoughts were these.

You will not need to pee before morning.

Why the tension between Welsted and Blanton?

I awoke to the sound of boots on plywood. Male voices beyond the partition to my left. Aircraft shrieking overhead.

I checked my watch.

6:50. How long had I slept? Not long enough.

I looked around, hoping I'd underestimated the dismal room the night before. I hadn't.

Naked walls, linoleum flooring, here and there a tacked and curling USO poster or photo. No window. One electrical outlet per bed. Typical barracks hut. Easy up, easy down. Life expectancy three to four years.

I dressed, gathered my toiletries and flashlight, and set off for my hundred-yard hike.

And got my first stunning glimpse of Bagram.

Mountains soared in a circle around me, high and commanding, their snowy peaks white against a sky slowly oozing from dawn into day.

Crunching past rows of B-huts, I remembered Katy's e-mailed comments. Not the Hilton, she'd said, but better than tents. Her main problem had been bugs. No Hershey bar remnants could be left around. No half-drunk sodas. I smiled at the thought of my daughter cleaning house every day.

And found myself searching. A pair of slim legs climbing the stairs. A blond head disappearing into a stall.

Could I bump into Katy in the dressing room? At the DFAC? Walking down a street?

While showering, I distracted myself by pulling up what I'd learned about Bagram before leaving home. There was little to pull.

Built as an airfield by the U.S. in the 1950s, the base was now the size of a small town. Its population of roughly six thousand military and twenty-four thousand civilians was composed of allied troops, international contractors, and Afghan day workers.

In addition to standard amenities, Bagram had coffee shops, fast-food joints, a tower left over from the days of Russian occupation, and a bazaar in which local vendors sold their wares. Disney Drive was the main drag, named in honor of a fallen soldier, not Uncle Walt.

Bagram Air Base lay close to the ancient Silk Road city for which it was named. And light-years distant.

Showered and shampooed, I hiked back to my quarters. And was delighted to find that the old PC actually allowed me Internet access.

Having twenty minutes to kill, I checked my e-mail. And found nothing from anyone I actually knew. I shot a note to Larabee, asking for an update on the hit-and-run case. Sent another to Slidell, knowing I'd get no response.

Blanton arrived at eight on the dot. While ingesting enough carbs to lay a rugby team flat, I learned that he held a BA in history, that he'd never been married, that he'd worked briefly as a cop, and that he was in his fourteenth year with NCIS.

Blanton was heading stateside as soon as the exhumation and analysis were completed. Surprisingly, he'd been born and raised in Gastonia.

Funny world. Come seven thousand miles and meet someone from right near home.

Blanton learned that I was board certified by the ABFA. And that I have a cat.

Why not share more? It might have been the way Blanton looked at me, never shifting his gaze, rarely blinking. Or the superior tone he used in phrasing some things. If asked, I couldn't articulate a reason. But an inner voice advised against candor.

I wondered if I'd been wise in talking about Katy. I'd been brain-dead from exhaustion. Too late. That was done.

When we returned, Welsted was leaning against a van outside my B-hut. Seeing us, her eyes went to her watch.

"Good morning, captain," I said brightly.

"Good morning." Welsted didn't smile or acknowledge Blanton. "Ready?"

"And eager." That was the third coffee talking.

Five minutes later, we arrived at a corrugated-metal building with a sign that identified it as the headquarters for base operations. We entered and climbed to the second floor.

Hearing boots, an Air Force sergeant popped from a doorway and led us to a conference room that would have looked right at home in a midsize law office. Blond oak table with chairs for a dozen. Blackboard. Sideboard with a coffee setup. Only the rough walls looked out of place.

A man was already present, filling a thick white porcelain mug. Navy. Lettering on his fatigues told me his name was Noonan. A Velcro patch told me he was with JAG, the Judge Advocate General's Corps.

Blanton took a seat at the table. Welsted and I crossed to Noonan.

Like Blanton, the Navy lawyer had hair that was fast parting ways with his scalp, and pale skin peeling from his nose and cheeks.

"Ruff Noonan, JAG." We shook. "I won't be going downrange for the festivities. Just sitting in on the briefing."

Hearing the door open, we all turned.

A black woman entered the room, short and large-breasted, with posture that made the most of her stature.

Dumping a pair of corrugated brown files on the table, the woman gestured us to sit.

"Shall we get started?"

Those standing took chairs.

"First off, let me introduce myself, Dr. Brennan. The rest of you know me." Quick smile. "I'm Gloria Fisher, commander of base operations here at Bagram. My staff and I are working to facilitate your mission. I trust your travel went well?"

"Yes."

"And that your quarters are satisfactory?"

"Yes, thank you."

"Captain Welsted is taking good care of you?"

"She's been very helpful. Everyone has been very helpful."

"And you've met the rest of your team?"

Assuming she meant Blanton and Noonan, I nodded.

"Good."

Fisher laced her fingers on the tabletop. Her nails, though uncolored, were better polished and manicured than mine.

"As you are undoubtedly aware, the tasking for a mission such as this is extremely complicated. And sensitive. The unearthing of an Afghan national is of concern not only to the DOD, but to the State Department, even the White House."

As Fisher spoke, Blanton eyed me without embarrassment. I met his gaze and, though listening to the colonel, stared back.

"Negotiations for this exhumation began almost immediately after accusations were laid. Only recently have discussions proved fruitful. It is my intent that all phases of this operation proceed smoothly and successfully."

Apparently no one felt the statement required feedback. Or those present knew Fisher would want none.

"So. Background." Fisher drew papers from the top file. "The incident took place in the village of Sheyn Bagh, twelve kilometers east of FOB Delaram."

"Forward operating base," Blanton explained for my benefit.

Fisher's eyes rolled to him, back to the page she was skimming.

"The accused, Marine Second Lieutenant John Gross, was at that time a platoon commander with the RCT 6, the 3/8."

Not wanting to interrupt, I made a note to obtain translation later.

"Intel had it that insurgents were storing illegal weapons in the village. Gross's mission was to perform a cordon-and-knock."

That one I knew. Surround the area and go house to house, banging on doors.

"Here is the full file." Fisher disengaged the bottom folder and slid it my way. "Mr. Blanton, I assume you have a copy? Lieutenant Noonan?"

Blanton and Noonan nodded.

Fisher directed her next comments to me.

"To summarize, on the day in question, a six-vehicle convoy rolled out of Delaram just before sunset. Upon arriving at Sheyn Bagh, Second Lieutenant Gross ordered his men to gather the villagers outside. Then, while some undertook a weapons search, others began interrogation. As the op was proceeding, an RPG detonated on the road outside the village wall, badly damaging a Humvee and injuring two of Gross's men. According to multiple witnesses, pandemonium ensued."

Fisher speed-read, choosing what she considered salient points.

"As per Lieutenant Gross's statement, at the time of the explosion he was covering two LNs, local nationals, who'd been identified as possible insurgents."

Fisher brought her eyes closer to the file.

"Ahmad Ali Aqsaee and Abdul Khalik Rasekh."

She straightened.

"According to Second Lieutenant Gross, Aqsaee and Rasekh ran at him. Though he ordered them to halt in English and Pashto, both continued in a threatening manner. Fearing for his life, he opened fire."

"Gross's version differs markedly from that of Eggers's."

"Yes, Lieutenant Noonan. That is why we are here."

Recognizing the rebuke, Noonan leaned back, lips compressed so tightly they blanched at the edges.

Fisher refocused on me.

"According to Corporal Grant Eggers, Aqsaee and Rasekh weren't rushing anyone. Terrified by the blast, they were attempting to move away from the road."

Several beats passed.

"The victims' bio profiles are in here?" I tapped the folder in front of me.

"Yes. Rasekh was significantly taller than Aqsaee. And the two differed in age."

"By how much?"

"Mr. Rasekh was fifty-two."

Fisher gave a tight shake of her head.

"Mr. Aqsaee was killed on his seventeenth birthday."

19

Fisher addressed a number of points concerning logistics, then, wishing us Godspeed, withdrew. Welsted took over.

"It's essential that we dot every *i* and cross every *t* while exhuming, transporting, and examining these remains. We screw up, go off task just once, the locals have the right to pull the plug. And we'll have eyes on us every minute."

"Friggin' nightmare."

"I realize that displeases you, Mr. Blanton. But that's the agreement. Two local nationals observe throughout."

Blanton pooched air through his lips but said nothing.

"The team will assemble at the staging area at oh-five-hundred tomorrow. Estimated flight time to Sheyn Bagh is two hours, which should put us wheels-down no later than oh-eight-hundred. Count an hour for a meet and greet with the mayor and his honchos, that puts us on-site at the cemetery by oh-nine-hundred. Wheels up by seventeen hundred. Either of you have a problem with that?"

"It's hard to estimate how long an exhumation will take without knowing what conditions we'll encounter," I said.

"You'll have eight hours." Read: end of discussion.

"Suits me," Blanton said. "No way I'm overnighting outside the wire."

"NCIS has final say during the dig and analysis, with input from

Doctor Brennan." Welsted looked my way. "But any disagreement, it's Blanton's call."

Though troubled, I nodded understanding.

"Blanton will oversee the actual digging. His crew will consist of two marines from Delaram and two LNs—"

"Like Ali Baba and his buddy will know how to trowel." Disdain dripped from Blanton's words. "Or how to keep their friggin' sandals from crushing the evidence."

"Lack of local participation was a deal breaker." Welsted's patience was wearing thin. "The Afghans insisted, the Pentagon agreed."

"Christ."

I looked at the NCIS agent, surprised by his contempt for the Afghan people.

But was that it? Was it the locals Blanton disliked? Or a malignancy that had taken root among them?

I try to be open-minded, to judge each individual on merit and accomplishment. I hold no bias against any belief system, sexual orientation, or skin color that differs from mine. I do not hate in stereotype.

But I have no tolerance for a creed that not only denies an education to girls, but condones, even encourages, the abuse of women. For dogma that allows men to beat, mutilate, even execute members of my gender.

My one prejudice. I despise the Taliban. And I firmly believe that the arrogance and cruelty of its followers stems from ignorance, fear, and male insecurity.

"Mr. Blanton will handle all video and photography," Welsted continued. "Villagers wishing to observe will be allowed to do so, but will be kept at a distance of at least ten yards."

"We gonna serve ice cream? Maybe sing a few camp songs?" Blanton slumped back in his chair. "Friggin' circus."

Welsted spoke to me. "You know your equipment needs?"

I pulled a list from my backpack and handed it to her.

Welsted looked around the table. "Any questions?"

I had one.

"Where will I perform my analysis?"

"At the hospital here on base."

"I'll need X-ray capability."

"All arranged."

I had another.

"Why couldn't we do this today?"

"The army is providing transport. The Blackhawk is available tomorrow."

Blanton started to speak. Welsted cut him off.

"Have a good one, people."

Blanton shot to his feet and strode from the room.

I gathered my backpack and jacket and made my way outside. As I reached the sidewalk, Blanton was disappearing around a corner of the building.

"Dr. Brennan?"

I turned. Welsted was coming through the door.

"Do you have plans right now?"

"Got a date with a case file."

"Are you qualified with a weapon?"

"I've done some shooting at Quantico, but—"

"I'm heading to the firing range. How about coming along?"

"Guns aren't really—"

"A woman needs skills, especially over here."

Taking my silence as assent, Welsted elbow-steered me toward the van that had brought us. During the drive, she exhibited an unsettling level of enthusiasm for, and encyclopedic knowledge of, firearms.

"You have your M16, M4 carbine, M27 automatic rifles. Sniper rifles like the M110, M40. The M1014 semiautomatic shotgun. Used by forces in Britain, Australia, Malaysia, Slovenia, the L.A. cops. Nice. Under a yard long. Less than nine pounds."

Welsted had never met a weapon she didn't like.

"I'll stick to handguns," I said.

"More useful stateside, if you get my meaning." Welsted actually winked.

The range was open-air and located on the periphery of the base. Beyond the uprights serving as targets, past the outer fence, stretched mile after mile of barren rock and sand. In the far distance, a walled village rose like a tiny, wavery bump in the endless expanse.

"Be right back," Welsted said after checking us in.

She was. With a weapon familiar to me.

"Beretta M9. Semi. Range of fifty meters. Fifteen-round detachable magazine."

I took the Beretta. Remembered why I liked it. Not too large, not too heavy. Nice heft. Grip that felt good in my hand.

"Reuben will assist you. See you in sixty."

Welsted moved to a target four down from mine.

Reuben was large and mustached, and definitely not a talker. He handed me earplugs and goggles, then set up a target and watched me shoot. After a few corrections to my grip and stance, he disappeared.

An hour after starting, I was leaving a tight circle of holes in the black bull's-eyed human form.

I was removing my earplugs when Welsted reappeared, face flushed either from heat or excitement.

"Good?"

"Good," I said.

Reuben materialized as Welsted called for the van. I handed over the Beretta and protective eyewear. Thanked him.

We were barely rolling when Welsted began punching keys on her mobile. Her end of the conversation suggested firming up of arrangements for the next day. Politeness was not the woman's strong suit.

I checked my iPhone. No signal.

"Pain in the ass dealing with these people." Welsted shoved the phone into a pocket of her fatigues. "Customs vary from tribe to tribe, subtle differences mostly. Pays to make sure everyone's on the same page."

"No surprises," I said.

"It's rare that a surprise here brings good news."

General rule or personal recollection?

After another two calls, Welsted turned and jabbed a thumb toward the window.

"You gotta try the Green Bean. Awesome coffee."

Except for the weapons, fatigues, and sign stating NO SALUTE AREA, I could have been viewing a gathering spot on any college campus.

Painfully young men sipped from paper cups in the shade of a gazebo. A couple held their heads close while reading something in their laps. A woman wrote alone at a picnic table, sun sparking her short brown hair.

Were the men just back from a convoy? Preparing to set out? Was the couple deciding what movie to see? Was the woman composing a postcard home?

In a year, how many would still be alive and intact?

My eyes began their reflex search for Katy.

And the guilt surged anew.

"Cup of java now?" Welsted asked.

"I should go back to my quarters and read the case file."

And check for messages.

"Your call."

Back in my room, I logged on to the dusty old PC. Found no word from either Katy or Blanton. No voicemail.

What the hell?

I checked my watch.

12:40.

I paced, agitated to be doing nothing. Anxious about my daughter.

I'd been at Bagram for twelve hours. Where was Katy? Why hadn't Blanton located her?

More senseless back-and-forth across the floor.

Why hadn't I brought Welsted into the loop?

I knew Katy's unit. Could find her myself.

No, a tiny voice advised.

For once, I listened.

Pulling a bottle of water from the cabinet, I shoved aside papers and magazines, pulled the Gross file from my backpack, and began reading.

Very quickly, my eyes grew heavy. My mind refused to focus.

Thinking food and a little exercise might reinvigorate me, I set out for the DFAC.

Forty minutes and an epic salad later, I rounded the corner of my B-hut row. My pulse quickened at the sight of a pink paper wedged into the doorjamb of my unit. I hurried forward, hoping it was a note from Katy.

It was.

Can't believe you're here. Awesome! Off with unit today, tomorrow. Meet tomorrow night. Lighthouse Coffeehouse. 10 pm. (Too late for you, old lady? Tee hee!) No comments on my hair.

Katy

Yes!

With a lighter heart and renewed energy, I returned to the file.

20

First I reviewed the naval criminal investigative service Summary of Incident report. Skimming the boilerplate, I focused on the salient facts.

A cordon-and-knock operation in Sheyn Bagh led to a firefight during which two unarmed Afghan civilians were fatally shot. The shooter was Second Lieutenant John Gross. Gross radioed his BDA to company HQ, and upon return to FOB Delaram reported in greater detail to his company commander, Captain Wayne Hightower.

I had to think for a minute. Recalled from my work at JPAC that BDA meant battle damage assessment.

Hightower ordered Gunnery Sergeant Werner Sharp to interview all participants and reported the incident to battalion HQ. Interviewees told Sharp that the drive to Sheyn Bagh had taken thirty minutes. The convoy of five Humvees and one seven-ton armored truck arrived at sunset. Two of the Humvees were augmented with M2 .50-caliber heavy machine guns. Though historically a friendly village, intel had reported probable weapons caches and explosives stores. The platoon was on high alert.

Sheyn Bagh was bordered on three sides by a wall and on the fourth by a steep hill. The front wall had two gaps for passage from the road to the village, one at each end.

I glanced at the NCIS photos. The place looked like a scene from a Ray Bradbury novel.

Back to the summary.

Light was fading. Three Humvees pulled inside the compound, and two set up outside the wall, one near each opening. The seven-ton positioned between them.

Fire teams from second and third squads began banging on doors and rousting occupants, starting at opposite ends and working toward the middle. First squad deployed to protect the vehicles and to provide covering fire to the searchers.

Lieutenant Gross, armed with an M16 and an M9 Beretta, remained in front to command the operation and to provide additional covering fire. Gross directed Corporal Grant Eggers, a SAW gunner with first squad, to also remain at the front with his light machine gun.

The first house entered was near the end closest to the lieutenant. Two AFG males were taken outside and ordered to remain in place. The searchers found nothing and advanced to an adjoining house. At that moment an explosion rocked the area next to one of the Humvees. The explosion sounded like an RPG. Two marines near the Humvee were hit.

Automatic-rifle fire from the hillside began kicking up dirt at the front of the compound. Lieutenant Gross screamed "contact front" and "engage, engage." He yelled to the Ma Deuce gunners to sweep the hillside. They tore up the hill and Eggers unleashed several bursts from his M249. Eggers at that point heard cries of "Allah Akbar" from his right and heard the lieutenant open fire. He turned and saw the two LNs from the first house twitching and staggering at an angle between the lieutenant and the house, in a direction away from where the RPG had hit.

The shorthand was all coming back. AFG was for Afghan and LN meant local national.

When Eggers saw the LNs, they were fifteen to twenty meters from the lieutenant, spinning sideways from the impact of the rounds. As they collapsed facedown, Lieutenant Gross ejected the clip from his M16 and jammed in another. Eggers turned to fire more bursts at the hill, but no enemy returned fire. The .50-cal gunners were still raking the hillside. Lieutenant Gross yelled to cease fire, and it got quiet.

Lieutenant Gross ordered everyone back to their vehicles and he and the medic moved to the wounded. Eggers checked the two LNs and both were dead. He did a cursory search and found no weapons or explosives on or near the bodies.

The medic declared the wounded stable but in need of medical attention. Deciding transport by vehicle would be quicker than waiting for a medevac chopper, Lieutenant Gross aborted the mission, had the wounded loaded into the seven-ton, and sped back to Delaram. The dead Afghans were left for the villagers to deal with.

I stopped reading to stand and stretch, and to contemplate what chaotic hell those minutes must have been. Then I turned to the gunny's assessment of the facts. Basically, Sharp had found the following.

Only Gross and Eggers saw the Afghans get shot, and Eggers did not see the first several seconds. Initially, the two were cooperative and nonthreatening. Only Gross and Eggers heard the men yell anything. Gross claimed the Afghans rushed him. Only Gross shot at them. It was undisputed that the men were unarmed.

The gunny paid particular attention to the statement given by Eggers, and summarized it in some detail:

> *Eggers was upset and thought both LNs had been shot in the back. Thought they were running from the RPG blast, not toward Gross. Why empty a 30-round clip at these guys? The hostile fire was coming from the hillside. Eggers thought he recognized the younger LN from prior sweeps of the vil. The kid had seemed friendly. Villagers had told him that bad guys would infiltrate the vil, fire at patrols, then melt away. Eggers was sure the dead were noncombatants.*

I read the statement by the company commander, Wayne Hightower, but learned nothing new. A file note by an NCIS special agent quoted Hightower as saying he did not intend to play Captain Medina to Gross's Lieutenant Calley, and that he'd made a full report to his superiors.

From the statement by battalion commander Lieutenant Colonel Walter Roberts, I learned that Roberts had informed the commanding officer of RCT 6, Colonel Craig Andrews. Roberts had also transferred Lieutenant Gross from command of his platoon to a staff assignment at battalion H&S Company. Headquarters and support. Roberts commented that the Gross case had the potential to develop into a major incident at the governmental level. He recommended that the inquiry proceed "by the book."

I read a directive from Andrews that the Gross matter be referred to the NCIS field office for an investigation into possible felony charges.

I got up for a stretch and shoulder roll. Then I turned to the NCIS scene investigation file.

Two things struck me immediately. First, the file was remarkably thin for an incident potentially leading to felony charges. Second, the special agent directing the scene investigation had not been Blanton. Somehow, that gave me more confidence.

As I worked my way through, I understood why the file was so sparse. By the time an NCIS site visit could be arranged, there was little to inspect. The bodies had been buried and the scene had been cleaned, then trampled by normal day-to-day activity.

One village elder produced thirty M16 shell casings and pointed out the area from which they'd been retrieved. The investigative team photographed damage to the wall where the RPG had landed, collected metal fragments blown from the Humvee, took telescopic photos of pockmarking on the hillside, and dug a handful of .50-cal slugs from the soft rock.

NCIS interpreters conducted interviews, but no one had witnessed the actual shooting. Everyone questioned told the same story. The dead were good men. No insurgents in village. No explosives. No bad weapons, just rifles for protection against thieves. Insurgents on the hill had come, then gone. Marines killed boy. Very bad thing.

Permission for an exhumation was repeatedly denied. With no bodies and no witnesses, that left only the scene examination report and statements from members of Gross's platoon.

Distilling the statements of the marines and the NCIS investigation down to the basics, a couple of facts stood out. One, the two witnesses to the shooting told conflicting stories. Two, rounds had struck the LNs either in the front or in the back.

I understood the importance of the exhumation. Wondered what Gross was thinking. Clearly he knew.

Perhaps because Eggers had no stake in the outcome, his statement carried enough weight to compel Colonel Andrews to prefer charges against Gross for murder and for conduct unbecoming an officer.

Yep, I thought, murder surely is unbecoming.

I read the DD Form 458s, the military charge sheets. The first identified the accused as Second Lieutenant John Gross, and alleged violations of the UCMJ Article 118 and UCMJ Article 133.

The specifications under 118 read: "That in Sheyn Bagh, Helmand Province, Republic of Afghanistan, the accused did unlawfully murder one Ahmad Ali Aqsaee, an Afghan national by shooting him multiple times with an M16 automatic weapon." It provided the time and date of the incident.

The specification under 133 referred to the same time and place but alleged that the accused engaged in conduct unbecoming an officer in unlawfully shooting said Ahmad Ali Aqsaee.

The second 458 alleged identical offenses as to one Abdul Khalik Rasekh. Both forms were signed by Colonel Andrews.

The chronology showed that after Colonel Andrews preferred charges, RCT 6 rotated back to Camp Lejeune, North Carolina, home of the Second Marine Division.

Once at Lejeune, Colonel Andrews appointed Lieutenant Colonel Frank Keever as Article 32 investigating officer and detailed Major Christopher Nelson as government counsel and Major Joseph Hawthorn as counsel for the accused.

Lieutenant Colonel Keever called the Article 32 hearing into session two months after RCT 6 returned to Lejeune. The file contained a transcript of the proceedings. I skimmed through it.

Hawthorn made a motion for continuance until an exhumation could be performed. Nelson objected, saying no exhumation was likely. There was discussion, after which Keever denied the motion.

The government's first witness was Grant Eggers, now out of the military. His testimony seemed in agreement with the statements he'd made to Gunny Sharp and the NCIS special agents.

To satisfy my curiosity, I read the portion of Hawthorn's cross-examination dealing with Eggers's motivation in accusing Gross.

Hawthorn: You're a civilian?
Eggers: Yes, sir.

Hawthorn: Is the reason you did not re-up the fact that Lt. Gross gave you a poor performance evaluation and told you that he would oppose your promotion to sergeant?

Eggers: No, sir. He did tell me that, but it was not the reason I did not reenlist.

Hawthorn: He demoted you, didn't he?

Eggers: No, sir. He reassigned me from fire team leader to SAW gunner, but I still had the same rank and pay.

Hawthorn: No one else in your platoon said they'd seen the LNs shot in the back, did they?

Eggers: No one else was in a position to see it.

Hawthorn: Did you actually see rounds strike those men in their backs?

Eggers: That's how it appeared to me, sir. They were being spun around by the impact of the bullets, but it looked like they were hit in the back.

Hawthorn: Would you describe Lt. Gross as a liar?

Eggers: Generally, no. But he has a lot at stake here.

The second government witness was Donald Drew, one of the NCIS special agents who'd examined the scene and interviewed marines. He testified an entire day, but added little.

The government concluded with testimony from three platoon members who said there had been an intense firefight during which they felt in peril, but that the fire came from the hillside, not from the area of the houses.

With that, the government rested.

The following morning, Major Hawthorn informed Keever that he'd received word that the Afghans had decided to let an exhumation go forward, and made a motion that the hearing be recessed pending an autopsy. After lengthy discussion, Keever reversed himself and agreed to a sixty-day recess, during which Hawthorn was to provide regular updates. Should an exhumation and autopsy be completed sooner, the hearing would resume immediately. Keever declared the hearing in recess.

I turned to the final document in the dossier, a handwritten page that appeared to have been torn from a journal.

And my interest level leapt.

The journal entry was written by the man himself.

July 15. 1142 AFT

Got into the shit last night. Ambushed on a cordon and knock. AK fire raining down. Usual Muj spray and pray shooting. Burn a lot of ammo, forget about aim.

We didn't know what to expect in Sheyn Bagh. Patrols had taken heat in the area, harassment by ambushes and IEDs. Intel had it weapons and explosives were stored in the vil. Our mission was to surprise the LNs at dusk, take the stuff before they used it on us.

We swept in, set up and began to toss the place. Adrenaline was pumping, and my guys were wired. The LNs didn't greet us with love.

We'd searched a couple houses when an RPG exploded. Two of my guys yelled they were hit. Rounds started peppering down from the hillside. AKs for sure. I ordered my men to take cover and return fire.

For a while the scene was all noise, streaming tracers, and flying debris. BA was no hits from the AKs, two WIAs from the RPG. No EKIAs or EWIAs. Two collateral KIAs in the vil. Our fire. Yours truly the shooter.

I paused for more alphabetic decryption. BA was battle assessment. KIA and WIA were easy—killed in action, wounded in action. I decided EK and EW referred to enemy casualties.

I see it every time I close my eyes. Two Muj rushing me, screaming about Allah. Only seconds to react. I figured the fucksticks were wired to blow. Gave them their tickets for the A train to martyrdom.

The hillside snipers went apeshit, but we had fire superiority. Eventually they shot their wad and disappeared.

WTF? The search found nothing strapped to the dead Muj. Couldn't have known that. Bedlam. Rounds hitting everywhere. Split-second choice. Easy decision. My ass over theirs.

I keep replaying it in my head. What did I hear? What did I see?

Gunfire. Shouting. Some wannabe martyr yelling Allah Akbar. Two LNs in disdahas rushing straight at me. Shit. You have to lay them flat.

Who knows what the assholes intended? I ordered them to

stop. They kept coming. I made sure the sorry bastards went down and stayed down. Emptied my clip.

Eggers had my six when the shitstorm started. Why the fuck didn't he turn his M-249 on the two coming at me? No big surprise. The guy's a train wreck.

While the Muj hauled ass, Doc and I checked the guys who were hit. They'd taken shrapnel, but could travel. We loaded them into the 7-ton, along with Doc and one fire team, and took off for Delaram.

Eggers is blowing smoke. Shortly before Sheyn Bagh, I had to shitcan him from fire team leader down to SAW gunner. He argued, but I told him my mind was made up.

How many warnings does the jackass deserve before he gets someone killed? Piss-poor inspections before taking his squad on patrol. Failures to properly search and secure areas under his responsibility. Improper deployments of his fire team in action. Guy's a fuckup waiting to happen.

Yesterday Eggers proved me right. His failure to take decisive action could have cost me my ass. If those Muj had been packing, I'd be going home in a box.

It's not like I wanted to waste those guys. Jesus. I'm practically puking about it. But it was a righteous kill. They were a clear threat.

Eggers doesn't get it. Doesn't think like a Marine. Or act like a Marine. CIVCAS from a mission sucks. But collateral damage is part of war.

I don't trust Eggers and he doesn't like me.

21

THE MH-60 BLACKHAWK LIFTED OFF, THEN BANKED LOW BETWEEN shale and limestone cliffs on the start of its three-hundred-mile run to Sheyn Bagh.

That was my best guess of the distance. Welsted had tried to fill me in, but between the throb of the rotors and the wind whooshing against the airframe, conversation wasn't happening. And lip-reading isn't one of my skills.

It was early, just past 0600, but after a bad night's sleep I was ready to move. Wall-to-wall nightmares. Katy's voice calling from darkness amid the thud of artillery shells. Birdie purring from the bottom of a deep well. Other scenarios, equally bizarre. The same images looping over and over.

I'd dressed in the predawn darkness, then bolted for a quick breakfast. After donning my IBA, I'd rendez-voused with Blanton and Welsted at the flight line.

The Blackhawk was a marvel of military engineering. Fourteen million dollars' worth of bulletproof steel and Lexan glass, powered by a pair of massive turboshaft engines.

We were sharing the bird with a half dozen soldiers. Stoic faces, intense eyes. Packed in like badass sardines in a tin. Welsted said they were going someplace north of Sheyn Bagh to quell a disturbance. She didn't elaborate and I didn't press.

The Blackhawk elevated at dizzying speed and hurtled toward our destination. The sun rose along the curve of the earth, throwing up spikes of early-morning light. The land was beautiful, the way Artic tundra can be beautiful. A narrow river looked like a dark ribbon twisting across the arid emptiness.

My gaze shifted to Welsted, then to Blanton. Something in their posture indicated a deep mutual dislike. When their eyes met they immediately jumped elsewhere, like magnets repulsing. The air between them crackled with pent-up tension.

I'd sensed the friction yesterday but couldn't pinpoint the source. Only an insistent tickle at the base of my brain stem telling me that something was off.

Did they have opposing views on the exhumation? Were they unhappy about being ordered into danger in a village of potentially hostile Muslims? Or was it personal?

Forget it. Focus on the task at hand.

I glanced out the Blackhawk's side window. The bulletproof glass was scarred with milky slashes where antiaircraft rounds had hit and ricocheted off. I charted the terrain below, wondered if anyone had us in his sights.

Concentrated on putting that out of my mind, too.

Thanks to a strong tailwind, we arrived at Delaram early, just before 0800. The Blackhawk's blades whipped up fans of yellow dust as we touched down. Blanton disembarked first, followed by the soldiers. All scuttled across the landing zone with heads lowered, shoulders hunched to the wind.

I followed Welsted off, sand stinging my face and collecting in the corners of my eyes. As the soldiers loaded onto a convoy truck and departed, Blanton waved us over to an idling Humvee with two grit-coated marines, one at the wheel, the other riding shotgun.

"World's biggest freakin' sandbox." Blanton pulled a wry smile.

Welsted breezed past us into the vehicle. Blanton and I joined her in the backseat.

The Humvee rumbled down an unpaved road that lay bleached and bone-white from the passage of military convoys. Nothing much to see. Sand molded by the wind into spiny formations. Stunted trees bearing withered fruit. The charred remains of a car half buried on the shoulder.

Our driver was young, Katy's age. No, younger. His cheeks were furred with peach fuzz. Shotgun wasn't much older.

I wondered what the parents thought of their sons being out here. A trapdoor sprung inside my head and suddenly I was seeing the hit-and-run vic back in Charlotte. The one with the pink barrette and kitty purse. The one in a body bag.

I glanced right and caught Blanton looking at me, eyes narrow, maybe even unfriendly. Calculating? If so, calculating what? What angle was there to play? Why would Blanton's goal, or that of NCIS, be any different from mine? From Welsted's?

Probably nothing. Blanton had made it clear he didn't like moving outside the wire. Maybe he was spooked. God knows I felt removed from my element. Everyone was keyed up. Still, I couldn't shake the feeling of his cold, appraising eyes.

The Humvee hit a VCP, a vehicle checkpoint that was nothing more than a cement pillbox. A pair of soldiers sat on folding chairs, sweating though the sun was barely up. One rose and trotted over, aviator shades hooding his eyes.

Welsted presented some documents. The soldier scanned them, then bent for a better view of the Humvee's interior.

"NCIS?"

Welsted tipped her head toward Blanton.

"Anthropologist?"

This time I got the nod.

The tinted shades swiveled my way. Lingered several beats. More hostility? Impossible to tell, since I couldn't see the guy's eyes. Did they figure I was there to buttress the prosecution of Second Lieutenant Gross? Paint him as a murderer? Stir up the locals once again and make everyone's job harder and more dangerous?

The soldier waved us through.

"We're nearly there." Welsted spoke without turning her head. "The village isn't much to look at. Typical of the sort you'll see in this province. Herding, some small-scale farming. Under normal circumstances you wouldn't find any open resentment."

"We aren't going in under normal circumstances."

"No, Mr. Blanton, we are not."

Blanton's jaw went rigid. Was the friction due to the same jurisdictional jockeying I was used to seeing in Charlotte and Montreal? Army versus Navy? Military versus civilian? I found the thought strangely calming.

No one spoke for a bumpy five or six minutes. Then, "I won't call these people ignorant, because that's wrong, not to mention potentially dangerous." Welsted squinted at the heat-shimmer rising at the horizon.

"But the life they lead is simple. We make a point of respecting their customs, insofar as they don't interfere with our own objectives."

"Which are?" I asked.

"Objective one is to protect the free world. Objective two, our specific goal in this operation, is to make sure that United States personnel acted properly in the pursuit of objective one."

After several more miles of nonconversational hitching and swaying, Sheyn Bagh took shape in the distance, a compound of squat stone structures enclosed within a low stone wall on three sides, backed up to a very steep hill on the fourth.

Welsted was right. The place wasn't much to look at. Unless your taste in architecture swung toward stark minimalism. But the setting was otherworldly.

Sheyn Bagh lay at the foot of a prominence, the south side of which rose sharply, maybe two hundred feet, to a mesa studded with oddly shaped boulders. The slope, more cliff than hill, was composed of peculiar, peaked formations that resembled upright ladyfinger cookies of differing heights. In the hazy morning light I could make out tiny holes in the rocks, like honeycomb. As we drew nearer those holes became doorways, windows, and staircases.

I was about to pose a question when Welsted explained.

"Half the village is built into the hillside. The rock is sturdy enough to provide a solid foundation, but porous enough to tunnel into."

"Maybe that's how Osama went to ground."

"These towns are like icebergs." As usual, Welsted ignored Blanton's comment. "Only a small percentage visible."

We drove through a gap in the wall and stopped in what probably served as the village green. At an opening between two low buildings, a goat raised its head, bleated, and clop-clopped slowly toward the Humvee.

Shotgun's fingers tightened on his rifle. Bringing the barrel into view in the window, he shouted in what I assumed was Pashto. A kid, maybe ten or eleven, ran forward and dragged the goat back toward the alley from which it had emerged.

"Bastards shove explosives up the asses of their barnyard pals." Blanton's voice sounded taut.

Shotgun shouldered open his door and got out. Welsted followed.

A trio of men approached wearing clothes the color of the desert itself. Striped kaffiyeh wrapped their heads. Sandals covered their dusty feet.

One man was taller than the others. One had a mole above his beard shaped like a daisy. All three were lean, their faces pitted and scarred. I couldn't guess their ages. Each had the look of living stone.

"I'll do the talking." Welsted circled the Humvee and advanced a short distance.

The men paused six feet from her. Solemn greetings were exchanged. No smiles.

Watching, I couldn't help but wonder. Was I looking into the face of the loathsome Taliban? Were these men who would beat women, cut off their ears and noses as they begged for mercy? Shoot them in their school buses for expressing their thoughts? Maim and shun them for being victims of rape? Men who would destroy schools lest little girls learn to read? Kill volunteer workers lest they supply vaccinations against polio?

Or were they simple farmers just trying to get on with life? With the struggle of herding goats, growing crops, and raising kids?

As Welsted conferred with our welcoming committee, I looked around.

Windows stared back at me, silent and empty. Or were they? Were hidden eyes tracking our every move?

An AK-47 propped open a door. Old, but undoubtedly functional. A lethal doorstop.

Here and there men in twos and threes watched with suspicion. Boys stood frozen, play forgotten. There wasn't a female in sight.

After a brief exchange, the trio withdrew, talked briefly, then returned to Welsted. The tallest of the three spoke. Welsted replied. The tall man hesitated, then nodded assent.

Welsted returned to the Humvee.

"They say there's been tension between U.S. troops and some of the locals. In light of the incident. He says the exhumation must be performed with caution and—"

"Dignity," I said.

"Exactly."

"Please tell them I'll treat the bodies with reverence."

Welsted translated. Again the men conversed. Again the tall one nodded.

"Let's get this freakin' show on the road." Blanton's eyes were bouncing from building to building, alley to alley, curious face to curious face. Veins were pumping in both his temples.

Two kids were summoned. Teenagers with long ropy limbs and wispy beards. Each carried a shovel on one bony shoulder.

The boys looked wary but excited. Digging in a graveyard. Forbidden, blasphemous, on this day condoned.

Eyes on the tall man, Blanton spoke to Welsted.

"Be sure this muj understands I'll be filming everything. I don't want any flak about pissing off ancestors or hijacking souls."

Welsted explained about the photography. The man responded.

"Don't film any women," Welsted relayed.

"There goes my fashion spread in *Cosmo*." Blanton spat in the dust. "Tell them to get their asses in gear."

"Lose the attitude, Mr. Blanton." Welsted's tone was toxic.

Blanton and I gathered our cameras, shovels, and other equipment. Welsted got the screen. The tall man gestured toward goat alley. Our driver moved to the front of the line, Shotgun to the rear. Both looked anxious, like deer in an open field.

As we moved in single file toward the western edge of the village, I felt unseen eyes on my back. Heard only our own boot falls and a wind chime somewhere out of sight.

The cemetery lay a few hundred feet outside the wall. The rocky outcrop loomed above, overshadowing the site like a mini-Masada.

The burials were modest, no ornate tombstones or carved statuary as in old-style American graveyards. A few had crude markers of the same rock used to construct the wall. Most were simply outlined with stones arranged in rough ovals.

Some burials were still mounded, but most slumped. The newly dead, the long departed. All were aligned in rows, as in a farmer's field. But bones, not seeds, lay beneath the ground.

Wordlessly, we wound our way to each of the graves. Aqsaee was buried just inside the cemetery entrance. Rasekh lay so far back his oval of stones sloped up the base of the hill.

Welsted looked at me. I told her we'd begin with Rasekh. No reason. We were gathered there.

Bodies coiled, eyes jumpy, the marines took up positions by the cemetery entrance. I wasn't sure if their tense vigilance heightened or lowered my sense of security.

As Blanton shot video and stills and the boys removed the perimeter stones, I used a long metal probe to check for differences in subsurface density to determine the configuration of Rasekh's grave.

Then, after brief instruction from Welsted, the boys sank their shovels into the dry desert soil. As they worked, feet spread, arms pumping, I squatted by the deepening trench, alert to color changes in the soil that would indicate decomposition.

For thirty minutes the air rang with the sound of blades gouging the earth. Of displaced earth *shish*ing onto a growing heap.

Men gathered at the village wall to watch in grim silence. Now and then I'd raise my eyes to glance at them. Though too far away to read their expressions, I knew they were scrutinizing us closely.

An hour passed. Ninety minutes. The sun rose, and with it the temperature.

After finishing a third series of photos, Blanton moved off to the edge of the group and lit up a smoke. An old man approached him, hand out. Blanton shook free a cigarette and placed it in his palm.

Finally I saw the telltale shift.

"Hold up," I said.

The boys stopped shoveling. Straightening, they looked at each other, then at me.

"Ask them to step away, please," I told Welsted.

The boys obeyed.

The hole was roughly three feet deep. At the bottom, a dark oval was emerging from the yellow-brown soil. Poking from it, I could see what looked like fabric.

I heard boots, then a shadow fell across the grave.

"Found one of our boys?"

Ignoring Blanton's question, I dropped to my belly, closed my eyes, and inhaled deeply through my nose.

The odor of decomposing flesh is unmistakable. Sweet and fetid, like residue spoiling in a trashcan.

I smelled only soil and a hint of something organic. Either the bodies had mummified or they had skeletonized completely.

Another shadow joined Blanton's.

"Need a hand?"

"Get the trowel and brush from my pack, please."

Welsted was back in less than a minute. "What do you have?"

"Probably the edge of a shroud."

"Time for a body bag?"

"Yes."

Using the trowel, I scraped dirt from around and below the fabric, slowly revealing the lumpy contours of what lay inside. When enough was exposed, I gently lifted one fragile edge.

The shroud contained exactly what I'd hoped. I recognized a clavicle, a scapula, some dark and leathery ligamentous tissue.

I gestured that the boys should now proceed with trowels, and gave a brief demonstration on how to do so.

An hour later, Rasekh's shrouded bones lay aboveground. I was on my knees, zipping the body bag, when, far off, I heard a noise. A low buzz, like a honeybee sluggish with sun.

I glanced up. Scanned the sky. Saw nothing.

The buzzing grew louder. Was joined by the sound of pounding feet.

I looked around.

Across the cemetery, Blanton's eyes were huge in a very white face. The villagers were gone from the wall. Back by the Humvee, Welsted was gazing skyward. So were the marines. My digging team was nowhere in sight.

The human brain is a switching station that operates on two levels. As my cortex processed these facts, my hypothalamus was already ordering adrenaline full throttle.

The buzz became a whine. Closer. Louder. The delicate hairs inside my ears vibrated uncomfortably.

"Get down!" Shotgun screamed. *"Now!"*

I curled and threw my hands over my head.

The world exploded.

22

I OPENED MY EYES.

Darkness.

I listened.

Absolute quiet.

By instinct I'd cupped a palm around my mouth to create an air pocket. And my helmet had helped. But the small bubble of space wasn't enough. My chest was compressed, my lungs squeezed too tightly to function. The heavy armor only made the pressure worse.

I tried to breathe. Couldn't.

I tried again. Got no air.

Panic began to set in.

How long could a person go without oxygen? Three minutes? Five?

How long had I been trapped?

I had no clue.

Again I tried to inhale. Again I failed.

My heart was banging. Pumping blood that was fast losing what little oxygen it held.

I tried moving the hand away from my mouth. Hit resistance within millimeters.

My other arm was numb. I had no sense of its position. The position of my legs.

A wave of dizziness flooded my brain. I saw images of the mesa. Of the ladyfinger rocks.

Rocks that now imprisoned me like a coffin.

How many feet? How many tons?

The panic increased. Adrenaline shot through me.

Breathe!

I tensed my neck and shoulder muscles. Bent my head forward as far as I could, then thrust it back.

My skull cracked rock. Pain exploded through my brain.

But the move worked. I heard the hiss of falling sand, felt a little less pressure on my chest.

I breathed in slowly. The dusty air coated my tongue, my throat. My lungs exploded in a series of hacking coughs. I breathed again. Coughed again.

The dizziness passed. My thoughts began to organize into coherent patterns.

Shout? But in what direction? How was I lying?

Was anyone out there? Was anyone alive to free me? Had the others also been buried?

I blinked sand from my eyes. Saw only inky blackness. Heard only stillness. No voices. No shovels. No movement.

Again, the panic.

Think. Forget the rubble. The dust. The deafening quiet.

I tried rolling to my left. My right leg was pinned. I could feel a sharp edge pressing the flesh of my calf.

I tried flexing my knee. A hot spike ripped up from my ankle.

I tried rolling to my right. Got nowhere. My shoulder was jammed tight against rock. Rock that moments before had overhung the graveyard. Rock that now buried me like the dead we'd just raised.

Think.

I willed myself calm. Willed my breathing steady. Willed the bulky armor to rise and fall.

In. Out. In. Out.

I tried yelling, but my mouth was too dry. I mustered what saliva I could and tried again.

My voice sounded dull, muffled. And which way was up? Down? Was I yelling into the sky or the earth?

My thoughts were again growing muddled. Oxygen deprivation? Or was it carbon dioxide overload? I knew the answer to that once. It was not coming to me now.

Questions winged.

An incoming mortar? A surface-to-surface missile? Launched by whom?

What did that matter?

Were Blanton and Welsted also buried? The two young diggers?

I closed my eyes. Heard only the soft hiss of sand worming through cracks.

Why was no one probing? Digging? Shouting? Had the villagers abandoned us? To let our people get us out or not?

Would I die? Of hypothermia? Asphyxia? How long would it take?

The thought of death filled me with a terrible sadness. In this place, so far from home, so far from the people I loved. Katy. Harry. Pete. Ryan. Yes, Ryan.

A tear traced a path sideways across my cheek and dropped to my hand.

My addled brain managed a deduction.

Dropped. Gravity. I was lying on my right side. The earth was somewhere below it. Dirt, rock, and sky were somewhere above my left shoulder.

I inhaled and began to test as far as my left hand could go.

My fingertips described a Lego jigsaw, gravity and pressure holding the pieces in place. Disturbing the balance might cause a shift, might bring more debris crashing down.

How much air did I have? The rocks were porous and most likely hadn't compacted tightly enough to exclude oxygen. But how deeply was I interred? When would help arrive? To find a survivor or a body?

Then I knew nothing.

Then I awoke. Heard sounds. Watery, indistinct.

Voices?

I froze.

Yes. Human voices. High and agitated.

Desperate, euphoric, I maneuvered my left hand to grope the farthest recesses of the small vacuum in front of my face. My fingers closed on a stone the size of my fist. My heart raced as I moved it in the small arc the limited space would permit, trying to bang against the rock above my head.

What was Morse code for SOS?

Mother of God. Who gives a shit?

I kept pounding with pathetically small strokes, desperate to make contact with the outside world.

The shouting intensified. Drew near. I heard staccato commands. Answers. Grinding. Dull thuds.

"Careful!" I bellowed. Or whispered. "I'm okay, just be careful."

The grinding continued. Separated into the sounds of individual rocks being shifted.

After what seemed a lifetime, a single shaft of light pierced the darkness. More grinding, then bright needles entered from all directions, a kaleidoscope sparkling dust suspended in the air around me.

Finally, a rock lifted and harsh, glorious sunlight poured in. I squinted up, blinded.

Blanton's face hung above me, skin flushed the color of boiled ham.

"Sit tight. We'll get you out in a jiff."

I could only smile.

Three hours later we were on our way back to Delaram. Aqsaee and Rasekh lay in body bags in the back of the vehicle.

When the mortar hit, both marines had been positioned behind the Humvee. Same for Welsted. Though scratched by flying shards, all three escaped injury.

Ironic. Blanton's need for nicotine saved his ass. He had also been standing clear of the impact zone. The diggers, being young and war-wise, heard the incoming round, understood, and ran.

In other words, I was the only one dumb enough to get hurt. Parked on my knees, I'd been too slow or too green to bolt. The impact of the blast had knocked me into the grave. The debris that fell on me wasn't that deep. Though it seemed an eternity, I'd been buried roughly ten minutes. The sides of the trench had sheltered me.

"Probably an M252A1," Welsted speculated as we rattled along. "You get so you can tell the difference. Each mortar sings its own song whistling through the air."

"Enlightening, but irrelevant. The important point is, who the hell fired the damn thing?"

"Impossible to say right now. Probably not friendly fire. Our people would have sent more than one." Though addressing Blanton's question, Welsted still spoke to me. "M252s are British-made, but our mortar platoons use them. Army and Marines. If troops are forced to retreat quickly, weapons can be left behind."

"And insurgents collect them."

Welsted nodded. "Pick them up and do what any savvy enemy would do."

"Were we the target?" I asked.

Welsted shrugged a who-knows. "Could be a scout spotted our vehicle and saw a chance to nail it, or it could be a misfire, an incorrect triangulation on a different objective. Could be—"

"Could be a world-class screw-up. I came out here to do a job, not get my nuts blown off."

Welsted slid a withering glance at Blanton.

"This is a war zone. Any assignment carries risk."

"Will you investigate where the round came from?" I asked.

"A recon team's already been dispatched, but I don't expect much. These launchers only weigh seventy pounds. A two-man crew can fire one and haul ass in no time. And the mortar's got a range of three and a half miles. That's a lot of sand to search. I'm surprised the shooters only launched one round. Probably only had one shell."

"Ain't the Tali grand." Blanton shook his head in disgust.

At that moment the Humvee hit a pothole. The sudden lurch sent fire from my ankle to my knee. Welsted noticed me wince.

"You ought to get that treated."

"I can take care of it."

"Suit yourself."

I would. I was embarrassed enough. Thanks to my body armor and helmet, my injuries were limited to cuts and abrasions. But the sprained ankle had forced me to direct the remainder of the disinterment while seated graveside.

Shaken by the blast, the initial diggers had refused to return. Their replacements were equally young, equally strong, but a lot less enthused. The required supervision had been significant.

Twenty minutes after setting out, we reached Delaram and our waiting Blackhawk. Hobbling toward it, I saw the body bags being placed in the cargo hold. I hurried to catch up to Welsted.

"I think the bodies should ride in the main bay," I said.

"Why?"

"Stowing them in cargo could be interpreted as disrespect. Like transporting a corpse in a car trunk."

Blanton watched as Welsted ordered the remains moved, but said nothing.

As I was buckling into my harness, the village trio pulled up in a rusted jeep. The tall man and the one with the mole got out and walked toward the chopper. They would travel with us to oversee the autopsy, as per the agreement. I wondered if Uncle Sam was providing round-trip transport, or if the driver would go overland to Bagram to collect them.

I stole glances at the men as we flew. Both sat grim-faced, staring at their hands. I couldn't imagine what they were thinking. Couldn't even guess.

We made good time but still arrived after sunset. The base glowed as a grid of light in a sea of unending darkness.

I was exhausted and my ankle hurt. Not unbearable, just a dull throb. My body felt gritty and leached of moisture by the sun and wind.

But still there was work to be done.

"I'll accompany the remains to the hospital," Welsted said. "You don't have to go."

I wanted to remove my IBA and filthy BDUs, shower, drink a gallon of water, and collapse into bed.

"Yes," I said. "I do."

"It's late. Let's move." From Blanton.

Surprised, Welsted and I both turned.

"I can take it from here," Welsted said.

"Not on your life."

Blanton strode toward a low-slung, retrofitted jeep and climbed in. I limped after him. When the body bags had been safely transferred to a van, Welsted joined us and told the driver to proceed. The LNs would follow.

"Growlers." Welsted slapped the side panel through her open window. "Two hundred thousand bucks a pop. Your tax dollars at work."

If Welsted wanted a shocked reaction, I disappointed her. Hadn't I read that the army paid six hundred dollars for a toilet seat?

En route, we removed our protective gear. Welsted opined that the fifty-bed facility to which we were headed rivaled any modern hospital stateside.

"The difference is they see fewer gunshot wounds here than back home in Texas."

Jesus. Where did the woman find the energy for humor? If it was a joke.

The Heathe N. Craig Joint Theater Hospital was located in a well-lit compound on the western edge of the base. The main structure was a squat tan affair with a half dozen smokestacks pumping on the roof. An Afghan flag hung on a pole beside Old Glory. Both standards looked indifferent to their surroundings.

The van pulled into a covered bay, followed closely by our Growler. Everyone got out. As the body bags were transferred to gurneys, I looked around.

An enormous American flag covered the ceiling above our heads. Vertically stenciled letters spelled out WARRIOR'S WAY on a pillar. Signs with slashed red circles warned of weapons not permitted beyond the doors.

The village overseers arrived in a second Growler. They alighted as the gurneys were rolled into the ER.

The hospital's interior was so cold I felt goose bumps pucker my flesh. The staff we passed watched with open curiosity, nurses and orderlies in fatigues or scrubs, doctors with surgical caps on their heads and masks half tied around their necks.

Aqsaee and Rasekh were wheeled down a long tiled hallway to a cooler not that different from the one back home at the MCME. They would remain there awaiting my examination.

I glanced at the village delegates, then turned to Welsted.

"It would speed things up tomorrow if a series of X-rays was done on each individual tonight. I need to know what's inside before I unwrap the shrouds."

"You could use some serious rack time."

"We all could," I said.

Welsted looked at me a very long moment. "If I'm present, do you trust a radiology tech to shoot your films?"

It was what I would do at home.

"Yes," I said.

Welsted crossed to the villagers, returned after a brief exchange.

"They're good with that. As long as we leave the bodies facing Mecca."

"I can stay," I said.

Welsted looked at her watch. "You call it a day." To everyone. "That's a wrap. We'll reconvene here at oh-seven-hundred hours."

Back at my B-hut, I dumped my IBA, removed my outerwear, and peeled off my sock. My ankle was a tequila sunrise of mottled flesh and abraded skin.

I knew I should ice down the injury. Hadn't the time to worry about swelling. Telling myself it could have been a whole lot worse, I changed to jeans and a sweatshirt, tied my boot as tightly as I could bear, and headed out, hoping I wasn't too late.

At 2200 hours the base was as busy as during the day. The roads rumbled with Humvees, pickups, jeeps, and bikes. Pedestrians hurried to or from meals, USO centers, or showers. Radio towers and light stanchions flickered against the night sky.

The air was cool, the wind fresh off the mountains. Insects swarmed the streetlamps overhead.

Asking directions, I made my way to a two-story yellow structure with a banner saying LIGHTHOUSE above its front door. A few patrons lingered outside, cigarette tips glowing orange in the dark.

"Mom! Mom, here!"

I looked up.

Katy was waving at me from the second-floor terrace.

"Come on up!"

Yes! Oh, yes!

Ankle forgotten, I beelined through the door and up the stairs.

The place was packed, only one free table. I was worming toward it when Katy swooped in, beaming, arms spread wide.

As we hugged, I was astounded by my daughter's strength. By the new hardness of her biceps.

"Holy fuck, Mom. You really are here."

"I really am."

"I went by your B-hut, but you were out."

"Yeah," was all I said.

A Marine lance corporal approached the empty table behind us. A look from Katy and he reversed course. We both sat.

"Something wrong with your foot?"

"Pulled a muscle."

"Wuss."

"Right. I got your note. Did Scott Blanton contact you?"

"Who?"

"Never mind."

Katy had cut her hair very short. Not required, but my daughter has never been a fan of half measures.

"I got your e-mails."

"And didn't reply?"

"Our unit's been outside the berm. Just got back."

"Doing what?" Casual as hell.

"Can't say. You're cool to that. Besides, we both know how you get."

"How I get?"

Katy bugged her eyes, opened her mouth, and slapped her cheeks with her palms. "Crazoid!"

"I do not get crazoid."

"Fine. But you worry too much."

"Or you don't worry enough." The fatigue. The ankle. I regretted the words as soon as they were out.

Katy's jaw set.

"Sorry," I said. "I've had a long day."

"I'm doing my job, Mom, same as you do yours. You came here. I came here. We both knew we weren't heading to Club Med."

"You're right. Crazoid. I'm sorry."

Katy's expression softened.

"Don't be sorry. I'd be crushed if you didn't worry. Who else will do it for me?"

We ordered snacks and coffee strong enough to give a pachyderm the shakes. Ongoing conversation was confined to safe subjects. Happenings back in Charlotte. Pete's upcoming wedding to Summer.

Before long Katy put her hand on mine.

"Early day tomorrow. And you look like you're flying on fumes."

"I am. And I also have to be up at dawn."

I paid the bill. We rose. Katy turned to go. Turned back, mischief in her eyes.

"And thanks."

"For what?" I had no idea.

"For not dissing my hair."

When Katy left, a good chunk of my heart went with her. But I would see her again soon.

Walking through the dark, I debated. Shower? Hit the DFAC for more food and ice to pack my ankle?

Screw it.

Back at the B-hut, I set my iPhone alarm, removed my jeans, and slipped into bed.

I drifted off to the sound of engines screaming overhead.

I AWOKE TO THE SOUND OF ENGINES SCREAMING OVERHEAD.

My ankle was better but my head throbbed, a combination of jet lag, lack of proper dinner, and thin desert air.

I dressed hurriedly and checked e-mail. Nothing from Larabee. Eight days since the girl had been found. I feared my hit-and-run case was rapidly cooling.

At the DFAC, I scored eggs and hash browns, poured coffee, and found an empty table. I'd barely started eating when Blanton slumped into the chair opposite, a dark crescent under each of his eyes.

"Another day in paradise."

Bits of bacon clung to the stubble above Blanton's lip. I considered telling him. Didn't.

"Sleep well?"

Blanton pulled down a lower lid to expose the bloodshot sclera. "Like a baby."

"That going to be a problem, Mr. Blanton? Lots of detail work today."

"By you, not me."

"I'll need everything documented."

"This ain't my first rodeo, my dear." Blanton smiled, saluted, and headed off.

As I finished my coffee, I considered. Did this jerk actually make Slidell look good? My mug hit the tray. No. But the gap was closing.

Welsted and the village delegates were already at the hospital when I arrived.

"The remains have been X-rayed." Welsted filled me in as we walked to the room we'd been assigned. "Shall I have them brought here?"

"Please. Where are the films?"

"On one of the gurneys."

When she'd gone I looked around.

White tiles, two spare gurneys, a floor-stand surgical light, portable illuminator boxes, two deep-basin steel sinks with counter, a small collection of cutting tools, calipers, and a magnifying lens. Not what I had in Charlotte or Montreal, but it would do.

Blanton joined us as an orderly wheeled the remains through the door and, without comment, began setting up his camera equipment. The two villagers observed, bodies tense, eyes never resting. Each looked jumpy enough to need pharmaceuticals.

I crossed to Welsted and spoke in a whisper. "It might be better if they watched from next door." I tipped my head toward an observation window in the wall above the sinks.

"I'll go with them," Welsted offered.

Moments later a light went on and the three appeared on the far side of the glass.

Nodding encouragement to them, I slipped Rasekh's X-rays from their envelope and popped them onto light boxes.

As I moved from plate to plate, flicking switches, my heart sank.

Rasekh had been aboveground when the mortar hit. We'd spent close to an hour re-excavating the body bag from under fallen soil and rock. All night I'd worried that the avalanche had damaged the bones.

I studied the remains glowing white inside the shroud. The long bones looked reasonably intact, but the torso was a jumble and the skull was crushed. Nothing was articulated. Rasekh was in much worse shape than I'd feared.

I sent a confident smile toward the faces in the window. Confidence I didn't feel.

"You ready?" To Blanton, as I blew into a latex glove.

"All systems go."

Blanton started the camcorder. I pulled out my iPhone and dictated the time, date, place, and names of those present. Then I masked.

As I unzipped Rasekh's bag, a musty, earthy smell wafted out. With cautious fingers, I unwound the shroud.

In a year, Mother Nature had worked her inevitable magic. Some remnants of ligament remained, the odd band that had once connected phalanges, a swatch that had once covered a joint capsule. Otherwise, the flesh was gone.

But what time and the desert had left, the landslide had demolished in seconds.

No part of Abdul Khalik Rasekh's skull or lower jaw measured more then five square centimeters, six max. I recognized an orbital ridge, a sliver of zygomatic arch, a mastoid process, a mandibular condyle, isolated teeth.

The postcranial skeleton had fared little better. While the femora and tibiae were whole, the rest of the leg bones were badly fractured. The pelvis was shattered.

The chest and upper limbs had taken the worst beating. The arm bones, clavicles, scapulae, sternum, vertebrae, and ribs were virtually pulverized.

Which wasn't good.

Marines are taught to aim for the center of mass on a target. Picture a human torso. Draw a line nipple to nipple, then another from each nipple to the throat. Any round striking this area will cause incapacitation due to paralysis, shock, or death.

The Triangle of Death.

Due either to the impact of the bullets or to the barrage of falling debris, Rasekh's triangle had been turned into hamburger.

Deep breath. Nod at the observers.

I began picking out recognizable elements and arranging them in a macabre sort of skeleton. As I positioned each fragment, I checked for evidence of gunshot trauma.

To keep focused, I ran through some basics in my head.

Gunshot wounds are categorized according to the distance between the shooter and the victim. A contact GSW, in which the gun is pressed to the flesh, can leave soot, a muzzle imprint, or even a laceration due to the effect of the bullet's propulsive gases. An intermediate GSW, in which the gun is fired at close range, can leave a zone of stippling, called a powder tattoo. A distance GSW is one in which the range of powder tattooing is exceeded.

But all that was irrelevant. There was no flesh. And witness statements already placed Gross approximately ten to fifteen meters from Aqsaee and Rasekh.

And I was seeing zip.

"What kind of weapon did Gross fire?" I asked. I remembered the NCIS file, but was confirming essential facts.

"An M16. Standard Marine artillery."

"How many shots?" I was also talking to mask my anxiety.

"The M16's got a thirty-round clip. Gross emptied his."

That was overkill, even for two targets.

"What kind of rounds?"

"NATO-standard five-point-five-six millimeter."

"Velocity?"

"Nine hundred and forty MPS. Anything under a thousand, popcorn!"

In his not so graceful way, Blanton was referring to a sequence of events that occurs with certain types of projectiles. If the bullet tumbles, or yaws, it can fragment, sending metal into the surrounding flesh. This type of wound can be much more damaging than a clean through-and-through shot.

"Do witness statements say anything about the sequence of fire?" I asked.

Blanton checked his notes.

"Witnesses reported hearing a burst, a pause, then another burst. But everyone says the same thing. The scene was chaos."

I glanced up at the delegates. Their faces were still at the glass, grim and resolute. I imagined mine looked the same.

When I'd sorted the entire contents of Rasekh's body bag, I began a running commentary on what I was seeing. As was my habit, I worked from the head toward the feet.

"Identifiable cranial features indicate a middle-aged male." I listed them. "Dentition fragmented and incomplete, but consistent in age and gender with the subject, Abdul Khalik Rasekh."

"That really necessary?" Blanton sounded impatient.

"Things get confused, memories fade. Identification is always a first step in any exhumation."

I continued through the wreckage, noting features relevant to

Rasekh's biological profile. A fragment of pubic symphysis confirmed my age estimate. Pubic bone shape said the remains were those of a male.

But the slivers, bits, and chunks that represented the torso were too shattered and abraded to yield any information as to cause of death.

Despite my resolve to stay calm, agitation crept into my voice. Blanton noticed.

"You okay, doc?"

"Peachy."

Backhanding hair from my forehead, I rechecked every fragment from Rasekh's midsection, this time using the magnifying lens. It was like viewing cookie crumbs smoothed by a tumbler.

As I worked, the morning's headache crept back. A tight feeling built in my chest. I'd said bullet trajectory was easy to analyze. They'd brought me seven thousand miles to do that. So far I was failing.

I was examining a sixty-centimeter segment of humerus when I noticed an almost invisible spray crosscutting the surface.

"There may be something here." I angled the bone so Blanton's camera could pick up the marks.

"Could be powder stippling. But it's evenly distributed."

"So no way to tell direction," Blanton guessed.

"No." After a few more moments of angling and squinting.

Disappointed, I dictated a description of the defect. Blanton took several more close-ups with a Nikon and scale, then shot backups with a Polaroid.

"These babies have come a long way from the clunkers we used in the old days." Blanton pulled the image free and laid it on the counter. "Fourteen megapixels, inkless three-by-five prints. The detail is passable in a pinch. I've seen way too many disasters with supposedly error-proof top-of-the-line equipment. I always shoot backups."

Hats off to you, Mr. Blanton.

I continued searching, fragment by fragment.

And came up blank.

Discouraged, I straightened and rolled my shoulders. The clock said 12:10.

"Break?" Blanton asked.

I shook my head. "Now that the bones are arranged, Rasekh goes back to radiology."

Blanton called for the tech who'd X-rayed the remains while still wrapped in their shroud. He arrived in moments. Harold. After instruction from me, Harold wheeled the gurney out through the doors.

"Unless the films pick up something I've missed, which is unlikely, Rasekh is a bust. Let's move on."

I dictated the second man's name. Ahmad Ali Aqsaee. After adding the other relevant information, I viewed the X-rays of Aqsaee in his shroud.

And relaxed a micron.

Aqsaee was in better condition than Rasekh. Made sense. He was still underground when the mortar hit. Nevertheless, normal postmortem damage appeared extensive.

Satisfied there was nothing amiss in the shroud, I crossed to the gurney, unzipped the body bag, and laid back the fabric.

Beside me, Blanton inhaled sharply.

Like Rasekh, Aqsaee had been reduced to bone. But his skeleton differed in one striking way.

The uninitiated think bone is white. They picture Halloween posters, instructional models from biology class, or the bleached cattle rib cages popular in western movies. But bone often takes on the pigment of the substrate in which it is buried.

That had happened with Aqsaee. His skeleton was the color of old saddle leather.

"That's not something you see every day."

"It's not uncommon," I told Blanton. "Most likely minerals leached from the rocks or soil."

"Why only this guy?"

"Could be the elemental makeup was different at the back of the cemetery. Maybe runoff from the hillside percolated through Rasekh's grave, washing the critical component away."

"The staining won't cause you problems?"

"No."

I approached the younger man exactly as I had the older. With only slightly less trepidation.

I confirmed that all skeletal and dental features were consistent with Aqsaee's bio profile. Male. Seventeen years old.

"Doc."

"I looked at Blanton.

"The rest of the team needs lunch."

Reluctantly, I agreed. Thirty minutes later we were back. I began my trauma analysis.

The skull was pristine. No fractures. No bullet holes.

Blanton shot close-ups from multiple angles.

Though the mandible was broken at the midline, I suspected the damage was postmortem and due to pressure from the overlying soil.

More photos.

The arms and legs showed no evidence of trauma. I moved on to the rib cage.

Aqsaee's midsection was damaged almost as badly as Rasekh's. Viewing the fragmented ribs, broken clavicles, and crushed and abraded vertebrae, scapulae, and sternum, I felt my chest tighten anew.

Unbidden, my eyes rolled to the observation window. On the far side, I could see Welsted and the delegates in heated discussion. The tall man was gesturing wildly. As I watched, he turned and stabbed a finger at the glass.

Blanton saw the argument, too.

"I'll check it out."

Pouring gasoline on a fire? Maybe, but I didn't try to stop him. My whole focus was on Aqsaee's thoracic region.

One by one, I lifted and inspected each fragment. I'd been at it ten minutes when I spotted a defect on a two-centimeter segment of rib. Though incomplete, the circular shape was classic. I set the segment aside.

Seven minutes later I found another partial defect. Then another.

With growing excitement, I identified and oriented four roughly triangular shards that, in life, had made up the sternum.

My heartbeat ratcheted up.

Moving carefully, I flipped and reconnected the shards in order to observe the back of the bone.

And had to restrain myself from raising the roof.

Bang! Bang!

My head swiveled to the window. The tall man had struck it with his fist. Blanton was trying to talk him down. I could no longer see Welsted.

I was too pumped to care what their issue was.

I'd send the bones for X-ray. Wouldn't matter.

I knew what had happened.

24

An hour after finishing, I was at the blond oak table in the conference room at base ops headquarters. The observers had been dispatched with promise of a full report and permission to transport Aqsaee and Rasekh back to Sheyn Bagh for reburial.

The others were in the exact same chairs they'd occupied on Tuesday. So was I. Weird how people do that.

Large crescents darkened Blanton's pits, mimicking the bags hanging under his eyes. He'd disappeared after we left the hospital. I wondered where he'd gone. What he'd done to work up such a sweat.

"You okay?" I asked, more to pass time than out of concern for Blanton's health. As before, we were waiting for Colonel Fisher.

Blanton shrugged one shoulder. "Might be coming down with something."

After that, we all sat in silence. Minutes passed. Blanton, Welsted, and I knew what we'd found. Noonan did not. He was tense.

Noonan and Welsted half rose when Fisher appeared. Blanton and I remained seated.

Fisher closed the door and took her place at the head of the table. "So." Quick smile to me. "You've finished."

"I have."

"I understand you saw some action out there."

"It wasn't dull."

"Proceed." Fisher leaned back, hands folded in her lap.

"It's the ever-popular good news and bad news," I said.

"Hit us with the bad."

"Mr. Rasekh's remains were far too damaged to allow any conclusion concerning bullet trajectory. Concerning cause or manner of death at all."

Fisher offered a tight nod. "And the good news?"

"Mr. Aqsaee was in better shape. Though postmortem damage was extensive, gunshot trauma was evident in the thoracic region. I was able to observe, describe, and record partial entrance and exit wounds on two rib fragments, one vertebra, and on the anterior and posterior surfaces of the sternum."

One of Fisher's brows arched slightly.

"His breast bone."

"Go on."

"Do you want a full biomechanical description of the fracture patterning?"

"Save that for your report. For our purposes, the bottom line will do."

"Second Lieutenant Gross did not shoot Ahmad Ali Aqsaee in the back."

Though quiet before, the room now went deathly still.

A beat, then Fisher said, "Maybe we could use a little more than that."

"I was able to identify three entrance wounds and two exit wounds. Together these impact sites described at least two bullet paths. The trajectory in both cases was anterior to posterior."

Same eyebrow.

"The bullet entered Mr. Aqsaee's chest and exited his back."

"A finding that corroborates Second Lieutenant Gross's account of the incident."

"Yes."

"How confident are you of your conclusion?"

"Very."

"Based on some little nicks in the bone?"

"In addition to the entrance and exit holes, metal fragments were visible on X-ray. Their orientation supports a conclusion of front-to-back movement." I'd spotted this when viewing the films of Aqsaee's unwrapped and semi-rearticulated bones.

Noonan leaned forward. "You're saying that the younger victim is a hundred percent?"

"Nothing is ever a hundred percent."

"Within reasonable medical certainty."

"Yes," I said.

Noonan ran a hand over his jaw. Exhaled through his nose.

Fisher still had questions.

"What about ricochets? Could a bullet go in from behind, bounce around the ribs or sternum or whatever, and double back?"

I shook my head. "Bullets don't boomerang like that. If a round enters through a victim's—"

"Can we stop calling them victims now?"

The sharpness of tone startled everyone. Fisher responded.

"What would you prefer, Mr. Blanton?"

"Insurgents? Or how about shooters?"

"There is no evidence that either Aqsaee or Rasekh was armed."

Blanton slumped back, shaking his head.

Fisher had one more query.

"Could he have shot him both in the chest and in the back?"

"That is theoretically possible, if he'd been spun around by continued bullet strikes, but I found no indications of back entry or front exits."

"So Gross may be innocent." Noonan's tone was flat, no surprise, relief, or skepticism.

"Please understand me," I cautioned. "All I am saying is that Mr. Aqsaee was either facing or approaching Lieutenant Gross when shot."

Gross's innocence or guilt was another matter, one involving variables not recorded in bone. Did the men behave in a threatening manner? Did Gross have a reasonable belief that he was in imminent danger? But that was for the lawyers, not for me.

Fisher said, "We appreciate your quick turnaround on this. Since the incident, relations with Sheyn Bagh have been shaky at best. If done poorly, this exhumation could have torpedoed what little goodwill we've reestablished."

"I doubt the villagers will take comfort in my findings."

Fisher thought about that. "No, they won't like the outcome. But, sadly, the Afghan people know the price of war. They will accept that, under duress, a soldier was forced to make a life-and-death decision. That, under threat, he acted to save himself and his men."

Perhaps. But I wondered what spin she and her team would use.

"You've done remarkable work here, Dr. Brennan. And it is truly appreciated. But I've been asked to impose upon you further. As you may or may not know, Second Lieutenant Gross's Article 32 hearing was suspended to allow for this operation. Your presence at Lejeune is requested."

I'd been anticipating this. "When?"

"Immediately."

Crap.

"I'll be there."

"Arrangements for your transport have already been made. The Marine Corps thanks you. As do I."

We all rose, shook hands, and went our separate ways.

Katy couldn't join me for dinner, so we'd made plans the previous night for a shopping trip.

As I walked the short distance from my B-hut to the PX, an exuberant sunset turned the snowcapped mountain peaks fiery red. The prefab buildings I passed glowed more warmly than during the day, and shadows split the ground into patches of sunlight and dark.

The store was packed. I scanned, but didn't see my daughter in the sea of camouflage.

"Hoo, boy." I felt a double tap on my backpack. "You'd make a lousy surveillance officer."

I turned. Katy was two feet behind me.

"Gotta watch your flank, Mom."

"Technically, you're not on my flank."

Katy smiled. She wore fatigues and boots. And an M16 slung over one shoulder.

So strange to see my daughter packing heat.

"Grab some caffeine?" she asked.

"Sure."

The Green Bean's interior looked like any café you'd find back home. A wall menu offered a zillion variations on coffee and tea. An espresso machine hissed intermittently in the background. Or was it cappuccino?

"What's your poison?" I asked. "I'm buying."

"Regular, just milk."

Another surprise. My daughter's preference in coffee now matched her new hairstyle. Simple and practical.

We settled into chairs by a wall covered with military patches. The leitmotif was all about combat: skulls, swords, iron crosses. The 335th FTR SQDN called themselves the Chiefs.

Katy noticed me eyeing the assemblage. "A lot of units have their own badges. They're kind of like family crests."

I knew that, but let her explain. I didn't care the topic of conversation, was just happy to be spending time with my kid.

At one point Katy asked about my investigation.

"It went well," I said.

"So you're done?"

"I leave tomorrow."

Katy didn't respond. I wondered. Was she sad I was going? Relieved? Had I invaded a world she wished to keep as her own?

"I met two women in Manas." She spoke after a pause that seemed to go on forever. "At Pete's Place."

"What's that?"

"A bar on base. At Manas, service members are allowed two drinks every twenty hours. Or something like that. Except marines."

"Why not marines?"

"I guess a few got overserved and blew it. I don't know the whole story. Anyway, it's much more civilized there than in Afghanistan."

"Not loving the no-alcohol policy?"

She rolled her eyes. "So these women were a mother-and-daughter team who'd enlisted, trained, and deployed together."

"Seriously?"

"They were Air Force, assigned to some sort of escort duty."

"Are you suggesting we buddy up?"

Loud guffaw. Another pause, then, "My unit's heading out again in two days."

"Heading where?"

"To the north. That's all I can say. Actually, that's all I know."

"I understand." I did. And hated it.

Katy finished the dregs of her oh-so-plain coffee and asked, "Ready to cruise the mall?"

We both laughed. The Bagram "mall" consisted of a warren of shops and kiosks, most selling locally manufactured products. Brass, wood, and fabric items. Jewelry. Rugs. That was about it.

"Lead on, empress of shopping," I said.

She did.

"Are the merchants all Afghans?" I asked as we walked.

"I think so. They come in the morning, clear security, operate their stalls, clear security again, and head home. We're talking sixteen-, seventeen-hour days."

As we passed, vendors entreated us gently to inspect their wares. Now and then we stopped. I was admiring an intricately woven scarf when something brushed my free hand. I turned.

An Afghan girl of about fifteen or sixteen was standing close, her large brown eyes fixed on my face.

"Hello." I smiled.

The girl whispered in Pashto or Dari. I caught only one word. *Allah*.

"I'm sorry," I said. "I don't understand."

Eyes cutting left and right, the girl repeated what she'd said. Maybe. Again, all I caught was *Allah*.

Did the girl want something? Or was she just trying to spread the word?

Katy was examining a scarf on another rack. I waved her over.

"Can you understand what she's saying?"

"Don't worry about it." Katy lowered her voice. "She's a little off."

"What do you mean?"

"I've seen her do this before."

"Do what?"

"Rag on women in civvies." Katy nudged me around the girl and up the street. "One of my bunkmates says the kid's nuts."

I allowed myself to be led. But when we stopped, I glanced over my shoulder.

The girl was still staring at me. As I watched, a man emerged from the shop and drew her inside.

"Mom."

I turned back.

"Come look at this."

Unsettled, I tried to focus on the rug that had drawn Katy's eye. I was about to comment when the sound of wailing split the air.

"Incoming." Katy dropped the rug. "Let's go."

We bolted across the road, took a hard right, and scrambled into a low concrete structure covered with sandbags. Others already occupied the benches. More followed us in.

In seconds the bunker was full. I sensed no panic, more the calm acceptance that comes with routine.

As we waited in the dark, sirens screaming, I again felt a light touch on my hand. I glanced left. Recognized the silhouette. The Allah girl was hunkered beside me. Beyond her was the man who'd taken her inside the shop.

Time passed.

The girl was so close I could feel her body trembling. At one point she whimpered. The man spoke to her sharply. I heard the word *Khandan*. Her name?

Finally, the all-clear sounded. We gathered our gear and scrambled out.

"You're pretty cool about this," I said, slinging my backpack over one shoulder.

Katy shrugged. "More a nuisance than anything. You get used to it. Life goes on."

Usually. But many had died at U.S. bases as a result of missile and mortar attacks.

As we spoke, the man and girl passed. Though he paid us no attention, her eyes again locked onto mine. Sad? Bewildered? Pleading?

Yes. That's what bothered me. The girl seemed so needy. But needy of what?

Then she was gone.

"What do you suppose that kid was trying to say?" I asked Katy.

"I told you. She's a nutjob. Forget it."

I tried.

But that night, alone in my bunk, the girl's face floated before me. Again and again I saw the dark, imploring eyes.

25

TWENTY-FOUR HOURS LATER I WAS STILL THINKING ABOUT THE girl.

Two girls, actually.

Khandan, at Bagram. Jane Doe, in Charlotte.

Welsted had organized my return flights. I'd risen with the sun to set out. The seven-thousand-mile trip, one to tax the resolve of even the most hardened traveler, started sadly, then quickly morphed into a nightmare.

First there was the tearful farewell with Katy. She met me at the flight line. We hugged tightly. She was so damn strong.

"You going to be okay?"

"I'm the one leaving. Promise you'll be careful?"

"Relax, Mom. I'll be fine."

Her calm certainty filled me with an odd sort of dread.

We'd hugged again. Then I'd made my way toward the lockdown hangar.

That's when the true misery began. Our C-130J had a blown rotor on one engine. Mechanics had been summoned. We all know what that means.

Already cleared for departure, I wasn't allowed to return to base. I spent hours dozing, watching football, drinking coffee, going to the head, and eating plastic sandwiches and muffins with a hundred sweaty soldiers, airmen, and marines.

Finally, we boarded and harnessed ourselves in. The plane muscled up through the desert air, broke the clouds, and leveled off. I leaned back against the icy vibrating bulkhead and closed my eyes.

And there were the girls.

Khandan. Something about her intrigued me. Katy said she was mentally challenged, but I wondered. She'd had an intensity that didn't square with that.

What had she been trying to say? I'd gotten one word. *Allah*. Was she seeking help? A handout? A sale? A convert? And why did the encounter bother me so?

Then there was Jane Doe in the MCME morgue cooler. Radio silence from Larabee. Dead ends, trails gone cold? Was Slidell still pushing? I needed to complete my testimony, get home, and rededicate myself to the case. To the promise I'd made her.

By the time we touched down at Manas International my head throbbed, a vein of fire ran my spine, and my ankle was causing me serious grief. This time I was met by a milk-faced soldier with a cornsilk mustache. His fatigues read ELKINS.

"Sergeant Mensforth is tied up." Elkins's voice was high and adenoidal. "I'll help get you processed."

I followed him through the labyrinth that was the transit center, weaving among U.S. service members and Kyrgyz guards with stone faces and very large guns.

Elkins pointed at a pile of luggage that looked identical to the one I'd rummaged on the way out.

I collected my bags and lugged them to customs. Where every item was removed and inspected as though my record showed multiple convictions for trafficking in heroin and guns.

We proceeded to passport control. Where I was refused clearance.

Not conversant in Kyrgyz, I failed to understand the problem. So did Elkins. A translator was summoned. Much discussion followed, during which my flight was called.

At long length, the interpreter explained that upon arrival I'd been issued a permit for one entry into Kyrgyzstan. Today's transit constituted a second entry.

Sixty minutes and a zillion phone calls later, the issue was resolved. Or a bribe was paid. I've no idea. I bolted to the gate and boarded as the door was closing.

Five hours after taking off, I landed in Istanbul. I was checking e-mail in the Turkish Airlines lounge when an annoyingly calm and sugary voice announced several flight delays. Mine was among them. Since the lounge was the most comfortable place I'd been in a week, I was not devastated.

Dawn was lighting the horizon when I finally settled into my little pod in business class. I was reading the menu when the captain's voice came over the intercom.

"Ladies and gentlemen, we've got a pesky little light flashing on the board up here. Probably nothing, but we're being advised to remain at the gate."

The cabin attendants immediately began dispensing alcohol to the business-class passengers. Little comfort to us nondrinkers.

It was late afternoon when we finally took off. Once airborne, I ate dinner, watched one movie, then lowered my seat and killed the light. Though fitfully, I did sleep.

Beyond knowing I'd gained seven hours, I was clueless about my exact ETA in DC. I collected my bags, dragged through customs and immigration, then on to my departure gate.

What are the odds? My flight was delayed.

There are times when all one can do is acknowledge the random futility of existing in this universe.

While waiting, I checked my phone messages. Ruff Noonan had called to say that Lejeune was aware of my situation, and that someone would meet me at wheels-down in Jacksonville, North Carolina.

Larabee wanted me to call as soon as I was back in Charlotte.

Pete asked that I phone when stateside.

Nothing from Ryan.

I e-mailed Katy to let her know I'd gotten back to the world.

It was just past midnight when I finally touched down at the Albert J. Ellis Airport in Jacksonville. A sergeant in fatigues approached as I was off-loading my belongings from the carousel. Stout, middle-aged, but looking like he could lift a Toyota.

"Master Sergeant Earl Rigg, ma'am. I'm your ride to Lejeune." Rigg heaved my duffel onto his shoulder. "Follow me."

We drove north on Route 258, lights strobing the windshield. Rigg wasn't a talker. Or maybe he sensed my exhaustion.

I stared out the window, barely taking in the passing tableau. A pawnshop awning saying WE BUY DRESS BLUES. Endless fast-food joints. Wilson Bay, the water an endless black mirror.

After some time, we pulled up to an imposing brick wall with signage stating CAMP LEJEUNE, HOME OF EXPEDITIONARY FORCES IN READINESS.

Rigg spoke when we'd cleared security.

"Looks like you could use some shut-eye."

"It's that obvious?" I smiled. I think.

"Yes, ma'am."

As Rigg drove across the base, I cracked the window and inhaled the warm night air. The smell of fresh-cut grass, pine, and red cedar made me realize how glad I was to be back in North Carolina.

The Lejeune Inn, built to provide temporary housing, was brick and strictly utilitarian. The Boxy and Plain School of architecture.

"Get yourself sorted with the front desk," said Rigg. "I'll bring your gear."

I drew a first-floor room. Rigg appeared as I was unlocking the door.

"Have a good night, ma'am." A curt nod, and he was gone.

I looked around.

A kitchenette. A table and two chairs. Built-in drawers and shelves, one holding a TV. Two double beds.

An electric alarm on a stand between the beds said 12:47. In the quiet, I could hear it humming softly.

After minimal toilette, I stripped down and crawled under the sheets. Sleep claimed me as soon as my head touched the pillow.

I awoke to the shrill of a phone.

"Mm."

"Sergeant Rigg, ma'am. Major Hawthorn would like to meet with you at ten hundred hours."

I glanced at the clock. 9:24.

"I'll be in the lobby in twenty minutes."

Quick shower, shampoo, teeth. A dab of blusher, one ghastly instant coffee, and I was out the door.

Rigg was waiting. He nodded, then turned quickly. I think he felt awkward, not being able to salute.

The morning was warm but overcast. Dozens of birds stood sentry on power lines and in overhead branches.

As we drove along the beach, I noticed a Marine unit doing nautical maneuvers, six-person crews humping Zodiacs into the surf. I could hear the drill sergeant barking orders over the sound of the waves.

The Legal Services and JAG office was located a short distance up Holcomb Boulevard. Rigg dropped me at the front door.

"Ask for Major Joe Hawthorn."

The receptionist had long legs, smooth skin, and amber hair piled high. Her drawl was thicker than Gran's cheese grits.

"Temperance Brennan for Joe Hawthorn," I said.

"I am so sorry." As though personally aggrieved. "Major Hawthorn's running a smidge late. Would you care to wait in his office?"

Smidge?

"That would be fine."

"Please come with me."

Smiling, she rose and turned right down a narrow hall, stilettos clicking on the shiny gray tile. We entered a door with a plaque bearing Hawthorn's name and rank.

"Can I get you anything? Coffee or tea? Perhaps a soda?"

"Coffee, please."

The office triggered a flash image of Mrs. Flowers. The blotter was positioned perfectly parallel to the edge of the desk. Everything on it was arranged with exactitude. A yellow tablet. A letter opener. Three pens equidistant from each other, nibs perfectly aligned.

A framed photo showcased a blandly handsome man, his blandly pretty wife, and two well-groomed boys. I was imagining names when Ms. Southern Apple Pie returned and handed me a napkin and a steaming Styrofoam cup. Hawthorn entered as she was leaving.

"I apologize for my tardiness."

Hawthorn's appearance mimicked the state of his office. Shoes gleaming, uniform pressed and sharply creased, mustache squarely edged, hair parted with laser precision.

I rose. We shook hands. Hawthorn's palm was dry, his nails and cuticles perfectly manicured.

"Thank you for coming. I know you must be tired."

"I'll catch a nap later."

"Please sit." Gesturing to the spot I'd just vacated.

I sat. Hawthorn moved to the chair behind his desk.

"As you know, the Article 32 hearing will resume tomorrow." Hawthorn tented his fingers and rested his chin atop them. "Do you know what an Article 32 is?"

"In general."

"Since the early 1950s, military justice has been administered in accordance with the UCMJ, the Uniform Code of Military Justice. It provides the statutory framework that is the bedrock of both substantive criminal law and criminal procedure in the U.S. military.

"Many of the substantive provisions are similar to those found in American state and federal jurisdictions. The procedural provisions can be quite different.

"Under Article 32 of the UCMJ, no charge may be referred to a general court-martial for trial until an impartial investigation of the truth of the matter has been made. This is similar to a grand jury proceeding for civilians."

Pete had always maintained that Article 32 actually affords an accused greater rights because it allows the accused and his counsel to be present at the hearing, to cross-examine government witnesses, and to present evidence, none of which is permitted before a grand jury.

I recalled how he'd bristle on hearing the old Groucho Marx gag that military justice is to justice as military music is to music.

Hawthorn's voice brought me back from my thoughts.

"The government has presented all its evidence. I intend to call only one witness, that being you. I have reviewed your report and plan to take you through it, just as any civilian lawyer would."

Hawthorn leaned back in his chair.

"I suppose you'd like to know a bit about the man of the hour?"

"Anything you think is pertinent, yes."

"Second Lieutenant Gross's father was Air Force, so he grew up a typical military brat. Base to base, hitch to hitch. Had the armed forces in his blood, you might say."

"Sometimes it goes the other way."

"Yes, but not for John. After graduating high school—as class valedictorian, I might add—he headed straight to a Marine recruiting office."

"Not Air Force?"

Hawthorn dropped his hands, palms flat on the blotter. "I suspect he felt the need to prove something to his father."

I didn't query the meaning of that.

"John enlisted on an 18x contract, which offered a direct shot at a combat assignment. After training, he volunteered, and was deployed, to Desert Storm. He served in the Middle East, on and off, from '91 to '94."

"That's a good stretch."

"Yes." Hawthorn appeared on the verge of a comment, decided against it. "At the completion of his last deployment, John did not reenlist. He'd proven what he needed to prove, to himself, to his father. He had other plans for his life. Using the GI bill to fund his education and working full-time, he enrolled at NC State University. After graduating with a degree in political science, he taught high school in Charlotte for several years. Or it might have been Charleston."

"Yet he must have reenlisted."

"November ninth, 2005. That date have any significance for you, Dr. Brennan?"

I shook my head.

"It did for John. On that date, suicide bombers hit three American hotels in Amman, Jordan. The Radisson SAS, the Grand Hyatt, and a Days Inn. The Radisson was the worst. Husband-and-wife bombers walked into a ballroom in which a nine-hundred-guest wedding was in progress. Thirty-eight people were killed, including the fathers of both the bride and groom."

I remembered the attacks now. Sixty killed, 120 injured.

"Reenlistments tend to rise after such incidents. In the wake of 9/11, lines ran out the doors of many recruiting centers."

Hawthorn's phone rang. He glanced at the caller ID but did not pick up.

"John experienced a sense of personal accountability. This is my interpretation, you understand. He never used those words specifically. It's what I've picked up from our many conversations."

"I understand."

"John had spent three years in Iraq, making the world safe. This massacre of civilians demonstrated that wasn't the case."

"But we're talking a different conflict, different perpetrators."

"Absolutely. But for some soldiers it's all one generalized evil. Saddam, Gadhafi, the Ayatollah, the Taliban—one evil with multiple faces. Like a hydra, a many-headed snake."

"This was John's thinking?"

"After those attacks, John viewed terrorism as a very real and very personal threat. To America, to our way of life."

"He quit his job and reenlisted."

"He applied for Officer Candidate School, which, given his age, was problematic."

I did some quick math. "He was in his early thirties by then."

"As in corporate America, the military prefers that its officers start out young. At his age, John should have been middle echelon. Nevertheless, he was accepted." Hawthorn straightened the letter opener. "John's status as a prior also worked to his disadvantage."

"A prior?"

"An enlisted man applying for OCS. It's tough to make the jump from the rank and file to officer class."

"But Gross managed it."

Hawthorn nodded. "Completed OCS at the top of his class, chose an infantry MOS, and volunteered for duty in Afghanistan. He was on his fourth tour when the incident at Sheyn Bagh took place."

"What did Gross's fellow officers think of him?" I set my napkin and empty cup on the edge of the desk.

"Hardworking, fair, cool under pressure. Excuse my French, but one called him a 'gung ho mofo.'"

I needed no translation.

"So John was intense."

Hawthorn gave a half smile. "Some might say a marine can never be too intense."

"What about those under his command?"

Hawthorn's eyes flicked to the cup and napkin ruining the careful symmetry on his desk. Unconsciously, his fingers squared the already square blotter.

"Opinions vary, of course. Most are positive."

"But not Grant Eggers."

"Corporal Eggers is the chief witness for the prosecution."

Enough said.

"How is Lieutenant Gross handling all this?"

"John loves his country and loves the Corps. But he feels betrayed. He hates being stuck in Jacksonville, and would prefer to return to Afghanistan. He is certain he will be vindicated. As am I."

Hawthorn smiled and pointed a finger at my offending debris. "May I?"

"Yes. Thank you."

He tossed the cup and napkin into something at his feet.

"So," he said, straightening. "Let's get into greater detail about your testimony."

For the next hour we went over the basics. Hawthorn listened, asked a few questions, made a few notes. When I'd finished, he rose and thanked me again.

"If you need anything further, I'm staying at the Lejeune Inn," I offered, sincerely hoping he wouldn't call.

Rigg met me outside with the van.

As we drove across base, I thought over Hawthorn's comments.

Intense was the word he'd used.

How intense? I wondered.

Rigg dropped me under the portico, said he'd collect me at oh-eight-thirty the following day. I went to my room and called Ryan. Got his machine. Although he'd responded to none of my earlier messages, I left another.

Frustrated and hungry, I walked to a Wendy's for a double with cheese and fries. God, it was good to be home.

Back in my room, the humming clock said 1:15. Already regretting the quart of grease I'd ingested, I lay down on the bed. Outside, the sentry birds were now twittering like mad.

I closed my eyes.

Again I was awakened by a ringing phone. The room had gone dark.

"Hello?"

Silence.

"Hello?"

The silence sounded hollow, as though someone was listening. Or cupping the receiver.

Click.

Apologies to you, too, shithead.

I walked down the hallway, bought a vending-machine Diet Coke, returned, and booted my laptop. As I moved images into a Power-Point presentation, my thoughts kept veering to Gross.

Would bones dug from the Afghan desert hold the key to his fate?

26

The courtroom was spartan: a raised bench stage center, defense and prosecution tables opposite, a witness stand adjacent to the bench and facing the courtroom, a court reporter's desk in front of the witness stand, an empty jury box, a few seats for spectators at the rear.

The investigating officer, Lieutenant Colonel Frank Keever, was a gray-haired guy, trim, with a no-nonsense air. Major Christopher Nelson had a blond buzz cut and what must have been a very long torso. The prosecutor looked much shorter standing than sitting.

A man and a woman were the only people in the three rows of benches at the back of the room. The only ones wearing civvies. Diligent note taking suggested both were journalists.

Lieutenant John Gross was already seated when I arrived, back rigid, fingers intertwined on the tabletop. He was built like a bulldog, compact but powerful, with a face that looked like chiseled granite. Every crease was sharp. Every hair was in place.

Promptly at 9:30, Keever brought the hearing to order and asked Hawthorn if he wished to proceed with evidence for the defense.

I was called to the stand.

Gross's eyes followed as I crossed the room. Otherwise, not a muscle, hair, or lash moved.

Hawthorn began with a review of my credentials. Some questions were the same as those posed during jury selection two weeks earlier in Charlotte.

Hawthorn brought out that I had a PhD in anthropology and was certified by the American Board of Forensic Anthropology, a group with less than a hundred members. I explained that I was not a medical doctor but specialized in the examination of skeletal material, and that I worked closely with pathologists in the evaluation of human remains.

Hawthorn mentioned my association with JPAC and my familiarity with the military. He pointed out that the bulk of my work had been on behalf of the prosecution rather than the defense.

I testified that I'd just returned from Afghanistan, where I'd supervised the exhumation of the bodies of Abdul Khalik Rasekh and Ahmad Ali Aqsaee, and performed skeletal autopsies at the Bagram Air Force Base hospital.

Gross watched with the intensity of a tomcat eyeing a sparrow. Now and then a subtle tremor twitched his left lower lid.

Hawthorn then got to the heart of it.

Hawthorn: "What conclusions, if any, did you draw concerning the entry and exit points of bullets?"

"As to Mr. Rasekh, none. As to Mr. Aqsaee, I concluded that bullets had struck him in the area of the chest and had exited at his back."

No reaction from Gross. Just the tic.

Hawthorn: "Why were you not able to determine trajectories with respect to Mr. Rasekh?"

"Bone destruction was too extensive to allow identification of entry or exit points."

Hawthorn: "But you were able to identify such points for Mr. Aqsaee?"

"Yes."

Hawthorn: "Please describe the findings that led you to that opinion."

"There were several. Defects on two rib segments, on bone shards that had been part of the sternum, and on one vertebrae all demonstrated classic fracture patterning for gunshot wounds in an anterior-to-posterior trajectory. Metal and bone fragments found on X-ray further supported that finding. Mr. Aqsaee was shot in the chest."

Gross remained absolutely motionless, his face a stone mask.

Hawthorn: "Can you explain briefly what happens when a bullet impacts tissue?"

I provided a jargon-free overview of the biomechanics of gunshot wounding, including the effects of projectile tumbling, cavitation, and fragmentation.

Hawthorn: "Tell us about bullet damage to bone."

"A projectile traveling at high speed subjects bone to sudden dynamic stress. Though bone is thought to be rigid, it actually has some elasticity. As with soft tissue, when a bullet penetrates bone, a temporary cavity is created."

Hawthorn: "What velocity is required for penetration of bone?"

"Studies suggest a minimum of two hundred feet per second. Much less than a bullet fired from an M16."

Hawthorn: "Tell us about exit and entrance wounds."

"Typically, when a bullet penetrates bone, a circular to oval defect is created at the point of entrance. The defect's edges are sharp, and its diameter may roughly approximate that of the bullet's caliber. An exit defect tends to be larger and more irregular in shape."

Hawthorn: "Why?"

"A number of factors, including the potential for bullet deformation or fragmentation, and the potential loss of much of the bullet's kinetic energy."

Hawthorn: "Larger size and irregular shape. Are those the only differences?"

"No. As a bullet exits bone, fragments are broken off the edges of the exit surface and propelled forward, accompanying the bullet on its path. As a result, an exit defect is beveled out in a conelike fashion. Schematic representations are included in my report. I also have photos and copies of X-rays."

"Have you transferred those to a computer-imaging format which you can display on our screen?"

"Yes."

I booted my laptop, opened my PowerPoint presentation, and advanced to an image of a section of rib.

"This photo shows the anterior aspect of a piece of Mr. Aqsaee's right fifth rib."

Hawthorn: "The part that faced front?"

"Yes." I ran the cursor around the upper border of a partially preserved circular defect. "Note the sharp, clean edges. This is a bullet entrance hole."

I advanced to the next image.

"This shows the posterior aspect of that same rib, the part that faced Mr. Aqsaee's spine. Note the beveled edges of the defect. The beveling indicates that this is a bullet exit point."

Hawthorn: "What does this fracture patterning tell you?"

"The bullet trajectory was front to back."

Gross remained impassive, but seemed to glance at the bench every so often to gauge how the lieutenant colonel was reacting.

I moved to the next image.

"This defect is located on the anterior aspect of Mr. Aqsaee's right seventh rib, at a point close to its articulation with the sternum."

Hawthorn: "His breast bone."

"Yes. Note that the defect characteristics are almost identical to those in the previous shot."

The next image showed a posterior view of that same rib. As with the exit defect on the fifth rib, spalling was evident around the edges. I moved on.

"This shows bullet damage on a segment of that same rib, the seventh, at a point close to its articulation with the spinal column."

Hawthorn: "Where it curves around to form the back of the rib cage?"

"Yes. This is an anterior view. Note the clean edges on the defect." Next image.

"This is a posterior view of that same segment of rib. Note the beveling."

Hawthorn: "So a bullet entered the front of the rib cage at the level of the seventh rib, then exited that same rib in back, near the spine."

"Yes." Next image. "This is a view of the anterior surface of Mr. Aqsaee's sternum, after rearticulation of the broken pieces."

"His breast bone."

"Yes."

Hawthorn: "You reconstructed it yourself?"

"Yes. Note the clean-edged circular defect at the middle right. This is a bullet entrance point."

Next image.

"This shows the posterior aspect of the sternal defect. Note its significantly larger size, irregular shape, and the fragmentation that exposes the underlying spongy bone. This is a bullet exit point. The fracture patterning demonstrated on these two images indicates that a bullet traveled through Mr. Aqsaee's sternum on a trajectory of front to back."

Hawthorn: "So. You are saying that three bullets entered Mr. Aqsaee's chest and exited his back."

"A minimum of three. There could have been more. I can only observe trauma evident on the skeleton."

Hawthorn: "Do the flight paths of these bullets suggest anything concerning Mr. Aqsaee's position relative to that of Lieutenant Gross at the time of the shooting?"

I projected a photograph to which I'd added graphics to illustrate this point. The reconstructed sternum, rib fragments, and vertebral fragments were placed in anatomically appropriate positions in a schematic of a skeleton. A red line connected each entrance wound with its associated exit wound, then extended forward and backward from the rib cage and spinal column. Each line ran roughly parallel to the skeleton's feet.

"The bullet trajectories suggest that Mr. Aqsaee was upright and facing Lieutenant Gross when he was shot."

Gross's lips tightened. His chin hitched up a millimeter, leveled.

"I can also project the X-rays."

I moved to an image in which brilliant white dots peppered a partial rib and two vertebral fragments.

"When a gun is fired, metal particulates can travel with the bullet as it moves through the body. These particulates appear here as white specks due to their greater density in comparison to bone."

I advanced to an image superimposing the X-ray over a schematic of a rib cage, and drew the cursor along a path from the rib to the vertebrae.

"Note how the metallic trace is more densely packed in the rib, less so in the vertebrae. Particles were lost as the bullet advanced along its path."

Hawthorn: "Its path being from the chest toward the spine."

"Yes. In addition to metallic trace, bone fragments can be displaced forward as a bullet moves through tissue."

I placed the cursor beside a minute sliver, not as intensely white as the metallic trace, but brighter than the vertebral bone in which it was embedded. Then I moved it to another sliver, and another.

"These bone fragments came from the blowout zone at the back of the sternum, from the area of bone loss we observed earlier. The orientation of the fragments suggests they were traveling from front to back with the bullet."

"So, in summary, this evidence substantiates your conclusion that Mr. Aqsaee was upright and facing Lieutenant Gross when shot in the chest."

"Yes."

"Did you prepare a report of your procedures, findings, and conclusions?"

"I did."

Hawthorn: "Let me show you defense exhibit one. Is that your report?"

"Yes, it is."

"Sir, the defense moves to admit exhibit one into evidence. A copy was previously provided to Major Nelson."

Nelson did not object to the report and had no questions for me. Keever advised that he would submit his conclusions and recommendations within a week, then adjourned the hearing.

Even while the flow of testimony was running decidedly in his favor, Gross never relaxed or smiled. He'd remained taut and erect throughout, battling his twitch.

As I passed the defense table, he disengaged from Hawthorn and strode toward me. His face revealed nothing, but his step and carriage radiated confidence.

"Thank you, ma'am."

Gross's hand shot out. Without thinking I responded.

Gross's cuff hiked up as we shook, revealing the lower part of a tattoo. I saw the bottom of the Marine Corps globe and anchor, the letters RIP circling below.

I'd heard that this version was favored by the most "gung ho mofo" types. Mess with the Corps and you'll rest in peace.

Noticing my glance at the tattoo, Gross came to attention, saluted, and said, "Semper fi, ma'am."

With that he stepped back, pivoted, and walked away.

PART THREE

27

Tuesday morning, I woke before the alarm bells bonged. Early dawn was seeping through the window, turning my room into a study in shades of gray. Outside, the first few mockingbirds were sending out tentative trills.

I ran sleepy eyes over the chair, the dresser, the antique wooden shelf with its collection of memorabilia. A conch shell from Maui. A silver Latvian bride's headband. Framed photos whose images I couldn't see. Didn't matter. I knew each like I knew my own features. Katy at her college graduation. Ryan and me in Guatemala City. Pete and Boyd on the beach at Isle of Palms. Birdie stretched full-length in the sun.

God, it was good to be home.

I rolled over.

The digits on the clock read 6:12.

I tried to fall back to sleep. Impossible. Would have helped to have Birdie there, snuggling and purring.

At 6:45, I gave up. A long hot shower and shampoo scrubbed away the last piggybacking grime from Bagram. Though still tender, my ankle was on the mend. The swelling was down and the bruising looked less flamboyant.

Down in the kitchen, I made coffee and popped bread into the toaster. Oddly, there was milk in the refrigerator. And cottage cheese, OJ, a plastic container of lasagna from Pasta and Provisions, fresh produce, lunch meat and cheese, and a number of other items I hadn't purchased. Including a Heineken.

More than a dozen *Observer*s had been dutifully brought inside during my absence. Making a mental note to thank my neighbor, I glanced through a few in a fast-forward manner, working from the oldest to the most recent. I got a general sense of what had happened in my absence. Which was the usual.

A student shot up a school in Montana, claiming he'd been bullied. Four dead. A couple was found with an arsenal of guns and explosives in their Trenton, New Jersey, apartment. Both were under arrest. The NRA was defending the right of every American to pack a semiautomatic and load it with a thirty-round clip. The video-game industry was claiming innocence in the fostering of a culture of violence.

On the local scene, a Gastonia plant closing was about to put hundreds out of work. Guns were found at two middle schools. Fraud was being alleged at a college. A kid reported missing from Mount Holly in 2004 was found living with his grandparents in northern Michigan. He was now fourteen.

I was on my sixth paper when a small headline caught my eye. Local section. Three column inches. I checked the date. The story had appeared the previous Saturday.

SEARCH FOR SUSPECT IN FATAL HIT AND RUN

The article started out by asking for the public's help in identifying a teenage hit-and-run victim. It provided a brief description of the girl and the date, approximate time, and Rountree–Old Pineville Road location of the accident. It stated that authorities were looking for witnesses or persons with information. My name was mentioned, as was Slidell's. Anyone with knowledge of the girl or the incident was urged to contact the CMPD.

My morgue-cooler face shot accompanied the text. So did a number for the homicide division at police headquarters.

The byline was Allison Stallings.

Second mental note. Another thank-you due. Though I could have done without personal mention. Seeing my name in the paper never thrills me. Unless I've finished the Charlotte 10K in under an hour.

The previous Sunday's edition had a follow-up piece on the MP case Slidell was working when I left for Afghanistan. Pictures of the missing woman, Cheryl Connelly, and her kids; background on her movements immediately prior to her disappearance; and a hint she might have had mental issues.

So Connelly was still whereabouts unknown as of two days ago. Great. Unless she'd turned up or was found on Monday, Slidell would still be distracted.

I took the papers to the recycling bin. Two empty Heineken bottles lay at the bottom.

Hm.

I went to the study. A PC sat on my desk, plugged into a wall switch. A Dell, minimally a decade out of date.

Pete and I have opposing views on cars and computers. I see the former as a means of transportation, the latter as a slick on-ramp to the knowledge of the world. My Mazda is too old to have resale value. My Mac is fast and new and will be gone as soon as an updated model comes out.

For my ex, automotive trumps cyber speed every time. I knew who'd been in my house. Suspected the reason.

I dialed Mrs. Flowers.

"Mecklenburg County Medical Examiner."

"It's Dr. Brennan."

"My, my, bless your heart. I couldn't believe my ears when I heard you'd gone to that terrible place. How are you?"

"I'm well, thank you."

"Did you see any of those dreadful Taliban?"

"I was mostly on base."

"I prayed for you every day. Will you be coming into the office soon?"

"Perhaps later. I just arrived home last night."

"Unpack right off. If you let it go, who knows what creatures will crawl out and move in with you. Happened to a friend of mine." Mrs. Flowers's voice dropped to a whisper. "I won't mention what took up residence in her house."

"I'll do that."

"You have several phone messages."

"I'll get to them first thing."

"And a new case."

Mrs. Flowers gave me a thumbnail. It involved hooligans, an out-house, and a noggin in doo-doo. I have to admit, I do enjoy her prose.

"Thank you. Could you transfer me to Dr. Larabee?"

"Certainly."

A soulless version of "Sailing" bridged me over until Larabee picked up. What is it with institutions and Muzak?

"Tempe, glad you're back. How was it?"

"I've got boundless respect for our troops."

"That bad?"

"Just tiring." And bugs, and body armor, and burial alive.

"Were you able to see Katy?"

"Yes. She's really something."

"The kid always was. Listen, I didn't respond to your messages because I didn't want to be a distraction."

"No problem."

"The DNA trace came up empty on our Jane Doe. She's not in the system."

"No big surprise."

"No. But you never know until you try."

I asked if he'd seen Allison Stallings's article. He had.

"Still no one's come forward."

"So we're no farther ahead than when I left."

"Au contraire. I got results back on the semen analysis. We were right. It came from more than one individual."

I sat up straighter in my chair. "This is where you tell me the DNA has names attached."

"The DNA has names attached. Two cold hits right here in the North Carolina database. I'll leave the reports on your desk. I've already forwarded them to Slidell."

"This could be big."

"Could be. I found something else which may or may not be big."

I waited.

"While going back over the X-rays, I spotted a small streak of radio-opacity near the right parieto-occipital junction. Hematoma was pretty extensive in that part of the brain, and the cortical bone is very thick there, so I hadn't noticed it at first. I double-checked, and sure enough something had gotten caught up when I retracted the scalp. Prob—"

"What did you find?"

"Looks like a sliver of bone. Pierced the scalp but didn't penetrate the ectocranial surface. I left that on your desk, along with the two DNA reports."

The line beeped.

"Hold on a sec."

As Larabee clicked over to answer the incoming call, I considered the implications of a bone fragment in a victim's scalp. A fall? A blow? Some sort of hair accessory? Before I got far, Larabee was back.

"Gotta go. Double suicide. Myers Park of all places. Thought the gentry were too well-bred to off themselves with rat pellets."

"I'll be in shortly."

"Good. You've got a skull from a crapper."

I hung up, totally pumped. About the DNA, not the latrine find.

When I left Charlotte, the hit-and-run case was going cold fast. Now there were leads. The names of men who'd had sex with the victim. Forced? For love? For fun? For money? It didn't matter. These men knew her.

I phoned Slidell, got voicemail. Left a message telling him to call me as soon as possible

I called ICE, figuring this new information might gain some traction with Luther Dew. Voicemail. Another message.

Irrational, but there are certain tasks I despise so much I conjure endless excuses to avoid them. Grocery shopping. Flossing. Car servicing.

Topping the list is unpacking luggage. Mrs. Flowers's advice was dead-on. Though for different reasons. Rational ones. But I knew I'd loathe myself later if I put it off.

Despite being anxious to see what Larabee had left on my desk, I went to the bedroom, dumped my duffel, and began to triage. Clothes to the laundry. Toiletries to the bathroom. Books, papers, and anthropology materials to the office.

I turned the duffel inside out in the yard, then stowed it on a shelf in the downstairs closet. Pleased with myself, I took a break to check my e-mail.

Katy had written to say she was glad I'd come. Opined I would forever be the only mother in her unit to do so. She also assured me she'd be careful.

Nothing from Ryan.

Why did I even bother to look?

Hurrying back up to the bedroom, I turned my attention to the backpack. I'd barely begun when the phone rang.

Thinking it was Slidell or Dew, I picked up without checking caller ID.

Click.

Dial tone.

Lejeune, now here. Twice in two days.

Nice.

Back to the pack. First I emptied the main compartment. Cap, jacket, sunglasses, books, a neck pillow I'd bought during the flight delay in Istanbul. The little goody bag the airlines give out in business class.

Then I worked my way through the outer pockets. Of which there are a bazillion on a military backpack. My efforts produced hand cream, batteries, two melted protein bars, at least a dozen used earplugs, and a whole lot of sand.

Ten minutes after starting, I ripped loose the last Velcro strap and reached into a side pocket, expecting nothing but wadded tissues. My hand closed on something that felt like plastic.

Curious, I withdrew the object.

Moments passed as I studied the thing, bewildered.

I turned it over.

My puzzlement grew.

28

I WAS STARING AT A PHOTOGRAPH, FADED AND WORN AROUND THE edges. Someone had placed it inside a clear plastic sleeve that was badly scratched.

Had Katy put the photo in my pack? Stashed it while I wasn't looking?

At first I thought that must be the answer. I wasn't focusing on the scene depicted, just on the fact of the picture's existence among my belongings.

Then I noticed a few technical details. The photo measured three by five and was printed on paper with a weight and finish that suggested a source other than a home computer or drugstore processor.

A recently stored memory flared. A comment about backups.

Of course. The print had been made with an instant camera, a Polaroid or some similar brand.

I brought the sleeve close to the window and studied the pic.

The image was grainy and slightly blurred, snapped quickly, or when the lens was in motion. Centered in it was a group of Afghan girls in head scarves and traditional dress.

I counted. Six in all. Five with arms linked, eyes all giggles and shyness. The sixth girl stood behind the group, forking "devil's horns" over the head of another.

That seemed wrong. Weren't devil's horns a very Christian reference?

Where had these kids learned it? Had they seen Western troops do it?

Five of the girls were facing directly into the lens. Though their heights varied, each appeared to be in her early teens, probably twelve to thirteen. The sixth girl was partially obscured but seemed a bit taller than the rest. All six had dark eyes and glossy black hair crossing their foreheads.

Adolescent girls caught in a playful moment. The subject matter argued against Katy as the source. Unless she'd taken the picture while out with her unit.

But Katy would use a smartphone or a digital camera, not an instant. And why sneak the photo into my pack? It seemed an odd memento. And, if that was her intent, why not simply give it to me?

My mind shifted from the question of how I'd gotten the picture to the question of its provenience. Afghanistan? Probably.

The girls stood a few yards from the corner of a modest stone house not unlike those I'd seen in Sheyn Bagh. Beyond the house, arid desert stretched in all directions. On the far left, a distant rock formation needled into a cloudless blue sky, dark and featureless, all detail lost to the camera's limited depth of field.

The moment could have been captured at any one of a hundred villages across Southwest Asia. Perhaps a thousand.

My mind shifted again. To the photographer.

Slim chance a local farmer would possess an instant camera. But it was possible. A gift from overseas. Maybe from one of the allied forces who'd visited the village.

Perhaps the photographer was a U.S. service member. Maybe picture taking was a ploy used to schmooze the locals. To win hearts and minds, as the military put it.

I moved my gaze from face to face. The girls looked excited but shy, the way kids are around strangers. That tracked with the soldier theory.

I flipped the sleeve and read what was written on the back of the print. A list, inked in block letters, all caps.

LAILA. KHANDAN. MAHTAB. ARA. TAAHIRA. HADIYA.

Six girls. Six names.

Definitely not Katy's handwriting. Her scrawl looked like tracks left behind by a snail on a bender.

What intrigued me was the fact that the names were written in English. Pashto and Dari both use versions of the Persian alphabet.

Perhaps a soldier or marine had taken the shot, then written the names as the girls provided them. That also tracked with the hearts-and-minds theory.

I pictured the scene. Wondered. Had adults looked on in silent disapproval? Had they enjoyed the smiles of their children? Had the girls agreed to a quick pic while off the parental radar?

I flipped the photo back and forth. Faces. Names. Did the order of the names match the lineup in which the girls stood? Was that order meaningful?

To which girl had the photo been given? Had she been allowed to keep it? Or had it been taken from her?

Another possibility. Had the soldier kept the photo, perhaps to mail to family back home? To give them a sense of the place. To assure a mother or a wife the locals were just ordinary people.

Or perhaps photos were taken for record keeping. More hearts-and-minds maneuvering. On the next sweep through the village, ask about the kids by name. Every parent loves that.

But it was all speculation. And no theory explained how the photo had ended up in my pack. At least I could eliminate or confirm one suspect.

Descending to the study, I slipped the print from its sleeve, photographed it with my iPhone, and attached it to an e-mail. Then I wrote the following note to Katy.

> Found this in my backpack. Your work? If so, thanks. If you met these girls I'd love to know the story. BTW, the print looks like a Polaroid. Are instant cameras common over there? (In other words, I'm curious why you didn't send the image by e-mail.)

Returning the three-by-five to its sleeve, I was struck by a realization. Whoever had taken the photo, and wherever, and for whatever reason, someone had cared enough to seal it in plastic. To preserve it.

So why give it to me?

Still puzzled, I placed the photo on my desk, stashed the empty backpack, dressed, and headed out.

*　　*　　*

I arrived at the MCME just past noon. The public area was deserted and there wasn't a pathologist, death investigator, or technician in sight.

Mrs. Flowers was not at her post. I guessed she was downing her usual tuna or chicken salad sandwich, or tending her section of the staff container garden in the courtyard. Her specialty was lettuce and basil.

I went straight to my office. The message light on my phone was flashing, and files and papers covered my desk.

After stowing my purse, I started on the mound. A request for expertise in anthropology lay on top. Mrs. Flowers's outhouse was actually a Porta-John, and the noggin was actually a partial cranium. Doo-doo needs no translation.

Though the prospect was unappealing, I hoped Joe had left cleaning of the skull to me. One never knows what might be trapped in adhering material. Shit happens?

I opened a file and placed the request in it. Then I dug out the reports on the semen. Each listed the case number under which the sample had been submitted, the name, age, last known address, and criminal history of the person whose genetic profile it matched.

The first DNA hit named Cecil Converse "CC" Creach. Creach's adult priors included multiple bumps for distribution of meth and weed, two for vandalism, and one for B&E. Of his forty-two years on the planet, Creach had spent seventeen behind bars. His juvie record was sealed and would require a warrant to open.

Creach's LKA was in an area of town known as Five Corners, near the Johnson C. Smith University campus. He was currently on parole, having served two of five years for hanging bad paper.

The second semen donor was Ray Earl Majerick. Before I could read his list of priors, my e-mail pinged.

A reply from Katy. Already?

Not guilty, but cute kids. Polaroids aren't uncommon here, or it could be a Fotorama, a knock-off made by Fuji. Some missions are tasked with taking pics of the LNs to jolly them up. Instant cameras are used because they spit out a snapshot you can hand over right away. For personal use, troops use digitals or smartphones.

I went back to the printout on Majerick. His arrest history told a different story from that of Creach. Armed robbery. Assault. False imprisonment. Forcible rape. The guy sounded like seriously bad news. No current tail, but Majerick's last known address came from the state parole board. It was in Concord.

I placed another call to Slidell. Voicemail. Didn't people answer their phones anymore?

Easy, Brennan. He may already be talking to Creach and Majerick.

I turned my attention to the bone Larabee had found in Jane Doe's scalp. As promised, it sat on the blotter, sealed inside a small plastic vial.

After gloving, I removed the vial's cap and slid the thing onto my palm. The fragment was off-white in color, triangular in shape, and measured approximately two centimeters long by a half centimeter across at the wider end. The narrow end tapered to a very sharp point.

The color looked right. The weight was okay.

I pressed the little triangle to my wrist. It felt cool against my skin. Good.

Yet something was off.

Uneasy, I dug a hand lens, matches, and a safety pin from my desk drawer.

Under magnification, the outer surface of bone should appear to have tiny pores, sometimes black or brown due to soil and other contaminants. Larabee's sliver looked strangely homogenous, like porcelain or china.

Plastic? Resin?

Placing the sliver on the blotter, I pulled out the business arm of the pin, lit a match, and heated the tip until it glowed red. Then I pressed the hot point to the sliver.

Though a faintly organic smell tinged the air, the surface did not burn. The sliver was not plastic or resin. That left bone or ivory.

But the material looked far too smooth and uniform for bone.

Mind buzzing, I hurried to the stinky room and positioned the sliver under the dissecting scope, fractured edge up. Then I adjusted lighting and magnification.

And there they were in the cross section. Schreger lines. Tiny angled marks, like stacked chevrons. Their presence meant the material came from an elephant or mammoth tusk. The angle of the little Vs could indicate which, but my memory failed me on that.

I stared, bewildered. How did ivory end up in the scalp of a hit-and-run victim?

Suddenly I was in a froth to talk to Slidell. Hurrying back to my office, I returned the sliver to its vial and punched in his number.

For the third time that day, I was rolled to voicemail.

"Sonofabitch!"

Agitated, and not wanting to scoop poop from a brainpan at that moment, I jabbed the message button on my phone, then, not so gently, entered my mailbox code.

One by one, I worked through ten days of accumulated drivel.

A question from the chief ME in Raleigh. Another from a colleague in Wisconsin. Those I saved. Two hang-ups. An interoffice appeal concerning abuse of the refrigerator in the staff lounge. Three queries from members of the media. All those I deleted.

The final message froze the fingers I was drumming on the blotter.

29

THE CALLER WAS FEMALE, THE WORDS WHISPERED IN ACCENTED English. Background noise obliterated much of what she said.

"... want to say, but ... girl that ... no accident ..."

The volume kept strengthening then fading, as though the woman had been repeatedly turning her head, sporadically distancing her lips from the receiver. Or maybe signal strength was erratic.

Somehow the voice was familiar. Or maybe it was the tone, the urgency.

Ping.

Was it the same person who'd contacted me from the pay phone at Seneca Square?

I held my breath, eager to catch every word, every nuance.

"... Passion Fruit ... place ... go ... not right ..."

I heard a shout in the background. Someone summoning the woman? Threatening her?

Either way, the call ended with the click of an abrupt hang-up.

I replayed the message again and again, pen poised over paper. I wrote almost nothing.

I receive hundreds of calls, listen to scores of messages, some useful, some crackpot, some the sad ramblings of bereaved next of kin. Over the years I've developed an instinct for those to take seriously. This call was among them.

I checked the messaging system information. The call had come into the switchboard the previous Friday, the day after Stallings's piece ran in the *Observer*.

I studied the few words I'd scribbled. My gut told me Passion Fruit did not refer to a produce market.

I hit Google. Bingo. The Passion Fruit Club was located on Griffith, along a stretch that catered to adult male tastes.

I picked up the phone and punched Mrs. Flowers's extension.

"Yes, Dr. Brennan."

"I got a call last Friday at one thirty-one P.M. It rolled to voicemail. Could you check the log to see if the number was recorded?"

After a few seconds, Mrs. Flowers read off a series of digits that began with 704, the local area code. I ran the number through a 411 reverse-lookup site, but got zip. No name, no address.

I was dialing Slidell when the man himself appeared at my door.

"Yo, doc." Dropping heavily into the chair opposite my desk, feet out, ankles crossed.

"Detective."

"How's it hanging?"

"Did you get my messages?"

Slidell reached out, snatched my tester safety pin from the blotter, and began cleaning a thumbnail. The scritching sound grated like a mosquito whining in the night.

"Didn't tangle with one of those mean-ass desert wolf spiders, did you?"

"Excuse me?"

"Big as golf balls." Slidell stopped excavating to splay his fingers. "Legs spread, they're big as dinner plates. And the little fuckers can jump. Guy told me—"

"Can we discuss my hit-and-run case?"

"Topping my dance card."

"It is?"

"Found our MP." More scritching.

"Cheryl Connelly."

"Ee-yuh. Car went off West Arrowood into a pond in the Moody Lake Office Park. Water barely covered the roof."

"I'm sorry to hear that." I was. Though I was glad Slidell was now free to focus on my Jane Doe. "Did you get my messages?"

"Seventy-two by my count."

"You received the DNA reports?"

"The many loves of Juanita Doe."

"That statement is presumptive and offensive."

Slidell raised a placating palm. "I'm just saying."

I leaned down to rub my ankle, which, for some reason, had begun to throb.

"Hurt your foot over there?"

"I'm fine. What do you know about Creach and Majerick?"

Slidell drew two printouts from an inside jacket pocket and tossed them onto my desk. Then he slumped back and reengaged with the thumb.

I unfolded and laid the papers side by side.

Two faces stared up at me. Mug shots in black and white.

CC Creach had close-set eyes above a nose that had clearly taken more than one hit. His lips were thick and hung partially open. A patch of depigmentation trailed from his right temple to his cheek, a pale footprint in a background of dark, acne-pocked skin. Descriptors said Creach was African-American, seventy-four inches tall, one hundred and eighty-nine pounds.

Ray Earl Majerick stared straight into the lens, smug and self-assured. His curly hair, square jaw, and straight nose made him handsome in a nondescript sort of way. But there was a coldness in the pale eyes, a meanness not tempered by the cocky smirk. Descriptors said Majerick was white, seventy inches tall, one hundred and seventy-five pounds.

"You know them?" I asked.

"I know the type."

"Meaning?"

Slidell leaned forward and jabbed a thumb at Creach. It was bleeding.

"In the way a rat catcher knows his rats. This guy, CJ—"

"CC."

"CC, CJ, PJ, BJ, who gives a flying fuck? Creach is your standard low-life dealer. If the turd has two working brain cells, which I doubt, he can't rub them together to form a thought. But he thinks he's slick, which will make it easy to run him to ground."

"Have you talked to his PO?"

"Not the sharpest knife in the drawer. The address she had for

Creach was a flophouse off Freedom Drive. She hadn't seen him in several months."

"Creach is on parole. Shouldn't he report in regularly?"

"Yes."

"She didn't follow up?"

Slidell shrugged.

"And she'd made no random house calls?"

"The lady said she was real overworked."

Jesus.

"And the other guy?"

"Ray 'Magic' Majerick. Him I do know. Paranoid and mean as a snake, which makes for a dangerous combination."

"What's his history?"

"Considers himself a ladies' man." The scritching halted momentarily, resumed. "He's a charmer, all right. Like Charlie Manson, or Al Bundy."

"Ted."

"What?"

"Never mind. Go on."

"Majerick's jacket's as thick as a phone book. Starts out tame, but turns ugly real quick. Battery. Assault with a deadly, B and E."

Slidell stopped to suck blood from his thumb.

"Could you stop that, please?"

Slidell rolled his eyes, but returned the pin to my desk.

"A few years back, Majerick busts into a home in Beverly Woods, slits the screen on a sliding glass door. Woman of the house is there alone, but gets lucky, manages to trip an alarm. We show up, Majerick's got her hog-tied in the basement. Inside a gym bag we find rope, pliers, and enough knives to start a circus act."

"Sounds like a torture kit."

"Ee-yuh. Ole Magic had a nasty little party planned."

"Why's he not in jail?"

"Suit got him off on straight B and E."

"Are you kidding me?"

"Asshole argued that word on the street was the house had cash in a safe, said the items in Majerick's kit were tools of the trade. Turned out there was a safe in a bedroom closet. The jury bought the story. Majerick served a nickel and walked."

"I assume you're looking for these two." I gestured at the print-outs.

"Issued BOLOs the minute I got the reports." Slidell used the cop term for "be on the lookout." "Checked LSAs, talked to the neighbors. Creach has a couple of sisters, but they knew nothing. Or wouldn't give it up. Couldn't find anyone who'd admit to knowing Majerick. These scumbags probably change addresses more often than I change shorts."

I refused that image entry into my mind.

"So Creach and Majerick are both in the wind."

"Yeah." Slidell raised the thumb to his mouth. Saw my face. Dropped the hand to his lap. "But not for long."

"We may have another lead."

I hit speakerphone and played the woman's message. As Slidell listened, I plucked a tissue and swept the bone-tester-turned-manicure-pin into the trash.

When the message ended, Slidell raised a questioning brow.

"I think it's the same woman who called once before."

"Think she's legit?"

"I do."

Slidell twirled a finger, directing me to play the voicemail again. I did.

When it ended, he said, "Sounds scared shitless."

"Yes. Can you trace the number?" Sliding him the sequence of digits I'd jotted.

Slidell glanced at the paper, unclipped his mobile, and punched a series of buttons. A voice answered. Slidell asked for an extension. Waited. Another voice answered.

"Slidell here. I need a trace." The voice said something. "No. I was hoping for next Thanksgiving."

The voice gave a decidedly clipped reply.

"Yeah? I'll see you get a medal."

"Moron," Slidell mouthed to me. I felt sympathy for the person on the other end of the line.

A full minute passed before the voice sounded again.

Slidell gestured for a pen. I handed him one. He shoulder-cupped the mobile as he wrote.

"Mix-coat-all?"

The voice responded.

"Spell it."

The voice did.

"I owe you one."

The voice had already gone silent.

"Call came from a Mexican joint off Old Pineville Road. Taqueria Mixed Coat All."

"Holy shit."

"Ay, caramba."

I was so jazzed I didn't bother to correct his Spanish. Old Pineville. The place my Jane Doe had died.

I yanked my purse from the drawer and shot to my feet.

"Up for a taco, detective?"

"Sí, señorita."

30

Taquería mixcoatl was located on a grotty little spur coming off Griffin Road, a two-lane winding west from Old Pineville to dead-end at the Charlotte Marriot Executive Park. The restaurant sat between a tattoo parlor and an auto-parts discounter. All three businesses had barred windows and grimy glass through which it was impossible to see.

Slidell swung into the lot and parked two doors down from the taquería. Only three other cars were present: a red Mini Cooper, a gray Lexus, and a jacked-up Chevy pickup with windows as dark as the glass in the shops.

"Mixed Coat All." Slidell was shaking his head at the sign. "What the hell's that supposed to mean?"

"Mixcoatl is the Aztec god of the hunt."

The restaurant was small and smelled of grilled meat. Inside the entrance, to the right, was a board filled with flyers, announcements, and posters, all in Spanish. On the left was a cash register counter. The tables were wood, the chairs high-backed, carved, and painted primary colors.

At midafternoon the place was deserted. Slidell and I held a moment, then seated ourselves by the front window.

In seconds a woman stepped through beads strung from a door-jamb to block the view into the kitchen. She wore a getup that looked vaguely Mexican. Puffy-sleeved white cotton blouse. Brightly colored textile skirt.

"*Buenos días,*" I said.

"Sorry you must wait," the woman replied.

"We're in no hurry." Big smile.

The woman handed us menus. They were laminated and featured pictures of standard Mexican fare.

"I know exactly what I want." I aimed another friendly grin her way. "Chicken enchiladas verdes and a Jarritos lime soda."

The woman nodded.

Slidell ordered a beef burrito and a Dr Pepper. One brow formed a comma as the woman clacked through the beads.

"*Buenos días?*"

"I wanted to get her talking."

"Think she's our gal?"

I gestured "Who knows?"

Thought a moment.

"The call came into my voicemail around one thirty. This place doesn't look like a big operation."

I scanned the restaurant, saw no landline or portable at the register.

"The phone must be in back."

"Meaning employee access only." Slidell got my meaning. Short list of possible callers.

Our food arrived quickly. Though I was friendly as hell, the woman ignored my attempts to engage her in conversation. In either language.

As she withdrew, I tried peering through the beads closing behind her. Caught a glimpse of an old man working the grill. His face looked bronzed by a thousand hours in the sun. A white apron looped his neck and was tied at the small of his back.

As we ate, my gaze drifted to the window, to the parking lot dimly visible on the far side. The Mini was gone, and the Lexus had been replaced by an SUV. The pickup hadn't budged. From this angle I could see what looked like a silhouette behind the wheel.

"—by the tracks you've got the Bronco Club. Can't tell me those ladies don't do double duty."

Slidell was still channeled on the idea that the hit-and-run victim was a hooker.

"There is no evidence the kid was turning tricks."

"Yeah? How about bingo-bingo on the DNA?" Slidell took a slug of his soda, smacked the can down. "I don't have all day. Let's do this thing."

Before I could stop him, he rapped his knuckles on the tabletop to summon the waitress. She appeared and crossed to us.

"How 'bout a check?"

The woman pulled a small tablet from her skirt pocket. As she totaled our bill, Slidell went straight for the kill.

"So, señorita. Made any interesting phone calls lately?"

The woman's eyes rolled up. She looked at Slidell, at me, then placed the check on the table and hurried back to the kitchen.

"That was not smart," I said.

"Yeah? Think she bolted because she ain't the happy dialer?"

"I think she bolted because you frightened her." Whispered, but angry. "Or she didn't understand the question."

"She understood."

"If that's true, I hope your haven't freaked her so much she refuses to talk." I snatched up the bill. "I'll meet you at the car."

I rose and walked to the cash register, hoping for the woman, not the old man. Once Slidell had left, she appeared.

"I apologize for my companion," I said in Spanish.

The woman gazed at me across the barrier of the counter, brows tight to each other over her nose.

Instead of presenting the check, I withdrew a card from my purse and positioned it facing her.

The woman glanced down, then her eyes rose and held mine. And I knew. Slidell was right.

"I'm Dr. Brennan," I said gently. "You phoned me last Friday."

The dark eyes revealed nothing.

"You saw a girl's picture in the paper. Perhaps on a flyer. That girl was hit by a car and left to die on the roadside."

The woman went very still. A vein pulsed in the hollow at the base of her throat, softly lifting and dropping a tiny heart-shaped birthmark.

"We don't know who she is. I think maybe you do."

"No."

"But you know something about her. And it troubles you."

The woman's eyes slid toward the kitchen. So did mine. Through the beads I could see the old man looking at something above what appeared to be a dairy case. Flickering light on his face suggested he was watching a wall-mounted TV.

The woman held out her hand. "Please. You pay."

"The man I am with is a police detective. He traced the call to this restaurant. He can tie you to it." Unlikely, but I knew Slidell was probably getting antsy. "If you have information and refuse to reveal it, he can charge you with obstruction of justice. Do you understand what that is?"

The woman shook her head. As I explained the term in Spanish, her eyes grew wide.

"What's your name?"

"Rosalie." Barely audible.

"Rosalie . . . ?"

"D'Ostillo. Rosalie D'Ostillo. Please. I am legal. I have—"

"I don't care about that, Rosalie."

Again her eyes flicked toward the kitchen.

"Or about anyone else's immigration status. A young girl is dead. It's my job to find out who she is and what happened to her. Every detail is important."

I touched her wrist gently.

"Rosalie . . ."

She yanked her hand free. For a moment I thought she was about to bolt.

"I . . . I make calls. Two."

"You did the right thing."

She allowed the slightest dip of her chin. I didn't push, just allowed her to speak at her own pace.

"I saw her picture. On a pole. I think to myself, Rosalie, you know this girl."

Again I waited.

"She was here. I remember because the"—she touched her hair, miming a clipping motion—"the pink thing."

"A barrette?" I felt a fizz in my chest. "Shaped like a cat?"

"*Sí*. I remember this cat when I see it in the photo. The face look different, but it is this girl who was here. She eat a cheese enchilada. They all do."

"Did the girl also have a pink purse shaped like a cat?" Fighting to keep my voice calm.

"A purse, yes. Pink like hair thing."

"When was this?"

Rosalie's eyes narrowed in thought.

"Dos semanas."

Two weeks. Around the time of Jane Doe's death.

"Did she come here often?"

"No. Just once."

"Was she with someone?"

Slidell chose that moment to stick his head through the door.

"Not getting any younger out here, doc."

"Just a few more minutes." I gave him my squinty-eye look.

Slidell sighed but didn't object. When the door closed, I urged Rosalie to continue.

"Three girls, one man. They eat, they leave. He pay."

"What was the mood?"

Rosalie looked at me, not understanding.

"Did the girls seem happy?"

Rosalie shook her head. *"Nerviosas."*

"Why do you say that?"

"They look at table, not my eye. No smile. No talk."

"Did you speak to them?"

"I say *hola*, they say nothing. I say *buenos días*, they say nothing."

"Did they talk to the man? Did he talk to you?"

"The man order cheese enchiladas. No friendly. *Muy frío.*"

"What did he look like?"

She shook her head. "Hat." She placed both hands level above her brows, like a visor. "I no see good."

"Was he tall, short, fat, skinny?"

She waggled a hand. "Not so tall, not so skinny or fat."

I pulled the mug shots of Creach and Majerick from my purse. Rosalie studied them, slowly shaking her head.

"The hat. And—" She mimed pulling up a collar. "And he no look into my eyes." She shrugged. "No face."

Great. A medium-size guy in a hat. Slidell would love that description.

"Did the man and the girls come by car?"

"Walking."

"Did you see where they went?"

Rosalie nodded. "After they leave I watch. From window."

With another quick glance toward the kitchen, she came around the counter, pushed open the door, and pointed to a storefront half a block up on the opposite side of the street.

"There. They walk there."

"What is it?"

She struggled, then, *"Sala de masaje."*

I had to think about that. Seeing my noncomprehension, Rosalie pantomimed rubbing her neck and shoulders.

"Massage parlor?"

"Yes." Her lips went thin. "Only men. Men go in, men come out. No women. But girls."

"The one with the pink barrette."

"Sí." She let the door swing shut, returned to the counter, and held out a hand. I gave her a twenty.

"May I ask one more question?"

She looked at me.

"Did you give the girl with the barrette a note about St. Vincent de Paul Church?"

"Sí. I think maybe these girls don't talk because they have no English." She shrugged. "Maybe, I think, they talk to Jesus."

"That was very kind."

"They don't say *gracias.* They don't say nothing."

She handed me change, slammed the register drawer, and drew in a breath. I sensed she had something further to say.

"I think those girls is scared. Then one is dead. I have to—" A hand rose to the heart-shaped splotch of brown at her throat. "I call you. Something is bad. Something is wrong."

"You did the right thing, Rosalie. Detective Slidell and I will find out who this poor girl is. Because of you she will go home to her family. And we will discover who hurt her. If other girls are being hurt, we will help them, too."

The door whipped open and two kids slouched through. Each wore an athletic jersey and jeans large enough for a party of four.

"Está abierto?"

"Sí." To me. "I go now."

"You have my number. Please call if you remember anything else or if you see the man in the hat again." I collected the printouts. "Or either of these two men."

Outside, Slidell was leaning against the Taurus.

"This better be good." He yanked open the door and slid behind the wheel.

"Drive past that building." I pointed to the massage parlor, then relayed what Rosalie had said about it.

"So the kid *was* turning tricks."

Was that it? Had Rosalie observed a meal shared by working girls and their pimp? I hated to admit it, but Slidell's theory was starting to have legs.

The massage parlor stood between a tattoo shop and a liquor store. Like its neighbors, the building was dirty-white brick with a glass door and large front window. Unlike its neighbors, every inch of glass was curtained. A small sign identified the place as the Passion Fruit Club.

Slidell and I observed in silence. No one entered or left any of the businesses.

After ten minutes, I said, "We should check the place out."

"Because a waitress disliked the look of the clientele?"

"She did see our Jane Doe enter the place." Testy.

Skinny didn't favor that with a reply.

Slidell was right. Still, it peeved me.

We watched another five minutes, then, without asking, Slidell put the car in gear and turned toward Griffin.

As we drove, I briefed him on everything I'd learned from D'Ostillo.

I'd barely finished when a phrase she'd used triggered a cerebral chain.

No face.

A hat pulled low and a collar raised high.

Who would hide their features?

A person with a disfigured face?

A vet with a disfigured face?

A vet involved in smuggling?

Dom Rockett?

Why would Rockett be in a taquería with a group of young girls?

One of whom now lay dead in our cooler.

31

IT WAS LATE AFTERNOON WHEN SLIDELL DROPPED ME BACK AT THE MCME. My ankle was kicking up, so at five I gathered what correspondence I hadn't gotten through along with my copies of the files on Creach and Majerick and headed home.

Pleasant surprise. Pete had returned Birdie. The cat met me at the door, wound my legs, then positioned himself for the stare-down bit.

Though it was early, I fed him. What the hell? I hadn't seen him in almost two weeks.

I watched the cat eat, then we both went to the study for some quality time on the sofa. I rubbed his ears. He purred. I scratched the base of his spine. He raised his tail and arched his back in approval.

My eyelids grew heavy. I yawned. Swung my feet up and laid my head on the armrest. The cat curled on my chest.

The landline rang. Softly. Too softly.

I rose and got the handset from the desk. Not seated squarely in its charger, the thing was dead.

Cursing, I positioned it properly, trudged up to the bedroom, and brought that handset down. The little screen identified the caller as Pete. Certain he'd try again, I lay back down. Birdie recurled on my chest.

Moments later the ring came again, this time at full volume.

"Mm."

"Welcome home, sugarbritches."

"What do you need?" Groggy. And fighting pulmonary compression caused by fifteen pounds of cat.

"Well, that's a fine thank-you."

"Thank you."

"You are graciously welcome."

"I mean it, Pete. Thanks."

"My pleasure. The little guy's not bad company."

"Mm."

"Are you napping, princess?"

"Jet lag."

"You claim to never get jet lag."

"I never get jet lag."

"Here's something to snap you awake. I just had a call from Hunter Gross. The Article 32 investigating officer has recommended that charges be dropped."

"That's great." Yawning.

"Did you hear what I said? John Gross is going to be cleared."

"I figured the hearing would go his way."

"You don't exactly sound over the moon."

"I'm happy for him."

"Of course, his career's probably in the toilet."

"Really?"

"Hell, what do I know?"

"Gross is one squared-away guy," I said.

"Imagine the stress he was feeling."

Pete was right. On two levels. Yes, I wasn't exactly over the moon. Somehow Gross had rubbed me wrong. Too cocky. Too tightly wound. And, yes, the pressure must have been dreadful. Especially for someone with his psychological makeup.

"Glad I could do my part," I said.

"You know you're famous."

"What?" That got me upright. To Birdie's annoyance.

"Google your name and *Stars and Stripes*."

"The military newspaper?"

"No. Old Glory."

I put Pete on speaker and set the handset on the cushion. Then I dug out and booted my laptop, followed his suggestion, and clicked on the link that came up.

FORENSIC EXPERT TESTIFIES ON BEHALF OF ACCUSED MARINE

The whole story was there. My name, as promised.

Dr. Temperance Brennan, working with NCIS, traveled to Afghanistan and performed dual exhumations and provided key testimony at the Article 32 hearing at Camp Lejeune, North Carolina . . .

I read no further. Two press mentions in a week. So much for keeping a low profile.

I snapped the computer shut.

"Hello-o."

I snatched up the phone. "Is Gross's attorney responsible for this?"

"Weren't journalists present at the hearing?"

"Could have been. There were a couple of spectators." Petulant.

"Come on. You saved the guy's ass. Enjoy the glory."

I rolled my eyes. Wasted, since Pete couldn't see me.

A few beats, then, "Did you leave a PC on my desk?"

"I did. It's acting sluggish, so I'm running a virus check."

"Have you considered the fact that the thing's an antique?"

"I only use it for personal e-mail. All my files are on the firm's system."

"Go crazy, Pete. Buy a new one."

"Maybe."

"Why here? Why can't you run your virus check at home?"

"Summer has every outlet tied up."

"What? She cooking meth?" That image brought a smile to my lips.

"She's charging some kind of weird little lights for the wedding reception. Must be a billion."

"Did you hang out at my place while I was gone?"

"I may have watched a little football."

"Thanks for the provisions."

"My pleasure, buttercup."

"How old is the lasagna?"

"Purchased yesterday. Get some shut-eye. You sound like you need it."

When we disconnected, I checked my e-mail. Nothing from Katy. Nothing from Ryan.

"Of course not." Louder than I'd intended.

Bird raised his head from his paws but said nothing.

The icon on my junk-mail folder showed seventy-four items. I deleted them one by one, expelling pent-up frustration with each irritated jab.

Until a subject line stopped my finger in midair.

You'll die, too, fucking slut.

What caused me to pause? Not the expletives. I'd just deleted several at least as obscene. Die? Die, too?

Ignoring the warning voice in my head, I opened the thing.

Blank.

I checked the delivery date. Yesterday. The *Stars and Stripes* piece had also been posted yesterday.

The e-mail's sender was citizenjustice@hotmail.com.

A political group? A crackpot? A kid with too much Web access and too little parental supervision?

Or was it personal? A threat specifically meant for me?

I had messages from several accounts routed into one central mail program. The e-mail had come through the ME system, not through my personal Gmail account. The address was easily obtainable. It was on my business cards. Hell, I'd posted it on flyers up and down Old Pineville Road and South Boulevard.

Was citizenjustice a disgruntled ex-con? Someone who'd served time because of my testimony? The reverse? A friend or family member unhappy that my findings had contributed to an acquittal? To loss of monetary recovery in a civil suit?

I racked my brain for other possibilities.

A student unhappy with a grade? A neighbor who doesn't like my cat? A psycho stranger I'd passed on the street?

I stared at the crude message. Tell Slidell? Screw it. I didn't need his skepticism. Or, worse, his paternalistic hovering.

It was probably nothing.

I closed the computer, ate the lasagna, took an aspirin for my ankle, and crawled into bed.

Sleep dropped like a curtain at the end of a play.

Sheee-chunk!

My lids flew up.

I listened, unsure if I'd dreamed or actually heard the sound.

Sheee-chunk!

The noise was definitely real. And inside the house.

My pulse kicked into high.

I blinked, urging my eyes to adjust. Held my breath.

I searched the room, alert to the slightest movement. Saw nothing but shadows. Heard only stillness.

The bedside clock read 2:38.

Sheee-chunk!

My pulse jackhammered harder.

The noise was coming from downstairs, a sound like a typewriter carriage slamming home.

I reached for the phone. Damn! I'd left the portable in the study, my iPhone in my purse.

I eased from bed and crept to the door, careful to avoid boards I knew would creak.

Breath suspended, I listened.

No stealthy footsteps. No whisper of fabric brushing a wall. No movement at all.

Something feathery touched my bare calf. I flinched and inhaled sharply. Looked down.

Two round eyes gleamed in the darkness.

I gestured at the cat with a downturned palm. Stay. He slipped through the door as the sound fired again.

Sheee-chunk!

A phrase flashed in my mind. Printed words.

You'll die, too, fucking slut.

Adrenaline shot through my body.

I glanced over my shoulder, searching the room for something to use as a weapon.

The troll from Norway? The LSJML mug? The MacKenzie-Childs vase?

I settled on the bronze of two monkeys holding hands. Heavy. Sharp.

Sculpture clutched in one hand, I inched into the hall. In the dimness, the wall mirror provided a ghostly view of the stairs.

No figure crouched below, knife or gun at the ready.

Birdie was poised on the first riser. Hearing me approach, he rose and started gliding down.

Sheee-chunk!

The cat froze. His tail flicked. Then he shot back up and disappeared into the bathroom.

Barely breathing, I took the treads one by one. My ankle floated little warning twinges.

At the bottom, I stopped to listen again.

Sheee-chunk!

Louder.

Jesus. What the hell was it?

I squinted into the parlor, the dining room beyond.

Seeing nothing alarming, I moved toward the study. The sound seemed to come from that direction.

I pushed open the door.

SHEEE-CHUNK!

My eyes darted, searching for a phone. One handset lay on the sofa. The other stood upright on the desk. The charger's tiny red light cast a patch of radiance across the blotter.

Something flicked in the glow. Flicked again.

My eyes flew to Pete's laptop.

As I watched, the CD tray spit forward, then quickly withdrew.

SHEEE-CHUNK!

What the hell?

I lowered the bronze primate, crossed to the desk, and lifted the top of the Dell to its full open position. On-screen, bright yellow script scrolled across a deep purple background.

PUNKED! PUNKED! PUNKED! PUNKED! PUNKED!

For once, my Luddite ex had been right. His computer had a virus.

I shut down, rebooted, and waited out the whole annoying Windows startup performance. The script was gone. The CD tray stayed put.

"You owe me, big guy," I whispered under my breath.

I was crossing the dining room when movement again caught my attention. A subtle alteration in shadows mottling the carpet. Below the window, on the far side of the table.

I paused. Was the adrenaline rush playing tricks with my brain? The whacked-out computer?

No. Like the sound of the tray, the shadowy ripple was real.

Back to the wall, I slid to the drapes and peeked out.

The night was moonless, the grounds of Sharon Hall dark as a tomb.

But there, below the magnolia. A wink of paleness. A silhouette?

I crouched a full minute, watching. But that was it. I saw nothing more. If I'd seen anything at all.

Sudden thought.

Had I locked up properly? Engaged the alarm? I'd been surprised to see Birdie. Distracted and exhausted, had I forgotten? Wouldn't be the first time. Though I'm conscientious when leaving, I'm often lax about security when at home.

My gaze fell on the files I'd dumped on the table. Creach and Majerick. Both burglars. One a violent offender.

I checked every door and window and set the alarm. As I grabbed a handset from the study, faint but distinct, I heard a car engine turn over.

A little uneasy, I returned to bed.

32

AGAIN MA BELL RANG ME AWAKE. I THINK I WAS SETTING SOME sort of record.

"We bagged Cecil Creach." Slidell sounded almost chirpy.

"Where?"

"Moosehead, over on Montford."

I'd been to the pub, knew the owner had a zero-tolerance policy.

"Creach wasn't dealing in that place," I said.

"Dumbass was drinking and shooting the breeze. With himself. Freaked the other customers, so the bouncer tossed him. Creach sat in the parking lot wailing about the injustice of life. Bouncer called the cops. Creach had a bellyful of booze, but wasn't holding."

"When was this?"

I heard paper rustle.

"Booked in just past one A.M."

If I'd had a nocturnal visitor, it hadn't been Creach. I debated telling Slidell about the previous night's incident. Tell him what? I'd been punked by a PC prankster?

"Did Creach resist?"

A snort from Slidell.

"What now?"

"I let him cook a while, then I sweat him."

"I want to be there."

"Show kicks off in an hour."

"Don't start without me."

Slidell made a noise that might have been agreement.

I fed Birdie, showered, and dressed. One coffee and a dollop of cold lasagna, and I was good to go. Despite the interrupted sleep, I actually felt energized. We were making progress.

I jammed the untouched files into my laptop case, grabbed my purse and keys, and opened the kitchen door.

And stopped.

A box sat on the mat, the kind you use for gifting a sweater or shirt. The top had no label, no printed or written name or address.

There was nothing overtly threatening about the thing. No wires. No sounds from inside. Still, every instinct went on alert.

The shadow play in the night. The movement under the tree.

And something else.

A ruby-brown blossom spread from the box's bottom up and across its left side.

I looked around.

My Mazda was sitting where I'd left it. No car idled curbside or looped the drive. The grounds were empty. Across the street, Myers Park Baptist Church was deserted. A few vehicles waited out the stoplight at Selwyn.

My eyes dropped back to the box. Inhaling deeply, I set down my laptop case and drew gloves from an outer pocket. After pulling them on, I crouched and carefully teased off the lid.

The box contained one single item. Gray-brown and shriveled, it looked like a hunk of mummified meat. The cardboard below it was dark and shiny.

At first I had no idea.

I turned the thing over with a fingertip. Took in detail.

Then comprehension.

Although the day was warm, I felt a chill run my spine.

"Jesus . . ."

I shot to my feet, stomach roiling. My hand flew to my mouth.

"Oh, Jesus . . ."

I swallowed. Swallowed again. Raised my chin and let the cool morning air play over my face. Willed myself calm.

One more check of my surroundings, then I replaced the cover, brought the box into the kitchen, and closed the door.

With a shaking hand, I pulled my iPhone from my purse and punched a speed-dial button.

Slidell picked up on the second ring.

"Where the hell are you?"

"Get over here. Now."

Slidell read the urgency in my voice.

"You okay, doc?"

"Yes. No. Just, please come now. And you may want to notify CSS."

To his credit, Slidell asked no questions.

I locked Birdie in the bedroom then returned to the kitchen. Slidell was at the door in less than twenty minutes. He looked anxious, concerned.

I let him in and showed him what I'd placed on the counter.

"It was on my doorstep this morning." Sounding much calmer than I felt. "I may have caught a glimpse of an intruder around two thirty A.M."

"Did you open it?"

I nodded. Raised my gloved hands.

"What is it?"

Without answering, I removed the lid and stepped aside.

Slidell bellied up to the counter and peered into the box.

"What the fuck?"

Slidell looked away, then quickly back. After a few seconds his brows drew together. "That what I think it is?"

"A tongue."

"Human?" His tone told me he knew the answer.

"Yes. Note the papillae."

"The little bumps that look like nipples."

"Yes."

Slidell ran a hand over his jaw. "Cut looks pretty clean."

"Yes. Though there are abrasions and lacerations probably caused by scraping against the dentition."

"Marks tell you anything?"

"I see curvature. Multiple arcs, so multiple attempts to cut through the flesh. I'm guessing small handheld pruning sheers with curved blades."

Slidell straightened and took a deep breath.

"Vic alive when this happened?"

"Staining on the box suggests significant hemorrhage."

Slidell raised both brows.

"Once the heart stops pumping blood to the vessels, bleeding stops." Greatly oversimplified, but sufficient for Slidell.

"You piss anyone off lately? I mean, more than usual." Slidell was coming back into character.

I shrugged. Who knows? "Do you think it's a threat? A warning?"

Slidell pulled out his mobile and punched some keys.

"Get CSS over here." He provided my address, then frowned at the information he was given. "As quick as you can, then."

Jamming the phone on his belt, he looked at me glumly. "What makes you think this is a threat and not just a windup?"

"Come into the study."

He did, head swiveling left and right.

I booted my laptop and opened the e-mail from citizenjustice@ hotmail.com.

"When did this land?"

"A few days ago."

"And you didn't mention it because . . . ?" There it was. That annoying paternalistic edge.

"I didn't see it until yesterday."

I told him what had happened in the wee hours of the morning. Maybe happened.

"It might have been nothing."

"Or it might have been the asshole delivering your door prize. I'm putting eyes on this place."

"Is surveillance really necessary?"

"Yeah," Slidell snapped. "It's really necessary. In the meantime, don't touch the box. Or the door. Or the mat. Or the stoop."

"I know how CSS works." Snippy. But Slidell's attitude was tripping that switch.

"Whoever did this was either angry or nuts. Which door you want, doc?"

"How about we go talk to Creach?"

Skinny gave me one of his Dirty Harry looks.

"Look, I have to submit a statement." I gestured at the box. "I might as well do it at headquarters."

Slidell pooched out his lips, then sighed.

"*I* talk to Creach." Jabbing at his phone. "You listen."

33

WHEN I FIRST STARTED WORKING FOR THE MCME, THE CHAR-
LOTTE Police Department had not yet merged with its Mecklenburg
County counterpart. CPD headquarters was an unremarkable beige
building at the corner of Fourth and McDowell.

Today the CMPD is located in a four-story Dixie neoclassic at
the intersection of East Trade and Davidson. Ten minutes after
leaving my town house, Slidell and I were walking through the
doors. After presenting ID, we rode an elevator to the second floor.
He led me past a row of interrogation rooms to one marked A.

"Creach is in C." Slidell popped the door. "You watch from here."

The small cubicle held the usual table and chairs, AV setup, and
wall phone. As I sat, the small screen came to life in grainy black-
and-white. Metallic sounds sputtered through the speakers.

CC Creach sat on a metal and gray plastic chair similar to the one
I occupied, elbows on the table, chin resting on his fists. His long
dark hair was pulled into a braid bound by elastic bands spaced
inches apart.

I heard a door open. Creach's head jerked up and spun toward
the sound.

Footsteps, then Slidell came into view. Creach followed his
progress, lower arms upright like long skinny poles, eyes wide and
skittish.

Slidell tossed a file onto the table. It landed with a sharp click.

Creach's hands dropped, allowing a better view of his face. The harsh fluorescent lighting turned the white patch on his cheek a pallid blue.

"Hey, man." Creach flicked a nervous grin. "What's happening?"

Slidell stared down at his subject, silent and unsmiling.

"Guess I got a little worked up." Creach made an odd giggling sound.

Slidell pulled out a chair.

"Dude has no sense of humor. I'll apologize. No harm no foul, right?"

Slidell sat. Opened the file. Slowly sorted and organized the contents.

Creach sat back. Sat forward.

Slidell checked that the AV equipment was on and working.

"This interview will be recorded. For your protection and for mine. Do you have any objection to that?"

Creach shook his head.

Slidell hit a button. "Present at this interview are Detective Erskine Slidell, Charlotte-Mecklenburg Police Department Felony Investigative Bureau/Homicide Unit, and Cecil Converse Creach." Slidell provided the date and time.

As Creach watched nervously, Slidell drew a paper from his stack and pretended to read. I knew what he was doing. And why he'd left Creach waiting so long. He wanted Creach anxious, vulnerable. More likely to make mistakes.

Slidell laid down the paper. "Class is now in session."

"What's that mean?"

"You ever go to school, CC? Maybe ride the special bus?"

"School of hard knocks." Creach giggled in a way that made me think of Jack Nicholson in *Easy Rider*.

"You think this is funny?"

"I thought you was joking. You know, that shit about going to school."

Slidell just stared.

Creach's right foot started pumping, sending one bony knee bouncing like a piston.

"I didn't do nothing."

"That's what we call a double negative, CC. If you didn't do nothing, then you done something. Which is why you're sitting here stinking up my interrogation room."

Some interviewers like to put their subjects at ease, gain their trust, then take advantage. Not Slidell. He believes in going straight for the kill.

"You're on parole, ain't that right?"

Creach nodded.

"A drunk and disorderly violates. Am I right again?"

No reaction.

"You don't cooperate, CC, your skinny black ass is back in the joint. I hear you're a popular guy inside."

Creach's eyes began jumping around the room.

"Look at me, dipshit. You lose focus, I lose patience. You don't want that."

"You got it wrong, man."

"Do I? Let's try this. Passion Fruit Club."

Creach looked genuinely confused.

"Ever get your pipe cleaned at the Passion Fruit?"

"What?"

"You need I should spell it out real slow?"

Creach opened his lips, but said nothing.

"I asked a question, asshole. You get your joystick tuned up at the"—Slidell hooked quotation marks—"massage parlor?"

Creach couldn't sit still. His fingers picked at the table edge. His sneaker went rat-tat-tat on the tile.

Slidell sighed and began gathering his papers.

Creach's hands flew up. "Fine, then. Yeah. I been there."

"When?"

"Couple times. Maybe three."

"When?"

"Like, a date?"

"Yeah, dipshit. Like a date."

"I'm not so good with dates."

"Dig real deep, CC."

Creach's eyes stilled as he thought about his recent timetable.

"A few weeks ago, maybe."

Slidell tipped his head.

"A Monday? Yeah. I remember. Two weeks ago Monday. I was with this guy Zeno. Zeno said they got fresh stuff dancing at the Bronco Club."

I grabbed my iPhone and opened the calendar. Two Mondays back. The day our Jane Doe died.

"What do you mean, 'fresh stuff'?"

"The owner brings new dancers in the first Monday of every month. When we're flush, Zeno and me go to check out the titties."

"How old are these titties?"

"I don't know."

Slidell drilled Creach with a look.

"The ones come those special Mondays, they're young."

"Kids?"

"Look, man. I don't ask their IDs."

"And sometimes these young ladies rock your world."

"No way." Creach's head wagged too fast and too many times. "One of them complained about something, it wasn't me. Or if they's underage or something."

"Uh-huh. Let me guess. You can't afford poontang at the Bronco, so you go down market to the Passion Fruit. What, the chicks a little older there? Maybe got all their molars?"

"No. They's young, too." Creach was too thick to catch Slidell's sarcasm. "I don't like old pussy."

"You're a real discriminating guy, CC."

Slidell sounded as revolted as I felt. After pausing a moment, he pulled a photo of Jane Doe from his assortment and whipped it across the table.

"You know her?"

Creach scratched an ear as he eyed the image. "Yeah."

Slidell's eyes rolled up to the camera.

I held my breath.

"What's her name?"

"Candy."

"Tell me about her."

"You're kidding, right?"

"Dead serious."

"The Passion Fruit's not a place for shooting the shit."

Slidell crossed his arms.

Creach shrugged. "She didn't speak no English, man. None of them did. They talked Spanish or some shit."

Slidell slid Ray Majerick's mug shot across the table.

Creach studied the face but said nothing.

"I'm gonna say something here maybe I shouldn't." Slidell inhaled deeply, exhaled through his nose. "I think you're trying, CC. But so far, it ain't enough. You give me something to work with, I'll do what I can to make the drunk-and-disorderly beef disappear."

"Yeah?"

"Yeah."

Creach tapped the photo. "This guy was always there."

"At the Passion Fruit."

"Yeah."

"He work there?"

"I don't know. Honest to fuck, I don't. The girls called him Magic. Acted scared of the dude."

"Why?"

"No fucking clue."

I hadn't noticed the pumping foot go quiet. Until it started again.

"This shit's all confidential, right? It gets out I talked to you, it's my balls to the wall."

Slidell flipped a pen and tablet across the table. "Write it down."

"I gave it up. Come on. We're talking my ass!"

Slidell was already heading for the door. He turned.

"Do yourself a favor. Calm the fuck down."

"Hey! Wait! What happens to me?"

I met Slidell in the hall.

"What do you think, doc?"

"His story seems to track."

"So we got Candy for our Jane Doe's street name. Maybe Majerick for her pimp."

"You figure Majerick works alone, or as a handler for someone else?"

"Magic's too mean and too crazy to run a string. If that's what we're looking at."

I thought about Creach's words. Young girls arriving every month. Arriving from where? Small towns? Middle-class burbs? Big-city ghettos? By buses? Trains? Vehicles in which they've thumbed free rides?

A revolving carousel of women, moving in young and naïve, then sliding down the ladder to places like the Passion Fruit, addicted, broken, youthful optimism gone forever. It was a dispiriting vision.

Suddenly one of Creach's comments clicked with something D'Ostillo had said.

"Show him Dom Rockett's photo."

"Why?"

"Will you just do it?"

"Why the hell not."

On-screen, I watched the third photo slide across the table, not sure myself what reaction I hoped for.

"Yeah. He was there."

"At the Passion Fruit Club."

"Yeah. Totally freaked the chicks out."

"They were afraid of him?"

"Scared shitless."

"Who is he?"

"Hell if I know."

Slidell placed Rockett's picture beside Majerick's. "Did these men know each other?"

"Same answer."

Slidell flicked impatient fingers.

"Hell if I know," Creach repeated himself.

"Did you ever see them talking to each other?"

Creach shook his head.

The monitor receded. The room around me. Facts were clicking together fast.

Dominick Rockett frequented the Passion Fruit Club. Our Jane Doe worked at the Passion Fruit using the street name Candy. Rosalie D'Ostillo saw Candy and other girls in the Taquería Mixcoatl. The taquería was near the intersection where Candy died. D'Ostillo and Creach thought Candy and the other girls spoke Spanish. Dom Rockett was an importer, probably a smuggler, who made frequent trips to South America.

I heard Slidell's footsteps click the tile in Interrogation Room C. The door open, close.

Creach began whining about his rights. His deal with Slidell. His safety.

The video and sound cut off.

I stood in the musty little space, a cold hollowness filling my chest.

Dear God.

Could that be it?

34

"SUPPOSE THESE GIRLS ARE BEING TRAFFICKED."

Slidell's expression was beyond dubious.

"Human trafficking. Think about it."

We stood outside the homicide unit squad room. Behind us, through a doorway, stretched a labyrinth of dividers, file cabinets, and desks. A few were occupied.

"Creach says the Bronco Club features special dancers every month. Very young girls. You think they're all hitching rides from Iowa and Nebraska?"

"They're strippers. They make a few bucks, they move on."

"And enroll in PhD programs at Yale," I snapped.

"That ain't what I meant."

"Consider this. Who would be well positioned to meet the demand for a constant supply of young women?"

Slidell gave me a skeptical look.

"Dom Rockett," I said.

"Just 'cause the guy smuggles dead dogs don't mean he'd smuggle live people."

I listed the points that had just toggled in my brain. Candy. The Passion Fruit. Spanish. Frequent buying trips to South America.

"And Rockett had cash to invest in S&S Enterprises. Where'd he get it?"

"You're saying he greases his pockets trafficking child sex slaves?"

Easy, Brennan.

"I'm saying we need to consider the possibility that girls are being brought here illegally then forced to work in the sex trade."

"And that Rockett's the doer."

"A number of factors point to him."

"Smuggling dead dogs is one thing. Smuggling kids is a mighty big leap."

"I understand that."

Slidell looked down at the file in his hand. Shifted his feet.

"Majerick I could see, but that kind of operation is above his skill set. Rockett, eh?" He scrunched one side of his face and shook his head.

I had to agree. My impression of Dom Rockett was conflicted. A scarred war hero. A man with no interest in helping ID a hit-and-run victim. I felt pity. I felt revulsion.

"Rockett has the skill set, as you put it. And the infrastructure. The trucks, the supply routes," I said. "Does he have the coldhearted ruthlessness to traffic helpless kids? I don't know."

The callousness to kill if they rebelled? That thought was too terrible to voice.

Two more neurons reached out.

A plastic vial. An antique tusk.

"Holy crap, Slidell. I just thought of something else. Larabee found a sliver of ivory in Candy's scalp."

"What's ivory doing in a hooker's hair?"

"Will you let me finish?"

Slidell looked at his watch.

"When we were in Rockett's house I saw a carved tusk in his living room. The thing looked old."

"And?"

"What do you mean, *and*?" Sharp. "The worldwide ban on ivory has been in effect for over twenty years. Who has the stuff just lying around?"

"I got an ivory marble my granddaddy give me."

"Are you listening to me?"

"Calm down, doc."

"I am calm. Did you know that, other than drugs and guns, human beings are the most smuggled commodity on earth?"

Slidell rubbed his chin.

A phone rang in the squad room behind us.

"I'll write up a warrant. Not saying I'll get one, but we've got Creach's admission the Passion Fruit is a rub and tug. I'll go with that. Once inside, we see what we see."

While Slidell tried to convince a judge to issue a search warrant, I headed back to the MCME to do some research. I learned the following.

A United Nations study put the estimated annual global profit from human trafficking at $31.6 billion. And that figure was a few years out of date. Given the industry's steep growth curve, some were placing the total closer to forty billion.

At any given time, 2.5 million people worldwide are in forced labor as a result of trafficking. One hundred and sixty-one countries are affected, 127 as exporters, 137 as importers. Asian and pan-Pacific countries are the most common source, followed by African, Middle Eastern, and Eastern Bloc nations.

The majority of victims are between eighteen and twenty-four years of age, but roughly 1.2 million children are also trafficked annually.

Trafficked individuals end up in bonded or forced labor, or in sexual servitude. Bonded laborers work to pay off a loan or service, often for years. Forced laborers work against their will, usually in domestic, farm, or sweatshop settings.

Forty-three percent of all trafficking victims end up in involuntary commercial sexual exploitation. Ninety-eight percent are women and girls.

After an hour I sat back, sickened.

Runaways hoping for better lives as nannies, models, or maids. Teens meeting an exciting new date, an exotic stranger, an older man. Kids playing or walking to school, grabbed and thrown into the back of a van. All ending up in an inescapable hell of strip clubs, brothels, and pornographic films.

I squeezed my eyes tight. The heartbreaking images remained.

Children jammed in a pen, hands clutching the wire, eyes begging for help. A girl with bound wrists, face devoid of hope. Young boys on mats in a filthy basement.

I hovered at the edge of a deep well of helpless rage.

An e-mail pinged me back.

I noted the sender. Read the subject line.

Felt needles of ice dance my skin.

You're next, bitch.

citizenjustice@hotmail.com.

"Bring it on, you bastard!"

I opened the vile thing.

A single image filled my screen, a .jpg transmitted as an attachment.

The picture showed a woman lying on her back, a dark puddle on the pavement below her head. The woman's eyes were open and fixed on nothing. Her face was swollen and discolored and streaked with blood.

My breath caught in my throat.

The woman's mouth gaped wide. Too wide.

"Oh, Jesus. Oh, no."

Despite the blood, I could see that the woman's mouth was empty.

I stared, shocked and sickened. Knowing. The woman's tongue had been severed, packaged, and left on my doorstep. Had I met her?

The woman's features were too distorted to allow recognition. If I even knew her.

I ran my gaze down the supine body. The clothing was unremarkable, a jacket, dark pants, sensible shoes.

I worked my way back up.

The jacket was stained with what I assumed to be blood.

My gaze fell on the woman's neck.

One heartbeat. Two. A dozen.

The icy needles burned hotter.

I grabbed my hand lens. Focused.

Saw a heart-shaped mark in the hollow of the woman's throat.

My fist slammed the desk.

Goddammit! Goddammit! Goddammit!

Tears burned the backs of my lids.

I got up. Paced. Furious. Miserable.

Culpable?

When the phone rang I nearly ignored it.

"What!" More expletive than question.

"You okay, doc?" Slidell.

"I . . . Are you near a computer?"

"Can be."

"I'm forwarding a photo to your e-mail."

"Could take a minute."

"Call as soon as you get it." I prayed my voice didn't reveal how gutted I felt.

"I thought you wanted—"

"Do it!"

More pacing.

The phone rang twelve minutes later.

"Citizenjustice. Who is this dickwad?"

I listened to Slidell's breathing, knew he was studying the image.

"It's D'Ostillo," I said.

"The waitress at the Mixcoatl?"

"Yes."

"You sure?"

"See the birthmark on her throat?"

Slidell grunted.

"It's D'Ostillo. She talked to us and was killed."

"Now don't go thinking this is your fault."

"Really? Whose is it? Whose idea was it to go to that restaurant?"

"She's the one called you."

"And for being a good Samaritan she gets her tongue hacked out!"

I was close to tears. And hating it. Especially when talking to Slidell.

Slidell was silent for so long I thought he'd disconnected. Given my rudeness, I wouldn't have blamed him.

"Getting sicker and sicker," he said.

"Whoever did this plays for bigger stakes than one teenage hooker."

"You're thinking Candy and D'Ostillo are connected?"

"You don't? Candy was killed near the taquería. D'Ostillo told us she'd seen Candy in there, said she worked at the Passion Fruit. D'Ostillo's dead, Candy's dead."

"Still liking Rockett?"

"Right now he's topping my list."

"I'll send the e-mail over to cyber crimes, see if they can capture an ISP. Techs can analyze the image. Filter it or enlarge it or whatever the fuck they do. Maybe we can nail the location."

"What are the chances the body's still there?"

Slidell made one of his Slidell noises. Then, "The Passion Fruit belongs to an outfit called SayDo, LLP."

"What?"

He started to repeat. I cut him off.

"Who are the owners?"

"They're not really into talking about themselves."

"Someone's looking into it?"

"As we speak. In the meantime, I got the warrant."

"When do you hit?"

"Tonight. Putting a team together now."

"I want in."

"Yeah, I figured that."

35

THE NIGHT WAS COOL, THE AIR TAINTED WITH THE SMELL OF DIESEL
and at least one peeved skunk. A full moon hung in the eastern sky,
crossed by wispy fingers of black.

"Nice night for a raid."

Slidell spoke from behind the wheel of a police cruiser. A uniformed cop named Rodriguez rode shotgun. I was in back.

Ours was one of four vehicles idling in an industrial lot on Griffin,
a bump north and fifty yards west of the Passion Fruit Club. Three
Chevy Suburbans held three SWAT guys each. Slidell had come
loaded for bear. His words.

My heart hammered inside my Kevlar vest. Slidell's idea. The thing
was bulkier than the IBA I'd worn in Afghanistan. My ankle ached
inside its boot.

Words spit from a radio clipped to Slidell's vest. He looked at
Rodriguez. Rodriguez nodded.

We got out. The others did the same, helmeted figures carrying
AR-15 Bushmasters and Remington 700P .308 sniper rifles equipped
with night vision. Bear.

"Place has two doors." Slidell's face was hard to see in the dark,
but the edge to his voice told me he was amped. "We're going in
pincers-style, Alpha and Charlie through the front, Beta and Delta
through the rear."

"Any weapons inside?"

"Proceed as though the place is an arsenal."

"We know how many are in there?"

"Negatory. You've been briefed on persons of interest. If Ray Majerick or Dominick Rockett is on the premises, bag 'em. By the book. No rough stuff. We don't want some asshole pinstripe arguing brutality."

We returned to our vehicles. Slidell cranked the engine, but not the lights. The armada rolled forward, silent but for the low growl of four motors and the crunch of sixteen tires on gravel.

As planned, two units stopped outside the tattoo parlor. Two others circled the buildings. A single car sat in front of the Passion Fruit.

Slidell cocked his head and pressed the transmit button on his rover. "Team Bravo in advance position?"

"Affirmative."

"Charlie?"

"Affirmative."

"Delta?"

"Affirmative."

"Alpha says green light. Let's boogie."

A million headlamps and cherries lit the night. Our car shot forward, stopped so fast the rear end lurched left. Slidell and Rodriguez fired from their seats.

I opened my door. Slidell pivoted and jabbed a finger in my face.

"Your cheeks stay glued to that seat!"

"Fine!"

That was the deal. Remain in the car or get left behind.

Slidell and Rodriguez crouch-ran forward, Glocks double-gripped and pointed up at the sides of their helmets. Charlie team joined them outside the Passion Fruit, one to either side, one in front of the door.

Slidell spoke into his rover, not so quietly now.

"Go!"

One Charlie guy booted the door. I heard metal bang an inside wall. Glass shatter.

Slidell and Rodriguez steamrolled in. Charlie team followed.

Something boomed. A rear door?

I heard Slidell's muffled bellow.

"Police! Everyone freeze!"

Someone screamed, high and shrill.

Men shouted.

Then nothing.

No bullets. No cries from disgruntled patrons. No shrieks from terrified women.

Seconds passed. A minute. A lifetime.

The quiet was deafening.

"Screw this." I launched myself from the car and ran toward the building.

Through the open door I could see a waiting room with taupe walls, orange plastic chairs, fake ferns, coffee and end tables scarred by cigarette burns.

One of the Charlie guys was there.

"Clear?" I panted, high on adrenaline.

"Yeah." He tipped the barrel of his Remington toward a doorway on the right. "Party's down there."

I followed a corridor toward the back of the building. As in the waiting area, the walls were taupe. Doors ran its length, all painted yellow. Three on the left, three on the right. Every door was open.

I glanced through each as I hurried past.

The rooms had plywood walls that didn't make it to the ceiling. Three were closet size and held only a bed, neatly made, and a straight-back chair. Two had your standard massage-table-and-boom-box setup. All were deserted.

Muffled voices emanated from the sixth room, the last on the right. One belonged to Slidell. The pitch and tenor told me he was barely containing his anger.

I entered.

This room was also cubicle size. It held a desk, a ratty upholstered chair, and an ancient rabbit-eared TV. A door stood open in one corner. Through it I could see stairs descending into gloom.

Another SWAT guy was in the room, Delta team, I think. His eyes followed me from below the rim of his helmet.

I pointed to the stairs.

He nodded.

The basement was dank and dismal. And, to my disgust, showed signs of habitation. Four cots, each with a tattered blanket. A mini-fridge. A hot plate. A sideboard with cabinets above and below. A

KATHY REICHS

table holding a lamp, a mug jammed with pens and pencils, empty ashtrays, a stack of magazines.

A wheeled clothes rack butted up to the sideboard. Every hanger was empty. A door opened onto a bath at the cellar's far end.

Slidell was glaring down at a woman who stood maybe five feet tall. She was returning the glare, clearly not backing off. In one hand she clutched a paper I guessed was the warrant.

Rodriguez was also present. Two more SWAT guys. I assumed the others were positioned outside the building, or checking adjacent properties.

"And you run this dump all by yourself?"

"Someone comes in to clean."

"Where are they, Mrs. Tarzec?" Slidell was looming over the woman. The man is a spectacular loomer.

"I told you. I don't know what you're talking about." Mrs. Tarzec sounded like decades of cigarettes. Her appearance matched her voice. Her hair was thin and fried, her skin sallow and wrinkled due to the diminished blood flow caused by smoking.

"I think you do."

Mrs. Tarzec shrugged.

Slidell's eyes rolled to Rodriguez.

Rodriguez gave an almost imperceptible shake of his head.

Slidell's jaw muscles bulged so large they jostled his helmet strap. "Who dimed you?"

"I have no idea what you're talking about." Slightly accented English. "We do massage therapy. Only massage therapy."

"Yeah?" Slidell made a show of looking around. "Where are the masseurs?" It came out *massers*.

"It's Wednesday. Business is slow. It's costing me more to keep the lights on than I'm taking in, so I gave the girls the night off. Girls. Making the proper term *masseuse*."

"The proper term is whorehouse."

"I love the way you do macho, officer. What are you? Four hundred pounds?"

"With my gun on." Slidell's face was hard, his cheeks the color of claret.

"You seem tense, officer. You might benefit from one of our aromatherapy packages."

« 262 »

"You might benefit from a little time in the box."

Mrs. Tarzec took two steps back, wagged her head slowly, and smiled. Her teeth were yellowed and seemed oddly small for her mouth.

"You going to arrest me?"

Slidell said nothing.

"I didn't think so. Whatever you're looking for, it's not here. Never was. You have nothing. You know it. I know it. So take your piece-of-shit guns and your piece-of-shit vans and get the hell off my premises."

"These masseuses"—pronounced *mass-ooses*—"where do they come from?"

"Licensed massage therapy training programs."

"What's SayDo?"

"Excuse me?"

"The outfit that owns this dump. The people funding your lavish pension."

At that moment a SWAT guy clomped down the stairs, Bushmaster angled toward the ground. I stepped sideways to allow him access to the room. He nodded thanks.

Slidell dragged his eyes from Mrs. Tarzec to look at the man. His deep frown deepened on seeing me.

The SWAT guy shook his head and raised a palm. Nothing.

"Toss it again," Slidell barked.

Mrs. Tarzec's tough exterior showed its first crack. "This is harassment. You can't do this."

"Yeah?" Slidell pointed at the warrant. "That says I can."

Mrs. Tarzec's eyes narrowed. "Can I get my cigarettes?"

"No. You can't." Slidell indicated one of the cots. "Park it."

Mrs. Tarzec sat and crossed both her legs and her arms.

The SWAT guys headed upstairs. In moments I heard boots on the floorboards above. I knew they'd recheck for people, not search for evidence.

Slidell knew that, too, and it was not improving his mood. He slammed through the desk, checking random papers, agitation obvious in his rapid breathing and jerky, heavy-handed movements.

Rodriguez moved to the sideboard and began pulling out ramen noodle packets, canned foods, and boxes of dried macaroni and spaghetti dinners. When each section was empty he knocked on the cheap laminated wood, testing for hollow spaces behind or below.

Slidell dug through the wastebasket. Empty. Pulled the blankets from the cots, the covers from the pillows. Nothing.

He disappeared into the bath. I heard the toilet seat bang, the tank cover scrape, the shower curtain screech across its rod.

Rodriguez opened the refrigerator. Found sodas and condiments, a few packages of cheese. Slidell emerged from the bath.

"You'll find nothing illegal." Mrs. Tarzec's voice now sounded high and stretched. Either nerves or the need for a nicotine hit.

"Good point. No client lists. No bills. No ledgers to square your ass with the IRS." Slidell drilled her a look. "Here's an interesting point. What ain't here can be as incriminating as what is."

"I doubt that."

Slidell strode over to her.

"What's SayDo?"

Mrs. Tarzec shrugged.

"Who you working for?"

"Darth Vader."

"You say you're sucking wind now? Let's see if business picks up with a cop parked on your ass twenty-four seven. Think Darth's gonna cut you a big bonus check?"

"That's what lawyers are for."

Slidell pulled out the picture I'd taken of Candy.

"Know her?"

Mrs. Tarzec glanced at the photo but said nothing.

"The kid's not looking tip-top, lying on a gurney at the morgue and all." Slidell waggled the photo. "Try again."

Mrs. Tarzec uncrossed and recrossed her legs, keeping her eyes averted from the image.

"Yeah. I don't like looking at dead kids either." Slidell's tone went harder than granite. "Last chance. Where did you take them?"

"You're crazy."

"Tell this to Darth. Wherever you turn, I'll be there, day or night. Here on in, I'm your worst nightmare. You're done."

No reaction.

"And here's the part you really won't like."

"Imagine that."

"See you tomorrow." Slidell clicked air through his teeth and winked.

Mrs. Tarzec's foot angled up and her leg started pumping. But she held her tongue.

"We're outta here," Slidell said to Rodriguez.

I got an angry scowl as he pushed past me to climb the stairs.

Rodriguez and I made our way up and out the front door. The SWAT guys were already piling into their SUVs.

Slidell was in the cruiser when Rodriguez and I got in. His anger felt like voltage sparking in the small space.

"Who the bloody fuck tipped them?" Slidell's palm slammed the wheel.

I knew better than to respond. So did Rodriguez.

Slidell swiveled to face me.

"And who the bloody blue fuck cleared you to leave this vehicle?"

"I waited a full—"

"This isn't done." Slidell twisted the key. "I'll get every document ever filed on this joint. Learn every penny ever earned or spent. The last time a fly was swatted or a toilet was flushed."

Rodriguez and I let him vent.

"And no more pussyfooting around with Rockett. That fuckwit's coming back in."

Slidell threw the car into gear and gunned from the lot.

I settled back, knowing my own castigation was far from over. But I understood. Slidell wasn't just frustrated at being outsmarted. Behind the bluster, he was feeling the same guilt he'd warned me to shake. We'd questioned D'Ostillo, and now she was dead.

And Slidell's anger wasn't all bad. An irate Skinny isn't a man you want on your trail.

36

THE NEXT MORNING I SLEPT LATER THAN ON ANY DAY SINCE MY return. Nevertheless, I awoke anxious and restless.

I had coffee and Raisin Bran, then washed my bowl and mug, feeling as though my skin wasn't properly sized. The failure of the Passion Fruit raid. Concern for other girls who might suffer Candy's fate. Frustration at still not knowing Candy's identity. Anticipation of Slidell's ongoing wrath. Guilt over D'Ostillo.

Guilt over avoiding Larabee's crapper skull.

Apprehension because some nutcase put a tongue on my stoop.

The ankle felt pretty good. I decided it was time to try it out.

I phoned the main switchboard at the MCME. Mrs. Flowers answered. I told her I was going for a run and that I'd be in shortly. She asked if I planned to do the Booty Loop. Surprised that she knew of it, I said yes, though I hadn't really decided on routing.

I donned my Nikes and usual spicy jogging attire—bike shorts and an oversized tee. The morning was cool but sunny. In tribute to Mrs. Flowers, I set off for the Booty Loop, a five-mile stretch circling the Queens University campus. Named for, well, that needs no explanation.

I hadn't run in weeks and the first mile was a slog. But the ankle felt strong.

By the second mile, lactic acid burned my leg muscles. I pumped on, determined to finish the circuit.

Sweating and panting, I finally reached the Clock Tower. I was doubled over, breathing hard, when someone called my name.

Straightening, I saw a man slide from a bench and walk toward me. He was tall and thin and wore a Tar Heels cap, jeans, and a black nylon jacket. A plastic bag dangled from one hand.

What the hell?

"I called your office. The woman who answered said I might find you here. She was very helpful with directions." Scott Blanton smiled, revealing the errant incisors. "I hope this isn't a bad time?"

A bad time? I was perspiring, drained, and puzzled. I'd last seen the NCIS agent at Bagram. Why was he lying in wait on my jogging route?

Blanton extended his free hand.

I raised mine high and offered an apologetic grin. "Sweaty."

Blanton scanned me from head to toe. "But looking very fit."

"Thanks." Suddenly conscious of the butt-molding spandex.

"How's the ankle sprain?"

"Completely healed."

"After the exhumation, I got sick as a dog. Was quarantined for two days before they let me come home."

I remembered a detail from one of our DFAC conversations. Blanton was from Gastonia.

"I'm sure your family is glad you're back." Lame. But I had no idea what the guy wanted.

"And I'll bet your cat was glad to see you."

The comment surprised me. Then I remembered that I'd also shared that in the DFAC.

"Yes." I brushed damp hair from my forehead.

Blanton reached into the bag and withdrew a cardboard box. Flat and rectangular.

Like the one that had held D'Ostillo's tongue.

Feeling slightly apprehensive, I checked my surroundings. Students crisscrossed the campus at our backs. Traffic passed on Radcliff, not a steady flow, but enough for comfort.

"For you, doctor." Blanton held out the box. "For being such a trouper."

"I was doing my job."

"Then consider it thanks for putting up with my obnoxious behavior."

I took the box and lifted the cover. Inside was a pashmina similar to those Katy and I had admired at the Bagram bazaar.

Blanton had come to Charlotte and tracked me down to present a two-dollar scarf?

"Your expression says stalker. Either that or you hate the color."

"It's beautiful. Just unexpected."

"I was in the area, thought you might like a memento."

Gastonia was a good forty minutes away. With light traffic.

"Look. I wasn't at my best over there. I was tense. The bugs. Welsted drove me nuts." Rascal smile. "Bygones?"

"Bygones."

Now that I'd stopped running, the breeze felt cold on my damp skin and clothes. I started to shiver. Blanton seemed not to notice.

"What we did was important, whatever the outcome. Sheyn Bagh was a bad situation with no winners. We helped see justice done."

"Have you spoken to Lieutenant Gross?"

"No. But I heard through the grapevine he's itchy to go back downrange." Blanton's look suggested he was trying to bore into my brain. "So how's business? As busy as over there?"

"Mm."

"Bad people doing bad things to other people. Hopefully to other bad people. But that's not always how it goes, is it?"

Blanton leaned close, conspiratorial. He smelled of stale coffee and Old Spice.

"We see it, don't we? Evil. Day in, day out. After a while it screws with your head. How does shit happen to good people? People like John Gross."

I thought it a poor example, but held my tongue.

"I don't know about you, but I've come to believe evil exists in this world. Real, tangible evil. You never know when you're going to wake up and find it sitting on our doorstep."

Blanton gave a self-deprecating grin.

"Listen to me, philosophizing. And look at you. You're freezing."

Blanton lifted the scarf from the box in my hands, unfolded it, and draped it over my shoulders. As he leaned close I noticed a tattoo low on his neck, a Chinese symbol of some sort.

Was I the only person left on the planet without inked skin?

"You take care, Dr. Brennan."

Before I could respond, Blanton turned and headed up the sidewalk. I watched until he vanished around the corner at Selwyn.

Feeling a sense of relief.

Jesus. Why did the guy creep me out so?

Suddenly my ankle didn't feel so great.

I did a slow jog home, showered, ate lunch, then headed to the MCME.

By 4:30 I'd finished with the skull. The unpleasant part was scraping off the caca. The easy part was ruling out foul play. No pun intended.

The skull was that of a young adult male, very possibly of Indian origin. The sutures and dentition gave me age. The bulging brow ridges, prominent nuchal crest, and large mastoid processes gave me gender.

The little screws, intended to hold the mandible in place, told me the skull was a biological supply house specimen. The exportation of real human bone stopped decades ago, but during the period it was legal, most human skeletons came from India. That fact, along with facial architecture, suggested South Asian ancestry.

I wrote a report stating the above. It would be up to Larabee, and, if he pursued it, the CMPD to figure out how the skull ended up in the dumper.

Motivated by my exemplary performance unpacking, jogging, and analyzing the skull, I hit a Harris Teeter on the way home to stock up on provisions. Who says I'm a procrastinator?

It was almost dusk by the time I got to the annex. Birdie darted from the hall closet and twined around my legs.

I picked him up and scratched his chin. He showed keen interest as I stashed my newly acquired rations. I left him wrestling with one of the plastic grocery bags.

I was upstairs stacking toilet paper and soap in the bathroom closet when I thought of the alarm and hurried down to set it. I'd seen a CMPD cruiser circling the drive as I arrived. Slidell's surveillance. Still.

Though I'd never admit it, I was glad the cops were out there. At least periodically. D'Ostillo's murder had my nerves on edge. Not to mention the delivery of her tongue to my house.

And Blanton's unannounced appearance bothered me. Why not

mail the scarf? Why buy it in the first place? That was one weird dude.

What had he said? Wake up and find evil sitting on our doorstep. Was he conveying a veiled threat?

The phone rang.

"Jeez, doc. I been calling for an hour."

"What is it, detective?"

"I brought Tarzec in for questioning. Didn't expect much, and that's what I got. Squat. Had nothing, so I had to kick her."

"What about tax returns, employee documentation, a lease or mortgage on the building?"

"I'm working on it. But I did touch base with the guy at ICE."

"Luther Dew."

"Yeah. What a donkey dick."

"Maybe if you tell him what D'Ostillo said—"

"I'm way ahead of you. I dropped by to share a few pics."

"The photo of D'Ostillo's body?"

"Thought he'd toss his lunch. But he gets it now. This could be about more than dead dogs. He shared some intel he'd just scored."

I waited.

"Rockett's a frequent traveler to the Lone Star State."

"How did Dew learn that?"

"ICE is digging hard. Cell phone records, credit card receipts, the usual."

"Does Rockett drive?"

"Sometimes. But get this. Sometimes he flies there, but not back."

"Where?"

"Houston. Or Phoenix, then on to El Paso."

"Where does he stay?"

"That ain't clear."

"Does he ever cross into Mexico?"

"Border patrol has records of Rockett flying to Guatemala, Ecuador, and Peru. Dew is guessing those are legitimate buying trips. There's no record of him driving from Texas into Mexico."

I started to ask a question. Slidell beat me to it.

"Or from Arizona, New Mexico, or California."

"Do his visits coincide with sales to accounts here?"

"That's just it. They don't. ICE cross-checked dates against invoices."

"Maybe the round-trip drives are to pick up legal shipments. Maybe the one-way flights are for something else."

I didn't need to spell it out. Every American has read about the porosity of our southern border. Two thousand miles, much of it unpatrolled. Most know about undocumented workers trudging through the desert or trying to swim the Rio Grande. We've all heard of coyotes, entrepreneurs who take money to smuggle illegals over-land into the country, sometimes abandoning them to die rather than face arrest.

"I doubt it's that simple," Slidell said. "Remember, Rockett got nailed at Charlotte-Douglas flying shit in."

"Cargo's simple. You pack it, you ship it. People present a much thornier problem. They have to eat, drink, breathe."

For a few beats we both thought about that.

"How's this play? Somehow, Rockett gets girls into Mexico. From South America, Eastern Europe, wherever. Either they got their own passports or he fixes them up with fakes. Maybe he don't even bother. Papers, no papers, he either marches them or trucks them over the border, then drives them east."

"That plays," I said.

"One thing's for sure. Rockett's not traveling to Texas to catch Cowboys games."

"No," I agreed.

More dead air. In the background I could hear phones, figured Slidell was at his desk in the squad room.

"Any luck with Ray Majerick?" I asked.

"Still in the wind. But we'll get him."

"What about citizenjustice? Any leads on that?"

"Shot it to the cyber boys, but they're swamped."

The doorbell rang. My fingers tightened on the handset. I was expecting no one.

The bell rang again.

Again.

"What's that?"

"Someone's here," I told Slidell. "You've got a cruiser outside, right?"

"Once every hour. Best I could do. The department's hamstrung for manpower."

"Stay on the line?"

"Yeah."

The doorbell rang again.

Again, too quickly.

Still clutching the portable, I climbed the stairs and tried to peek through the window overlooking the front steps. The porch light was off. Below the eaves I could make out part of a man's shoulder and leg, scuffed loafers.

"You want I should dispatch a car?" Slidell asked.

I put the phone to my ear.

"Wait."

I ran downstairs, crept to the door, and pressed my eye to the peephole.

"Oh, my God . . ."

"Yo, doc? You okay?"

Shocked, I slid back the deadbolt and opened the door.

37

H<small>IS FACE WAS A HALLOWEEN MASK, EYES SHADOWY RECESSES,</small> cheeks hollow, jaws stubble-dark.

"Talk to me." Slidell's barked demand spit from the phone.

I raised the device to my ear, gaze locked with that of the man on my doorstep.

"I'm fine."

"What the—"

"It's a friend." Level, camouflaging the emotion roiling inside me. "I'm good. Thank you."

I disconnected. Stood frozen, unsure how to play it. Joyful? Angry? Indifferent?

I flipped on the porch light. In the soft yellow glow I could see red spiderwebbing the whites of his eyes.

"You look like hell." Opting for humor.

"Thanks." Ryan's voice sounded gravelly and hoarse.

"Shall I to try to reboot you?"

"Doesn't work."

"Come in."

He didn't move.

"If I leave you out there, you'll run down and terrify the villagers."

Normally, Ryan would have hit me with a snappy retort.

"This a bad time?" No snap.

"I was about to clean lint from the dryer." Keeping it light.

"Fire hazard if you let that go."

I smiled.

Ryan smiled. Sort of.

I stood back.

Ryan reached down and grasped the handle of a draped cube at his feet. As he brushed past me I heard a bell jingle. Scratching. His clothes stank of sweat and cigarette smoke.

I closed the door and turned.

Ryan stood in the center of the room, unsure what to do. He'd lost weight and looked gaunt and haggard.

"He expressed a desire to go south." Pulling the cover from the cage.

Charlie, our shared cockatiel, looked startled. But birds always look startled.

I gestured to the dining room. Ryan set the bird on the table, replaced the cover, then returned to the parlor. I dropped into an armchair and drew my feet up.

Ryan sat on the sofa but didn't lean back. "Place looks good."

"Been a while," I said.

"Yeah."

"I'm glad to see both of you."

Gran's clock ticked off a full thirty seconds. The silence felt strained and awkward.

"How's the birdcat?" Ryan asked.

"Still king of the lab."

Ryan nodded, but didn't call out or search for Birdie as he normally would.

"Coffee?" I asked.

"Sure."

I went to the kitchen. Ryan didn't follow. Cranking up the Krups, I thought of the times we'd shared the task, grinding beans, measuring water, arguing the mix was too strong or too weak. What the hell had happened?

When I returned to the parlor, Ryan was sitting forward, elbows on knees, hands clasped and hanging between them.

He accepted the steaming mug, then turned his head to stare out the window. To stare away from me?

I resumed my place in the armchair, legs tucked beneath my bum. Steeled for the words I was about to hear. The final severance.

At length, Ryan's eyes rolled my way. He set down his untouched coffee. Cleared his throat. Swallowed.

"She's dead."

"Who?" Totally thrown. "Who's dead?"

"Lily." A strangled whisper.

Saying his daughter's name unleashed a torrent of emotions Ryan had been battling to hide. His nostrils blanched and his breathing turned ragged.

A bubble of heat formed in my chest. Tears threatened.

No!

I flew to the sofa, pulled Ryan to me, and held him close. Sobs racked his shoulders. I felt hot dampness on my shirt.

"I'm so sorry," I murmured again and again, feeling helpless in the face of such devastating grief. "I'm so, so sorry."

At length, Ryan tensed. He pushed from me, sat back, and ran his palms down his cheeks.

"Captain America, reporting for duty." He smiled, clearly embarrassed.

"Crying is good, Ryan." I took his hand.

"Man tears."

"Yes."

He drew a deep breath, let it out slowly. "I thought you should know."

"Of course."

Ryan yanked a hanky from a jeans pocket and blew his nose.

"When?" I asked softly.

"Ten days ago."

No wonder he'd returned none of my calls. Remorse overwhelmed me. But with undertones of pain. Why hadn't he reached out for my support?

"What happened?" I asked.

I was certain of the answer. Ryan had shared his daughter's recent history. The drug escalation, culminating in heroin addiction. The dealer boyfriend. The arrest for shoplifting. I was one of the few in whom he'd confided.

The past year, Lily had appeared to be turning a corner. She'd seemed happy, was attending rehab.

What do we really know about others?

"Overdose." Ryan patted a pocket. Remembered where he was. Dropped his hand to his lap.

"It's okay to smoke." It wasn't. I hate the smell, hate what cigarettes do to the carpets and drapes. To people. But Ryan needed a crutch to steady his nerves.

I went to the kitchen for an ashtray, knowing I had none. Returned with a saucer.

Ryan shook a Camel from its pack. As he lit up, I noticed a tremor in his hand.

"Guess we each choose our own poison," he said.

I watched Ryan inhale hard, hold the smoke deep in his lungs, let it out slowly through his nose.

"They found her in an abandoned duplex being used as a shooting gallery."

I'd been to a heroin den once, as part of a team to collect a corpse. I could still picture the horror. Stained mattress. Used needles. Bugs. The reek of urine and feces.

"She was wearing a T-shirt we bought in Honolulu. She loved it, made me memorize the proverb." His voice again sounded husky. "Hele me kahau 'oli."

I reached out and stroked his face.

"Go with joy," he translated.

"You did everything you could, Ryan."

A tear broke free and rolled down his cheek. He backhanded it roughly. Took another drag of his Camel.

"Guess it wasn't enough." Bitter.

What could I say?

When Ryan learned of Lily's existence, she was already in her teens. He'd never cradled her as an infant, never shared her joys or comforted her fears as a child. I knew he regretted his absence from her life. Knew he felt responsible for her addictions. Her death.

Under the law, Lily was an adult. Ryan couldn't tell her how to live or what to do. Still. I could imagine my own sorrow and self-recrimination should something happen to Katy.

Parenting transcends rationality. Always you think you could have done more. Always you blame yourself when things go wrong.

"I should have concentrated more on Lily and less on the job, on strangers who don't even know my name. I should have focused on *her*. My own daughter."

Ryan's pain was a raw wound. There was nothing I could do but listen.

"Funny. The things that come back. Meaningless moments. One night she came into my bedroom to play a song she'd downloaded from iTunes. I remember exactly what it was. Israel Kamakawiwo-ʻole's 'Over the Rainbow/Wonderful World.'"

Ryan's haunted eyes searched my face. "Is that all we had, Tempe? All I ever gave her? One lousy vacation in Hawaii?"

I placed my hand on his. "Of course not."

"Then why is every memory tied to that trip?"

"It's still too soon."

He snorted softly. Shook his head.

"You should stay here," I said. "As long as you like."

"I have to go." He drew deeply, then stubbed out the Camel.

"Now?" Disbelieving.

"I'm sorry." He shot a hand through his unwashed hair. A gesture so familiar it tore my heart.

"Go where?" I asked.

"Away."

I looked a question at him.

"I need to move. Move and keep moving."

"Ryan—"

"I'm sorry." He rose and started for the door.

"Please." Imploring. "Stay."

"I'm not fit to be around people."

"Where are you headed?"

He hesitated. "South."

"You can have the study. I'm busy with a case. You'll hardly see me."

"I can't. I'm sorry."

He read my expression to mean something it wasn't.

"You're right. This was a mistake. I just . . ."

"A mistake?" Masking the anger and hurt.

"I didn't know where else to go."

"Stay, Andy."

"There's nothing you can do. There's nothing anyone can do."
With that, he left.

I hurried to the door and watched him recede into shadow, tears hot on my cheeks.

Halfway down the walk he paused, turned, and slowly walked back toward the porch.

"I'm so sorry."

"I wish you'd let me help."

"You have."

He spread his arms. I ran into them. They closed around me. I molded my body to his.

He hugged me hard. I smelled stale smoke, leather, and a hint of cologne.

As we embraced, headlights curved the drive and lit our bodies. Blinded, I couldn't tell if the car belonged to Slidell's surveillance team.

The vehicle accelerated, blew past us, and turned right onto Queens.

Flashbulb images. A box. A severed tongue. A bloated, bloody face.

Mistaking my sudden stiffness for dismissal, Ryan pulled away.

"I'll miss you." Kissing his fingertips and pressing them to my cheek.

"Don't go." I may have spoken the words, may only have thought them.

Ryan strode down the walk and rounded the corner. A car door slammed. An engine kicked to life.

I shut and bolted the door. Leaned against it, struggling to process. He hadn't asked about Katy. About my travels. I'd been to a war and he didn't give a damn.

In his time of suffering, Ryan had shut me out. The rejection felt like a knife to my heart.

Seriously? The man's daughter is dead and you're miffed he didn't call or query your recent concerns? Have you become that self-centered?

I pushed from the door, ashamed of my pettiness. I had one foot on the stairs when the phone rang.

Excited, I snatched up the handset.

It wasn't Ryan.

"Yo, doc."

"What is it, detective?"

"That sounds as enthused as a dead trout."

"Why are you phoning?"

"Got a shocker for you."

It was.

38

"REMEMBER ARCHER STORY?"

"The younger brother of John-Henry, the man who died in the flea market fire." Maybe. "What about him?"

"Archer and John-Henry were partners in S&S Enterprises."

"Right." Drawn out and ending high. A question. I had no idea where this was going.

"S&S. Story and Story. They owned John-Henry's Tavern, a string of convenience stores, a whack of storage centers, and a bunch of other shit. Nice little money machine. But they were tanking on other investments."

"The Saturn dealerships and the pizzerias."

"You got it. But the bros weren't exactly circling the drain. They'd diversified. And buried their investments in layers and layers of umbrella LPs and LLPs and other legal bullshit."

"What does this have to do with Candy and Rosalie?" Ryan's visit had left me drained. I wanted to curl up and sleep until the pain receded.

No. What I wanted was a drink. Cabernet or pinot noir until euphoria, then oblivion. But I knew how a binge would end. Knew the self-loathing that would follow. I'd been down that road. Wouldn't travel it again.

"Will you let me finish?" Slidell snapped.

My sigh conveyed impatience equal to his.

"Turns out one of these little shelters is SayDo."

That got my attention. "The Passion Fruit Club."

"The Passion Fruit and four other massage joints. Names are real magic. I'll spare you."

"Holy shit." Facts were winging. John-Henry Story. The US Airways club card in Candy's purse. The Passion Fruit.

"Yeah. Holy shit."

"How did we miss that?"

"It took time to untangle the mess. The guy I had working it got diverted to another case. And I got sidelined with the damn MP."

"Now what?"

"Now I figure out how to get to Archer Story."

"Just bring him in."

"I do that, he'll lawyer up tighter than a frog's nuts."

I ignored the metaphor. "You can't even question him?"

"Based on what? He owns skin joints and we think maybe the personnel director offed one of the hookers?"

"What about a nasty habit called human trafficking?" I felt like screaming.

"The raid turned up dick."

"Of course it did. Someone tipped Tarzec, so she moved the girls and sanitized the place."

Silence.

"Will you at least check out the other massage parlors?"

"I got nothing to get a warrant. And, needless to say, my credibility took a nosedive after the fiasco at the Passion Fruit."

"Jesus, Slidell. These people killed Candy. And D'Ostillo. They'll kill again if they feel threatened. These girls mean nothing to them."

Slidell was silent a moment.

"There's a SayDo joint up in NoDa. I'll swing by tonight. Unofficial like."

"Keep me looped in."

"If it makes you any happier, I dropped in on Rockett for a little more face time."

Slidell didn't seize the opportunity for humor on that. Good sign.

"And?"

"He told me I could suck his dick."

When we'd disconnected, I went upstairs for a long, hot bath. And realized I still hadn't seen Birdie. I'd been distracted by Slidell's call. Then Ryan showed up. Then Slidell phoned again.

Had the scamp slipped through the open door while Ryan and I were on the sidewalk? Stupid not closing it. He loves to sneak out, I suspect mainly to get my attention. I always find him in the shrubbery, within inches of the foundation.

Cursing, I trudged back downstairs and out the front door. Called his name. No cat.

I circled the building, my annoyance increasing each time my summoning went unanswered. Eventually, I expanded my search onto the grounds.

After fifteen minutes, I gave up. Told myself to relax. He'd done this before. He'd come home when hungry.

The bath was a bust. I lay in bubbles up to my chin, sadness and worry foreclosing any relaxation.

Lily, dying before her twentieth birthday.

Ryan, excluding me in his time of sorrow. Forever?

Katy, fighting in Afghanistan.

Pete, marrying a bimbo with a boob size exceeding her IQ.

D'Ostillo, trying to do right, getting murdered and mutilated.

Candy, perishing on a two-lane, alone and terrified.

How had Candy ended up on that dark stretch of road? Was she trafficked? Lured by someone she trusted? Stolen and caged like stock?

What fate awaited her had she lived? To be brutalized, her body a commodity exploited until its value was gone? What then?

Were others out there suffering the same hell?

My mind was in overdrive. I had to do something to squelch the terrible thoughts and images ping-ponging in my skull.

I got out, dried off, and pulled on sweats. Yanked my hair into a pony and headed downstairs.

I shouted through both the front and kitchen doors. Shook a bag of his favorite treats. Still no Birdie. My annoyance was joined by a tickle of apprehension. Why?

Ping.

Blanton had mentioned my cat. He'd been waiting just a block from the annex.

Paranoia, Brennan.

I brewed coffee, went to the study closet, and pulled out a large erasable board I use for structuring lectures. Then I got Scotch tape and a marker from the desk.

After propping the board on the mantel in the parlor, I collected every picture I'd accumulated over the past two and a half weeks. Snapshots, crime-scene photos, Polaroids, printouts, mug shots.

I started by taping up a picture of Candy, the hit-and-run victim whose real name we still didn't know. Beside it I placed one of the snapshots I'd liberated from John-Henry's Tavern. Pictured was John-Henry Story, the man whose US Airways club card Candy had inside her purse lining.

Using the marker, I drew a line between Candy and John-Henry.

Next I posted the second "borrowed" snapshot, Dominick Rockett at the tavern with John-Henry Story. Rockett, the smuggler who traveled to South America and made mysterious trips to Texas. Rockett, customer or maybe more than a customer at the Passion Fruit Club, owned by John-Henry and his brother, Archer, via SayDo. And employer of Candy.

I drew lines connecting Candy and Rockett, Rockett and John-Henry Story.

After jotting the name Passion Fruit on the right side of the board, I drew lines connecting the massage parlor to Candy, Rockett, and John-Henry.

Next in the lineup went the mug shot of CC Creach. Creach's semen was found on Candy. Creach was a patron of the Passion Fruit, and said Candy and the other girls were afraid of Rockett. And of Ray Majerick, who was often there.

I added Majerick to the row. Majerick's semen was also found on Candy. Majerick had a history as a sexual predator.

I drew lines between Candy and Creach, Candy and Majerick, Majerick and Creach, Majerick and Rockett, Majerick and John-Henry Story. Then between both Creach and Majerick and the words "Passion Fruit."

I paused to consider.

Majerick had been seen at the Passion Fruit and had sex with Candy. Did that mean he knew John-Henry Story? I erased parts of that line, converting it to a dotted connector.

The last photo to go up was Rosalie D'Ostillo. My stomach still tightened on seeing the hideous mutilation.

D'Ostillo saw Candy at the Mixcoatl. The taquería was located close to the Passion Fruit. Like Creach, D'Ostillo thought Candy and the other girls spoke Spanish. D'Ostillo was murdered within hours of talking to me. Her tongue was left on my doorstep.

I drew a line from D'Ostillo to Candy, a dotted link to the words "Passion Fruit."

Then I stepped back and surveyed my work.

The board showed a maze of interconnections. Which ones were meaningful? Which were spurious? Was Candy's killer one of the men whose pictures I'd posted? Was I staring at his face right now?

How did the lines link up?

I moved my eyes from photo to photo.

Candy, lying on her morgue gurney. How did John-Henry Story's US Airways club card end up in her purse? How did semen from Creach and Majerick end up on her skin? Turning tricks? Voluntary sex? Rape?

Dom Rockett and John-Henry Story sharing a beer. The two were partners in S&S. How had Rockett acquired the money to invest? Aware of his illegal trafficking in antiquities, did Story approach Rockett about doing the same with humans? Rockett was a smuggler, knew the routes, the cops and agents who could be bribed, the border-crossing points most easily breached.

Or had it gone the other way? Had Rockett proposed a money-making scheme to John-Henry, knowing Story had the infrastructure to make it work?

I thought of something. Jotted the identifier citizenjustice on the left side of the board.

The bearer of that name had sent threatening e-mails to me. Had that same person murdered D'Ostillo and delivered her tongue as a warning?

I stared at D'Ostillo's ravaged face. Wondered. Who was the man in the hat and upturned collar she'd served in the taquería? Rockett was only a best guess.

Ray Majerick? Someone of whom we were unaware? A male counterpart to Mrs. Tarzec?

I jotted Mrs. Tarzec's name and drew lines to Candy, John-Henry, and the words "Passion Fruit."

I squeezed my eyes shut. Pinched the bridge of my nose.

A tiny itch in my brain kept pestering. Asking to be scratched.
What was I missing?

The lines were crisscrossing like an Etch A Sketch pattern gone wrong. What threads were important? What intersections?

Clearly the Passion Fruit. A lot of lines converged there. Candy. Creach. Majerick. Story. Rockett. D'Ostillo. Tarzec.

Ditto for Candy. Every line led to her.

Still the itch.

What was the subliminal memory I couldn't call up? What hidden data byte dozed in my id?

I stared at the crazy quilt of photos, names, and lines, willing the answer to make itself known. Stared at Candy's bloodless face, frustrated, desperate to fulfill my promise to her.

What was eluding me?

Rockett. Why did he make trips to Texas and come back empty? Or did he?

John-Henry Story. Why was his lounge card in Candy's purse? Was Story really dead?

Discouraged, I got a hand lens from the study and started moving from picture to picture.

Candy, face bruised and fractured. Blond hair bound by the little-girl barrette.

No. No tears.

I sipped some coffee, now tepid, checked on Charlie, then turned back to the photos.

Story and Rockett at John-Henry's Tavern, neither man smiling. Story rodent-lean. Rockett's mangled features shadowed by a hat pulled down to his brows.

I moved the lens across the snapshot, taking in details.

A brass rail paralleled the right edge of the bar, a strip of brightness lighting the curvature of its surface.

"Camera flash," I muttered to no one.

Beyond the table, a jukebox. On the wall above, three or four decals, none larger than a man's palm.

No, not decals. Military patches. I hadn't noticed them on my visit with Slidell. The patches were similar to the ones I'd seen at the Green Bean at Bagram.

Was that the heads-up my hindbrain was offering?

I raised and lowered the lens, trying to make out unit totems or names. The image quality was too poor. Tomorrow I'd take the photo to the MCME and view it under higher power with the dissecting scope.

My eyes continued tracking across the magnified image.

Suddenly stopped.

I nearly dropped the glass.

The photo's upper left corner caught a section of the old mirror in the main eating area. The glass was angled, not flush with the wall. I guessed it hung by a horizontal wire placed a bit too low.

The mirror reflected a ten-foot bubble of space in front of the table at which Rockett and Story were seated. In it stood a man, arms raised, elbows flexed, face largely obscured by a small box camera and the sunburst of its flash.

The man's body was visible from the neck down. He was in jeans and a dark T-shirt. And had a tattoo I'd seen before.

I felt adrenaline start to seep into my blood.

All my theories skidded sideways.

39

Impossible.

Yet there he was.

Coincidence?

I don't believe in coincidence.

But how did he work it?

Didn't matter.

I retrieved a brown corrugated file from the study, emptied the contents onto the dining room table, and began reading every page.

It didn't take long.

How had I missed it?

Oblivious to the possibility.

Careless?

Sudden realization. Another possibility overlooked?

I went to the parlor, took Candy's photo from the lineup, and studied it again under magnification.

The dusky skin. The dark-rooted blond hair.

Rosalie D'Ostillo spoke Spanish to the girls but got no response. Fear of their handler? Or another explanation?

My mind was on fire now, spitting data forgotten since the time it was stored.

I raced upstairs and snatched a photo from the bureau. Sat on the bed. Placed the bureau photo on my knees beside the morgue shot of Candy. Looked from one to the other, forcing the lens steady in my hand.

Holy shit.

I flipped the bureau photo. Read the handwritten list on the back.

Holy free-flying shit.

I grabbed the phone and dialed.

Got Slidell's voicemail.

"Jesus H. Christ!"

My eyes flew to the clock. 10:40. Slidell was probably at the massage parlor in NoDa.

I left a message. Call me ASAP. It's urgent.

I disconnected. Tossed the handset onto the bed. Got up and paced.

Everyone carries a mobile. Why couldn't Slidell keep his turned on?

10:45.

Come on. Come on.

More pacing.

10:50.

Keep busy.

I double-stepped down the stairs and made myself more coffee, knowing caffeine was the last thing I needed. To keep my mind occupied, I returned to the papers covering the dining room table.

Verified.

Thought about the implications.

Of course. That had to be it.

11:05.

Where the hell was Slidell?

I ran to the study. Punched speed dial on that handset.

"'Lo." Pete sounded groggy.

"It's Tempe."

"Yes." Pete yawned. "I know that."

"I need a favor."

A woman spoke in the background, words also sleepy thick.

"You're up late. Partying?"

"Does it sound like there's a party here?" I snapped.

"Whoa. Bad day?"

"I have a question for you."

"Bring it on."

I asked.

"Maria . . . no, Marianna. Mariette? No, definitely Marianna."

"What was her maiden name?"

"Is it important to know this now?"

"Yes."

"Hold on."

I heard bed linens swish. A whiny protest from Summer. Then the ambient sound changed, as though Pete had moved to another room.

In moments I had my answer.

"Thanks, Pete. I have to . . ."

"You okay? You sound strange."

"I'm fine. I've got to go. Thanks."

11:10.

I disconnected and called Slidell again. Left the same message.

It all made sense. Terrible, improbable sense.

I returned to the lineup on the mantel. Stared at the photo from John-Henry's Tavern. At the man hidden by the camera flash.

"You vile sonofabitch," I whispered under my breath.

But now what? It was nearing midnight.

Wait to hear from Slidell? Wait until morning?

Other girls were in danger. I knew it in my gut. If they weren't dead already. Like Candy.

Or had they been taken to another town, another state? To disappear forever into the pipeline.

No. They were still in Charlotte. I was certain.

A million places to hold girls prisoner.

Two million to bury their bodies.

Slidell had talked to Rockett, to Tarzec. These animals knew the knot was tightening. And had zero respect for human life.

If alive, would the girls survive to see daylight?

Where the hell was Slidell?

Where the hell was Birdie?

I dashed outside for another look. Another round of shouting. No cat.

I pictured e-mails. Citizenjustice. A tongue in a box.

An icy hand clutched my chest.

Had these bastards taken my cat?

I slammed inside. Paced the parlor, frantic what to do.

Breathe.

Breathe.

To keep from going crazy, I opened the bright yellow file lying on the desk in the study.

I began with the crime-scene shots. A lonely road. A vinyl boot. A pathetic little mound under a red wool blanket.

I moved to the autopsy photos. X-rays showing a fractured chin and crushed hand. White cotton panties with pale blue dots. A shoulder, bruised in a pattern of dashes.

The last half dozen photos were new to me. Larabee or Hawkins had taken the close-ups from different angles. They showed a skull peeled bare of its face and hair. A blood-coated object shaped like a long, slender triangle.

I stared at the sliver Larabee had removed from Candy's scalp.

Ivory, not bone.

How had Candy ended up with ivory in her head?

I'd seen a carved tusk in Dominick Rockett's home. Did ivory often pass through his hands?

I got my laptop and Googled the phrase "ivory uses."

Statuary, carvings, decorative embellishments, billiard balls, bathroom handles, piano keys, signature seals, radar and airplane guidance components.

Useless.

I decided to try another tack.

Where had Candy been seen? The Taquería Mixcoatl. The Passion Fruit Club. The Yum-Tum convenience store. They all clustered in a fairly tight radius not far from the Rountree–Old Pineville intersection where her body had been found.

Were the missing girls being held in that area?

I clicked over to Google Maps and zoomed in on the Passion Fruit. Around it spread a warren of roofs and empty lots.

The roofs varied in size and shape but revealed nothing of what lay below them. Most properties were fenced. Some fences were topped with razor wire.

Pausing the cursor generated labels on a few of the buildings. A storage facility. A warehouse. The Bronco Club.

It was the kind of district that exists in most cities. A place where things are manufactured, stashed, or left to rust.

Had the girls been taken to a location somewhere in that maze?

Frustrated, I returned to the file.

Gran's clock ticked softly as I worked through the pages.

Ten minutes later, I heard a soft noise, like scratching. Elated, I flew to the front door. No feline sat on the porch.

I tried the kitchen door. Empty stoop.

I was on the patio, calling Bird's name, when headlights swept the drive. Seconds later, a cruiser passed. I waved. The cop waved. Dejected, and frightened for my cat, I went back inside.

The amber light on the landline was flashing.

Sonofabitch!

Slidell's message was short. The massage parlor in NoDa was closed and padlocked. That was it. Nothing else.

I hit redial. Got his goddamn voicemail.

Dismayed and exhausted, I forced myself to read the last printout in the yellow file. An FBI report.

I was skimming through jargon about solvents and binders and pigments and additives when I remembered something Slidell had said.

Methyl this and hydrofluoro that.

Hydrofluorocarbons?

I took a closer look at the list of components found in the smear on Candy's purse.

Difluoroethane.

The dispatcher in my subconscious sat up and took notice.

Sudden flash. Pete on the phone in his Beemer. Summer, fixing up antique bottles for the tables at her wedding.

Difluoroethane.

In vehicular paint?

I Googled the term. Pulled out the relevant and dismissed the background noise.

. . . propellant necessary . . . initially chlorofluorocarbons, banned in 1978 . . . propane and butane abandoned in the '80s . . . since 2011, hydrofluorocarbons such as difluoroethane and tetrafluoroethane . . .

My pulse kicked up a notch.

I closed my eyes. Saw a building. A NO TRESPASSING sign in the rain.

Facts toggled.

Images cascaded.

My lids flew open.

I shot to my feet. Raced for the phone.

Again, my call rolled to Slidell's voicemail.

Mother of God!

"I know where the trafficked girls have been taken. I'm going there." I left the address and disconnected.

Adrenaline pounding, I grabbed a jacket, shoved a flashlight into one pocket, snatched up keys, and bolted for my car.

40

I PEERED THROUGH RUSTY CHAIN LINKING. A FINGERNAIL MOON crisscrossed by pewter tendrils revealed the scene beyond the fence in charcoal and black.

The warehouse loomed dark and menacing. Though shadowed, I recognized the loading dock and its motley collection of rusty kegs, rickety table, and defaced piano.

A truck was parked at the base of the dock.

At my back, across the street, the small bungalow brooded silent and empty.

Stepping gingerly, I worked my way around the perimeter of the property, searching for an opening in the fence. It didn't take long. Opposite the building's south side, the chain linking had been cut and bent inward.

Thanking the vagrants so disparaged by Slidell, I slipped through the breach. Six feet inside, a rusted sign kinked up from the ground on bent metal legs. Carefully shielding the bulb with my palm, I thumbed on my flashlight.

The sign announced the coming of thirty-six luxury lofts. I crouched behind it to listen.

The night was alive with sound. Leaves skittering across gravel-coated concrete. The muted whistle of a distant train. My own terrified breathing.

No one shouted at me to show myself or get lost.

I didn't really have a plan. In a fever to rescue the girls, I'd simply raced here.

I stared at the building. It stared back, yielding none of its secrets.

My breath caught. Had a shadow crossed one of the upper-floor windows? I studied the broken, dirt-caked glass. Detected no movement.

Ten yards of concrete yawned between the fence and the building. Here and there a puddle gleamed darkly iridescent. Rocks and objects of indeterminate function dotted the expanse. Nothing big enough to provide cover.

I waited out a count of thirty, then fired forward.

Reaching the murky dimness below the dock, I pressed my back to the brick and listened again.

Dripping water. The cooing of startled pigeons.

I eyeballed the pickup, a Chevy with deeply tinted windows. Like the one I'd seen outside the Mixcoatl.

Citizenjustice? The man who'd left a severed tongue at my home? Was he here? Had he been at the taquería, watching? Already planning D'Ostillo's murder?

I tiptoed up the rusty metal stairs. A door stood open at the far end of the dock. I crossed to it and slipped inside.

The smell hit me like a roundhouse punch. Stagnant water, urine, mold, pigeon droppings.

I desperately wanted to relight the flash. Decided it was too risky until I'd established who was present.

Heart yammering, I crept forward. Liquid sloshed beneath my sneakers. Between the pooled water, bird shit crunched.

Slowly, my pupils adjusted. I took in details made visible by patchy moonlight oozing through gaps in the windows high above.

The warehouse was cavernous. One brick wall was scorched with long black serpentine tongues. One was painted with graffiti. A bird, an Egyptian ankh, the words WORTH THE WAIT on a bright pink heart.

I looked up. Nests lined the rafters, some topped by billed silhouettes. I sensed a thousand avian eyes on my back.

Something rustled by my right foot. Claws skittered.

I fought the impulse to scream. Imagined more eyes, beady and red. Yellowed teeth and long naked tails.

Palms slick, I moved deeper into the gloom. Dust coated my tongue. Or atomized guano. I swallowed, immediately regretted it.

I'd gone maybe thirty feet when an unmistakable sound touched my ears.

I froze.

The first footfall was followed by another.

From above? Behind? Outside? Echoes distorted the soft scraping, making it impossible to pinpoint the source.

Blood racing, I ducked into a recess and dropped to a squat, praying the shadows were thick enough to conceal me.

I strained for the faintest indication of a human presence. Heard nothing but intermittent cooing.

Time passed. How much? Enough for my pulse to slow somewhat.

I started to get to my feet. My knees buckled from lack of circulation. I pitched forward.

My hands impacted something firm yet yielding, molded hardness beneath.

Fingertip memories triggered an image.

I jumped back in horror.

The man sat propped against a wall, head angled toward but not touching his left shoulder. One shoe was off, and a tube sock winked white in the gloom.

Between the tuque on his head and the darkness in the alcove, I couldn't make out the man's features.

But I could make out that he was no threat.

Blood trickled from below the hat to pool in the recess of his right eye. As I stared, a drop broke free from the bridge of his nose.

Pulse galloping anew, I took a shaky step closer. A Beretta 9mm lay beside the man's hip. Still, I couldn't see his face clearly.

A few inches more and, with trembling fingers, I Braille-read the man's features. Rutted oatmeal channels. Rubbery smooth bands. A bulging brow. A mangled nostril.

Cognitive liftoff.

My hand recoiled in shock.

Without thinking, I plucked the man's cap from his head and shined my light on his face.

Dom Rockett's good eye stared into a future he would never enjoy. Blood snaked from a hole above his right temple.

I felt, what? Pity? Anger? Yeah, anger. I'd wanted Rockett alive to face justice. Fear? Yeah, a boatload of fear.

Mostly, I felt confusion.

Before I could ponder the implications of Rockett's death, another footstep snapped my head up. I killed the beam and dove deeper into the alcove.

Other footsteps followed. Grew louder.

Heart pounding, I crawled toward the brick angling down to form the edge of the recess. Craned out.

More footfalls. Then boots appeared at the top of the stairs, beside them a pair of small feet, one bare, the other in a platform pump.

The feet started to descend, the small ones wobbly, their owner somehow impaired. The lower legs angled oddly, suggesting the knees bore little weight.

Anger burned hot in my chest. The woman was drugged. The bastard was dragging her.

Four treads lower, the man and woman crossed an arrow of moonlight. Not a woman, a girl. Her hair was long, her arms and legs refugee thin. I could see a triangle of white tee below the man's chin. A pistol grip jutting from his waistband.

The pair again passed into darkness. Their tightly pressed bodies formed a two-headed black silhouette.

Stepping from the bottom tread, the man started muscling the girl toward the loading-dock door, pushing her with a one-handed neck hold. She stumbled. He yanked her up. Her head flopped like a Bobblehead doll's.

The girl took a few more staggering steps. Then her chin lifted and her body bucked. A cry broke the stillness.

The man's free arm shot out. The silhouette recongealed. I heard a scream of pain, then the girl pitched forward onto the concrete.

The man dropped to one knee. His elbow pumped as he pummeled the inert little body.

"Fight me, you little bitch?"

The man punched and punched until his breath grew ragged.

Rage flamed white-hot in my brain, overriding any instinct for personal safety.

I scuttled over and grabbed the gun. Checked the safety, thankful for the practice I'd put in at the range.

Satisfied, I reached for my phone. It wasn't with the flashlight.

I searched my other pocket. No phone.

Had I dropped it? In my frenzied dash, had I left it at home?

The panic was almost overwhelming. I was off the grid. What to do?

A tiny voice advised caution. Remain hidden. Wait. Slidell knows where you are.

"You are so dead." The voice boomed, cruel and malicious.

I whipped around.

The man was wrenching the girl up by her hair.

Holding the Beretta two-handed in front of me, I darted from the alcove. The man froze at the sound of movement. I stopped five yards from him. Using a pillar for cover, I spread my feet and leveled the barrel.

"Let her go." My shout reverberated off brick and concrete.

The man maintained his grasp on the girl's hair. His back was to me.

"Hands up."

The man let go and straightened. His palms rose to the level of his ears.

"Turn around."

As the man rotated, another fragment of light caught him. For a second I saw his face with total clarity.

The face in the mug shot.

Ray Majerick.

On spotting his foe, Majerick's hands dipped slightly. Sensing he could see me better than I could see him, I squeezed further behind the pillar.

"The fucking slut lives."

You'll die, too, fucking slut.

"Lose the gun."

Majerick didn't move.

"Now!" I racked back the slide on the Beretta.

Majerick pulled the gun from his waistband and tossed it. I heard it hit somewhere near the loading-dock door.

"Takes balls to send threats by e-mail." My voice sounded much more confident than I felt. "To bully defenseless little girls."

"Debt to pay? You know the rules."

"Your debt-collecting days are over, you sick sonofabitch."

"Says who?"

"Says a dozen cops racing here now."

Majerick cupped an upraised hand to one ear. "I don't hear no sirens."

"Move away from the girl," I ordered.

He took a token step.

"Move," I snarled. Majerick's fuck-you attitude was making me want to smash the Beretta across his skull.

"Or what? You're gonna shoot me?"

"Yeah." Cold steel. "I'm gonna shoot you."

Would I? I'd never fired at a human being.

Where the hell was Slidell? I knew my bluff was being sustained by coffee and adrenaline. Knew both would eventually wear off.

The girl groaned.

In that split second I lost the advantage that might have allowed Majerick to live.

I looked down.

He lunged.

Fresh adrenaline blasted through me.

I raised the gun.

Majerick closed in.

I sited on the white triangle.

Fired.

The explosion echoed brutally loud. The concussion knocked my hands up, but I held position.

Majerick dropped.

In the dimness I saw the triangle go dark. Knew crimson was spreading across it. A perfect hit. The Triangle of Death.

Silence, but for my own rasping breath.

Then my higher centers caught up with my brain stem.

I'd killed a man.

My hands shook. Bile filled my throat.

I swallowed. Steadied the gun and stole forward.

The girl lay motionless. I squatted and placed trembling fingers on her throat. Felt a pulse, faint but steady.

I swiveled. Gazed at Majerick's mute, malevolent eyes. Did nothing.

Suddenly I was exhausted. Revolted by what I'd just done.

I wondered. In my state, could I make good decisions? Carry through? My phone was back at the house.

I wanted to sit, hold my head in my hands, and let the tears flow.

Instead I drew a few steadying breaths, rose, and crossed what seemed a thousand miles of darkness. Climbed the stairs on rubbery legs.

A single passage cut right at the top. I followed it to the only closed door.

Gun tight in one clammy hand, I reached out and turned the knob with the other.

The door swung in.

I stared into pure horror.

41

THE SCENE STILL HAUNTS ME. WILL THE REST OF MY LIFE.

The room held four girls. Their hair was tangled and dirty. One wore only a long dirty sweatshirt. The others weren't dressed like pastors' wives.

Each had an ankle shackled to a pipe running the length of one wall. One was sitting with her arms up, wrists bound by a zip tie looping an overhead pipe. Her head hung between her upraised shoulders, snarled hair hiding her face.

Three pairs of empty handcuffs dangled from the lower pipe. A discarded zip tie lay below.

A half dozen filthy blankets were scattered across the floor. A bucket of urine and feces overflowed in one corner. The smell was unbelievable.

The girls stared at me with the same eyes I'd seen in online images. Blank, devoid of hope. Perhaps high on heroin.

I felt bile rise again. Fought it down.

"It's all right," I whispered. "I won't hurt you."

The zip-tied girl raised her head. Otherwise, no one moved or spoke.

What to do? I couldn't leave to call the cops. The girls might be taken while I was gone. I couldn't chance that.

Stupid! Stupid! How had I forgotten my phone?

As I stood, undecided, one of the girls whispered to another. I didn't understand the words, but the cadence seemed familiar.

I was about to speak again when the hum of a car engine froze my lips. I darted down the hall, rose on my toes, and peeked over a windowsill.

The glass was frosted and coated with grime. All I could see were twin beams slashing the darkness below.

The engine cut off. The headlights. A door slammed. Boots rattled up the rusted loading-dock steps.

Shit! Shit! Shit!

I raced back up the hall, slipped into the room, and signaled to the girls with an index finger over my lips. They stared. Not understanding? Too numb to react?

Heart rate in the stratosphere, I pressed my back to the wall, gun barrel up and as steady as I could keep it. Mind racing. I'd used one bullet. Had Rockett fired? How many remained in the chamber?

Boots sloshed and crunched across the warehouse floor. Stopped abruptly.

"What the fuck? Ray?"

A moment, then the footsteps charged upstairs.

My finger tightened on the trigger.

The footsteps hurried toward the door, paused, then, to my shock, retreated. I held my breath. Were they moving back down the stairs?

Silence enveloped the warehouse.

Thinking back, I still have no sense of how long I waited.

Pigeons cooed.

My heart thumped.

The car engine did not start up.

Was he gone? Checking Majerick? The girl? Calling in backup?

I had to do something.

I pictured the targets at the Bagram range. Conjured an image of the Triangle of Death.

Palms tight on the grip, I peeked around the door frame.

The blow knocked me sideways. My head cracked brick. My vision swam as my ass hit the floor.

A boot stomped hard on my hand. As pain shot up my arm, my wrist was viciously hyperextended. Something popped. The gun jerked from my fingers.

I screamed and lashed out with a foot. Connected. Heard the gun hit, then skitter. An echoing clink marked its impact with the floor below.

Scrabbling on all fours, I circled to the top of the stairs. Either my opponent was armed or he wasn't. I had no choice. Bent low, I pelted down, taking two treads at a time.

My pursuer thundered behind.

I ran past Majerick, out the door, and down the loading-dock steps. The Chevy pickup had been joined by a Porsche 911.

I cut left past the vehicles and fired toward the breach in the fence, my pursuer close on my heels.

I almost made it.

Two yards from the developer's sign, a hand clamped down on my shoulder. I twisted and raked my nails over the skin. Saw parallel trails darken the word RIPPER.

The clamp relaxed a micron. I tore free, lurched forward, and ducked behind the sign.

The man shook the injured hand, clutched a gun in the other.

I hunkered low, pulse throbbing in my temples, my throat, my chest. Why didn't he pull the trigger?

Then I heard a click.

No bullet pinged metal. Or tore through my flesh.

Another click. Still nothing.

Cursing, the man pocketed his weapon and started toward me.

I bolted for the fence. He was on me with breathtaking speed.

We went down and rolled. Scrap metal and rock jabbed my belly and ribs. Oily water splashed my face and soaked my clothing. Our frantic breathing obliterated all other sound.

Knowing nothing of hand-to-hand combat, I thrashed wildly, stoked on adrenaline and driven by panic.

A miracle. I broke free and began to scrabble toward the opening.

A hand clawed my foot. As my body jerked backward over the ground, my fingers closed on a rusty metal object. The thing was long and cylindrical, I guessed a section of pipe.

With a visceral snarl, I pivoted my torso and swung like a batter going for the upper deck.

And hit a homer.

The force of the impact dropped my attacker to his knees. His hands flew to his head.

I clambered to my feet, pipe gripped so tightly rust particles showered my arms.

My enemy's face stood out pale in the moonlight. It didn't surprise me.

"It's over, lieutenant."

Gross looked up, eyes unfocused, expression equidistant between rage and pain.

But I was in a bind. If I went through the fence, he would be gone, maybe first dispatching the girls. Could I hold him at bay? I had to. Had to stall. Had to keep the bastard there until Slidell arrived. Whack him again? No, that could be murder!

"You had me fooled." Between panting breaths.

Gross swayed on his knees, but said nothing.

"How's it work?" I asked. "You buy the girls then fly them stateside using fake passports? Or do you skip the niceties and just ship them like cargo?"

Still no response.

"Semper fi, eh, John-Henry?"

Gross's chin cocked up in surprise. His hands detached from his temples, slowly drifted down.

"The middle initial 'H' on the Article 32 charge sheet. Didn't take a genius to tie you to Uncle John-Henry. You two should make his sister proud. She's your mother, right? Marianna Story Gross?" I had Pete to thank for that puzzle piece.

"Leave my mother out of this." Slurred.

I rolled on, desperate for the sound of sirens.

"How's it feel to dishonor the Corps?" Images flashed in my brain. Tattoos. Badges. "And Ripper. I assume you and Rockett hooked up during Desert Storm. Was the scheme his idea?"

"Rockett couldn't scheme his way off a toilet seat." Still woolly, but stronger.

"Was Rockett about to blow the whistle on his old task-force buddy? That why he had to go?"

Gross's shoulders hitched. For a moment I thought he might laugh.

"What was Candy's sin? She try to escape? Threaten to talk? Pain in the ass, so just run her down? Was Majerick your muscle on that one, too?"

"Aren't you the fucking hotshot. Got all the answers."

I kept talking, and, though my wrist was on fire, tightened my grip on the pipe.

KATHY REICHS

"That why you killed the kid at Sheyn Bagh?"

"Collateral damage."

"Aqsaee came at you, all right. But not as an insurgent. He wanted to confront you about Ara. That's what he yelled, right? Ara, not Allah. I guess Eggers's hearing it wrong helped you with your story."

"Eggers is a jackass."

"Aqsaee identified you as the man who stole Ara. He would have told the village elders."

Remembering the Polaroid in my backpack, my loathing burned more fiercely.

"Why Ara? Why not Khandan or Mahtab or Laila or Taahira? Or were they in the crosshairs, too, you miserable sonofabitch?"

"Girls have shit going for them over there." Cold now. Controlled. I again tightened my grip.

"And you were going to make the world their dance floor."

Gross brought one knee up and planted his foot. Swayed. Steadied himself.

I raised the pipe. "One move and I bash in your skull."

Our eyes locked. Gone was any trace of the falsely accused war hero. Before me was a calculating predator.

Several beats, then Gross made his move. Too slow, too obvious. I read it and sidestepped his kick. Thrown off balance, Gross stumbled, then spun to face me.

I raised the pipe, ready to swing harder than I've ever swung in my life. But my action was also signaled. Gross lifted his forearms to parry the blow.

I checked my motion, dropped the pipe low, and brought it up in his crotch with all the power I could muster.

Gross doubled over.

Giving me time.

I hammered his shins. His kneecaps.

Gross dropped and curled fetal.

I stepped close and raised the pipe over his head.

My heart pounded. My breath wheezed in jagged gulps.

A thin wail penetrated the pandemonium in my ears and chest.

I stood, weapon poised, muscles flexed.

The wailing separated into sirens.

« 304 »

Reason overrode primal fury.

Or maybe I knew help was at hand.

I did not bring the pipe down.

Shortly, cruisers screamed up to the fence. Doors slammed. Lights pulsed red and blue on the house of horror at my back.

EPILOGUE

October is schizophrenic in Charlotte. One day you're in shirtsleeves. The next you're pulling on jacket and gloves.

The cold arrived on Sunday. It was a bitch bringing plants inside one-handed.

Monday I decided to build a fire. After much clumsy choreography, flames danced behind the antique brass screen shielding the hearth. The parlor smelled faintly of smoke and pine.

I'd done my duty in the wee hours of Friday morning. Seated in the back of a cruiser, I'd answered a barrage of questions from Slidell, a few from reporters who'd caught word via police-band receivers. I'd even given Allison Stallings a heads-up.

I'd seen Gross and his victims placed aboard ambulances. Heard Slidell contact headquarters to ensure that the girls were met by interpreters and SANE nurses. Watched Majerick and Rockett loaded into an ME van. Then, at Slidell's insistence, I'd accepted a ride to the emergency department at CMC.

Thanks to Skinny's phone bluster, I was treated immediately. X-rays revealed a broken scaphoid and a linear fracture of the distal radial border in my right wrist. The ED doc was astounded at my tale of hefting a pipe. I went home in a thumb spica splint the size of a mallet.

Perhaps he knew the strength of the painkillers I'd been issued. Perhaps he was busy grilling Story and Gross. Slidell gave me the weekend before coming to visit. Bearing a floral arrangement the size of an offshore rig.

In the intervening days Slidell had learned the following.

The bullet Larabee dug from Rockett's brain was fired from Majerick's gun. So were the two dug from his gut, and one dug from the brick behind him.

The bullet in Majerick needed no explanation. I would not be charged. The shoot had been ruled self-defense, and extremely lucky.

Luck was with me twice, actually. Once when I pulled the trigger. Once when Gross did. He'd scooped up Majerick's gun while chasing me from the warehouse. The magazine wasn't full when Majerick arrived. He'd emptied it while shooting Rockett.

Raids on the other SayDo massage parlors had turned up eleven more girls, all Afghan. Those from the NoDa operation were found in the basement of a closed beauty parlor, in conditions similar to those at the South End warehouse.

None of the girls spoke English. None had a legitimate visa or passport. Their ages appeared to range from thirteen to seventeen. All were now in the custody of ICE.

The girl Majerick was beating when I surprised him was named Huma. Little Bird. She came from a village not far from Sheyn Bagh. Huma had contusions, abrasions, and a broken nose, but was doing well.

Archer Story had been arrested and charged with conspiracy to commit murder as to both Ara and Rosalie D'Ostillo, with maintaining establishments for prostitution, and with promoting the prostitution of minors. He was also charged with multiple counts of human trafficking.

John-Henry Gross was charged with all of those offenses, plus attempted murder as to me.

The madams of all four establishments were charged with participating in the prostitution of minors and with human trafficking.

North Carolina statutes state that an individual commits the offense of human trafficking by knowingly recruiting, enticing, harboring, transporting, providing, or obtaining by any means a person to be held in involuntary or sexual servitude.

If the person is a minor, that constitutes a class C felony. At forty years per offense times at least sixteen victims, the defendants were looking at 640 years just on the trafficking counts. No wonder they were all scrambling to make deals. Story and the madams were singing like canaries on crack.

Story was claiming ignorance of any knowledge of trafficking or prostitution. His lawyers were proposing full cooperation in return for a sentence not to exceed fifteen years. Mrs. Tarzec and the other madams were offering guilty pleas in exchange for maximum sentences of eight years.

Gross's attorney had approached the DA about a plea to reduced charges. The DA wasn't biting.

"Will any of the girls testify?" I asked.

Slidell snorted. "They're so freaked they won't even raise their eyeballs when I'm talking to them."

"But Majerick is dead and Gross is behind bars."

"The pigfucks kept them cowed by threatening harm to their families. Majerick made the rounds with your morgue shot of Ara and Majerick's pic of D'Ostillo. Said if anyone tried to run or slack off they'd get the same."

"Majerick was citizenjustice?"

"Ee-yuh. Smarmy little bastard was watching from a truck outside the taquería. He dimed Gross to report that D'Ostillo was talking to us. Gross ordered her taken out in a way that would impress."

"D'Ostillo saw Majerick with Ara and the other girls."

Slidell nodded glumly.

"More coffee?"

"You able to pour with that sledgehammer you got for a mitt?"

"Funny. Three sugars, right?"

I went to the kitchen, returned, and handed Slidell his refill.

"Did that bird just tell me to kiss its ass?"

Charlie was raised in a brothel, rescued by Ryan, and gifted to me following the raid. His was not your standard "pretty bird" repertoire. I didn't feel up to explaining that to Slidell.

"Why kill Ara?" I asked, resuming my seat.

"Majerick was driving her to the joint in NoDa. The version he gave Story was that she jumped from the truck. Archer was shocked when he learned about the accident. After the fact, of course."

"Of course."

"Majerick was violent and had a hair-trigger temper. When the kid rebelled, he probably lost it and ran her down."

I pictured an imp in a group of six, holding mischievous fingers above her friend's head. Knew it was true. Knew Ara had possessed the spirit to resist.

"And the monster just left her there."

"Majerick told Story there was too much traffic to collect the body without being seen. And no chance he'd take her to a hospital, anyway."

I recalled the empty stretch on which Ara had died. Felt tears start to form. Slidell's question brought me back from the brink.

"How'd you finger Gross for the doer? He was never on our radar."

"His tattoo."

Slidell's brows floated up in question.

"I saw it at the Article 32 hearing at Camp Lejeune. But only part of the lower half, below his cuff, so I got it wrong. I thought it said RIP, meaning rest in peace."

"No better friend, no worse enemy."

It surprised me that Slidell knew a Corps slogan.

"Except Gross is a disgrace to the military," I said.

"Fuckin' A. He ain't what marines are about."

I wondered if Slidell had history with the Corps unknown to me. Was sure I wouldn't ask.

"Anyway, I saw the tattoo again in the tavern snapshot of John-Henry Story and Dom Rockett, but it didn't register. The image was reflected in a mirror, so everything was reversed. When I was going over photos Thursday night, it suddenly clicked. I'd seen the Task Force Ripper patch hanging in Rockett's living room. RIP. Ripper. Gross was the guy shooting the pic. That connected him to Rockett and Story."

"I hear you."

"I checked the Article 32 charge sheet, saw that Gross's middle initial was H. Henry. Then I confirmed that his mother was born Marianna Story. John-Henry Gross was the nephew of John-Henry and Archer Story. After that, it all started tumbling.

"Gross was on his fourth deployment to Afghanistan. I compared the photo I'd found in my backpack to the one I'd taken of the hit-and-run victim. Our Jane Doe's hair had been bleached, but it was definitely the same kid. Also in the shot was Khandan, the girl who spoke to me at Bagram. When I looked carefully, I could identify a distinct rock formation behind the village of Sheyn Bagh."

"The place you dug up the bones."

"Yes. That's when it all made terrible sense. The man I had helped at Camp Lejeune had in fact murdered Aqsaee and Rasekh. Aqsaee had seen Gross take Ara away. When Aqsaee recognized Gross at the cordon-and-knock he ran toward him yelling 'Ara,' not 'Allah.' Gross panicked and used the firefight to gun him down. Rasekh as well."

"You think this kid Khandan slipped the Polaroid into your backpack?"

I nodded. "Shortly after she approached me we spent time sitting side by side in a bunker."

"Who snapped it?"

"We may never know that."

"How'd Khandan come to have it?"

"No idea. But she must have treasured that photo. She'd put the thing in a plastic sleeve."

I was about to ask a question when Slidell beat me to it.

"How'd Ara come to have John-Henry Story's US Airways club card?"

"Has Archer commented on his brother's involvement with the massage parlors?"

"He claims to know shit." Dripping with disgust. "But Mrs. Tarzec said John-Henry had been a regular customer."

"Maybe John-Henry dropped the card. Maybe Ara lifted it from him. For whatever reason, she kept it."

"Good thing. That hunk of plastic was our first leg up."

For a beat we both gnawed on that. Then, "You sure Story died in that fire?"

"Larabee reviewed the entire file," I said. "He still feels confident about the ID."

For several moments we watched orange tendrils twist and curl behind the filigreed brass. Charlie used the interlude to squawk one of his favorites.

"I want your sex!"

Slidell's eyes stayed on the flames. I felt compelled to explain.

"It's a line from an old George Michael song."

"Tell me this." Slidell looked my way. "How'd you know to go to that warehouse?"

"An inspired guess, really. Larabee found a sliver of ivory embedded in Ara's scalp. Not many uses of ivory these days, but it was once common on piano keys. Impact against a keyboard explained the patterned injury on Ara's shoulder."

Slidell hitched his shoulders. And?

"The FBI report listed difluoroethane among the ingredients in the smear on Ara's purse. Difluoroethane is a propellant added to aerosol paints."

Again the shoulders.

"The warehouse across from John-Henry's Tavern was supposed to be converted into lofts, but the project never went forward. So it was empty. The day we talked to Sam Poland, I saw an old piano on the loading dock."

"Spray-painted with graffiti." Slidell snapped a finger and pointed it at me. "Not bad, doc. And by the way, that's the last time you go swanning off after one of your hunches without me. I'm the detective. You're the anthropologist."

"Noted."

Slidell nodded sharply, as though he'd scored a point.

"Ara must have been at the warehouse the night she died," I continued. "As Majerick tried to force her into his truck, she probably struggled, and her head and shoulder struck the piano."

My mind flashed an image of the Huma-Majerick silhouette wrestling in the dark. Another of a hatted corpse.

"Rockett was never part of the trafficking, was he?" I asked.

"Dew's getting the whole story, but it looks that way."

"Why did he lie about knowing John-Henry?"

"The guy was a dick, but he probably suspected something. He was a customer at the Passion Fruit, must have noticed that the girls didn't speak English. He had to wonder where they came from."

Slidell slipped the faux Ray-Bans onto his nose.

"We're gonna need you to write all this up." He gestured at my cast. "When you're good."

I smiled and lifted both hands. "No problem. I'm amphibious."

Either Slidell missed the reference to the Charles Shackelford amphibious-ambidextrous gaffe, or he didn't get the humor. I let him out with a promise to e-mail a statement.

When Slidell had gone, a shocking realization struck.

Dirty Harry hadn't once chastised, ridiculed, or laughed at me.

An hour later, Dew showed up. He was wearing a black suit, blue tie, and eye-blistering white shirt. Still no fedora.

Dew and I assumed the same chair and sofa positions as dur-

ing my visit with Slidell. Unlike Skinny, Dew sat ramrod straight
with heels together, enormous hands cupping enormous knees. He
declined my offer of coffee or tea.

Dew had the following to report.

Early in his second deployment, John-Henry Gross hooked up
with a French private security contract worker named Jean Pruet.
Pruet had spent six years in Afghanistan, and, over that period,
deposited almost $2 million in a Swiss account. Pruet was returning
to Europe, and, for a fee, rolled his network over to Gross.

The scheme was far from original. But it was lucrative.

Central to the operation was an Afghan national named Maroof
Hayel, the man I'd seen reprimanding Khandan the day she
approached me at the Bagram shops. Hayel was Khandan's father
and Ara's uncle.

Hayel recruited young girls by promising them, or their parents,
jobs in the United States. He drew mostly from the slums of Kabul,
Charikar, and Jalalabad, but also from villages in the surrounding
provinces.

Hayel was paid $200 for each girl he delivered. A Photoshop whiz
kid in Kabul supplied false passports and visas at $40 a pop. The
girls were escorted from Khwaja Rawash Airport in Kabul to Wash-
ington Dulles by an Afghan woman named Reja Hamidi. Each ticket
cost around $1,600.

The girls were met by Mrs. Tarzec or one of her counterparts
and driven to various locations in North Carolina. John-Henry Story
paid his nephew $50,000 for each "employee" supplied, no ques-
tions asked.

"Counting round-trip tickets for Hamidi, Gross's outlay was less
than five thousand dollars per girl." I couldn't keep the loathing from
my voice. "Placing his profit at roughly forty-five thousand dollars
per transaction."

"Yes. Pruet had made approximately the same sending them to
France."

"Sweet Jesus. How could someone sell his own flesh and blood?"

"In Ara's case, it was 'her.'"

"Sorry?" I didn't get Dew's meaning.

"Ara's mother turned her over to Hayel."

"She sold her own daughter?"

The snowy cotton stretched, eased as Dew inhaled then exhaled slowly.

"Ara's mother is a woman named Gulpari. At age seven Gulpari saw her mother raped by Taliban fighters. When Gulpari's father tried to intervene, the men shot him.

"Following the rape, the dishonored widow was shunned. With no prospects for remarriage, she kept her daughters, Gulpari and Noushin, clothed and fed by begging and performing menial tasks.

"At fourteen, Noushin was sent to marry a man in a neighboring village. The man's family worked the girl sixteen hours per day and forced her to sleep in their unheated barn. When Noushin was caught trying to escape, her husband and father-in-law held her down and doused her with acid. Two days later, Noushin managed to return to her mother's house. She died of infection resulting from her burns. Gulpari was twelve."

Dew stared at his hands as he continued.

"Gulpari was raped by the Taliban at age fifteen. Like her mother, she was spurned by the village and treated with scorn. Ara was born on Gulpari's sixteenth birthday."

"Gulpari wanted a better life for Ara." Barely trusting my voice.

Dew nodded, still looking down. "When Hayel talked of jobs in America, Gulpari believed him. He was her brother. Why would he lie?"

"Hayel sold Ara to Gross."

"For two hundred dollars."

I got up to stir the embers. Pointless, but I needed to move. To divert the anger and grief threatening to overwhelm me.

"After John-Henry died, did Archer continue with business as usual?" When I'd returned to my chair.

Dew cleared his throat. Twice. Met my eyes.

"Of the sixteen girls currently in ICE custody, two were brought into the country after Archer assumed management of the various Story enterprises, including SayDo."

"How does he explain that?"

"Mr. Story claims to know nothing of his employees' histories. And he vehemently denies any knowledge of prostitution at his establishments, forced or otherwise."

"You buy that?"

The pink-lemonade face darkened. "I believe the government's star witness is being less than forthcoming. But, thanks to you, our investigation has shifted focus. We *will* learn more. Much more."

"What about Dominick Rockett?"

Dew was quiet a moment, probably deciding what best to say.

"The mummified dogs will be returned to Peru. Mr. Rockett's files have been confiscated to check for information on other illegally trafficked antiquities."

"Dom Rockett never smuggled human beings." I'd given that question a whole lot of thought.

"It seems not."

"Rockett met John-Henry Story through his nephew?"

"Mr. Rockett and Lieutenant Gross served together in Desert Storm. Perhaps out of pity, perhaps at his nephew's urging, John-Henry hired the disfigured vet. Rockett was compensated in part with shares in the company. At least that's the version Archer Story gives."

"What did Rockett do for S&S?"

"Whatever needed doing. Driving. Security. Hiring contractors and workers for maintenance and repair. Rockett also sold articles at S&S flea markets, items legally imported from South America."

"Rockett had no involvement with SayDo?"

"It looks that way."

"But CC Creach saw him at the Passion Fruit."

Dew raised both palms, dropped them back to his knees. "Due to his condition, Mr. Rockett enjoyed limited access to women."

Delicately put.

"Why did Rockett make the trips to Texas?" I asked.

"He was assisting Story in the closing of his car dealerships. John-Henry was selling off inventory, and, occasionally, delivery was required. Rockett would fly to Texas and drive cars wherever they needed to go."

"What was Rockett doing at the warehouse last Thursday?"

"According to Mrs. Tarzec, he showed up at the Passion Fruit that evening very agitated and wanting to look around. She told him no one was there. He demanded the truth about the girls, said he knew they were trafficked because the cops had told him. Then he asked where they'd been taken. When threatened at gunpoint, Mrs.

Tarzec revealed the location. After Rockett stormed off, she phoned Majerick."

"Rockett went looking for Gross. Or maybe he just planned to free the girls. Either way, he'd had enough. He died trying to undo at least some of the evil."

"I believe you are correct."

"What will happen to the girls now?"

"That must be worked out. If they are deported back to Afghanistan, there is an NGO-run shelter in Kabul for victims of trafficking."

"Will Ara's body be returned to Sheyn Bagh for burial?"

"If funds allow."

"I'm happy to help if money is an issue."

A sad promise kept.

"Your offer is very generous, Dr. Brennan. I'll do all in my power to assure that is not necessary."

Dew smiled sadly.

"We accomplish what we can. But, worldwide, human trafficking generates billions of dollars annually. Think of this. A gram of cocaine or heroin can be sold only once. A human being can generate income for years. Did you know that North Carolina is the eighth most likely state in the U.S. for trafficking to take place?"

"At least the problem is gaining attention."

"Yes. It is. But the picture is still bleak. In December of 2012, the United Nations Office on Drugs and Crime published a global report on trafficking in persons. Almost one third of all trafficking victims are children. Two thirds are girls."

Dew rose to his feet with Baryshnikov grace.

"On a more positive note, one hundred and fifty-four governments have now ratified the UNDOC Trafficking in Persons Protocol, and eighty-three percent of countries now have a law that criminalizes trafficking in persons that is in accordance with the protocol."

Dew really did speak as though reading aloud.

"Including the U.S.," I said.

"Yes. United States Code Title 18, Section 1591 stipulates severe penalties for anyone involved in human trafficking, and, as you no doubt know, North Carolina also has very strong laws. The difficulty comes in catching the traffickers because victims are so powerless and afraid."

"It's a start," I said.

"It's a start," Dew agreed.

Wishing me a speedy recovery, Dew departed.

That evening it was Pete. His ninety-pound fruit basket had arrived on Saturday, so he came bearing Chinese takeout and at least one of everything sold at Dean and DeLuca.

As I watched him stock my pantry and fridge, I wondered why Summer was elsewhere. Didn't ask.

While Pete opened little white cartons, I set two places at the table. Then we helped ourselves to brown rice, seafood lo mein, cashew chicken, and eggplant in garlic sauce.

Way to go, Pete. My Baoding favorites.

Over dinner, we discussed Katy, Majerick, Rockett, the Story brothers, D'Ostillo, Ara, and her mother. And of course John-Henry Gross.

"I'm sorry I dragged you into the whole mess, sugarbritches."

"Don't be."

"It seems impossible that Hunter has a nephew capable of such cruelty. He's such an ethical person."

"John's behavior is no reflection on Hunter."

A few beats passed. When Pete spoke his voice was taut.

"John Gross dishonored his oath. And shamed the Corps."

"Gross was an aberration. He shamed himself, not the Corps. When Eggers made accusations, the Corps played it by the book, did Gross no favors. The command investigated and prosecuted in an honest and forthright manner."

Pete's jaw tensed, but he didn't disagree.

"I mean it. The Marine Corps dealt with Gross's actions in Sheyn Bagh in a straightforward way. As did I in looking at the bones of his victims. Eventually Gross's involvement in trafficking would have come to light. And the same impartial process would have kicked into gear."

"Hopefully with better results."

"Ironic, isn't it?"

Pete tipped his head.

"Rockett and Gross. The man who seemed a monster was the one with a conscience. The man who seemed a patriot warrior had venom in his veins."

We talked about Katy. About the fact that the military had reversed its traditional stance and was now opening frontline combat positions to women.

Seeing I found the subject less than calming, Pete changed tack.

"So this troll Blanton was actually harmless?"

"Just one weird dude."

"What was Blanton's beef with Welsted?"

"Just didn't like each other."

"What's with the cockatiel?"

"He's visiting."

"Where's the birdcat?"

"Holler 'lo mein.' He'll be here in the flick of a whisker."

Thursday night, I'd closed Birdie in the closet when digging out the erasable board. Consumed by the firestorm swirling in my brain, I'd mistaken his scratching for sounds outside the annex. By the time I got home, the cat had been captive for hours. Since that distressing misadventure, he'd ventured downstairs only to eat.

Or maybe it was Charlie. The two had never really bonded.

Pete shouted. In seconds Birdie padded through the door.

Pete placed noodles and shrimp on a saucer, smiled as he watched the feline scarf it up. Then the smile faded. When Pete spoke again, his voice carried a tone I hadn't heard before.

"That night." Pete stopped to regroup. "I came here Thursday night. You were outside on the walk."

Ryan. The embrace. Headlights sweeping the drive, continuing past.

"That was you?"

Pete nodded.

"Why didn't you stop?"

"You were with someone."

I said nothing.

Pete studied his napkin as though he'd never seen one before. Then his eyes rolled up to mine.

"I've called off the wedding."

I chuckled. "As I predicted. Wait a few—"

"I've broken our engagement."

"What?" I hadn't expected that.

"The marriage wouldn't have worked. I've known that for a while. When I saw you with—" Pete raised a hand. "It wouldn't have worked."

"Where's Summer?"

"Gone back to her place."

"How is she?"

"Not happy."

"Oh, Pete. I'm so sorry."

"It's better this way."

Pete dropped the upraised hand onto my good one. Our eyes locked. His thumb began stroking my skin.

The moment became embarrassingly long.

"Is there anything I can do to help?" Slipping free of Pete's grasp.

"You already have."

Pete left me sitting in my chair, staring at half-empty cartons of my Chinese favorites.

As I got up to clear the table, a sudden thought struck me. Had Pete filed the divorce papers? Was he at long last officially my ex?

When finished with the dishes, I went up to my room. Lying in bed with Birdie, I thought about loss.

Aqsaee and Rasekh.

Ara and Rosalie.

Lily.

ICE agents would care for Gross's victims. Find out who they are, where they came from, what happened to them. They would return the girls to their homes. Or set them on the road to better lives.

La Police Nationale would track Jean Pruet and the girls he had trafficked into France.

Canadian authorities would probe Lily's death. They would shut down the shooting gallery where she died. Arrest the dealers who led her to that time and place.

All three investigations would involve grim, gut-wrenching tasks.

Cuddling with my cat, I resolved one thing.

The world is rife with evil and misfortune, but it is also full of good people determined to right wrongs. I would not sink into sadness. I would celebrate those who refuse to give up. Those who battle to make things better.

But who, I wondered, would battle for Ryan in his agony?

Ryan.

Pete.

I needed to be alone.

Needed time to consider and digest all that had happened.

FROM THE FORENSIC FILES
OF DR. KATHY REICHS

OF BONES, BODIES, BULLETS, BLACK HAWKS,
AND BONDAGE

**Spoiler alert! If you haven't yet finished *Bones of the Lost*,
you might want to read this later.**

As with each Temperance Brennan novel, the ideas for *Bones of the Lost* came from both the professional and personal parts of my life.

My professional background offers no shortage of inspiring material. Most everyone knows what forensic anthropologists do. In the opening chapter Tempe explains the job while being questioned for jury duty. Forensic anthropology is all about bones and compromised bodies.

Here's a surprise: Now and then my colleagues and I examine fleshed individuals, sometimes even living, breathing people.

Occasionally the subject is an adolescent whose exact age is unclear. Should he or she be tried as an adult? Granted asylum? Allowed to make his or her own medical decisions? In such cases anthropological analysis focuses on whether the individual is above or below an age significant for legal reasons.

Occasionally the subject has died recently but remains unidentified, and age or ethnicity is uncertain. Or the fracture patterning due to trauma is complicated. In such cases, skeletal analysis can add valuable information to the soft-tissue autopsy.

A real-life situation inspired Tempe's involvement with the hit-and-run Jane Doe. A driver was found dead on the floor of a large truck depot. One story had him accidentally struck by a vehicle while standing upright. Another had him intentionally run over while lying facedown, following a fistfight.

The pathologist wanted to know if analysis of the cranial trauma could resolve the question. It did. A skull subjected to enormous weight loading while compressed against concrete fractures differently from one striking concrete as a result of a fall.

So. Change the trucker to a young girl on a lonely two-lane.

And what of the bullet trajectory dilemma?

Some years ago I was asked to serve as an expert adviser for a public inquiry into the 1969 death of a police detective. The man was found in his car, dead of a gunshot wound to the chest. When the manner of death was ruled suicide, the family cried foul, insisting their father/husband had been murdered for testifying about police corruption. They claimed he'd been shot in the back and that the wound on his chest was from a bullet exiting, not entering, as stated by the coroner. Twenty-seven years postmortem they found a pathologist who agreed with their version of events, based on his viewing of the old black-and-white autopsy and scene photos.

A government commission formed and a team was assembled to exhume the deceased. Michael Baden was the pathologist. I was the forensic anthropologist.

Though three decades underground had reduced the remains to bone, the fracture patterning on the sternum was classic. The bullet had entered anteriorly and exited posteriorly, taking breakaway fragments with it. Dr. Baden and I were in agreement concerning a front-to-back trajectory.

Suicide? Homicide? Not our call. But the man had not been shot in the back.

Desperate, the family's pathologist then argued that the defect was a developmental anomaly called a sternal foramen, and, later still, that the damage was produced not by a projectile at all but by our analysis.

To no avail. The original finding of suicide stood.

So. Change the police detective to an Afghan man and boy. Change the question of suicide versus homicide to one of murder versus self-defense.

But why Afghanistan?

That's where the personal enters the picture.

In the fall of 2011 I was honored and privileged to be invited by the USO (United Services Organizations) and the ITW (International Thriller Writers) to travel with Clive Cussler, Mark Bowden, Sandra Brown, and Andrew Peterson to Afghanistan and Kyrgyzstan to thank our troops for their courage and dedication. I was overwhelmed by the bravery, selflessness, and optimism of every service member I met.

My time in the Middle East remains a collage of vivid memories. Rising at five and dropping into my bunk at midnight. Trekking from our B-hut to the head with my roomie, Sandra. Plunging earthward in a pitch-black C-130J Hercules. Riding in Black Hawk helicopters with Mark Bowden, author of *Black Hawk Down*. (We good, Mark?) Wearing a helmet and forty pounds of body armor.

But mostly I remember the people: The army sergeant penning his first novel. The air force mother-daughter team who'd enlisted, trained, and deployed together. The marine lieutenant serving in a war zone as her baby was cutting his first teeth.

Being part of Operation Thriller II was humbling, moving, and gratifying. Before touching down stateside I'd decided to share the experience with my readers.

Why human trafficking?

Same answer. Personal.

In many of my books I use Tempe's exploits to illuminate an important societal issue: The predatory nature of cults. Trafficking in endangered species. The tragedy of human rights abuse. Black marketeering in human body parts. Child pornography on the Internet. *Bones of the Lost* follows in this tradition.

My daughter Courtney Reichs Mixon is a nurse. BA, BSN, RN, ONC. (Point of information: My offspring maintain a friendly rivalry over post-signature credentialing. Though both of her siblings are attorneys, at the moment Courtney holds the lead in alphabetic certification.)

Since obtaining her RN, Courtney has pursued an interest in forensic nursing and has worked alongside sexual assault nurse examiners (SANE). She has come to understand that sexual assault victims are often severely psychologically traumatized, and she feels a particular calling to help those who have suffered as a result of human trafficking.

Courtney belongs to several organizations dedicated to this goal, including NC Stop Human Trafficking (www.ncstophumantrafficking .wordpress.com) and All We Want Is Love: Liberation of Victims Everywhere (www.allwewantislove.org). She labels soap with a trafficking hotline number for placement in hotel, motel, and truck-stop bathrooms; organizes fund-raising events; answers hotline calls; and is training to be a speaker/educator for school groups, book clubs, churches, and other organizations.

It was Courtney's passion on the subject of human trafficking (along with her relentless nagging each time I started a new book) that spurred me to highlight this tragic and heartbreaking problem.

Professional. Personal. Free-ranging data bytes in my brain. Disconnected facts, memories, and impressions reconfigured.

Voilà: a new Temperance Brennan novel is born.